A DELICATE MATTER

Jack Taggart Mysteries

Loose Ends (2005)
Above Ground (2007)
Angel in the Full Moon (2008)
Samurai Code (2010)
Dead Ends (2011)
Birds of a Feather (2012)
Corporate Asset (2013)
The Benefactor (2014)
Art and Murder (2015)

A DELICATE MATTER

A Jack Taggart Mystery

Don Easton

DUNDURN
TORONTO

Editor: Maryan Gibson
Design: Courtney Horner
Cover Design: Laura Boyle
Front Cover: 123RF.com/Mariuz Blach
Printer: Webcom

Library and Archives Canada Cataloguing in Publication

Easton, Don, author
      A delicate matter / Don Easton.

(A Jack Taggart mystery)
Issued in print and electronic formats.
ISBN 978-1-4597-3427-2 (paperback).--ISBN 978-1-4597-3428-9 (pdf).--
ISBN 978-1-4597-3429-6 (epub)

      I. Title. II. Series: Easton, Don. Jack Taggart mystery.

PS8609.A78D44 2016   C813'.6   C2016-900385-X
                                                 C2016-900386-8

1   2   3   4   5   20 19 18 17 16

Conseil des Arts   Canada Council   ONTARIO ARTS COUNCIL
du Canada   for the Arts   CONSEIL DES ARTS DE L'ONTARIO
                   Canada   an Ontario government agency
                                             un organisme du gouvernement de l'Ontario

We acknowledge the support of the **Canada Council for the Arts** and the **Ontario Arts Council** for our publishing program. We also acknowledge the financial support of the **Government of Canada** through the **Canada Book Fund** and **Livres Canada Books**, and the **Government of Ontario** through the **Ontario Book Publishing Tax Credit** and the **Ontario Media Development Corporation**.

Care has been taken to trace the ownership of copyright material used in this book. The author and the publisher welcome any information enabling them to rectify any references or credits in subsequent editions.

— *J. Kirk Howard, President*

The publisher is not responsible for websites or their content unless they are owned by the publisher.

Printed and bound in Canada.

VISIT US AT
Dundurn.com | @dundurnpress | Facebook.com/dundurnpress | Pinterest.com/dundurnpress

Dundurn
3 Church Street, Suite 500
Toronto, Ontario, Canada
M5E 1M2

To Piper and Kei ... you weren't forgotten

Chapter One

It was the second Wednesday in September and a sprinkle of rain caused many of the shoppers to quicken their pace as they went to and from their cars. Young moms were enjoying the freedom of having their children back at school, and this morning the mall parking garage in Surrey, British Columbia, was busy. For one man it was the ideal time to go hunting. He selected his prey and kept his head down so that the hoodie he wore hid his face.

He guessed she was in her early thirties. Her raincoat was open, revealing an attractive figure, and her black hair cascaded over a white blouse. Her slacks were charcoal-coloured. She carried several shopping bags from high-end clothing stores. *Expensive tastes … exactly the kind of snooty rich bitch I'm looking for.*

He approached her. She hesitated at the elevator beside the stairwell, then cast a glance in his direction. She turned and walked up the ramp in the parkade, taking the more visible and open route designed for cars.

What's the matter, bitch? Aren't I your type? He felt the blood surge in his groin and took the stairs two at a time to the second level, then eyed her through the glass pane in the door. She had one hand rummaging through her purse, probably seeking her keys, while she continued walking to the third level. He scampered up the stairwell again and saw her stop at the end of a row of cars and hold out a key fob. The trunk to a white Lexus obediently opened and she bent over to tuck her packages inside.

He pulled the drawstrings on his hoodie tight around his face as he crept toward her. He was within a couple of steps before he saw her body momentarily freeze, then spin around, her eyes riveted on his. He gave an evil grin when her gaze shifted down to his open fly and his engorged penis.

"How 'bout you bend over again and I pack this in your trunk, bitch!"

The woman looked curiously at his penis. "Why is it so tiny?"

"What?" he spluttered as his penis promptly wilted. "What did you say?"

"Is your problem achieving an erection due to feelings of insecurity around women? Do you only achieve physical gratification and a feeling of empowerment over a woman if she displays fear — or are you hoping to arouse me?"

His eyebrows furrowed. "You whore!" he snarled, stepping forward with his fist raised.

"I don't mind if you talk dirty to me." Her voice had turned sultry. "I've fantasized about this moment. Hoping it would happen."

He stopped. "You have?" He lowered his fist.

"Yes," she answered while rummaging in her purse again. "Would you like to join me in the back seat of my car?"

"Are ... are ...," he stuttered before finding the words. "Are you serious?"

"Definitely. I hope you're into bondage," she added, taking a set of handcuffs from her purse.

He heard a van door slide open two spaces down and turned to see a couple of men leap out. He looked back at the woman. The cuffs were gone and she was pointing a pistol at him.

"You're under arrest!" she yelled. "Put your hands over your head!"

"You fucking bitch!" he screamed, ignoring her command and running for the ramp. When he saw other police officers closing in on him, his mouth fell open in panic.

Seconds later Constable Sophie White's jaw also went slack when her suspect ran to the edge of the parkade, gave a glance back, then leaped over the side of the retaining wall. She, along with her colleagues, rushed to the wall and looked down. Three storeys below, the culprit lay sprawled face down on the sidewalk.

"Think he's dead?" one of the officers asked in a tone that showed his indifference.

"Maybe," Sophie replied. "Glad he didn't land on anyone."

As they watched, the culprit squirmed and rolled over onto his side.

"Nope, guess we don't need the coroner," Sophie said, taking a portable radio out of her purse.

The culprit managed to stand on one leg. After a few failed attempts to put his other foot down, he started to hop away.

Sophie rolled her eyes, then clicked the transmit button.

Constable Chuck Field was in a car near the parkade exit when he received the call.

"Field, we tried to arrest our man," Sophie radioed, "but he leaped over the wall on the opposite side of the building from where you are. Drive around and pick him up. We've got the eye from up here."

"You got it."

The sound of screeching tires echoing up from the street said that Field would not take long. His voice crackled over the radio again. "What's he look like?"

"If you see a guy hopping down the street on one leg with his dick hanging out, that'll be him."

Chapter Two

Corporal Jack Taggart drove into the parking lot of the Steinhouse Pub in Port Coquitlam. The pub was about a forty-minute drive from Vancouver, where he worked undercover for the Intelligence unit of the Royal Canadian Mounted Police.

He was driving a black SUV with tinted windows. Constable Laura Secord, who was both his partner and subordinate, sat beside him. Today her long auburn hair was pulled back in a ponytail and she wore a green rain jacket over blue jeans and a denim shirt.

Jack had shoulder-length hair and a bushy beard that was showing a hint of grey. He wore a black T-shirt under an open brown kangaroo jacket and black jeans.

Both Jack and Laura had received special training by the RCMP to work undercover. Their assignment was to combat organized crime. At the top of their list was Satans Wrath, a motorcycle gang involved in drug trafficking, prostitution, murder, and a host of other criminal activities.

Satans Wrath had developed over the years into a sophisticated criminal empire with seventy chapters in forty countries around the globe. It had, for the most part, insulated itself from its criminal activities by using other gangs as middlemen. Satans Wrath would use a puppet club to do its dirty work for a few years, after which some puppet-club members might be selected to join Satans Wrath. At that time the remainder of the puppet club would soon find it in its best interests to disband. In September, during the Labour Day ride, it was noted that the Gypsy Devils had been invited to tag along.

Bikers wear their club logo, called their "colours," on the backs of sleeveless jackets, which for the Gypsy Devils was a skull adorned with a green bandana and a black patch over one eye. The name of the club, or the "top rocker," was above the skull, while the "bottom rocker" beneath denoted the area they're from. For the Gypsy Devils it simply read "Poco," to denote Port Coquitlam.

Satans Wrath colours bore a full face-on skull with horns, purple eyes, and a sinister grin. Their bottom rockers bore the names of countless cities from many regions of the world.

Probationary members of the clubs, referred to as "prospects," had only bottom rockers on their jackets. Prospects generally took part in the riskier areas of Satans Wrath's criminal activity and then, after they'd been thoroughly screened for a couple of years, Satans Wrath members would vote on whether to allow the prospects entry into the club. If accepted, a prospect would receive the top rocker and complete logo, which was known as getting the "full patch," or "colours." Currently, the Gypsy Devils had nine full-patch members and three prospects.

What surprised Jack was that the Gypsy Devils tended to represent the more degenerate and filthy image of what outlaw biker clubs were thirty-five years ago. Although Satans Wrath didn't hesitate to use extreme violence to protect its turf or expand its criminal tentacles, the members generally wore clean clothes and tried not to attract police attention and thereby jeopardize the financial gains from their criminal activity. The Gypsy Devils had not displayed the same intelligence.

In the past clubs like the Gypsy Devils would receive a warning from Satans Wrath to shut down, and if they didn't the ramifications would involve lengthy hospital stays — if they were lucky.

Jack felt that Satans Wrath had displayed a friendlier attitude toward the Gypsy Devils than it had other puppet clubs. He believed the Gypsy Devils had something Satans Wrath wanted and he intended to find out what. All bikers were well aware of police wiretaps and seldom said anything of value over their phones. Biker informants were also a rare commodity, as loyalty and devotion to their respective clubs was extremely high.

Today Jack hoped that surveillance might lead to his discreetly busting someone the Gypsy Devils dealt with. He intended to try to turn that person into an informant and work his way up from there.

Laura eyed the cluster of Harley-Davidson motorcycles in the pub parking lot. One of the bikes, which had the logo of the Gypsy Devils painted on the gas tank, belonged to the club president, Carl Shepherd. "Looks like we're in luck today," she said.

Jack gave a satisfied nod. "This is their favourite watering hole. They were bound to turn up sooner or later."

"You sure you want to go in there alone?"

"I'll be fine," Jack assured her. "These guys don't know me. Besides, I've got Smith and Wesson to help, if need be. Stay put, collect the plate numbers, and act like the paparazzi."

Laura frowned. "These guys don't know you, but some of Satans Wrath do. What if they show up? I know you used to have a goatee, but even with your beard and longer hair, they could still recognize you."

"I doubt any full-patch members of Satans Wrath would lower themselves to hang out with these yokels. Maybe one or two of their prospects might show up to conduct business, but those guys don't know me. Besides, even if Satans Wrath members do show up, they aren't stupid. They'd probably send me a beer to let me know I'd been spotted."

"Yes, a beer with the date-rape drug so they could bend you over a table and … *do* you."

Jack smiled to himself. Despite the years on the job and the type of work Laura did, she seldom used foul language. "Don't worry if they do show. It's the Gypsy Devils we need to be concerned about. They're more dangerous because of their lack of cerebral development. I'll call you if I need a hand. Speaking of which, time for a radio check."

Laura flicked on a portable police radio and Jack whispered, "Test, test, test," into a microphone hidden in his sleeve. His words echoed over Laura's portable radio. He then tucked a receiver into his ear and covered it with his hair. Laura clicked her portable and Jack heard the click on his receiver. He gave her a thumbs-up and reached for a ball cap.

"The cap makes you look like Forrest Gump," Laura noted. "You look meaner and tougher without it."

"I know," Jack replied. "Looking tough around these guys is inviting trouble. They'd want to find out who I am — or worse, how tough I really am."

Moments later he wandered into the bar. It was relatively small and well lit. The Gypsy Devils had been forced by law to not display their colours in the pub, but were still easily identified by their appearance. They, along with an assortment of other representatives of the criminal element, occupied one side of the pub, while the other side was favoured by people from local businesses who often came in for lunch.

Jack found a small table on the fringe of where the bikers were and ordered a beer. Sitting alone tended to make him stand out, but Laura was a very attractive woman and he feared she'd attract unwanted attention from the Gypsy Devils. Unwanted attention that'd require a bare-knuckled response ... or the need to use the 9mm Smith & Wesson pistol tucked in the back of his jeans and thereby blow his cover.

He'd only taken his first sip when he saw that he'd caught the attention of two women at the next table. One was a brunette in an outfit that looked like a chauffeur's uniform. The other had her blonde hair in a braid over her shoulder and wore a blouse and slacks. She looked like an office worker.

The women gave him a friendly smile, then each said, "Hi."

Jack nodded in response.

"You look lonely sitting there," said the blonde. "My name's Roxie."

Yeah, and I guess I look stupid, too. Jack gave a curt nod and stood up. "Excuse me, I have to find a quiet place to make a call." As he glanced around for another place to sit, he thought, *Okay … the ripple effect … fourth table away should be okay.* A Gypsy Devil by the name of Thorsen, who was the sergeant-at-arms for the club, was talking to a couple of his buddies at a nearby table. *Ah, the guy they call Thor … looks like a gorilla and only half as smart. I better pick five tables away.*

The women exchanged annoyed looks as Jack picked up his beer and moved five tables away from the bikers. He was no longer able to hear any of their conversation but he still had a good view.

Some minutes passed and Jack discreetly radioed Laura the descriptions of the few men who'd left the pub after sitting with the Gypsy Devils. He then saw two men enter and walk past him. Both were clean-cut and one was wearing a black leather bomber jacket and the other a light windbreaker. Jack noticed that the man with the bomber jacket had a jailhouse tattoo — a Celtic cross — on the crux of his thumb and forefinger. *So his nice-boy image hides a sinister past,* he thought.

Once, on an undercover assignment in prison, Jack watched a group of convicts use a lighter to melt a green plastic comb, then dip a pin into the melting plastic. Next they used the pin to make a row of prick marks on the recipient's arm. The resulting tattoo was less than what one might call professional, but it did the trick.

Both men looked around the bar for a place to sit. It didn't appear that they knew anyone. They then opted to sit at the table where Jack had originally sat.

Jack whispered into his sleeve, "Laura, you see the two guys who just entered? Black bomber jacket on one and a blue windbreaker on the other?"

"Ten-four. I got close-ups of both their faces. The driver is the one wearing the bomber jacket. I ran his name. He's got a record for armed robbery and sexual assault."

Jack grinned when he saw the two men being chatted up by the same two women who'd spoken to him minutes before. *Oh, yeah, here it comes.*

"You copy, Jack?"

"I copied. Sexual assault, eh? That's perfect."

"Why is it perfect?" Laura asked.

"I'll explain later."

"Are they with the GDs?"

"Definitely not," Jack whispered. "Talk to you later." He picked up his beer and held it above the table without taking a sip.

"You trying to fuck our women?" Thor roared at the newcomers, shoving himself back from his table.

Before the two men could respond, Thor lunged out of his chair, along with the other bikers, and attacked. Chairs and tables tipped over, sending drinks crashing to the floor, as the bikers pummelled their victims with a flurry of fists and boots.

The man in the windbreaker was knocked backward onto the floor, where he was kicked and given several rib-breaking stomps.

The man in the bomber jacket rose and managed to get one punch in, an action he'd soon regret. Seconds later he was on the floor being kicked and stomped on. Then he was dragged to his feet and thrust back against a pillar, where Thor pressed and twisted the jagged end of a broken beer bottle to his nose and mouth. The man's lip drooped like a piece of liver. Another twist of the bottle around his eye gouged out a section of his eyebrow, along with the flesh on the bridge of his nose.

The bartender timidly approached. "Please, guys, can you take it outside? We'll lose our licence again if you keep doing this in here."

Thor hesitated, then nodded to the others. Two bikers dragged Thor's bloody victim toward the exit. As they did, one biker backhanded the victim on the side of his face to gain his attention and said, "We're gonna scoop your licence. If you're stupid enough to say anything, remember that we know you and where you live."

Seconds later they opened the door and flung the hapless victim outside, along with his looted wallet. In the meantime three other bikers took turns kicking the other man as he crawled toward the exit. Eventually they let him get to his feet and stumble outside.

The two women, who were both laughing, joined the Gypsy Devils while the overturned chairs and tables were righted.

Jack noted that the ripple effect of displaced beer and furniture had stopped next to where he sat. *Hey, that's pretty good. I predicted that one right on.*

"Jack, what did you do to those two guys?" Laura radioed. "I know you don't like sex offenders but … oh, man."

"Wasn't me," Jack whispered. "Just the good ol' boys and a couple of their women having some fun."

"One guy's face is covered in blood. His buddy's trying to help him across the parking lot to their wheels … but he looks pretty messed up, too. I'm getting some close-ups but, hey, what happened?"

"Karma," Jack replied. "Hang on, someone's calling me on my cell." He took the vibrating phone from his pocket and held it close to his ear.

"Jack, it's Sophie White. I got your number from your boss and she said to call you direct."

"Sophie White?" Jack asked. "Do I know you?"

"Now my feelings are really hurt," she replied, sounding miffed. "We met seven years ago. You shoved me into the back seat of a car and climbed in on top of me. Guess I didn't make much of an impression."

Jack snorted. "*Now* I know who you are," he said. "How's your nose?"

"You mean the one you broke?"

"How many do you have?" Jack asked.

Sophie snickered, then her voice became serious. "You saved my life that night. I'll never forget it."

"We both got lucky that night," Jack replied sombrely. "What can I do for you?"

"Maybe it's what I can do for you. I'm still working uniform in Surrey, but I know you're the guy to talk to about Satans Wrath. I caught one and he wants to talk."

"Give me a sec," Jack said. "I'm in a bar — let me step outside where I can talk." Seconds later he continued his conversation while walking across the parking lot to where Laura waited in the SUV. "Who'd you catch?"

"His name's Mack Cockerill. What I caught him on is nothing. Maybe probation if we're lucky, but he says he's willing to talk if I'll drop the matter."

"What's he offering? A pipe bomb or a gun?"

"You got it," Sophie said. "Also some bullshit about someone planning to shoot up an abortion clinic."

"All of which he'll arrange if you drop his charge."

"Yeah, that's what I figured, but I thought I should call you. He seems really stressed. Mind you, he might be in pain. He leaped off the third storey of a parkade when I tried to arrest him and broke his ankle."

"You didn't tell me what you're charging him with," Jack said, stifling a yawn as he watched the man in the bomber jacket stumble and leave a bloody hand-streak down the side of a white Toyota Camry. His buddy was holding him by the other arm and trying to steer him while grasping his own rib cage.

"He's a weenie wagger," Sophie replied.

Jack immediately forgot about the victims in the parking lot. "You've got to be kidding," he said. "You got him for exposing himself?"

"Yeah. We've had three complaints in the last two weeks from women saying some guy has been jumping out at them in a parkade and waving his dick. We set up a sting and today he did the same thing with me. We've got it all on video. Enough that Defence won't be able to say he had a bladder infection and was simply relieving himself."

"That's fantastic," Jack said. "I mean it."

"Why? It's no big deal as far as the courts go. The judge will probably think it's funny and give him thirty hours of community service. Maybe less if his lawyer can convince the court that his client suffered enough by having broken his ankle."

"The judge might find it amusing, but Satans Wrath wouldn't," Jack said. "It'd be a huge embarrassment to the club. The jokes would be flying around the country saying they should change their top rocker from Satans Wrath to the Weenie Waggers."

"That'd make for a good laugh."

"They'd kill him if they found out — or put him in the intensive-care unit for a year and kick him out of the club. Personally I think it'd be the first option."

"Think maybe he'll give us more than he's pretending to offer?"

"Damn right. Once he realizes you won't go along with the bullshit he offered, he'll offer you something genuine. Likely stolen property or dope to start with, but handle him right and he could be a gold mine for you."

"For me?" Sophie sounded doubtful. "You should be the guy to talk to him. I'm smart enough to know that I don't have the experience to handle a guy like him. The asshole would probably end up running *me* instead of me running him."

"That wouldn't be the first time that's happened," Jack said. "I'd be glad to take a run at him. I'm in Port Coquitlam at the moment, so I could be there in less than half an hour. Maybe we could work him together if you like."

"I've got all the work I can handle," Sophie responded. "Besides, I'm still in uniform. This guy's more your department. If he doesn't cooperate, I'll charge him afterwards."

"Oh, he'll cooperate," Jack said. "I'm sure about that."

"Then he's all yours if you want him."

Jack smiled. *Oh, yeah, I want him all right. Goodbye Gypsy Devils. You've been outtrumped by one weenie-wagger.*

Chapter Three

Jack and Laura sat in an office with Sophie White at the Surrey RCMP detachment and listened as she recounted the circumstances leading to Mack Cockerill's arrest. "After that, we took him to the hospital where he received a walking cast. Now he's in an interview room," Sophie said, gesturing with her thumb behind her. "Hope he can really do a number on the club for you."

"I wish," Jack replied, "but even if he wants to spill his guts, it won't affect the club as a whole that much."

Sophie looked puzzled. "Why not?"

"They tend to operate in cells independent from one another to prevent someone from ever doing that. Even if he was willing to wear a wire and testify, all I'd expect to get would be some high-level dealers who score from the club, maybe a couple of prospects, and one or two colour-wearing members. For the moment we need to aim our sights lower. If all goes well perhaps down the road we can convince him to stick his neck out further."

Sophie nodded. "Would you mind if I sat in and listened? I don't have much experience with guys like him and I'd like to see how you do it."

"I don't mind, but let me clue you in about a few things before we see him," Jack replied. "First of all, these guys are usually extremely loyal. If I push him too hard he may decide to clam up and face the consequences, dire as they would be. I'll tread slowly at first, then lead him into deeper water, which may or may not be today. If things go the way I want, eventually he'll realize there's no turning back."

"I see," Sophie said.

"First, though, we'll shake him up a bit. Is he wearing his colours?"

"Yes. He was wearing a hoodie over the colours, but I seized that as evidence. It matches what the three victims said the suspect was wearing."

"Perfect." Jack rose to his feet. "Let's talk to him. Laura will wait here."

Sophie looked at Laura. "You're not coming with us?"

Laura smiled. "Jack discussed a plan with me on the way over. It'll be more fun for you to watch it unfold than to explain it to you."

A moment later Cockerill looked up as Jack and Sophie entered the interview room. He eyed Jack suspiciously.

"Get to your feet," Jack ordered.

Cockerill scowled and slowly got up.

Jack used his cellphone to take a picture of Cockerill, then ordered him to turn around. After taking another picture depicting his colours, he told Cockerill to sit down.

The biker obeyed and Jack pulled a chair up so their faces were only an arm's length apart.

"Who the fuck are you?" Cockerill asked defiantly. "A narc?"

"My name's Jack Taggart," Jack replied evenly. "I'm not a narc."

Cockerill studied Jack's face, then muttered, "Fuck."

"You've heard of me," Jack replied.

Cockerill nodded. "I didn't recognize you — but now I do. I saw you years ago when you climbed over the wall behind Damien's place."

The mere mention of Damien made Jack feel agitated. Damien Zabat, the national president of Satans Wrath, was Jack's nemesis. The two men had been involved in several confrontations over the years. Despite that, Jack had never been able to put him in jail, even though Damien had ordered dozens of murders and orchestrated a wide variety of criminal activities.

Damien, now almost sixty, was still intimidating. He was a huge bear of a man, as well as highly intelligent and perceptive at reading people. The years had, however, taken their toll. He had recently decided to retire while he still had everyone's respect. A new national president had been elected to replace him at the end of the month. For Jack, Damien was the one who got away, and it bothered him intensely.

To make matters worse, Jack knew that Damien's son, Buck, had been a prospect for the past two years. *Soon he, too, will be a full-patch member and the cycle will continue. Like father, like son, and it seems all I can do is sit back and watch.*

"So what're you doing here?" Cockerill asked, breaking Jack's train of thought. "This ain't got nothin' to do with you."

Jack sneered. "I'm here because Constable White isn't swallowing any of your bullshit about what you're offering for us to drop the beef — and neither am I."

"What the fuck? You don't think some guy shootin' up an abortion clinic is worth me being pinched for trying to have a piss in a parkade?"

"Cut the crap," Jack said. "You were caught on video, as well as audio."

Cockerill frowned. "Okay, okay, you got me on that." He made a palms-down gesture to drop the subject. "Still, I know this guy, and once he shoots up the clinic, I'll be able to give him to ya. Bust him quick and he'll still have the gun to match the bullets."

"Which'll be the gun you'll have given him after you shoot up the clinic." Jack shook his head in disgust. "I'm done talking to you," he said abruptly. "I need to make a phone call."

"But —"

Jack gave a dismissive wave of his hand and placed a call. A female voice, audible over the phone in the small interview room, answered.

"Hey, good lookin'! It's Jack Taggart. Remember me?"

"Jack! You bet I remember you. Are you still working in the Intelligence unit?"

"Yes."

"Hang on. I'm doing a story on the six-o'clock news tonight … I've got someone here. Give me a sec."

The look of fear on Cockerill's face told Jack that he'd heard. Laura sounded like she was talking to someone in the background. "Yep, I'll follow the lead story." Then her voice became louder. "Okay, Jack. I'm back."

"I'm going to send you two photos," Jack said. "Hang up and call me back. Later I might be able to get you a copy of a video and audio, as well." He hung up and thumbed his phone.

"You can't do this!" Cockerill snarled, waving his hand in the air in an unsuccessful bid to gain Jack's attention. "I've got my rights! You can't do this!"

"Already did," Jack said, finally glancing up.

"My lawyer'll sue you!"

Jack smiled. "That should take about seven years to get through the courts. Think you'll be above ground that long?"

Cockerill stared open-mouthed at him before turning to Sophie for support. His eyes widened when she busied herself examining her fingernails. He looked at Jack again. "You can't —"

Jack's phone vibrated and he answered. Cockerill stopped in mid-sentence.

"Hey ... Satans Wrath!" Laura exclaimed. "Was it you who put him in the cast?"

"No, he did it himself," Jack replied, "but wait'll you hear what he was doing."

"Don't do this to me!" Cockerill pleaded.

Jack put his hand over the receiver and looked at Cockerill. "An abortion clinic? Yeah, right." He turned his attention back to his phone. "This'll be a really funny story. I'm sure it'll be picked up by networks and newspapers across the country. Figured I'd let you be the first one to break the —"

"I'll ... I'll give you something!" Cockerill's face was awash in fear and panic. "Please ... don't tell her."

Jack paused as if contemplating the offer, then spoke to Laura. "Hang on a moment while I put you on hold. Someone wants to speak to me." He looked at Cockerill. "Speak fast — and cut the bullshit."

"I can give you a grow-op," Cockerill said rapidly. "About a thousand plants. It's hidden in the bush. Nobody'd ever find it."

"You think I'm interested in busting some farmer? It isn't worth the trouble. Quit wasting my time."

"You work bikers, right?" Cockerill asked.

"Yeah, a club called the Weenie Waggers. I heard you were president."

"No, please, listen!" Cockerill wailed. "The ones picking up the weed are with the Gypsy Devils." He paused, his eyes searching Jack's face in the vain hope of seeing interest. "The crop is being harvested and the GDs are picking it up next Wednesday or Thursday." He sounded enthusiastic. "They do it in the wee hours of the morning when nobody's around. That way they can check for heat, make sure they're not being followed. What do you think?"

Jack's face remained without expression.

"I can tell you where it is," Cockerill hastened to say. "You could watch it and either grab the GDs when they pick up, or if the grower delivers, then follow him and bust 'em when he hands it over."

"Gypsy Devils," Jack noted. "Could be something for you to show good faith until you give us something better."

"Good faith?" Cockerill's eyes darted nervously between Jack and Sophie. "Come on, busting bikers with dope has gotta be better than catching me with my fly undone."

"Want me to ask Damien if it's better?" Jack asked.

Cockerill briefly locked eyes with Jack, then his head dropped. "No," he whispered.

"Not to mention, busting someone in the bush at night could be a problem."

"You can only get to it by boat," Cockerill offered.

"That doesn't help. Makes it more difficult. Give me some details. How many growers are looking after it and which of the GDs will be involved?"

Cockerill pointed at the phone in Jack's hand. "You gonna hang up?"

Jack stared blankly at Cockerill, stalling long enough to cause him further stress, then said, "One weed deal won't cut it. I'll probably end up with some farmer and a Gypsy Devil, who in my opinion is only a wannabe biker."

Cockerill swallowed nervously.

Jack leaned forward so that their faces were a hand-width apart. "If I suspect anything you tell me is bullshit, I'll be calling her back."

"It won't be bullshit," Cockerill promised.

Jack spoke into his phone. "Hi, I'm back."

"What's it all about?" Laura asked.

"The biker we were doing surveillance on tried to play hopscotch with some little kids on a sidewalk. He fell off the curb and broke his ankle. Later he was brought in for unpaid tickets and we photographed him."

"That's not all that funny," Laura replied. "My boss wouldn't be impressed. I thought you were going to give me something juicy."

"For a tough guy it seemed funny to me," he said. "Maybe next time." He hung up.

"I broke it playing fucking hopscotch?" Cockerill looked displeased. He took a deep breath, slowly exhaled, then said, "Okay, as far as I know, there's only one guy looking after the crop. His name's Larry. I don't know his last name. There should be a couple of GDs picking it up."

"Which ones?" Jack asked. "I need to know everything. It'll help me come up with a plan to protect you from anyone ever finding out how we knew."

Cockerill snorted. "Nobody'd suspect me. The blame would be laid on either Larry getting careless or on the GDs because they're a bunch of stupid fucks anyway. I'm full-patch Satans Wrath. Ain't nobody gonna point a finger at me over this."

Over this, no … but what will you tell me in the future? I don't want anyone to connect the dots, you dumbass. Jack cleared his throat. "Who from the GDs are picking it up?"

"I dunno. Could be one of three guys or maybe all three."

"You're talking about their prospects," Jack replied.

"Yeah," Cockerill admitted.

"I expect to nail full-patch members at a minimum. The GDs should have I-D-I-O-T-S for their top rocker." He leaned closer and spoke harshly. "Come on, you can do better than this! I can't believe you're trying to stand up for those goofs. I've a hard time thinking of them as real bikers."

Cockerill brooded. "Okay, I'll give you the full package." He paused to adjust his pant leg where his jeans had been cut to make room for his cast, then looked at Jack. "Their prospects will be picking up from four different grow-ops next week. Two on Wednesday night and the other two on Thursday. I don't know where the other three grow-ops are, but I know where it'll end up."

"How much?"

"Total of about five hundred keys." He paused to see Jack's reaction.

Jack shrugged indifferently. "Keep going."

"The prospects take the weed to a stash house where they press it into kilo bricks and wrap it. Out of that, two-hundred-and-fifty keys are picked up by a full-patch GD by the name of Neal. He passes it on to his brother, Bob, who's an independent trucker."

"They hide it in the trailer with a load of something legit?" Jack asked.

Cockerill shook his head. "We had the sleeper cab in his truck custom built in Mexico. It's got double walls and roof to hide dope." He paused. "Neal and Bob ... I don't know their last name."

"Is Neal a big fat greasy guy with a long braided goatee?"

"Yeah, that's him."

"Neal Barlow," Jack said.

Cockerill nodded. "The other half of the weed is sold off piecemeal to local players."

"Where's the stash house the GDs use to press and brick it up?"

"I dunno. That sort of shit is beneath me."

"Why don't the prospects deliver it straight to Bob? Neal is full-patch. I would've thought, as you put it, that doing that sort of shit is beneath him."

"Neal lives with Bob in an old farmhouse out in Delta, so any raid on Bob would be on Neal, too."

"I see."

"Neal brags that he's good at spottin' heat and would never lead the cops to the semi."

Jack nodded. "I'll bear it in mind."

"So this works out better for you, don't it?" Cockerill said. "All you gotta do is watch Bob's semi and wait for Neal to arrive. That'll probably be about four o'clock Friday morning once it's all packaged up. Then you'll get to arrest him and Bob, along with scoopin' up two-hundred-and-fifty keys. Not only that, if you watch their prospects and find out where the stash house is, you'd get the rest." Cockerill leaned back in his chair and smiled, wiping the palms of his hands together like he was washing them. "That oughtta make us even."

Jack ignored Cockerill's last comment. "Regarding the two-fifty keys in the semi … sounds like it's going to one customer."

Cockerill nodded.

"Doesn't anyone from your club swing by to confirm the dope is there or at least crack a brick open to check the quality?" His question caused Cockerill to tense. *The idea of ratting on one of your own not to your liking?*

"Ah … not much anymore," Cockerill replied. "It used to be that we'd have one of our prospects drop by to inspect it, but we trust the GDs now. Even if that did happen, Neal might not be around. He's the only full-patch who touches the stuff — so that's who you really want. You'd be better off to bust Neal and Bob when they're loadin'."

No, who I really want are full-patch Satans Wrath members. He saw Cockerill waiting for a response. "You're right. Neal and Bob it is."

Cockerill looked relieved.

Why do I have the feeling that you're holding something back from me?

Cockerill grinned and cast a sideways glance at Sophie.

"What's so funny?" Jack asked.

Cockerill chuckled. "Ah, it's nothin'. We joke by saying, hey, Neal and Bob, are those your names or is that what you do?" He gave a wry smile. "Guess they'll be kneelin' and bobbin' in jail after this."

Jack faked a smile. "Good one." He saw Cockerill relax further. "How is it that you know where the grow-op is?" he asked casually. "You're not some flunky prospect. It seems odd that you'd be involved at that low of a level."

"Fuck, what's the deal on how I know where it is?" Cockerill said in annoyance. "What's important is that I know."

What're you hiding? Jack's face hardened. "Because I'm not going to call people out to say we're going after a ton of weed only to find out that it's a ton of bullshit! If I'm suspicious about something, I ask questions. Right now I'm suspicious. Generally you'd use one of your flunky prospects to deal with Neal on something risky like going to a grow-op. It'd also be an opportunity for you to throw it in Neal's face that the two of you aren't equals. An opportunity I know your club would use."

Cockerill looked edgy, then made an obvious effort to look nonchalant. "Yeah, what you said is right, but it's no big deal. One of our prospects once told me that Neal wanted to take me out to do a little salmon fishin' and drink some beer. I took him up on the offer and the four of us went out. That's when I met Larry, 'cause it was his boat we used. Larry ain't all that bright and pointed out where his grow-op was when we trolled past."

Telling me that shouldn't have freaked you out — so what is it? "Okay, that makes sense," Jack said. "Can you point out the location on a map?"

"Yeah, it's on an island. Get me a map and I'll show you."

Jack looked at Sophie and raised an eyebrow.

"Be right back." She returned a moment later and unfolded a map. Cockerill pointed to a remote region on an island near the coastline.

"West side of Bowen Island," Jack noted.

"Satisfied?" Cockerill asked. "You'll let me go now?"

"A couple more questions," Jack replied. "What does Larry's boat look like?"

"It's an aluminum job with a red canvas cover over the wheelhouse, but it's small enough that you could pull it up on shore. It won't be hard to spot because the bow is painted like it's on fire. Same kinda thing you see on hotrods. He keeps it at the Hidden Bay Marina. If it's not there, then he's probably at the grow-op, which is about an hour away. Maybe a little less — we were fishin' and not going all that fast."

Jack eyed Cockerill curiously. "Which of your prospects was with you on the boat?"

Cockerill's eyebrows pinched as if he was trying hard to recall. "I can't remember. It was a coupla months ago."

"You remember Larry's name but can't remember one of your own guys?" Jack said sarcastically. "There were four of you drinking beer and crowded into a small boat. Why are you lying?"

Cockerill locked eyes with Jack but didn't respond.

Jack knew why. He leaned back in his chair, folded his arms across his chest, and smiled.

Chapter Four

Cockerill's shoulders slumped and his head hung like a cowering dog's. Jack saw Sophie looking at the situation in bewilderment. "Prospects usually aren't important to the club," he explained. "There's no reason to hide his name. That is, except for one." He looked at Cockerill. "It was Buck Zabat, wasn't it? He's detailed to check the shipment."

Cockerill slowly looked up. "Yeah," he mumbled. His sombre look said he'd crossed a line that he never intended to cross.

Jack looked at Sophie. "Buck is the son of the national president of Satans Wrath."

"Oh." Sophie looked unsure of what it meant or how to respond.

Jack refocused on Cockerill. "So if I don't bust Neal and Bob when they're loading the truck, I'll probably catch Buck checking out the dope later. Maybe even nail them all with a conspiracy charge."

Cockerill swallowed.

"Mind you, that's only one option," Jack continued. "What if I don't bust anyone when it's being loaded, but wait'll the truck's unloaded? There'd be less heat on you and I could catch whoever is buying it."

Optimism flashed across Cockerill's face. "Better yet, they're takin' it to the States. You could get 'em at the border! They'd get big time for importing into the States."

"They?" Jack questioned. "Does Neal go with Bob?"

"No, not Neal. Bob has an ol' lady. Her name's Roxie. She drives the rig, as well."

"Down to the States," Jack confirmed.

"Yup. They make regular runs hauling freight and cross the border in Alberta at the Aden crossing. Roxie's sister works at U.S Customs there. She trusts them and never checks the cargo. Even if she did, she wouldn't find it."

"Because it's hidden in a secret compartment in the sleeper cab," Jack said.

"Yeah. Two-fifty of weed is the most the cab will hold, but with the regular runs they make, supplyin' orders larger than that works out fine."

"So that's why you guys are courting the GDs," Jack said. "You need their Customs connection to deliver to the States."

"It ain't like they got anything else going for them," Cockerill sneered.

"What does Roxie look like?"

"Tall, good-lookin' … blonde hair with a long braid that hangs down to her tits."

"Do Bob and Roxie hang out with the GDs at the Steinhouse Pub in Port Coquitlam?" Jack asked.

"Probably … if they're not out on the road," Cockerill replied. "The GDs hold their monthly 'church meetings' in a barn beside where they live — so Bob and Roxie are pretty tight with the club."

"I've seen Roxie," Jack said. "She's got a real wicked sense of humour."

"Maybe." Cockerill looked dubious. "I've never spoken with her."

"Too bad," Jack said sardonically.

Cockerill looked quizzically at Jack, then shrugged. "Anyway, it'd be easy to nail them at the border. They'd get big time in Montana."

"Where exactly do they deliver it in the States?" Jack asked.

"Texas."

"In exchange for cocaine?"

"Usually," Cockerill admitted, "but lately things have changed and the truck doesn't bring anything back. If you wait until the return trip, you won't get anything."

"Why not bring the coke back in the truck?" Jack asked. "Don't you trust the GDs with your blow?"

A fleeting instance of fear crossed Cockerill's face, then he sat back and stretched his arms in a pretence of looking calm. "Nah, it's not that. Too many eggs in one basket. We worry about you guys provin' conspiracies."

That I know, but why did the question scare you? Jack had heard rumours that Satans Wrath was on the verge of opening up a cocaine distribution network in Europe. *Is the cocaine being allocated for there?* He eyed Cockerill. "Who do you deal with in Texas? If we don't pop the semi at the border, it might be better to do it when they're unloading. It'd put the heat on the buyers instead of up here."

Cockerill grimaced. No doubt he'd already given more information than he wanted to give.

"Come on," Jack demanded. "You might think you're safe with us taking them down at the border, but I don't take chances. With Roxie's sister working at Customs, we can't make it look like some random search. She'd know and I couldn't count on her to keep her mouth shut with Roxie. If we're going to do this, it'd be better for you if we made it look like the heat came from Texas. It's not like your club would have a hard time finding new customers."

Cockerill scratched his nose. "Yeah ... okay. It goes to Dallas. We deal with a group called the West 12th Street gang. The truck's leaving Friday morning. They got some legitimate freight they haul, as well, but should unload the weed in Dallas on Sunday."

"Good." Jack nodded. "And what's your role?"

"I handle the money on this end. Usually, though, I end up giving it to Buck, who hands it off to Neal. If Neal isn't around, sometimes it gets handed off to a GD by the name of Mouse."

"Mickey O'Bryan, alias Mouse," Jack said.

"Yeah ... you know your stuff," Cockerill noted. "He runs a limousine service."

"I didn't know that," Jack admitted.

"He's only got one car. A six-passenger stretch limo. Buck said it's pretty cool, though."

Buck being in Mouse's limousine was an important piece of information. Jack would apply for a wiretap that'd include the limo, but he didn't want Cockerill to realize the significance of what he'd let slip. "I don't care about some car," he replied. "Tell me about the money. How and when are the growers paid?"

"A day after the weed is pressed and the bricks counted, Buck pays Neal, who hands it off to their prospects to pay the growers. The GDs get their cut after the weed is delivered to Dallas, then Bob and Roxie get paid by Neal when they return."

"I would've thought Bob and Roxie received the money from the West 12th Street boys and brought it back themselves for disbursement."

"Nope, it don't come back with them. I got no idea how that works other than it takes a coupla weeks before I get it. I think only the exec in our club know those details. All I know is that eventually I get my cut, along with the payment for the GDs."

Jack nodded. *Damien is too smart to ever let those details be known to someone like Cockerill.* He decided on a different approach. "Who passes the money to you?"

"Sometimes the chapter treasurer, sometimes different guys. I never know who until it happens."

Something about the tone of Cockerill's voice said he was protecting his own financial interests. Jack knew that to push it any further might cause him to clam up. "Which is when you hand some money over to Buck to pay the GDs," Jack said.

"Yeah. Then the GDs divvy it up amongst themselves. It won't be Buck I hand it to next time. He'll be getting his full patch soon. We're supposed to vote on it, but everyone knows it's a done deal."

"How soon?"

"September twenty-seventh. That's when Pure E takes over as national prez."

"Current president of the Winnipeg chapter," Jack said.

"Was. He's moving here this weekend. Guess he's sick of the mosquitos and the snow in Winterpeg."

Jack glanced at Sophie. "The man's real name is Purvis Evans. He was nicknamed Pure E — short for pure evil. A name, I'm told, that's well earned."

"Sounds like a nice guy," Sophie said.

"It'll be a big party with Damien stepping down on the same day Buck gets his patch," Cockerill added. "Another prospect will then be picked to deal with the GDs."

A big party for Damien to celebrate his success. Jack sighed. "Damien must've made a fortune over the years. Has he ever told you what he's done with it or where he plans to retire?"

Cockerill smirked. "Nope. I'm too low on the ladder for Damien to even acknowledge, let alone talk about shit like that. He surpassed my league long ago."

Jack realized he'd clenched his own fist in anger. *Cool it. This asshole is already smirking because Damien got away with it. Don't give him the satisfaction of seeing how pissed off it makes me feel.*

"Same goes for the other guys at the executive level," Cockerill continued. "I don't know how they get their cut or what they do with it. For the rest of us guys doin' the work, we take the cash."

"Which guys?"

"It varies. Depends on who happens to be around when we need something done or to oversee a shipment of cocaine or something coming in."

"Speaking of cocaine, I've heard a rumour that you guys are opening up a new connection in Europe," Jack said.

Cockerill looked startled. "I've never heard anything about that," he lied. "Who told you that?"

Jack gave Cockerill a hard cold stare in response. A new plan formed. His primary target would not be the Gypsy Devils or Bob and Roxie. Neither would it be the West 12th Street gang.

Damien, I missed my chance with you, but nailing Buck and your top execs would sure lessen the bitter taste of defeat.

Chapter Five

It was eleven o'clock the following morning when Jack eased the throttle back on the small boat he and Laura had rented. Earlier they'd checked the marina but didn't see Larry's boat.

As they slowly cruised past the location where Cockerill had told them the grow-op was located, Laura used binoculars to scan the shoreline. "I see it," she said. "Red flames painted on the bow."

"Good. At least it confirms some of what Weenie Wagger told us," Jack replied. "I'll feel a little better passing on our intel to Drug Section."

Laura nodded. The mandate of the Intelligence unit was to gather information to the point that they could point the appropriate investigative unit in the right direction, but not become so involved themselves that it'd necessitate testifying in court. Not being required to testify would help protect their own undercover identities and prevent gruelling questioning by defence lawyers attempting to identify informants.

"We'll continue on past for about twenty minutes," Jack said, "then head back to the marina."

Movement on shore caught Laura's attention. She toyed with the adjustment on the binoculars. "There's someone at the front of the boat now. He's untying a rope."

Moments later Larry's boat headed out behind them and went in the opposite direction.

"What do you think?" Laura asked. "If he's going to the marina, it'll take him close to two hours for a round trip. Would be nice to verify the crop is there and how big it really is."

Jack nodded. "If I moor about a ten-minute walk farther down the shore we can walk in. If he comes back sooner we'll walk along the shoreline like a couple of beachcombers. I doubt it'd heat him up that much."

Twenty minutes later Jack and Laura made their way along the rocky shoreline until they came to a length of blue nylon rope tied to several concrete blocks. It was where Larry had moored his boat. A small path led away from the shore up a slope into a forest. Jack glanced back at the ocean once more. It was calm, and the sound of an approaching boat would be easily heard. He gave Laura a reassuring nod and they silently made their way up the path.

Soon they came to a No Trespassing sign and Jack smiled. "Pretty good indication we're on the right path, considering we're on Crown land."

A minute later the blast from a shotgun sent pellets ripping into the trees and bushes around them. Instinctively they dived for cover behind trees on each side of the path.

"Son of a bitch!" Jack exclaimed. He glanced at Laura. "You okay?"

"Yes." Like Jack, she already had her pistol in her hand. "You?"

He gave her a thumbs-up.

"You-you guys get away from here!" yelled a man from a ridge above them.

Jack peered out from behind the tree and glimpsed a man wearing camouflage clothing and holding a shotgun. He spotted Jack and raised the gun again, but Jack ducked and the man held his fire.

"Saw one man," he whispered to Laura. "He's too far away to be effective with what he's using. The spray pattern will be too large."

"You might think so," Laura replied, "but it only takes one slug and a few of them already whizzed past me."

"Go away!" the man hollered again. He sounded like he was about to cry. "You-you guys are stupid. Can't you read? You can't come here!"

"Think he's stoned?" Laura asked.

"More like mentally challenged." Jack then yelled, "Okay, okay, we're really sorry! We want to go, but we're afraid to move, 'cause you'll shoot us."

"You shouldn't be here!" the man wailed.

"Take over and keep him talking," Jack whispered. "I'll slide back a bit and circle around behind."

"Better hurry," Laura said tersely. "Sounds like we're about to have company."

The sound of a boat approaching at high speed told Jack that Laura was right. He slid back down the slope and quickly circled around while Laura did her best to distract the man with conversation.

"I'm really, really sorry!" she shouted. "My boyfriend

and I were looking for wild mushrooms."

"But the sign says No Trespassing. You're s'posed to turn around!"

"I'm sorry. We thought it was an old sign. We know better now."

The conversation continued between Laura and the shotgun wielder while Jack circled around. Through the bushes he saw the man standing with his back to him in a small clearing beside a tent. As Jack crept closer, the sound of the boat engine stopped.

"Dwayne!" a male voice yelled from the direction of the boat.

"A man and a lady are here!" Dwayne yelled back. "I told them to leave but they're still here."

"Police!" Jack shouted, peering out from behind a cedar tree with his pistol pointed at Dwayne. "Drop your weapon!"

Dwayne spun around, discharging another round as he did. The shot was so far from Jack that he knew it was accidental.

"Drop it!" Jack shouted again. "Don't make me kill you!"

Dwayne ignored the command and turned toward the shore. "Larry, he's got a gun! Larry!"

"Put your hands up!" Laura ordered from below.

Jack knew that Larry was no longer a problem. He concentrated on Dwayne. "I said drop it!"

Dwayne turned and nervously raised the shotgun toward Jack. "You go away!"

"I'm a police officer," Jack declared. "I'm not going away because I'm doing my job. Drop the gun!"

The next yell was from Larry. "Dwayne! Do what they say! It's okay."

"But nobody's s'posed to be here," Dwayne cried.

"Damn it, Dwayne," Larry responded. "Drop the fuckin' shotgun or I'll kick your arse!"

Dwayne let go of the shotgun like it had given him an electric shock.

Guess I should've told him I'd kick his arse.

A few minutes later both Larry and Dwayne were sitting on the ground with their hands handcuffed behind their backs. Jack retrieved a Newfoundland driver's licence from Larry's wallet identifying him as Lawrence Beggs. Dwayne didn't have identification and said he didn't know how to drive.

Jack handed Larry's licence and wallet to Laura to check for criminal records and warrants. He then went exploring. When he returned, he motioned for her to step away from their captives so they could talk in private.

"There's a small stream up there they've been using for irrigation," Jack said. "They have lots of plants hidden in several patches through the bush. Could be a thousand. Also saw a generator, hydroponic equipment, camouflage netting, and a pump to get water from the stream. They've got quite the operation going."

"No criminal records and no warrants," Laura said. "They're brothers and you're right about Dwayne being mentally challenged. The two of them talked a little while you were gone. Larry isn't what you would call sharp, either. He's four years older than Dwayne and is being protective. He told me all the plants are his and that Dwayne has nothing to do with it."

"Nothing to do with it except shooting at us with a shotgun," Jack said sarcastically.

"So what now?" Laura asked.

"Busting these two would screw up our investigation. Satans Wrath would know that someone talked. They could end up putting the Gypsy Devils on hold for who knows how long."

"So much for rushing to get a tracker on the semi or doing a major conspiracy."

"A conspiracy that includes Satans Wrath and the West 12th Street gang. Not these two yahoos."

"Hey," Larry hollered. "As I was sayin', the dope's all mine. Let Dwayne go and I'll cop to it."

"I'll talk with you in a minute!" Jack said.

"So what should we do?" Laura asked. "After what happened we can't turn them loose. They'd blab."

"Not if we turn them into informants."

"We're already a couple of levels above these guys. Whatever Larry and Dwayne tell us won't matter … but you're right. It should keep them from talking."

"What's the big deal?" Larry again. "Let Dwayne go!"

"This might be your lucky day," Jack said, walking closer to the two captives. "Give me who you're selling the weed to and we won't bust you."

"I'm not sayin'," Larry replied.

"Yeah, we're not sayin'," Dwayne echoed.

"Dwayne, you stay out of this!" Larry reprimanded him. "You don't know nothin' and you ain't got nothin' to do with nothin'."

Jack squatted beside Larry. "Are you forgetting that Dwayne tried to kill us?"

"I was shooting above your head," Dwayne said. "I was only scaring you."

"Oh, it scared us, all right," Jack replied. "We were lucky that the spray pattern was so wide that the slugs went past us. But then you fired again when I told you to drop your weapon."

"That was an accident. The gun went off by itself. Wasn't me who did it."

"I told you to never touch it," Larry scolded him. "Why? Why'd you do it?"

Dwayne hung his head and started blubbering.

Jack cast Larry a sympathetic look. "I feel bad, but trying to kill two police officers over a grow-op … Do you realize that Dwayne may be spending the rest of his life in prison?"

"Larry!" Dwayne cried. "I don't wanna go to jail! I wanna stay here!"

Larry swallowed as he looked at his weeping brother.

"Talk to us and tell the truth," Jack said. "We'll make sure nobody finds out you talked. Your brother's awfully vulnerable. Think what they'll do to him in prison."

Larry's eyes welled up, then he nodded.

Jack and Laura helped him to his feet and they led him a short distance away to talk. Larry told them that by the next Tuesday he was to have the crop harvested and put in duffle bags. He'd then get a call from someone nicknamed Banjo, who'd ask him how many crabs he caught, which was code for how many duffle bags he had. Banjo would then tell him to bring them to the party, which would be on either Wednesday or Thursday, depending upon which night the delivery was to take place. The night of the delivery he'd take the duffle bags to the marina, then wait for another call before meeting Banjo on a highway in a remote area.

Jack knew from an intelligence report that Frederick Smith, a criminal who went by the alias Banjo, had attended the Labour Day ride. At that time Smith wore the bottom rocker for the Gypsy Devils which identified him as one of their prospects. Larry was telling the truth. "Do you have Banjo's phone number?" he asked.

"It's on a piece of paper in my wallet." Larry looked at Laura. "It's the one I saw you write down a few minutes ago."

Laura tapped her notebook to indicate she'd recorded it.

Jack continued. "Have you done this before?"

"Yeah, last year," Larry admitted.

"Was it Banjo you dealt with before?"

"Yeah. He's really rich. He arrived in a big black car like a movie star to pick up the dope. Even had a lady driver."

"Do you know any of Banjo's friends?"

"I met a guy who hangs out with Banjo by the name of Neal. I took him and a couple of his buddies fishin' once, but that's all."

Jack nodded. He knew from what Cockerill told him that it was one of the Gypsy Devils, a guy called Mouse, who ran the limousine service. Banjo was far from rich. Using a limo was a way to avoid prosecution if they were caught. Police would have a hard time proving that the drugs belonged to the limo driver and not the passenger.

"It's only me that takes it to Banjo," Larry said. "Dwayne ain't too good at stuff like that. I only got him helpin' me so I can look after him."

"Don't you have any other relatives to look after him?" Jack asked.

"None I ever knowed. Me and Dwayne lived in about a dozen foster homes all over Newfoundland when we was growing up, but … well, I guess he was a handful. Ain't nobody I know would be willing to look after him." Larry frowned. "It's kind of a worry for me when I get older. That's why I was hopin' to make some money, so he'd be taken care of."

"How much money did you make last year?"

"I got thirty grand, but my operation was only half the size. I reinvested the money to buy good equipment and make it bigger."

"I'll give you my phone number," Jack said. "I want you to tell me any time you hear from Banjo."

"Larry! Am I goin' to jail?" Dwayne cried from where he sat.

"Nah, everything's okay!" Larry shouted back. "We ain't goin' to jail. It was all a mistake."

"Yeah … they shouldn't have come up here. We had a *sign* and they shoulda —"

"Shut up Dwayne! Lard Jesus, you got more lip than a coal bucket! I told you never to touch the gun."

"I'm sorry. I won't do it again. Can I get up now?"

"No. Stay where you're at. I'll be dere da-rackley."

"What did he say?" Laura whispered to Jack.

"I speak a little Newfie. I think he said he'd be there directly."

Larry returned his attention to Jack. "Are you gonna arrest Banjo as soon as I give him the weed?"

"No. Later I plan to arrest the people Banjo hands it to. He might not ever be charged."

"Then they won't know it was me who opened my yap." Larry looked relieved.

"Definitely not. I'll always protect you as long as you tell me the truth."

A minute later the handcuffs were removed from Larry and Dwayne.

"Are we goin' to jail?" Dwayne asked.

"No, I told ya we ain't and you're not to ever tell anyone about this," Larry said.

"How come?"

"Because we're secretly working for the police now."

Dwayne looked surprised, then delighted. "You mean we're deputies?"

"Yes, and you're not to tell anyone," Larry said again. "It's a secret."

"I understand. I'm not stupid. I watch television, you know. I'm not stupid."

"Once you deliver the dope to Banjo I'll consider us even," Jack said, "on one condition."

"What's that?" Larry asked.

"That you go straight afterwards. If you don't, I'll charge your brother. You got that?"

It was a moment before Larry answered, "Okay, let's shake on that."

Jack hid his amusement and shook his hand, after which Dwayne stuck out his hand. Jack shook it.

"One last thing," Jack said. "We're taking the shotgun with us."

Chapter Six

Late that afternoon, Jack and Laura met with their boss. Staff Sergeant Rose Wood leaned forward in her chair, listening attentively as Jack outlined his goal and his plan to achieve it. When he was done, Rose nodded thoughtfully. "You want satellite trackers on Mouse's limo and Bob's semi?"

"Along with bugs in both," Jack stressed. "I'll get the DEA to take over surveillance of the semi when it crosses the border."

"Where you hope to identify the weed for cocaine connection and nail them all in a conspiracy," Rose said.

"That's the plan. It's a good opportunity to gather evidence from the ground up."

"Literally," added Laura. "From the marijuana grown here to the cocoa plants in South America."

"Maybe when the truck is being unloaded and the DEA bust them, they'll find evidence to support the rumour about Satans Wrath widening its cocaine-distribution network into Europe," Rose noted.

"Probably not any direct evidence," Jack said. "There won't be any full-patch Satans Wrath going anywhere close to Bob's truck … either here or in the States. I also doubt that the coke connection would show up in person when the truck arrives in Dallas."

"You don't think catching full-patch Satans Wrath is a possibility?" Rose asked.

"There's always hope that the DEA will come up with a lead on the money trail to connect the dots, but so far we've never been successful in that regard."

"So I've noticed," Rose said. "What do you know about the West 12th Street gang in Dallas?"

"I called a friend in the DEA. He says the gang is well connected with the Mexican mafia and are affiliated with other gangs in several major U.S. cities."

"Mexican mafia," mused Rose. "Explains the coke connection."

"Exactly, but knowing and proving are different things. My idea is to let the semi return without any arrests being made, then see if we can discover how they move the money by working back when everyone gets paid."

"Tracking the money trail has never progressed beyond the bottom end before," Rose said. "What makes you think you'll succeed this time?"

Jack made a face. "It probably won't succeed the first time, but it's a start. At least we know the money's not being brought back with whoever delivers the dope. We may have to watch several deliveries take place before we can figure out how the money is distributed."

"You're talking months, perhaps even a year or two."

"One way to really hurt Satans Wrath is to take away their money. I think it's worth the gamble. All we'd risk losing is the chance to arrest a bunch of chumps with some weed. I've talked with Sammy Crofton in the Drug Section. He's a good guy and in charge of a team. He's on board with the idea. I told him we'd assist his team with getting a wiretap and do a bit more preliminary work, then the operation would basically be in their ball park."

"Are the DEA willing to let two-hundred-and-fifty keys of marijuana go?" Rose asked.

"I'm sure of it," Jack replied. "They'll be interested in linking the cocaine connection and looking into the money-laundering aspect, as well."

"Not to mention, the truck makes regular runs," Laura put in. "If things work out, they'll get the opportunity to bust them another time."

"The DEA might also be able to do some side busts on the marijuana without heating anything up," Jack added. "That'd provide more evidence for the conspiracy. If we surreptitiously get a sample of the weed here before the truck leaves Vancouver, it would tie in nicely."

"Surreptitiously get a sample?" Rose looked doubtful.

"I'll think of something."

Rose raised an eyebrow. "I'm sure you would." She smiled to show she was joking. "The thing is, when it comes to the point of being surreptitious, we're talking about testifying in court — which means Drug Section should be in control of the investigation, along with the DEA. Ultimately it will be their decision of what should be done and when."

"Certainly," Jack agreed, "but I still have a vested interest to protect my informant. Both Drug Section and the DEA will appreciate that."

"Is your informant in jeopardy?"

Jack grinned. "No, but it's a good excuse to maintain some control over the investigation."

Rose nodded. "You said you wanted the trackers and bugs in place by next Tuesday. Do you think that between you and Drug Section you can get a wiretap order prepared that fast?"

"If Laura and I work double shifts we should manage. Sammy will apply for the wiretap, but we'll help him with the paperwork. His team will also do surveillance on the limo and the truck. Then when the wiretap's approved, we'll have an idea of the best time and location for the team to sneak in and plant the bugs and the trackers."

"Speaking of bug planters, have you checked with their office to see if they currently have the space to monitor the wiretaps for us?"

"I called them. They said they could handle it."

"Sounds like you have your ducks in a row," Rose said. "Why are you sitting here? Get to work."

The next several days were hectic for Jack and Laura, but by Monday afternoon a judge had approved the wiretap order. It named Buck Zabat, Mickey O'Bryan, alias Mouse, Frederick Smith, alias Banjo, and Neal, Bob, and Roxie Barlow. An attempt to obtain a wiretap order on the other

Gypsy Devil prospects had been turned down by the prosecutor, who deemed there was insufficient evidence.

By late Monday night, an electronics team was successful in planting a satellite tracker and listening device in Mouse's limo.

Bob stored his semi in the barn next to his house in Delta, which was about a twenty-minute drive out of Vancouver. A pit bull was observed chained in the yard, and any attempt to place electronic equipment in the semi wasn't possible because someone had always been home.

At noon on Tuesday Jack was at his desk when he received a call from Nicole Purney, who was a civilian member tasked with monitoring the wiretaps. Informants' identities were not disclosed in the wiretap, but simply referred to as "informant A" or "informant B." Nicole knew that Jack was one of the lead investigators conducting a drug investigation involving the named targets with the Gypsy Devils and Satans Wrath, but that was all.

"Banjo made his first call," Nicole said, "and I'm certain it's a good one. He asked some guy how many crabs he caught and the guy said seven. The guy then told him to hang onto them and bring them to the party on Thursday."

"Any idea who Banjo was calling?" Jack asked.

"No, it's a disposable phone. The guy was complaining that he might have food poisoning. He sounded like he was in pain."

"Give me the guy's number. I'll talk to my informant later and see if I can match it with other names and numbers he might have." Jack smiled when he saw that the number Nicole gave him was Larry's number, which he already had in his notebook.

"Hold a sec," said Nicole. "Banjo has called someone else … asking how many cases of beer the guy is bringing to Thursday's party."

"Maybe they're having a party drinking beer and eating crab," Jack suggested, pretending to question Nicole's assessment.

"I don't think so. Doing my job, you get a feeling for people's tone of voice after a while. I think these calls are dirty."

"I believe you," Jack replied. "Have you told Drug Section?"

"Not yet, but I'll give Sammy a call."

"Thanks." Jack felt his phone vibrate. "I've got another call. Talk to you later."

Jack answered his phone and was pleased that it was Larry, telling him that Banjo had called him to say the delivery was set for Thursday night.

"You're grunting like you hurt yourself," Jack noted. "Is something wrong?"

"I've been throwin' up," Larry replied. "I think I got food poisoning." He yelped in pain.

"Cramps in your abdomen?" Jack asked.

Larry moaned. "The pain was around my belly button earlier, but it's now down on my lower right side. Maybe what I haven't puked is workin' its way out."

"It could be appendicitis. You need to see a doctor. If your appendix ruptures and you're stuck out there, you could die."

"Yeah, but the weed … Our deal needs to — Shit dat 'urts!" Larry moaned. "I've already cleared out most of my hydro equipment and got it back at my apartment. All I need is for Banjo to get the weed. Another two days and — Lard tunderin' Jesus b'y, she 'urts."

"Get your ass to a doctor now," Jack ordered. "Then call me back."

"But what if you're right? Won't they put me in the hospital?"

"Yes, but only for a couple of days if it isn't ruptured."

"A coupla days? I gotta be here Thursday. Dwayne can't handle the delivery. He can't even drive."

"One step at a time. See what the doctor says. Maybe it's nothing, but if worse comes to worst we'll figure something out. If it's appendicitis, the GDs will just have to wait or pick it up themselves."

"They won't go out in the middle of the night in my dinky little boat to get it," Larry muttered. "I got six duffle bags of it stored at the campsite now. Got about one more to go." He hesitated before going on, "Still, me nerves is rubbed right raw wit da pain."

"Look, if it ruptures, you'll be a lot worse."

"You really think it'd kill me?"

"Definitely."

"That's all I need is to wake up dead. Okay, I'll do it. Dwayne can take care of the remainin' bag. Except …"

"Except what?"

"If I's gone a coupla days, Dwayne'll be stranded out there … but guess it's okay. He's got food."

"Give him my number," Jack suggested. "If you end up in the hospital and he needs anything, tell him to call me."

"Yeah … okay."

———

It was 6:00 p.m. and Jack was on his way home from work when Larry called back and said, "I'm at Vancouver General. You was right, b'y. It's me appendix. I'm goin' in for surgery in a few minutes. They think it just ruptured an' said I'll be here for at least five days. I better call Banjo and —" A cry of pain and a nurse's voice in the background interrupted his sentence.

"Forget about Banjo until after your surgery," Jack said.

"I ... okay, okay."

Two hours later Jack received a call that would haunt him for the rest of his life.

"Officer Taggart! Officer Taggart! It's Dwayne! I can't get hold of Larry! He won't answer!"

"It's okay, Dwayne, settle down," Jack said calmly. "Your brother had to go to the hospital, but he'll be okay."

"I know! He tol' me, but they're stealing all our bags," Dwayne said excitedly. "I gotta stop 'em."

"Who's stealing the bags?" Jack's tone sharpened.

"Three men in a boat. They got three bags already and went back for the rest."

"Do they know you're there?"

"No, I was hiding — but I'm gonna trick them and smash their motor," Dwayne said, sounding pleased with himself.

"No, stay hiding," Jack ordered.

"I got a rock."

"No! Don't do anything except stay hidden."

The sound of rock smashing on metal told Jack he wasn't heard. "Stop!" Jack screamed into the phone. "Can you hear me? Stop!"

The noise stopped and Dwayne said, "Uh-oh, they're coming. Uh-oh."

"Run!" Jack yelled. "Get away from there!"

Then he heard Dwayne shout, "I'm a deputy! You-you're in big trouble!"

"Think you can fuck with my boat and get away with it?" a distant man yelled.

"Stay away from me! I'm warning you!" Dwayne shrieked.

"Why you little fucker!" The man sounded surprised, as well as angry.

The sound of a gunshot caused Jack's arm to twitch.

"He shot me, Officer Taggart!" Dwayne cried. "In my tummy. I'm gonna die, aren't I? Oh no, oh no …"

"Dwayne! Fall down! Pretend you're dead!"

"It really hurts," Dwayne sobbed. "I — Stay away!" he cried. "You go away!"

A second gunshot echoed over the phone, followed by what sounded like the phone bouncing off a rock and into water. Jack stood with his mouth agape, holding his breath as he strained to listen. All he heard was his own conscience screaming at him. Telling him he'd screwed up and that Dwayne had been murdered as a result.

Chapter Seven

It was an hour and forty-five minutes later when Jack and Laura arrived in a high-speed Zodiac boat in the company of officers from the Integrated Border Enforcement Team.

Powerful spotlights cut through the darkness and illuminated the shoreline. As the boat approached the shore, Jack leaped off into the knee-deep water of the rising tide and ran toward the pathway. His calls to Dwayne went unanswered.

It was midnight by the time Corporal Connie Crane of the Integrated Homicide Investigation Team arrived on another I-BET boat, along with officers from the Forensic Science and Identification Service.

Jack took Connie aside and tersely told her the background of the situation, starting with his and Laura's first meeting with Larry and Dwayne and ending with the details of the call he'd received from Dwayne earlier.

"I take it you've checked the area?" Connie asked, glancing around.

"I-BET searched the shoreline and out in the ocean while we were waiting for you. They didn't find anything. Laura and I went to where Larry and Dwayne have a tent, but there was also nobody there. We stayed off the path so as not to contaminate the scene. Same goes for where the tent is pitched. I did look inside, but was careful not to step on any footprints — not that I saw any. The ground is matted with pine needles. There's one thing I noticed later," Jack said, looking forlornly back at the entrance to the path.

"What's that?"

"Larry had a blue nylon rope tied to some cement blocks that he used for mooring his boat. The rope and the blocks are gone."

"I'll call the dive team out in the morning," Connie said. "For now, I want a written statement. Word for word of the phone call you got tonight, if you can remember."

Remember? I'll never forget it. "Already done," Jack replied. "It's on the boat I arrived in." He pointed to the I-BET Zodiac.

"Do you think you'd be able to recognize the voice of whoever yelled at Dwayne for screwing with his boat?"

"The guy wasn't close enough to the phone. Maybe even running. With the sound of the waves … well, I'd never recognize the voice."

"You sure?" Connie asked, a hint of suspicion in her voice.

Jack knew she was thinking about previous cases they'd worked where some people he investigated turned up dead. "If I could identify the voice, I'd be after you to let me listen to whatever suspects you might come up with — but I can't."

"How'd you and Laura know to come here the first time and look for a grow-op?"

"From another informant." Jack swallowed some bile. *Christ, I wonder if my voice sounds as acidic as my throat feels.*

"Is there any way this other informant could've had something to do with —"

"No. He wanted the drugs to be delivered by Larry to save his own ass. He's definitely not involved."

"Could the Gypsy Devils have come to do a rip-off ... maybe not realizing Larry had a brother?"

"Possible, but I don't think so," Jack replied. "The GDs would definitely rip someone off — but not Satans Wrath. They wouldn't risk pissing those guys off."

"Maybe Larry will have some potential suspects," Connie suggested.

"Maybe. I'll talk to him. Find out who else knew about this place."

"I want to be with you when you talk to him," Connie stated flatly.

"I expected you would." Jack nodded. "I'll send Laura back to the office to compile a dossier for you of all the Gypsy Devils and their known associates. While she's doing that, you and I can notify Larry."

"I appreciate that." As they returned to the boats, Connie gave Jack a sideways glance. "Do you have any suspicions at all as to who did it? Even an inkling?"

"If I did, I wouldn't have been here waiting for you," he replied coldly.

It was 6:00 a.m. when Jack and Connie identified them-selves at the nurses' station and explained they were there to do a next-of-kin notification. The nurse led them to where Larry was sleeping. Three other patients were sleeping in the room and the nurse pulled a curtain around Larry's bed for privacy before leaving.

Jack stared at Larry, then took a deep breath and slowly exhaled before gently shaking him awake.

Larry mumbled as he awoke, then his eyes widened. "What're you doing here? Who's she?"

"Corporal Crane," Jack replied. "She and I are working together at the moment."

"Whaddaya doin' here?"

"I've some bad news," Jack said. "I think Dwayne was murdered last night by someone ripping off your stash."

"What? No! What do you mean, you think?" Larry demanded.

Jack quietly relayed the phone call he'd received, along with the news that Dwayne could not be found and that the nylon anchor rope and cement blocks were missing.

"Maybe they took him to scare him," Larry suggested, apparently unable to accept the reality of the situation.

"I told you that Dwayne said he was shot in the stomach," Jack reminded him. "Then there was that other shot and he never spoke again."

Larry squeezed his eyes tight, but that didn't stop the tears from running down his cheeks. "I shouldn't have left 'im out dere alone," he said.

Jack laid a hand on his shoulder and gave a sympathetic squeeze. A moment later Larry's face clouded with anger and he jerked back. "You took the shotgun away," he said accusingly. "The poor boy had nothin' to defend himself with!"

"I'm sorry, but —"

"You're sorry?" Larry was almost yelling now. "That's it? Me brother's dead and you're sorry? You said you'd protect us!"

Jack lowered his voice. "You're angry right now. So am I. Whoever did it will be caught. That I promise," he said adamantly.

"Like you promised to look after us and not let anything happen?" Larry snorted contemptuously.

"I understand why you're pissed off at me and we can talk about that later, but now we need to ask you some questions."

Larry acted like he hadn't heard. The anger on his face changed to grief. "Aw fuck. Who am I kiddin'? It ain't your fault. I should never've got him involved. It's me who got 'im killed."

"You were looking after your brother the best you could," Jack said. "Sometimes the consequences of our actions are never what we expected or wanted. It wasn't you who murdered Dwayne. You need to realize that."

Larry stared glumly toward his feet without replying.

Connie cleared her throat. "I'm sorry we have to ask you questions at a time like this, but every second we waste helps the killer. Who else knew where the grow-op was?"

Larry ignored Connie and looked sharply at Jack. "Banjo! You think Banjo —"

"I don't think Banjo did it," Jack said, "but if he did, I'll find out."

"How? He'll just lie to ya."

Jack didn't want Larry to know about the wiretap, let alone that he had an informant in Satans Wrath, so he decided to lie. "The same way I knew where your grow-op was."

"How'd ya know?"

"You have to swear to me that you'll never tell anyone," Jack said.

"I swear," Larry said solemnly.

"One of the Gypsy Devils is talking to me. I'll soon know if they're responsible."

"They gotta be the ones," Larry said decisively. "Only them knows where it is."

"You sure?"

"Yeah, I'm sure."

"Could Dwayne have told someone where the grow-op is?" Connie asked.

"Nah. He don't even know how to get to it on his own. Besides, I keeps a close eye on 'im. Ain't no way he told anyone." Larry looked at Jack. "Forget about trying to protect me. I'll testify or do anything you want. I don't care what happens to me now."

"There *is* something you could help us with immediately," Jack told him. "I want you to call Banjo. Tell him that it was you Dwayne called last night and say that you called the cops to try to save him because you're in the hospital. Then say that Corporal Crane from Homicide came by to tell you that Dwayne couldn't be found. Banjo will want to know what you told the police about the weed, so tell him that you said it was yours and that you planned to sell it yourself."

"He might ask if I'm being charged," Larry said, looking at Jack and Connie for an answer. "With having a grow-op I mean."

Connie shook her head. "Your cooperation … and loss in this matter will ensure that you're not charged."

"And all my hydro equipment?" Larry asked. "Are ya takin' dat?"

"Damn it, Larry," Jack said. "The deal we made was for you to go straight after —"

"I intend to," Larry protested, "but the equipment cost me a lotta money. If you don't take it, I could sell it on eBay or somethin'."

"Cooperate with us and I'll let you keep it," Connie said. "Make the call."

Larry did as requested. When he was finished, he hung up and scowled.

"What did he say?" Jack asked.

"At first he was surprised. Then he pretended to be all sympathetic. I could tell it was an act. The fucker was more concerned about losing the weed than what happened to Dwayne. He was worried, too, about what I told the cops. Seemed okay, though, when I told 'im what you said to tell 'im."

"Anything else?" Jack asked.

"Yeah, well I guess you heard me goin' on 'bout how it was only his guys who knew about the grow-op an' he better find out who did it."

"What did he say?" asked Connie.

"Said he'd get back to me."

"We'll find out who did it," Jack said. "You can't be certain it was the Gypsy Devils. Personally I don't think it was."

"They're the only ones who know about it. It has —"

"It could be that one of them told someone else," Jack interrupted him. "It may take some time for us to find out."

"Wish I could find out right now," Larry said bitterly.

"We all do," said Connie, "and believe me, we'll do everything possible to catch the killer."

Jack pointed his finger at Larry's face and spoke harshly. "You leave this to us! You hear me?"

"Yeah ... of course."

Chapter Eight

At 8:30 a.m. Jack and Connie entered the monitoring room and listened to the call that Larry had made to Banjo, then to a call that Banjo made immediately afterwards to Carl Shepherd.

"Who's Shepherd?" Connie asked as the call began.

"President of the Gypsy Devils," Jack explained. "If it was Satans Wrath, there is no way a prospect would talk to the president direct. It shows how undisciplined this club really is."

They listened as Banjo told Shepherd about the call he received from Larry.

"Fuck, another rip," Shepherd responded. "Who the fuck's doing it?"

"If it's the same ones," Banjo growled, "this is the first time that someone's been murdered. It could cause some heat."

"At least Larry was smart enough not to mention us," Shepherd noted.

"Yeah ... but now what?"

"Contact Neal and tell him to let his buddy know. There's a possibility we may come up short."

"Hopefully the other three will have enough to cover it, but yeah, I'll let Neal know."

"Also get a new phone. Did Larry call you on the one you're using now?"

"Yeah."

"Keep it in case he calls, but in the future don't talk business on it. Meet him in person if you need to. Also check and make sure he isn't wired if you do."

"Figure Larry will rat?" Banjo asked.

"Fuck, his brother was whacked," Shepherd replied. "What if he thinks we were involved? Who knows what he'll do?"

"Yeah, guess it don't hurt to be careful."

"Let's hope the cops solve it quick," Shepherd added before disconnecting.

Jack looked at Connie. "So much for the GDs being involved."

"Also this isn't the first rip," Connie said. "When Shepherd said Neal needed to contact his buddy, I presume he was talking about someone in Satans Wrath, wasn't he?"

"Yes, likely one of their prospects or maybe a full-patch member," Jack replied, not wanting to divulge any more than he needed to in order to protect his informant.

Connie nodded, then reached for her phone to take a call. When it was done she said, "That was one of my guys — Lyle Roster. He's still at the scene. He said Forensics found a cellphone when the tide went out. Judging by the distance it was from shore and the height of the tide at the time, someone threw it."

"Dwayne's phone. Did they find anything else? Keel marks from a boat, footprints, or the rock Dwayne used to strike their motor?"

"Nothing. The dive team is still searching. Roster said Forensics sectioned off the shore into squares the size of floor mats when the tide was out. Usually when we say 'no stone was left unturned,' it's just an expression. In this case it wasn't. No sign of any stones with fresh scrapings or anything to indicate a rock had been used to bash a motor."

"What about elsewhere — up at the camp?"

"They found a few footprints where the plants were growing, but nothing of value around the campsite."

"Those footprints will belong to Larry and Dwayne," Jack said. "They'd already harvested the weed and put it into duffle bags at the campsite."

"Forensics will be there all day. Maybe something will turn up."

"Like a body," Jack said grimly.

"A body? Are you holding something back from me?" Connie asked suspiciously.

"I'm referring to Dwayne," Jack replied. "Come on, Connie, give me a break."

"Sorry. I'm so bloody tired I can't think straight."

"Any thoughts on how you want to work this?" he asked. "Maybe let me focus on the bikers and you check for other possibilities?"

"Christ, Jack, it's me you're talking to," Connie replied in exasperation. "I don't need any more bodies turning up — and I am thinking straight about that."

"Connie, I want whoever did it arrested as much as you."

"Arrested? I know you. Having one of your informants murdered — you take this personal."

"You're damn right I do. Larry was actually my informant, but Dwayne … well, I guess he was my informant, too. He was trying to be one of the good guys and was calling me for help." He grimaced. "It's eating away at me that I should've done something different. Maybe arrested them both to start with. I don't know." He met Connie's gaze. "Of course I want the case solved. I'm a police officer. Not some lunatic looking to kill someone."

"Maybe so, but I want you to stay out of the investigation," she said forcefully.

Jack suppressed his emotions. In his heart he knew she was right and gave a nod of agreement. "I understand. Defence would claim I was biased because of some sort of personal rage. They'd imply that I tampered with the evidence and was lying about whatever testimony I gave."

"You're damn right they would, which is why you can't be involved."

"Still, I've got these wiretaps," Jack said. "I told you I didn't think the bikers were involved. The call between Shepherd and Banjo proves it. I'm not dropping the biker investigation."

Connie was silent.

"What're you thinking?" Jack asked.

"That I haven't been to bed in twenty-six hours. I'm going back to the office, do a quick report, and assign day shift to work on it. Then I'm going home and starting fresh tomorrow morning."

"Sounds like a plan," Jack agreed.

"How about we meet tomorrow morning at ten o'clock with our bosses to update everyone in person and discuss the matter?" Connie suggested.

"To have me put in my place," Jack replied. "Sure, if it'll make you feel better."

Connie snorted. "I'd only feel better if you were assigned to highway patrol — and even then I'd wonder every time a body turned up alongside the highway."

Chapter Nine

Jack returned to the office and met up with Laura, after which they went to Staff Sergeant Rose Wood's office. Laura had already briefed Rose up to the point where Jack had gone with Connie to the hospital, but Rose wanted to hear it again from Jack, starting at the beginning.

Lack of sleep coupled with feelings of depression and anger caused Jack to rephrase and repeat his words a few times, but Rose got a clear picture.

"So what do you plan to do?" she asked.

"Carry on as before," Jack replied.

"I've seen how you've carried on before," Rose said quietly.

"What do you mean?"

"You've never lost an informant before, have you?" Rose asked.

"Never."

"It shows — and you know what I mean. I don't want you taking the law into your own hands."

"You sound like Connie." Jack was exasperated. "I went over the same thing with her. It's her case — I know that. I'll stick to working on the bikers and leave Dwayne to her."

"Swear to God?"

Jack allowed his anger to spill out in his voice. "You know I'm an atheist. What're you doing, testing to see how truthful I'm being?"

Rose stared at him. "Yes … and I'm sorry. Go home and get some sleep. We'll talk tomorrow. You need to settle down and get your mind focused."

Jack glared in response, but realized he couldn't deny what she said. "I am tired," he admitted. "I'll go home, but first I should call Sammy in Drug Section to let him know, in case anything else comes in on the wire."

"Swear on a three-olive martini that you'll go home?" Rose asked.

Jack gave a lopsided grin as he stood up. "Swearing on that means more to me than some Bible."

"Out of curiosity, have you ever even read the Bible?"

"Nah, I'm more of a non-fiction kind of reader."

Jack returned to his desk and called Sammy. He told him how he and Laura had turned Larry and Dwayne into informants and the details of Dwayne's call to Jack.

"Man, what a horrible thing to hear," Sammy said sombrely. "What do you want me to do?"

"There's nothing we can do as far as Dwayne goes," Jack replied. "That'll be up to Connie." *At least, for now.*

"We were going to set up on Banjo later today," Sammy said.

"Good. The GDs should be picking up weed from two other grow-ops tonight. Banjo will be involved, along with the other two prospects, Kyle Fennel and Arnold Hoster."

"Yeah, I've got their pictures from the reports you gave me."

"It'd be nice to discover where they press it and brick up," Jack said.

"For sure. Later on, if we could get video and audio in the place, it'd make for strong evidence. I also want to get a sample of the dope before it leaves, but so far it doesn't look good. Either Bob or Roxie or both have been staying close to home. Neal comes and goes at all hours. What with their dog, I doubt we'll get into the truck."

"Maybe you'll have more luck with the prospects," Jack said. "In the meantime I need to get some sleep. If anything interesting happens, give me a call."

"Will do — and Jack, I'm sorry about Dwayne. I know you're really protective of your sources. All I can say is … well, shit happens. It doesn't sound like there was anything you could've done different."

"It'll bother me a lot less when I find out who did it — and justice is served."

After arriving home late in the afternoon, Jack forced himself to stay awake until after dinner. An hour later he was brushing his teeth in preparation for bed when his phone vibrated.

It was Mack Cockerill. "What's happening?" he asked nervously. "I heard someone ripped off Larry's grow-op and whacked his brother."

"I heard," Jack said. "Homicide contacted me because I had an alert on the computer for me to be notified if Larry was ever checked."

"I didn't know he had a brother," Cockerill said.

"Likewise," Jack replied.

"You can still watch the truck. The GDs are actin' a little paranoid, though. Neal said he's gonna run whatever they brick up tonight over to Bob, then do the next run tomorrow — so everything's still a go. Sounds like there's still lots to make up for what was taken." Cockerill hesitated a moment, then said, "You're quiet. This doesn't change anything, does it?"

"A murder taking place does put a different spin on things."

"That ain't my fault! I didn't know that —"

"Relax," Jack interjected. "I'm not blaming you as long as you're straight with me."

"I've been straight," Cockerill insisted. "Tellin' you everything."

"I'm talking about you telling me what's going on with your own club. You think you're the only Satans Wrath talking?" Cockerill was the only informant Jack had in Satans Wrath, but if Cockerill believed someone else was talking, it would help ensure that he told Jack the truth and kept him up-to-date. On a psychological level, it would also ease the guy's conscience to think someone besides him was disloyal to the club.

Cockerill appeared to mull over what Jack said. "I didn't think talking about my own club was part of the deal."

"And I didn't think that a guy in the grow-op you gave me would be murdered. Makes me wonder if you were trying to prevent me from doing my job."

"I had nothing to do with it! Fuck, I want this done and over."

"It'll be over when I say it's over. Keep me in the loop about everything … and I mean everything. Which means about your club, too."

"Yeah, but my club wasn't part of the deal!"

"Neither was murder," Jack said angrily. "When someone is arrested for it, then we'll talk about whether or not we're even. In the meantime I want to know who did the rip and what you guys are doing about it."

"We got no suspects at the moment," Cockerill replied. "Ain't nothin' for us to do."

"If I hear of something that you should've told me, I'll do more than burn you to the media."

"Okay, okay." Jack could hear the sudden fear in Cockerill's voice. "I'll keep my ears open. No need to get all pissed off. It don't change nothin' as far as the truck goes. We got lots of weed to make up the difference. It'll still be packin' two-fifty down to Dallas."

"Good."

"I still think you'd be better off to take 'em down at the border," Cockerill added. "They'd never suspect me."

"It's not only your skin I have to worry about." Jack didn't want to let Cockerill know that his real plan was to get evidence on Satans Wrath. "Like I said, you're not the only guy talking to me, so don't even go there. How did you find out about Larry's brother being murdered?"

"I found out 'cause Larry called the GDs. Neal then told Buck, who told me. Apparently three guys showed up to do the rip and shot his brother. Larry was in the hospital at the time with a ruptured appendix and his brother was on the phone to him when it happened. He heard everything and called the cops."

"What did you do after Buck told you?" Jack asked.

"Passed it up the ladder to the chapter prez."

"Lance Morgan," Jack noted.

"Yeah. He's really pissed. We had two grow-ops ripped last year. Word is that other grow-ops have also been ripped."

"You think it's the same guys?"

"We don't know. At one rip, three guys were seen, but the other rip happened when nobody was around. At one time we wondered if it was the GDs rippin' us off."

"I don't see the GDs having the balls to rip you guys off," Jack said, "although they're pretty stupid."

"That's exactly what Lance said. We think whoever did it doesn't know it was our stuff. They'll pay big time if we find out."

"So it was only Lance you met with? Damien didn't show up?"

"Nah, no way the national prez would ever talk about somethin' like that in front of me."

"Even over this? You're full-patch. Doesn't he trust you?"

"Fuck, I was surprised that Lance let me talk to him about it. I went through the sergeant-at-arms first. The only reason Lance met me face to face is because I'm the only full-patch assigned to act as a go-between with the GDs. Buck deals with 'em, too, but he's still a prospect, and even though he's Damien's son, he still isn't allowed to talk to the prez direct about anything. He's gotta follow the rules like anyone else."

"Any thoughts as to what'll happen if your club finds out who the three guys are? Will it be physical retribution — or cash payback with interest?"

"Dunno, but am inclined to think they'd be joining Larry's brother."

I'll keep that in mind.

Jack placed a quick call to Sammy to tell him that Neal would be picking up whatever marijuana was bricked up tonight and then meeting with Bob to stash it in the semi.

"Perfect," Sammy said. "I'll divide the team. Half will continue watching Banjo and the other half will sit on Neal's and Bob's place. If we lose one, it'll give us a second chance."

"Neal prides himself on his surveillance-detection ability," Jack warned.

"The acreage they live on is down some backwater road in Delta," Sammy replied, "but eventually these roads funnel out to a main artery where there's more traffic. I'll have my guys watch from there. Worse comes to worst, we'll let him go rather than heat him up. Besides, we still have tomorrow night."

"Sounds good. Happy hunting." Jack hung up and climbed into bed. It was seven-thirty in the evening and he was exhausted. But as he lay there, the sound of the gunshot and Dwayne's plea for help kept replaying in his head, along with the shot that followed.

What should I have done different? Let them keep the shotgun for protection? What if they'd then killed some innocent schmuck ... maybe I should've arrested them both ... would it have changed the course of the investigation? Dwayne, I'm sorry.

Four hours later he was still awake and frustrated that he couldn't seem to stop rehashing the events over and over again. He knew he was in desperate need of sleep.

Tomorrow is going to be another long day.

Chapter Ten

Assistant Commissioner Isaac was the Operations Officer in charge of the RCMP Pacific Command. He was reading the report from I-HIT — the Integrated Homicide Investigation Team — concerning the murder of Dwayne Beggs. The mention of Jack Taggart's involvement with the victim caught his attention.

Isaac sighed, then looked at his desk calendar and flipped over a page to view the following month. Sunday, October twelfth, was circled in red. That was when he'd have done thirty-five years of service. He'd submitted his retirement papers to make it his last official day. Briefly he brooded about his replacement. *Ralphy Mortimer. Can't believe they promoted that pudgy little man to Assistant Commissioner. Guess being a sycophant in Ottawa does have its rewards.*

He returned his attention to the report from I-HIT. *Taggart — how many investigations has he been involved in where suspected murderers died before ever going to court?*

Some were self-defence ... but others? Written off to coincidences? He shook his head in wonder. *All these years and I still don't know ... is he a saint or a sinner? One thing for certain, he's not coming near this investigation.*

Jack arrived at work and immediately called Nicole Purney in the monitoring room for an update.

"You'll like this," Nicole said. "I read some debriefing notes from last night. At 11:00 p.m. Sammy and his team followed Banjo to another prospect's house — Kyle Fennel. Shortly after that, another prospect arrived by the name of ... Hang on, I need to grab the report."

"Arnold Hoster," Jack stated, giving a polite nod to Laura as she arrived at work.

"Yes, the one and only," Nicole confirmed. "What I was about to say is that they saw Hoster unload several stuffed duffle bags from his trunk and haul them into Fennel's house."

"Super! Sammy found the stash house where the press is," Jack said for Laura's benefit. "Did they also follow Neal to the stash house?"

"They broke off surveillance on him when they found the stash house, but he did show up at two in the morning. He was driving a pickup truck with a shell on the back. They saw him load two duffle bags into the back and confirmed that he turned off the main highway onto a gravel road leading to his and his brother's place a short time later."

"Only two duffle bags?" Jack questioned. "I was expecting there'd be at least four with about thirty to thirty-five keys in each."

"Your math is good," said Nicole. "Let me finish. He made a second trip to the stash house at 4:00 a.m. Guess he's paranoid about getting caught with all the eggs in one basket. Surveillance saw him take two empty duffle bags into the house and lug them, filled, back out a few minutes later. He took them to the Delta acreage, as well. Banjo and Hoster left the stash house at about 5:00 a.m. and returned to their own places."

"This is great," Jack said. "I expect they'll do the same thing again tonight."

"I've a note that said Sammy worked until 6:00 a.m., but will be back in at noon. In the meantime a couple of other guys from his office are watching Fennel's house."

"Perfect. Maybe tonight we'll get our hands on some of that weed." Jack noticed Rose waiting to talk to him, so he said goodbye to Nicole.

"You look happier this morning," Rose noted.

"I am. Last night Sammy found the stash house and confirmed Neal made two deliveries from the stash house back to where he lives with Bob and Roxie."

"Nice to get good news," Rose said. "I also have some news. I received a call from Isaac's secretary. He wants to see the three of us in one hour."

"No surprise," Jack said. "I had a feeling that Connie didn't take me at my word when I told her Dwayne's murder was all hers."

"Maybe because she has a memory," Rose replied dryly.

An hour later Jack, Laura, and Rose were walking down the hall to meet Assistant Commissioner Isaac when they met Inspector Dyck and Connie heading for the same meeting.

Connie looked uncomfortable when she saw Jack. She motioned for him to walk with her as they followed the others down the hall. "It wasn't my idea to get Isaac involved," she whispered. "When I told you we needed to have a meeting with our bosses, I meant Rose and Inspector Dyck."

"Don't worry about it," Jack said. "Isaac and I have a bit of history together. I suspect he reviews all my cases under a magnifying glass."

"Can you blame him?"

Jack shrugged. "Guess not. There has been the odd unfortunate coincidence in some of my past investigations."

Connie frowned. "Unfortunate coincidences in that the perps ended up dead."

"Sometimes," Jack admitted. "Maybe 'unfortunate' is the wrong word. I should've said 'fortunate.'"

"Speaking like that, maybe it's a good thing Isaac's involved." Connie's voice had a distinct edge. "I want to make it loud and clear that you're not to —"

"Relax, Connie, before you burst an aneurysm," Jack said. "Sure I'd love to be involved, but I'm not naive. I know it'd be ammo for a defence lawyer."

"Guaranteed," Connie stated.

"Know something? The lawyer'd be right. It *is* personal to me. I'd never lie in court or fabricate evidence as would be suggested, but it'd only take one person out of twelve to believe the defence lawyer and toss the case. You're a good investigator. I'm happy to let you solve it."

"Solve it and bring the perp before a judge." Connie enunciated every word.

"Isn't that what we all want?" Jack replied before turning

his attention to Isaac's secretary, who said that Isaac was ready to receive them.

Moments later Isaac referred to the reports he'd received and gave a brief synopsis of the chain of events leading to Dwayne's disappearance and probable murder. Upon confirming that he was up-to-date, he looked at Jack. "You're investigating the bikers for exporting marijuana to the United States — possibly in exchange for cocaine, which you think Satans Wrath may be using to open a new pipeline to Europe."

"Yes, sir," Jack replied. "As of last night, Drug Section located the stash house that the Gypsy Devils are using to package the marijuana. The investigation is currently in its infancy, but with the assistance of the DEA, we hope to get a lead on the money trail to lead us back to Satans Wrath."

"Why should it be different this time?" Isaac asked skeptically.

"I know from my informant that the money isn't being returned in the semi and that there is a one- or two-week delay in getting the money. That's new information for us. I hope that in time, perhaps through surveillance, we'll identify who hands out the money on this end and work our way back from there. If we're to hurt Satans Wrath, we'll do far more damage by finding out how they launder their money or where it goes, rather than busting some low-level drug dealers."

"You're also hoping that the DEA in Dallas may uncover some connection to who the West 12th Street gang is involved with in Mexico — which I take it would be an integral part of the suspected pipeline of cocaine bound for Europe."

"Yes, sir. Satans Wrath recently opened a chapter in Bogotá, Colombia, but for years they've dealt with the Mexicans for their cocaine. If money is not being paid immediately upon delivery for the marijuana, then I feel the Mexicans must still be involved, as they're connected to the gang in Dallas."

"It would appear there are still a lot of unanswered questions," Isaac noted, "but I concur with you, Corporal. Finding their money would certainly put a damper on them." He turned to Inspector Dyck. "Am I to understand that your homicide investigation has revealed that the bikers are not involved with the disappearance of the victim — Dwayne Beggs?"

"Yes, sir," Inspector Dyck confirmed. "It was clearly established through a Drug Section wiretap that someone other than the bikers were responsible. A wiretap, I might add, that Drug Section obtained through the efforts of Corporal Taggart and Constable Secord."

"Then that being the case," Isaac said, looking at Jack, "I see no reason why you shouldn't continue with your investigation while I-HIT pursues their investigation."

"Thank you, sir," Jack replied. "I expect to be turning the bulk of the work over to our drug section and the DEA, but will have some involvement due to my informants."

"That's fine, but under no circumstances are you to take any action in regard to the homicide investigation unless it's at the specific request of I-HIT."

"Yes, sir."

Isaac eyed Jack carefully. "I'm not criticizing your ability and I am sure you have a particularly strong desire to see the homicide solved, but in this instance, I'm ordering you to sit back and watch from the sidelines."

"I understand completely," Jack replied. "I spoke with Connie earlier and am happy to leave it in her capable hands. I understand the reason to stay out of it."

Minutes after the meeting with Isaac ended, Rose spoke to Jack as he was about to enter his office. "I think that went well," she commented.

"Me, too," Jack said. "Connie can handle the murder and Laura and I are free to go after Satans Wrath."

"I noticed you told Isaac that you're happy to let Connie handle it ... but what if she doesn't solve it? What'll you do then?"

Jack's face darkened. "I'll cross that bridge if and when I need to," he replied.

Rose stared after him as he walked to his desk. *And no doubt that bridge will cross a deep chasm with slippery slopes. Hope for your sake that a body doesn't show up at the bottom.*

Chapter Eleven

Jack and Laura spent most of the day writing reports and exchanging phone calls with Sammy. He confirmed that his team was watching the stash house and Bob's semi, but had nothing of importance to report.

Late in the afternoon Sammy called again. "It doesn't look good for us to scoop up a sample of weed before the truck leaves. Neal, Bob, and Roxie have been home all day."

"Then steal it from Neal when he's making his last delivery tonight," Jack suggested. "If he makes two deliveries like he did last night, he should have about seventy-five kilos. Taking that much won't affect their delivery to Dallas. They'd probably have enough at the stash house to cover it."

"That would be one hell of a big sample, but as nice as that would be, I don't think we'll get a chance to steal any of it," Sammy replied. "Neal takes it straight from the stash house to home. It's not like he stops for a beer along the way."

"Is Benny Saunders still on your team?" Jack asked.

"Yeah … why?"

"He's a good undercover operator. Get him to help you steal it when Neal is hauling the last load back."

"How can we do that without Neal knowing we're on to him?"

"And you call yourself an operator," Jack said mockingly. "Guess I better get someone in uniform to help you. Do you know Constable Sophie White from Surrey Detachment?"

"We can't have uniform seize it! They'd be heated up for sure. You don't want to chance that."

"That's not what I had in mind," Jack said.

Moments later Sammy chuckled as he listened to Jack's plan.

Minutes after talking with Sammy, Jack received a call from Connie.

"What do you know about a gang called the Cobras?" she asked bluntly.

"Not a lot," Jack replied. "They're a low-level street gang, maybe comprising a dozen dealers. Their territory is in New Westminster and they hang out in a bar called the Shot Glass. Why?"

"Do you know one of them by the name of Jamie King?"

"He's the ringleader. He used to live in Vancouver. Don't know if he still does or not. At one time they were calling themselves King Cobras, but later it got shortened. They deal a lot of dope on the street, but are still too low level for us to pay much attention to. The Anti-Gang Unit has photos and dossiers on them. We do, too, but ours are a few years old. Theirs might be newer."

"They do. I've already got copies, but like you, they haven't had much time to work on them."

"Why are you interested?"

"When I got back to the office this morning, I found out that King has a boat in the same marina as Larry. I did a walk past on the pier. It's a small speedboat and I saw what looks like blood splatter inside on the stern. It also has twin Evinrude motors and there's a fresh scrape on one of the cowlings, like from a rock. Everything fits. I've got someone watching his boat while I get a warrant to seize it and search his house."

"That's fantastic! They're definitely the type of guys who'd do rips." Jack smiled at Laura and gave her a thumbs-up. "I knew you were the right person for the job, Connie."

"Yeah, well, there's still a long way to go. I showed the photos to Larry. He recognized King from seeing him at the marina, along with another Cobra by the name of Craig Dutton."

"Dutton's a skinny little guy they nicknamed Weasel," Jack said.

"Yeah, I can see the similarity in the photo. Larry made several trips hauling hydro equipment and fertilizer to the island. King and Weasel may have clued in and followed him."

"How'd Larry respond to seeing the pictures?" Jack asked.

"What do you mean, how'd he respond? He's thrilled. What're you getting at?"

"Do you remember how he acted when we told him his brother had been murdered?"

"Yeah. He was upset. Blaming you to start with."

"Not that," Jack replied. "It was his demeanour later on. He was angry and thinking of taking matters into his own hands. I called him on it. Remember?"

"I remember, but the poor guy — his brother had just been murdered. Of course he was angry, but he never said he was going to take matters into his own hands."

"He didn't say in so many words, but he was thinking it."

Connie gave an unladylike snort. "Not everybody thinks like you."

"I'm serious. He's also not that bright. I suspect doing stupid things comes natural to him."

"I hope you're wrong, but even if you're not, I doubt he'll get the chance. He'll be in hospital for another two days and King is already in custody."

"You've caught him?"

"About ten minutes ago. He's still living in a run-down house in Vancouver. I had an arrest team waiting for him to show up. They're bringing him in now."

"That's great, Connie. Good police work. Let me know how it goes, will you?"

"Be glad to. Maybe you being ordered to watch from the sidelines isn't a bad thing," she joked. "This time I managed to bring in a live one."

"King's not at your office yet," Jack cautioned.

Connie laughed. "You asshole. I'll call you after I interview him."

That evening, Jack was at home when Cockerill called him. "I got somethin' you should probably hear," he said.

"Can you speak up? We've got a bad reception. Are you calling from a parkade at some mall?"

"That … that's not funny," Cockerill stammered. "Do you wanna hear what I got to say or not?"

Jack could tell by the sound of Cockerill's voice that he'd been drinking and decided not to fuel the anger. "I'm listening."

"We found out it's a chicken-shit gang out of New West-minster that's been doin' the rips. They call themselves the Cobras."

"How do you know it was them?" Jack asked, knowing full well how they knew.

"The cops sort of tipped us off," Cockerill replied. "They showed pictures to Larry, who recognized two of 'em from being at the marina. Larry's still in hospital, but called one of the GDs, who went over and talked to him."

"What are you guys going to do about it?"

"We met with the Cobras a few minutes ago."

"You should've told me before the meeting," Jack said tersely.

"I didn't know until I got there, then it was too late to be callin' anyone. The Cobras hang out at a bar called the Shot Glass. We paid 'em a surprise visit."

"Bust any skulls?"

"Not yet. 'Cause I'm still gimpin' around with my cast, I was told to stand six by the door. I wasn't able to hear everything that was said, but it went smooth like it was supposed to. Nobody got spanked. They were told that we knew they were doin' the weed rips and that they had to pay up. They denied it. Their main guy, King, wasn't there. Bet you guys have already scooped him, haven't you?"

Jack ignored the question. "How was it left — seeing as they denied it?"

"We gave 'em two days. Told 'em if they didn't pay us by nine Saturday night there'd be consequences."

"Consequences?"

"If they don't pay by then, we'll put a couple of 'em in hospital for incentive. Might use the GDs for that, or maybe have a couple of our guys tag along. Then they'll be given another couple days. After that, we won't be so nice."

"You know where some of them live?"

"Nah, but we'll find them if need be."

"What if they really didn't do it," Jack said. "Did you consider that?"

"Who the fuck cares? At least it'd send a message to whoever *is* doin' it. Besides, it's time the Cobras were taught a little respect. We'll make them pay regardless — one way or another."

After hanging up, Jack reflected on his previous conversation with Isaac. *I'm only authorized to watch from the sidelines.* He gave a half smile. *This could get interesting.*

Chapter Twelve

Twenty minutes after speaking with Cockerill, Jack received a call from Connie.

"Bad news," she grumbled. "King demanded a lawyer immediately. I couldn't get a word out of him. A search of his house didn't turn up any guns. There was a little weed and coke for personal use, but that was it. The guy you call Weasel lives with him."

"What about his boat?"

"The lab says the blood on the stern is fish blood. I had to cut him loose."

"Damn it." Jack's clenched his fist and had to make a conscious effort not to punch the wall in frustration. "What about the marks or scrapes on the engine cowlings?" he asked.

"One scrape is fresh, but without the rock to match, it means squat."

"Son of a bitch."

"It doesn't mean I'm giving up on him," Connie said.

Jack took a deep breath and slowly relaxed his fist, then stared at his fingers as he opened and closed them a couple of times. "He may wish he was still in custody," he muttered.

Connie became hostile. "What do you mean by that?"

"Satans Wrath paid some of his guys a visit tonight. They're blaming them for the rip and demanding payment."

"Oh." Connie's tone returned to normal. "I must be on the right track if Satans Wrath think they did it, too."

"Not necessarily."

"Why do you say that?"

"Satans Wrath think the Cobras were involved because of what you told Larry. After you showed him the photos, he passed on the info to the Gypsy Devils, who then told Satans Wrath."

"That jerk! Wait'ill I get my hands on him."

"Don't," Jack replied. "If he knows we know, it could jeopardize my informant. Leave it for now."

"What are Satans Wrath going to do?" Connie asked.

"They gave them until Saturday night to pay up. If they don't … well, I think you get the picture. At that point a few of them will end up in hospital and the deadline will be extended for another two days."

"And if they still don't come up with the money after the next two days, then what?"

"Then I'm told that Satans Wrath won't be so nice to them."

"Crap," Connie muttered. "I've got more work now than I can handle. When did you find this out? Isaac told you explicitly —"

"To watch from the sidelines. Yes, I know. I received the information from my informant right before you called me. I'm at home. It wasn't like I was out investigating the Cobras. I simply heard about it."

"Oh." Connie said. "Still makes me think the Cobras had something to do with the murder for Satans Wrath to become involved this fast."

"Possibly, but it was intimated the Cobras needed to be taught some respect. I think Satans Wrath are using it as an excuse — not that they need an excuse."

"The Anti-Gang Unit also told me that the Cobras move a lot of weed on the street, which supports my belief that King did it."

"Weed is everywhere," Jack said. "You can get it by the truckload."

"Yeah. So how's it going with your semi full of weed?"

"I'm pretty much out of that one too," Jack replied. "Drug Section is taking over the investigation and they'll be working with the DEA. So far it looks like everything is going according to plan."

"That's good."

"So what do you plan on doing about King?"

"Forensics hasn't finished," she said. "We still have his boat and will be checking for DNA."

"They might have towed the body out."

"Gee, don't you think I thought of that? We also found rags and rope in his boat and seized some dirty laundry from his room."

"So you'll check for DNA, gunpowder residue, blood —"

"Jack?"

"Yes?"

"I know my job," Connie said firmly, "and to tell you the truth, I'm too tired and too busy to listen to you trying to tell me how to do it."

"I didn't mean to be telling you how —" He quit talking when he realized she'd hung up. *You think you're tired and busy now? We've got the Cobras, Gypsy Devils, Satans Wrath ... and me. Connie, your murder count can only go up.*

Chapter Thirteen

It was 4:15 a.m. when Neal Barlow turned off the main highway to complete the last delivery of marijuana to his brother's semi. He yawned as he glanced in the side mirror of his pickup truck — nobody following. The gravel road was narrow and without street lights. If anyone was tailing him it would be obvious. Not that he was concerned. To ensure he was alone, he'd already driven through several quiet residential areas after leaving the stash house.

Minutes later, his senses came alive and he braked to a stop. A car was parked in the middle of the road with the driver's door open and the interior light on. He rolled down his window and listened. The car's engine was not running and he could see a toddler's car seat in the back. Nobody appeared to be around. He tapped his horn, wondering if someone was slumped over in the car. It was then that he felt the muzzle of a pistol in his ear.

"Put your hands on the dash, you fucker, or I'll blow your brains out!"

Neal gasped as his head spun around to look. A man in a ski mask pointed a pistol directly at his face. He saw the hard cold eyes staring at him — and the latex-gloved hand holding the gun.

"Grab a piece of the dash now!" the man ordered.

Neal slowly put his hands on the dash, afraid that any sudden movement might get him killed.

"Behave yourself and you won't get hurt," the man said, opening the door. "All we want is your wheels." He glanced over the hood and barked a command. "Mad Dog! Get over here and search this fucker. Make sure he don't have a phone to call the cops."

Neal saw Mad Dog glance through the passenger window, then run to the driver's side. He was also wearing a ski mask and latex gloves. Although he was considerably shorter than the man with the gun, he had a powerful build, and he grabbed Neal by the collar and flung him out of the truck. Neal landed on his hands and knees. "Face down on the road!"

Neal quickly complied. Mad Dog searched him and took away his phone, which he handed to the man with the gun.

"Good, load 'er up while I cover him," the man ordered.

Neal watched as Mad Dog opened the trunk of the car and took out a flat-screen television, which he loaded into the back of his pickup truck. *Oh, shit. They're taking my truck. The weed! Fuck! They're going to get the weed.* Next he retrieved a pillowcase containing bulky items. On the way back to the truck he dropped the pillowcase.

"Be careful with that shit!" the man with the gun said. "I tossed a camera in there."

"Yeah, yeah," Mad Dog replied, scooping up the pillow-case and stowing it in the back of Neal's truck.

Neal felt a nudge in his ribs from the toe of the man's shoe. *You fuckin' goof. I'll kill ya someday.*

"Listen to what I'm sayin'," the man said. "We got your wheels and registration. We'll know where you live. Give us one hour before callin' the cops. You rat us out before then and we'll come back someday — and it won't be a happy day for you. Got it?"

"You don't know who you're fuckin' with!" Neal snarled.

"Yeah?" The man crouched and pointed the gun at Neal's eye. "You tellin' me that you're somebody danger-ous? Somebody I better kill now?"

Neal felt his throat go dry and swallowed. "No ... I ... I didn't mean it. Take my truck. I don't care. I'll do what you want."

"You better, if you ever wanna collect old age security."

Seconds later Neal watched as the two men turned his truck around and drove off. He immediately got up and ran to the car. There were no keys in the ignition and a quick rummage through the glove box and ashtray came up empty. He stood for a moment, panting from stress. He wasn't in shape to run, but figured he could walk the remaining distance home in about twenty minutes.

Ten minutes later he was trudging along the road when he heard a car approach from behind. He turned to look as a spotlight illuminated him. Behind the glare of the light, he saw the symbol of the Royal Canadian Mounted Police on the side of the car.

"Put your hands up!" a policewoman ordered from the passenger seat.

Neal swore under his breath and raised his hands.

"We found a stolen car down the road," the officer said. "We already ordered it to be towed in for examination. Are we going to find your prints in it?"

"Shit no! Well, yes, my prints might be in it, but I didn't steal it!" Neal exclaimed. "About fifteen minutes ago I was stopped on the road and carjacked by two guys who were in that car. One of 'em goes by the name Mad Dog. They took my truck and my phone. I was heading home to call you."

Moments later Neal sat in the back of the police car and gave a description of his pickup truck. When he finished, the policewoman turned to her male companion. "Phone it in, verify that the plate he gave us is accurate, then have them put out an APB." She turned to Neal. "We were in a high-speed pursuit of that car earlier, but had to break it off because it was becoming too dangerous for the public. The car's real owner had GPS installed, so we were eventually able to track it. Sorry we couldn't get here sooner."

Neal nodded. "Do you have any idea who they are?"

"Not yet. You said one guy called the other guy Mad Dog?"

"Yup."

"Helps a little, but every jail in the country has had someone called Mad Dog," the policewoman said.

"There's a farmhouse not far from where the car was parked," her partner put in. "Bet they were planning on stealing a vehicle from there until you came along."

"Yeah, sort of what I was thinkin', too."

"I'm going to need a statement," the policewoman said, taking out a pad of lined notepaper from her briefcase.

The next hour dragged past as the policewoman took his statement. She asked numerous questions about the sound of the carjackers' voices, what they were wearing, and estimated heights. When she finished writing, she read the statement aloud.

"Yup, that's right," Neal said.

"So to clarify, you said they took a flat-screen television, two duffle bags, and something in a pillowcase out of the car and loaded it into your truck?"

"Yup. Got no idea what was in the duffle bags, but they looked heavy." *At least if you catch 'em with the weed it won't come back on me …*

"Probably more stuff they stole from houses," the policewoman said. "I'm surprised they didn't steal your wallet."

"Yeah, I thought that, too." Neal shrugged. "They were in a hurry. Guess they forgot."

The policewoman glanced at the statement. "Okay, I think we're done here. We'll give you a lift home." She nodded at her partner.

"Hang on a sec," her partner said. "Got a call."

Neal watched as the officer spoke briefly into his phone, pausing momentarily to give him a thumbs-up before turning his attention back to his phone. "The owner says they wearing latex gloves." A moment later he hung up, then smiled at Neal. "Your truck's been located in a shopping mall in Surrey. Your keys are in it and a cellphone is on the floor. It's turned off, but I'm betting it's yours."

"Hey, that's good news," the policewoman said. "Rather than take you home, we'll drive you over to pick it up."

"What about the two guys?" Neal asked nervously. "The, uh, stuff they put in the back of it? Is it still there?"

"The truck was abandoned and the back of it is completely empty," he replied. "Whoever stole it got away."

Neal's face reddened with rage.

The policewoman stared at him. "I can see how angry you are, but count yourself lucky that you weren't hurt. Plus we got your truck back."

"Yeah? Well fuckin' hallelujah," Neal spluttered. "You got no idea how pissed I am! If I ever get my hands on Mad Dog, he'll be Dead Dog."

Chapter Fourteen

Early Friday morning Jack was on his way to work when Cockerill called and told him that Neal had been robbed on his way home with the last shipment.

"You're kidding," Jack replied. "This is the second time the weed has been ripped. Do you figure it's the same guys?"

"Nah, fuck," he slurred. "From what Neal says, it was a fooke."

"Fooke?"

"Yeah, a fuckin' fooke. I mean, fluke. Some guys in stolen wheels were being chased earlier by the cops. They hijacked Neal's truck to switch rides. He was just in the wrong place at the wrong time. They didn't know when they took it that there was seventy-five keys in the back. Must've thought they won the jackpot when they saw it."

"Is Bob going to be short on this trip?" Jack asked.

"Nah. It took everything left at the stash house to cover it, but they'll leave with a full load. No fuckin' problem, man."

"Good. One more thing. How much have you had to drink?"

"What the fuck? So I popped a couple pills and drank a bit. What's it to you?"

"Popping pills? Didn't think the club went for that."

"Yeah, well … they don't go for me talkin' to you, either."

"What kind of pills?" Jack asked.

"I dunno. Pharmaceutical shit."

"That can be a deadly combo."

"You trying to be my mother now?"

"No, I'm trying to take care of you. I know you're under a lot of stress."

"No shit, Sherlock."

"If you're changing how you behave, guys in the club will notice. Someone could get suspicious."

"Yeah, well … we wouldn't want that, would we?" Cockerill snarled, then hung up.

Jack arrived at the office and learned that after Neal retrieved his pickup truck, he'd been witnessed by Drug Section making another trip to the stash house before returning to his own house. The semi, with Bob and Roxie in the cab, left a short time later. It was currently eastbound on the Trans-Canada Highway.

It had already been arranged for the DEA to take over surveillance once the semi crossed the border and then try to make a few sideline busts of marijuana a day or two after the semi left Dallas, so as not to alert the criminals that the police knew about the shipment.

It was midafternoon when Jack and Laura finished doing their reports. Laura turned to Jack. "What now?"

"I know it's been a fun day watching from the sidelines," Jack said facetiously, "so how about we celebrate and go for a drink?"

"Olive soup?" Laura replied. "I haven't had a martini in weeks. Sounds good."

"No, I'm thinking beer," Jack said. "The place I'm thinking of isn't all that swanky. You'll need to dress down. Try to look ... like a hag." He gave an ironic smile. "If you can."

"I've got a change of clothes in my locker." Laura got to her feet. "I'm sure I can pull it off. Where we going? The Steinhouse?"

"It's not the Gypsy Devils I'm interested in at the moment. I want to see how many Cobras are about. Let's view their photos again, then go for a drive."

One hour later Jack and Laura each ordered a Kokanee beer as they sat in a corner of the Shot Glass.

Jack waited until the waitress left, then turned to Laura. "See anyone of note?"

"Yes, I'd say almost everyone here has seen the inside of a jail cell," Laura replied. "Don't recognize anyone from the Cobras, though."

"Noticeably conspicuous by their absence." Jack grimaced. "We'll stay for a couple of hours in case they show, but I've a feeling they won't."

"What do you make of it?"

"They've gone to ground. They're scared of what'll happen when Satans Wrath come back."

"You seem upset. I thought you'd take delight in seeing the Cobras get a thumping from the bikers."

"Normally I would, but you have to ask yourself — why have they gone into hiding? If they were going to play the tough-guy role and refuse to pay, they wouldn't be hiding. Same if they were going to pay it back."

"Meaning?"

"Meaning they can't pay it back. They don't have the weed or the cash from having sold it."

Laura clued in to why Jack was unhappy. "It's not them," she said. "The Cobras aren't behind Dwayne's murder."

"That'd be my conclusion," Jack said bitterly. "I think Connie is barking up the wrong tree."

"Then who did it?" Laura asked. "The grow-op was really well hidden. Only the GDs, Weenie Wagger, and Buck knew about it."

"That's the million-dollar question," Jack said.

The waitress brought them their beer and they each sipped in silence for a moment. "I've a theory," Jack said. "What if some of these grow-ops were robbed by different people? Not even connected with each other?"

"There's a good chance of that, but how does that help?"

"How many grow-ops do you think are in southern B.C.?"

Laura shrugged. "Hundreds for sure ... maybe thousands. It's hard to say. Most of our members hardly take the time to charge them anymore. They get nothing for it in court. The growers are more upset about losing their equipment than whatever fines they have to pay." She eyed Jack curiously. "What're you getting at?"

"I-HIT and Forensics would've done a thorough search of Larry's grow-op right down to the shore."

"And the water beyond the shore," Laura added.

"Yes, but how far did they search in the hills behind the grow-op?"

"Nothing in that area except wilderness," Laura pointed out.

"Unless there's another grow-op hidden somewhere nearby," Jack said. "There are deer trails all over the place. It'd be easy for someone to spy on them and know when they were harvesting. Depending upon how far back, they could also access from someplace else."

"Someone who still might have seen or heard Larry and Dwayne coming and going," Laura said when she understood what Jack was getting at.

"Want to go on a little boat ride tomorrow morning?" Jack asked. "I know it's Saturday, but we can take Monday off in lieu."

"Fine with me." Laura nodded.

"If there's another grow-op up there, they'll be limited by the need to access water. All we have to do is follow the stream that Larry was using farther back into the hills."

"Providing we don't find other streams," Laura said.

"Even if we do, it shouldn't take us long to find out if there was or is someone else up there."

"Is this what you call watching from the sidelines?"

"If we find something, I'll pass on my theory to Connie and she can go look for herself," Jack said. "She won't need to know we were there."

"Unless someone takes another go at us with a shotgun." Laura's tone was wry. "Then you may need to include a body in your theory — and hopefully not mine."

Chapter Fifteen

Jack and Laura arrived at what had been Larry's grow-op at nine-thirty Saturday morning. Three hours later Jack had to admit defeat. The time they'd spent searching for another grow-op turned out to be fruitless.

"Well, it was worth a shot," Laura said when they returned to where they'd moored the boat. It was the same spot where Dwayne had been murdered. The tide had gone out and she saw a couple of wire markers on the exposed and quadrated beach that Forensics had left, indicating where Dwayne's phone had been located.

Jack glanced at the markers, then picked up a fist-size stone and threw it as far as he could. The stone landed short of the quadrated area.

"The cell phone would've been lighter," Laura said.

Jack didn't reply as he stared out at the ocean.

"They would've found the stone if there were any markings left on it," Laura said next. "Forensics searched all the way out."

Jack still didn't reply. He replayed Dwayne's last call over again in his mind. *Stay away from me! I'm warning you!* He briefly closed his eyes to concentrate on what followed. *You little fucker!* He winced at what he remembered next and opened his eyes.

"What're you thinking?" Laura asked.

"Whoever shot Dwayne swore at him first, calling him a little fucker. He sounded surprised. I'm guessing that Dwayne threw a rock at him." Jack picked up another fist-size rock. This time he threw it in the opposite direction, toward the path that emerged from the forest. It bounced off rocks along the shoreline and went sideways.

"How well did Forensics search in the opposite direction?" Jack wondered aloud.

"We're here. Let's find out," Laura said.

They searched the area where Jack's rock had landed but came up empty-handed.

Jack stood and stretched his back muscles, then pointed at a thicket of blackberry bushes across from them. "Maybe it bounced or landed in there."

Laura looked at the thorny bushes. "Be my guest. I'll cover you," she joked.

Jack picked up a dead branch and used it to defend himself from the thorns as he slowly progressed. The branch offered only partial protection

"You look like you lost a fight with about a dozen tomcats," Laura said as Jack continued to make his way deeper.

Jack didn't respond. His eyes were focused on the ground and he knelt to peer at something. When he stood, his smile told Laura what he'd found.

———

"You what?" Connie exclaimed into her phone. "You're telling me you found the rock that Dwayne used to smash the boat engine?"

"I think so," Jack replied. "I haven't touched it, but it has what looks like fresh scrape marks on it and bits of blue paint."

"What were you doing out there?" Connie asked.

Jack told her about looking for a second grow-op, then his idea to throw a rock in the opposite direction from where the cellphone had been tossed.

"You're thinking that Dwayne threw the rock at whoever killed him," Connie said.

"Yes."

"Why the hell didn't Forensics find it?"

"It wasn't easy to find," Jack replied. "I almost missed it myself. Come out and take a look. It's in the middle of a huge clump of blackberry bushes."

"You were ordered not to stick your nose into my investigation."

"You angry with me?" Jack asked in surprise.

"Hell, no … not me," Connie replied. "I can't accuse you of butting in by going to an area that we'd given up on. If we can match the rock to paint and scrapes on King's boat, we'll have him."

"I don't think it *was* King," Jack said. "That's why Laura and I went looking for another grow-op in the area."

"Even if you're right, it'll still be good physical evidence. If it is paint on the rock from a boat motor, give the lab a couple of weeks and they should be able to tell us the make and maybe the size of the engine. It'd be a big step in pointing us in the right direction. Will you wait there until I arrive?"

"You bet."

"It's noon now. I better let Inspector Dyck know and call Forensics back out. We should be there within two hours."

"Wear gloves and heavy clothing. Tell Forensics to do the same."

"To hell with them," Connie snapped. "It'll be justice for them not finding the rock to start with."

At two-fifteen Connie arrived with two Forensic investigators. Jack and Laura watched as they went to work taking photographs, then used gardening shears to expose where the rock was lying. When Forensics began measuring distances from the shore and taking more photographs, Jack and Laura said goodbye to a thankful Connie and returned to the marina.

It was four o'clock when they paid for the boat rental in the marina office. As they did so a uniformed RCMP officer came out of an office in the rear and walked outside toward his patrol car. Jack and Laura caught up to him and identified themselves.

"You here over something to do with the homicide four days ago on Bowen Island?" Jack asked.

"I've nothing to do with that," the officer replied. "I'm here because the marina reported a break-in last night."

Jack's brow furrowed. "Much stolen?"

"Nothing. I'm wondering if there really was a break-in. There was no sign of a forced entry and the door was locked when they arrived. I'm betting someone forgot to lock it when they closed the office and doesn't want to admit it. They're claiming someone broke in because a lamp had been knocked over and broken. They also said they could tell that someone had rifled through their files. They don't keep any cash on the premises, so if it was a break-in, whoever did it didn't get anything."

"Hardly worth your time and effort to come out here," Jack said.

"You got it, but a friend of mine lives out this way. Good excuse to come out for a coffee."

Jack said goodbye, then quickly headed for where he'd parked his SUV.

"Hey, can you slow down a bit?" Laura complained. "My legs aren't as long as yours."

"We have to hustle," Jack said. "We need to return to the office and pick up the video recorder and grab King's address. Hopefully the ultimatum takes place after nine tonight and not some other night."

"The ultimatum?"

"Satans Wrath gave King and the Cobras an ultimatum to pay by nine tonight or face the consequences. I think Satans Wrath did the break-in — at least one or two of their guys have taken locksmithing and could pick locks. If someone hadn't knocked the desk lamp over, nobody would've been the wiser. I think that whoever broke into the marina last night did get what they were looking for."

"King's address," Laura said.

"You got it. How about we go and do what we were ordered to do?"

"What's that?"

"Watch from the sidelines."

Chapter Sixteen

It was 7:30 p.m. when Jack and Laura drove past King's house, a single-storey box-shaped place situated next to an empty lot partway up the block. It had a garage off the rear alley and the yard was overgrown with weeds. A white bedsheet hung over the living-room window to provide privacy from the street.

"The living room has a side window facing the empty lot — I can look in there, see if anyone's home," Jack said. "Let me out at the end of the block. I'll walk down the street, cut through the lot, and look through the window, then return up the alley."

Moments later Jack crept up to the house and looked through the side window. He recognized King and Weasel, both sitting on a sofa. A coffee table in front of them held numerous beer bottles and an ashtray overflowing with butts. They each held game controllers in their hands and were concentrating on the television screen across from them.

Jack then cut through the lot to the rear alley. A clunker was parked in front of the garage behind the house. As he continued up the alley he noticed a pickup truck parked there. He recognized Neal behind the steering wheel.

Jack looked away and pretended to scratch his head as he neared, so as not to show his face. Neil did likewise. Jack smiled to himself. *You don't want to be seen, either, Neal. Be careful you don't get robbed. You never know when Mad Dog might leap out ...*

"Anything?" Laura asked when Jack returned to the SUV.

"Yes. I'd say that King is going to get some unwanted guests tonight."

Laura listened as Jack told her what he'd seen. "So Satans Wrath are going to have the Gypsy Devils do their dirty work for them," she concluded.

"Looks that way. Although I'm sure a representative from Satans Wrath will be present to ensure that King knows that the message is from them. Also to order the GDs around to make clear who's in charge."

"Maybe it'll be Weenie Wagger. He's their liaison."

"I doubt it," Jack said. "He's still hobbling around in a cast. They'll want someone who looks tougher and meaner for this job, but he still should've called to let us know."

"You told me he's been getting drunk a lot."

"He's not handling the stress too well, that's for sure." Jack gave a nod toward King's house. "As long as the action takes place in the living room, I should be able to video it."

"While remaining on the sidelines as ordered," Laura mused.

Jack grinned. "Of course. Weenie Wagger said they planned on putting a couple of them in hospital this time. I like seeing bad guys spank each other."

"Even if we get video, what do you plan on doing with it?"

"Later on, if the Cobras don't pay up, I'm sure one or two of them will get whacked. If that happens, I'll turn the video over to Connie. It'll be a good place for her to start her investigation."

Laura raised an eyebrow. "That could prove interesting. Are you hoping to rub her nose in it that we've been sidelined?"

"Only a little. I know we had to take a back seat in this, but it might be a small inducement for them to decide that we shouldn't be sidelined completely."

Dusk had fallen when Jack returned to spy on King and Weasel as the two continued to play video games and drink beer.

Drink lots, guys. It might numb the pain …

Laura hid in a backyard a few houses down to watch Neal, who was still sitting in his truck.

It was after ten when Jack saw two cars drive past in the alley. Seconds later he pressed his finger to his earpiece and listened to Laura's hushed voice. "They've arrived. Headlights turned off … can't tell how many got out. They've popped their trunks and it looks like a couple of them are baseball players. One might have a sawed-off rifle or shotgun, as well, tucked inside his jacket."

"Copy that," Jack replied.

"They're coming down the alley ... going past me ... count about eight guys. One is wearing full-patch SW colours."

"Can you make out who it is?"

"Too dark. Hang on, there's a prospect with him — but I don't see any GD colours at all."

"Makes the message clearer about who's running the show."

"They're stopped in the alley behind the house and are whispering to each other."

"Showtime," Jack said.

"Oh, man. I just realized — Neal continued walking your way. He's almost where you are. Copy?"

"Copy and out." Jack cursed silently when he heard Neal's footsteps and realized he didn't have time to hide. He looked at the empty lot next to where he was standing and dived into a patch of tall weeds and flattened himself on the ground.

Neal crossed the empty lot close to where Jack lay motionless, but his attention was focused on the open living-room window. He crept across the lot onto King's property and looked in. Seconds later he retraced his steps down the alley.

Jack got to his feet and radioed, "I'm back. He didn't see me."

"Good. Sorry about that," Laura whispered. "Okay, I can confirm there's eight altogether ... they've broken into two groups ... five, including the two SWs are heading for the rear door. The other three are going around front. Can I come to where you are?"

"As long as you make sure they don't leave someone outside standing six," Jack cautioned her. "I don't want you spotted."

"Copy."

Jack crept closer to the open window and stopped at the edge of the shadows. He turned on the camera and focused it on the two men playing video games.

Seconds later the front and rear doors of the house were kicked open simultaneously. King and Weasel looked at each other in panic. Before they could get to their feet, six Gypsy Devils rushed into the room. Two of the bikers were brandishing baseball bats, one had a pistol, and another held a sawed-off shotgun.

"What the —" Weasel screamed. A baseball bat landed a bone-crunching blow to his chest. He emitted a gurgle and gasped for air.

King looked on dumbfounded, then a melee of fists, kicks, and wallops with bats followed. Both King and Weasel ended up on the floor, where the assault continued.

When the beating stopped, both victims lay moaning. Then they were searched and roughly thrown back onto the sofa. Weasel sat slumped over, coughing up blood that had trickled down his throat from a broken nose. King had a gash over his eye, but tried to sit upright and look defiant.

Jack nodded at Laura as she joined him in time to see the group of GDs part in the middle to make way for the full-patch member of Satans Wrath. Jack knew him by the nickname of Hammer and focused the camera on him.

Hammer strutted past the two helpless victims to ensure they saw his colours, then made a pretence of glancing at his watch. "Your time was up an hour ago," he told King. "You gonna pay for what you stole from us?"

"We didn't steal it," King said angrily. "My guys had nothin' to do with it!"

Jack's view was blocked when another biker stepped in the way. The bottom rocker said he was a Satans Wrath prospect. Hammer's voice was still loud and clear. "You think we're runnin' a fuckin' courtroom where y'can enter a not guilty plea? Judgment has been passed. You've been found guilty and now it's time to pay up!"

"But we didn't do it," Weasel whined.

"They ain't listening," Hammer declared. "Show 'im what happens when you don't listen!"

The prospect moved in time for Jack to see the Gypsy Devil named Thor swing a baseball bat and shatter Weasel's leg below his knee. The Cobra emitted a blood-gurgling scream and grabbed his leg.

"You fucker!" King yelled, leaping to his feet and trying to wrestle the bat from Thor's grip.

The prospect pulled a pistol from his waistband and smashed the butt end on King's temple. One blow was enough and King fell to the floor like a boneless sack of skin. The prospect was not deterred, however, and aimed a well-directed kick at his groin, followed by a stomp on his ribs.

"See what happens when you don't show respect!" the prospect said as he turned and pointed his pistol at Weasel.

It was the first time that Jack was able to see the prospect's face and his adrenalin soared. *Buck Zabat!* He steadied the camera and continued to record.

"Please, don't kill me," Weasel begged.

Hammer's voice came again. "We won't this time. Tell King when he's done napping that we're giving you another three days to come up with what you owe us. Don't make us come looking for you next time!"

"I'll tell him," Weasel snivelled.

All the bikers left through the rear door of the house, but Jack kept filming the contorted look of pain on Weasel's face as he steadied his broken leg with one hand while reaching down and shaking King on the shoulder.

A full minute passed before Weasel came to the same realization that Jack and Laura did. King was dead.

Chapter Seventeen

Jack and Laura listened to Weasel's frantic 911 call. He told the dispatcher that three men wearing masks had broken into their house and killed King with a baseball bat. He said he tried to stop them and had been hit himself.

Laura saw a grim smile cross Jack's face. She knew what he was thinking: *Weasel is smart enough not to name the bikers and become a witness.* Jack gave her a nod and they hurried back to their SUV, where she stuck the keys in the ignition, but Jack brushed her hand away before she could start the engine.

"We need to talk," he said.

"No kidding we need to talk," she replied emphatically. "We just witnessed a murder and it's obvious Weasel isn't going to say who did it!"

"Yes, I never dreamed things would turn out so good," he said excitedly.

"Turn out good?" *Oh, man.* "So you're thinking of scooping Buck up and charging him with murder?"

"No, it'd be more like manslaughter if we did. The murder wouldn't be ruled intentional by the courts. Everything considered — even if the prosecutor brought criminal-organization charges into play, I bet he'd still only be looking at five to ten years of actual time."

"Better than his dad ever got."

"Damien," Jack said as if the word itself was bitter. "I'm very much aware of that — which is why I don't want Buck charged."

"You don't want him charged?" Laura was surprised. "What're you thinking? That we can turn him into an informant?"

"I don't think he'd turn," Jack replied. "He's too young, gung-ho and impressionable. He's been brainwashed all his life by Damien that loyalty to the club supersedes anything else in life."

Laura heard the far-off sound of sirens approaching. "So what, then?" she asked. "In a couple of minutes this place will be crawling with uniform and then VPD Homicide."

"It's not Buck I'm after," Jack said. "How do you think Mr. Damien Zabat and Mrs. Vicki Zabat will feel about their son going to jail?"

"You're going to try to turn Damien? No way!"

"I'll use Vicki to put the heat on him," Jack said.

"You actually think Damien would turn against the club?"

"The chances are low, but despite being ruthless, he's still a family man. If he co-operates, it'll be worth a lot more than putting Buck away. If he doesn't, we still have that option — and it'll definitely put a rift in their marriage."

"A legacy of murders and all we can do is cause a rift in his marriage?" Laura said. "That's just depressing."

"I know, small satisfaction," Jack admitted, "but anything that'll make Damien's retirement years more miserable makes me happier. Worrying about how his son is surviving in prison will be part of that."

Laura's reply was without enthusiasm. "I guess."

"There are a few things we need to consider."

"Such as?"

"If this does go to court, defence will do their utmost to rule our video inadmissible. They'll try to block our testimony by saying we didn't have the right to trespass on King's property. A jury would never know what we saw."

"We had grounds because we believed bodily harm was about to befall King and Weasel."

"I know, but there's always the possibility that a judge would decide our informant wasn't a reliable person and that we shouldn't have acted on the information. Another consideration is Damien might decide that Weasel is a loose end. He might not live to testify."

"Bet you're right. Weasel better pack his bags. You said a few things to consider. What else?"

"Hang on, I just got a text," Jack said, reaching for his phone. He scanned the message quickly. "It's from Sammy. The DEA in Dallas say that the semi has arrived and is parked at a truck stop. Looks like Bob and Roxie went to bed in the sleeper. They'll stay on them until delivery is made."

"Good," Laura said. "Back to what we were talking about. What else should we consider?"

"Damien is going to wonder how we knew about it."

"Think we might be putting Weenie Wagger in jeopardy?" Laura asked.

"No, there were plenty of Gypsy Devils present. I think Damien will blame them."

"Cause a little animosity amongst the ranks," Laura said musingly. "Sounds good."

Jack's voice became sombre. "There's something else. Damien may decide that the two of us are loose ends."

Oh, man. "Meaning we'll be transferred to some remote spot for protection. Are you telling me I might be eating whale blubber and reindeer meat the rest of my life?"

"Whale blubber? Hell, no. I'd kill him first before putting that in my mouth. Besides, I hate snow."

"What then?"

"I'm going to tell him that another member of the Intelligence unit was with us and say that the original video is at our office. If it were true, killing us wouldn't solve his problem."

"If it were true," Laura repeated. *Wonderful.*

It was 2:00 a.m. when Jack parked under the powerful security lights outside the electronic gates to Damien's estate. Beyond the gates, the interior of the mansion was in darkness, but the landscape around it was lit up.

"Maybe he won't let us in," Laura commented as they got out to approach the intercom.

"He will when I tell them it's about one of their children. They used to have two daughters, but one died of meningitis. The pain of losing one child … the panic they'll feel. We'll get in," he said confidently, then buzzed the intercom.

Moments later the closed-circuit security camera hummed as it zeroed in and they turned to face it.

"Taggart!" Damien's voice sounded hollow over the intercom. "What do you want? Show me your warrant … or considering that I only see Secord with you, I'm guessing you don't have one."

"We're not here with a warrant," Jack said. "We're here on a family matter. Let us in. We have some … bad news to talk to you and Vicki about."

"Oh, my God!" Vicki's voice cried over the intercom. "Something has happened to Katie or Buck!"

Damien was waiting in the front doorway as Jack and Laura exited their SUV and approached. He was wearing a white terry housecoat that, coupled with his physic, made him look like a polar bear. Vicki stood in the foyer behind him. She was also wearing a housecoat, but hers was a clingy cream-coloured silk affair patterned with blossoming Japanese plum trees.

Jack gestured to his laptop. "It's better if we come inside and show you something. It'll answer a lot of questions."

Damien looked at the laptop. "You said this was a personal family matter. Why do I get the feeling I should be calling my lawyer?"

"Can if you want," Jack replied. "But I think it's in your best interests to see a short video first."

"Is it about Katie or Buck?" Vicki asked in a trembling voice.

Jack nodded.

"Did one of them …?" Vicki apparently couldn't bring herself to say the word.

Jack remained expressionless, his gaze fixed on Damien. He knew he was being cruel by not telling them that both their children were alive. He told himself that the reason he was tormenting them was not because of his hatred for Damien, but to gain an edge. The more Damien was rattled, the more he might realize how much he loved his children and be more inclined to provide information in exchange for Buck's freedom. Jack told himself that was the reason, but he did enjoy seeing the look of anguish on Damien's face.

"Oh, my God!" Vicki cried again. She clutched Damien's terry robe for support. "Katie's dead, isn't she? A drug overdose?"

"A drug overdose?" Jack gave Damien a puzzled look.

"We've put her in rehab," Damien said tersely. "Nobody knows."

"Well ... this isn't about her," Jack replied.

"Oh no, it's Buck!" Vicki said.

"Yes, it's about Buck."

"Oh God, oh no, oh no, oh no!" Vicki wailed.

Jack saw Damien close his eyes to suppress the pain he felt.

"What...? How...?" Vicki asked.

"How?" Jack responded. "Oh, he's not dead, if that's what you're thinking."

"He's alive?" Vicki said.

"Then why the hell are you here?" Damien demanded.

"Buck is in trouble."

"Trouble?" Vicki asked fearfully.

"The sooner you watch the video, the sooner you'll understand what happened — and could happen."

"Let's go into the kitchen," Damien said. Vicki's fear was contagious and his face had paled. He wrapped an arm around his wife's shoulders and gestured with his head for them to follow.

Damien and Vicki sat together on one side of the kitchen table and Laura took a seat across from them. Jack put the laptop on the table and sat on the end, close to Damien.

"Well? Let's see it," Damien said impatiently.

Jack reached for the laptop, but let his finger linger over the start button as he spoke. "Four hours ago, an officer who will remain unnamed, along with Constable Secord and me, had occasion to record this video. What we brought is a copy of what we have back at our office. In the event something should ever happen to the two of us, it wouldn't jeopardize the evidentiary process."

"You think I might kill you for whatever it is you want to show me?" Damien asked, looking puzzled.

"Murder does appear to be one of your family traits," Jack said coldly.

Chapter Eighteen

The tension was palpable as the video played. When it reached the point where the Gypsy Devils rushed into the room and beat King and Weasel, Vicki turned to Damien to see his reaction. "These guys aren't even with our club," he said.

Vicki gave Jack a smug look, but when Hammer appeared, wearing his full Satans Wrath colours, she looked at Damien again. He ignored her, choosing instead to direct an angry scowl at Jack.

Jack's face remained impassive. *Putting it together, Damien?*

Upon Buck's appearance, his back to the camera, Damien looked at Jack again and the two men locked eyes. This time Damien's eyes revealed his rage. *You recognize your son's colours — great.* A vein on Damien's temple throbbed visibly as he turned to watch the video.

Vicki showed no sign of recognition and her face remained stoic, even when Weasel's leg was shattered with a baseball bat. *Guess violence doesn't bother you as long as it isn't against someone in your family.*

It was after Buck smashed King's temple with his pistol, then kicked and stomped on him before turning toward the camera, that Vicki recognized her son. She gasped, then her mother's instinct to defend took over. "That guy asked for it. He shouldn't have tried to grab the bat. Buck was only —"

"Shut up," Damien said tersely, "and listen."

Vicki's eyes betrayed her panic as she continued to watch.

Jack leaned back and folded his arms across his chest. Soon he got the response he expected. Vicki's eyes widened in terror when she realized that her son had murdered a man. She looked at Damien, no doubt hoping for some sign that everything would be okay, that somehow he'd make it all go away.

Damien shut his eyes and briefly placed his hand over them in a failed attempt to hide his anguish. Seconds later his beefy paw fell to the table. He swallowed, then looked at Vicki. "I'll call Basil."

"Don't be in a hurry to do that," Jack said, ignoring the look of fury that Vicki gave him. "At least, not him."

"Why not?" Damien growled. "I presume you haven't picked Buck up yet, or I would've heard. But I'm sure you're about to —"

"Basil Westmount is the lawyer you keep on retainer for the club," Jack explained. "His loyalty lies with Satans Wrath — which might not be in your son's best interests."

"So that's why you're here." Damien glowered. "You're hoping to turn Buck into a rat. You want us to convince him to go along with you."

"Uh, that's —"

"Forget it!" Damien said, slamming his fist on the table. "Satans Wrath is family! I didn't raise my son to be a squealer. We don't turn on our brothers."

"It isn't him I'm looking to cut a deal with," Jack said. "It's you."

"Me?" Damien looked shocked. He snorted a laugh, but his throat was dry and it sounded forced. He swallowed and cleared his throat. "You're out of your fucking mind."

"Give me something worthy and I'll make all this go away," Jack said calmly.

Damien shook his head, but Jack could see fear in his eyes.

"Damien?" Vicki put her hand on her husband's cheek.

"Don't talk to me now," he said, twisting away.

"Come on, Damien," Jack coaxed. "You say Satans Wrath is your family. What about your *real* family? Your children?"

Damien continued to glower at Jack.

"I can only imagine the grief each of you felt when you lost a daughter to meningitis," Jack said softly. "Now with Katie in drug rehab … I hope it works out, but of course, when it comes to addicts and their overdoses … well, some things are beyond our control."

Vicki threw him a filthy look. She turned to Damien for support. He acted like she wasn't even there.

Jack continued, "That being said, you still have Buck. His fate is something you can control."

Vicki released a tearful sob and gripped Damien's wrist in an attempt to connect on an emotional level. Her eyes were pleading and she gave a slight nod toward Jack, urging her husband to accept Jack's offer.

Damien continued to ignore her. He looked at Jack. "I'm retiring at the end of the month," he said bluntly. "It's a done deal. I couldn't help you even if I wanted."

Jack rolled his eyes. "Who are your trying to bullshit? Are you hoping to convince Vicki that you're unable to help — rather than tell her that your loyalty to the club is greater than your love for your children?"

Damien clenched his jaw.

"Damn it, Damien!" Vicki cried. "He's our son! You don't leave him hanging out there!"

"Yeah … and what do you think would happen when the club found out?" Damien shook his head. "You really think a video like this would be kept secret? It's probably already on YouTube."

"More excuses," Jack said. "If you're worried about someone finding out about the video, I could tell the prosecutor that I didn't know that either of the two victims were going to be hurt — which means we didn't have grounds to go on the property. The video wouldn't be admissible and neither would our testimony. It'd be an easy victory for civil liberties. The case would never go ahead and be written off as police incompetence."

"That'd work!" Vicki exclaimed excitedly. She looked earnestly at Damien. "Give him something!" Damien didn't respond so she turned to Jack. "What do you need? What would it take for you not to charge Buck?"

"Vicki, shut the fuck up!" Damien ordered harshly.

Vicki looked taken back. It was evident she wasn't used to being spoken to in that manner.

"Buck is her son, too," Jack went on. "Besides, like you said, you're retiring next month. Isn't Buck's future more important? I know there's a new European connection being set up for you guys to distribute coke."

"I've no idea what you're talking about," Damien said.

Jack continued as if he hadn't heard. "The delivery has to be by boat or air. Give me the details. Let me arrange the busts to sever the connection in Europe and I'll say we're even. Then you can retire and go about enjoying life the way you intended."

Damien gazed stone-faced at Jack, not betraying his thoughts, but the fact that he hadn't immediately dismissed the notion gave Jack hope. "Come on, Damien," Jack urged. "This is your own kid here. Being your son will make it tough for him in jail. You've got a lot of enemies. What're his odds of surviving ten or twenty years in prison?"

"Oh, my God!" Vicki looked at her husband again. "Damien, come on!"

Damien sneered at Jack. "Ten or twenty? That's a load of crap and you know —"

"We'd lay charges of belonging to a criminal organization on top of the murder one," Jack said. "That allows for a life sentence."

"B.C. has never declared us to be a criminal organization," Damien countered. "Other provinces have, but not here."

"He was with the Gypsy Devils. They're not as sophisticated. I'd say there's a good chance of getting them declared. If that happened and the judge decided Buck was there to supervise the GDs, he'd get more time."

"Even if you did lay charges, there's no fucking way he'd draw more than a fin," Damien replied.

"Five years? For this?" Jack chuckled. "I don't think so, but say you were right. It's a matter of semantics. Would you chance one minute of allowing your son to be killed, let alone years?"

Damien gritted his teeth and a muscle rippled up the side of his jaw.

"Besides," Jack continued, "I'm damned certain you've made your millions, so what's Europe to you? I could cover off the arrests by leaking a false news report to say the investigation started over there."

Damien hesitated and Jack could see the pain in his eyes, which changed to anger. "You came here tonight to poison Vicki with your fucking bullshit! You think I don't see that?"

"We came here because Buck is your son. Yours and Vicki's."

"Get the fuck out of my house!" Damien roared, leaping to his feet and sending his chair toppling over.

"Have it your way," Jack replied, getting to his feet. As Laura picked up the laptop he looked at Damien and tossed his business card on the table. "I know this came as a shock, so I'll give you two days to think it over. Same as the two days your guys gave King. My cell number is on the card. If I don't hear from you by Tuesday morning, it'll be too late to save your son."

"I don't need two days! Thirty minutes with you has been long enough. The answer is no. Get the hell out of my house!"

Jack nodded. *You think thirty minutes with me is a long time? Wait until you spend the next two days with Vicki and see how that goes.*

Once Jack and Laura stepped outside, Damien slammed the door behind them. As they walked away they could hear Vicki screaming at Damien, demanding that he do something.

Laura glanced over her shoulder. "If she keeps that up, he's liable to kill her."

"Good. It'd be just reward for her living a life of luxury based on money earned from the misery and death of others."

"Maybe we should hang around," Laura suggested. "We might get him for murder."

"He won't go that far. He knows she's upset. Besides … I know he loves her."

"Once she cools off, she has to realize that her son isn't some innocent kid caught up in the wrong crowd. He's a killer."

"A mother's love can sometimes be blind — which is what I want."

"Which is what you want?" Laura echoed.

"He won't be retiring in peace. Vicki will hold this against him for the rest of his life. Anything I can do to hurt him makes me happy, petty as that sounds."

"You hurt him tonight, but speaking of a mother's love, there's something you should consider."

"That being?"

"She'll do anything to protect her family. I saw the look she gave you when you spoke about Katie in rehab. I thought she was going to leap across the table and gouge your eyes out. Same when she realized you'd videoed Buck."

"It wasn't only me who was there tonight," Jack replied. "You were there, too."

"Yes, but she focused on you," Laura said pointedly. "You're the one she blames."

"Satans Wrath are to blame. We were simply watching from the sidelines."

"Think she'll see it that way?"

"Probably not," Jack replied.

Chapter Nineteen

"You're just going to stand there? Say something!" demanded Vicki as she crossed the foyer to where Damien stood.

Damien grimaced. "There's nothing I can do." *Damn you, Taggart. You intentionally riled her up.*

"Bullshit!" Vicki seethed. "You're telling me you're going to let some guy walk into our house and tell us he's taking our son away from us?"

"He's not taking him from us. At worst, Buck will serve a couple years."

"A couple years? You heard what he said! You got enemies! What about the guy he killed? Who's he with?"

Damien put his finger to his lips. "Outside. We're not talking in here."

Moments later Damien and Vicki were on a path that meandered through the back garden of their estate. After passing a koi pond, they stopped alongside a clump of California lilac bushes that partially covered the stone wall at the far end of their property.

"Okay," Damien said. "There's no need to worry about the chump who got killed. He's nobody. He was the leader of some piss-ant little club called the Cobras. There won't be any retaliation from them."

"Was he really given two days to pay up?"

"Probably. Stuff like that doesn't need my approval."

Vicki looked at Damien accusingly. "Someone in the club had to have ratted for Taggart to know. You guys aren't as close as you think. It shouldn't bother you to do the same and give Taggart what he wants if it means saving Buck."

"The rat wouldn't be one of our guys," Damien said assuredly. "Buck was with a bunch of wannabes called the Gypsy Devils. It'd be one of them who screwed up. Most likely by being stupid and saying something over a phone or a bug than actually ratting. Either way, the GDs'll pay. I'll give them two weeks to find out who and take care of him. Otherwise we'll find out *for* them — and take out a couple more for allowing it to happen."

"Two weeks! For what this jerk did to Buck? Make 'em pay now!"

"Calm down there, Mama Bear. Rushing out and killing the wrong person could make the situation worse. Give the Gypsy Devils time to look after it themselves. Don't worry, whoever ratted won't be above ground very long."

"Guess what's really important is what's going to happen to Buck!" Vicki said hotly. She eyed Damien reflectively. "What Taggart said about you having enemies — I know you do. Some are bound to be in jail. If not, they'll have connections inside."

"We have people on the inside, too," Damien told her. "If Buck goes to jail, he won't be on his own."

"So you're talking about warring gangs in prison? You think it's okay to put our son into that?" she said angrily.

"If things don't look safe, Buck would be moved to solitary. He'd be safe there. That's if he's convicted in the first place."

"Which is what we should be talking about! Do something so he isn't charged and sent to jail."

"I can't stop Taggart from having him charged," Damien said grimly.

"Can't? Or won't?" Vicki snapped. "Give him that European thing he was asking for."

"I'm not ratting on the club."

"You heard Taggart. He could put all the heat on the other side. The club would never suspect you."

"I don't give a fuck about that! I won't do it because I'd never sell out my guys!"

"Aaagh…!" she yelled in frustration. "Then kill the bastard! Secord, too. Let it be a lesson for everyone. Nobody messes with our family!"

"Calm down. Are you forgetting that Taggart and Secord saved your life once? Katie's, too."

"So what?" Vicki replied contemptuously. "That was their job."

Damien shook his head. "Tonight Taggart said there was another cop with them when they videoed. I've got the feeling he lied, but either way, killing them isn't a viable option."

"Why not? I'll shoot him myself if I have to. He's not getting away with this!"

"Lower your voice, damn it, and quit talking stupid." Damien watched as she wiped the tears from her eyes. *She's been weepy and stressed all month, ever since her dad entered the hospice. Guess she knows what's coming, seeing as her mom died four years ago from smoking like a chimney.*

Vicki took a deep breath, then exhaled. "I'm not talking stupid," she insisted. "I'm talking about our son."

Damien sighed. "You're not being rational. I'm not going to start murdering cops over Buck going to jail for a couple of years." He eyed her closely. "I've never heard you talk like this before."

Vicki's eyes flashed. "You're right. I've never talked like this before or asked for anything. Even when Katie and I were kidnapped by the Colombians over one of your dope deals, did I ever complain?"

God, don't remind me. He swallowed. "No, you didn't."

Vicki raised her hand to expose a missing finger. "Even when they cut this off, along with my wedding ring, I never complained."

That was horrible.

Vicki continued, "Since then you've made me pack a gun in my purse when I go anywhere. Do you think that actually puts my mind at rest?"

"I guess not, but what else can —"

"You're damned right it doesn't! I also never complained either time you gave me chlamydia."

"I told you I used condoms. They broke. Wasn't like I gave you AIDS or something."

"That's all you got to say about it?"

Damien looked at her coldly. "If you wanted to marry a saint, you should've hung out at a church. You knew what I was like. You enjoyed hanging out with the bad boys. You thought it was cool."

"What're you saying? That I'm just one of your desperate pathetic tramps who clings to a pole in a nightclub?"

"No, you're the opposite," Damien replied evenly. "Most of them are drug addicted, have low intelligence, and come from dysfunctional families. Your dad was an engineer. You come from money and are educated — and smart enough when we met to know what I was about."

"I was young. Only twenty-one when we got married and pregnant with Buck. What the hell did I know? You were thirty-nine. I looked up to you as someone who was strong and would look after me."

"Are you telling me you haven't been well looked after? Take a look around. I never heard you complaining when we moved here, and certainly not about all the shopping you do. Clothes, jewellery."

"I've also put up with all your other crap," she said. "Trying to raise three kids and putting up with gang wars, your business deals. I never complained or asked for anything." Vicki gestured with her hands. "This time is different. This time I am asking that —"

"My business deals have brought in a lot of money." Damien scowled. "Millions. You've never complained about that, either."

"I was short-sighted. Christ, when I'm in my early sixties, you'll be eighty. I'll probably be pushing you around in a wheelchair. Some future I've got to look forward to. You ever think of that?"

"Is that what this conversation is about? Your future? I thought it was about Buck."

Vicki looked at Damien contemptuously. "I didn't even blame you when our own daughter got addicted, and I sure as hell should've."

"Blame me? I sent Katie to Italy and put her in the best

rehab place there is."

"Yeah? Or are you hiding her out of embarrassment?"

"Our daughter's sick. I'm not embarrassed about it."

"Ever wonder if her addiction came from the dope you imported?"

Damien was taken back. "That's bullshit! Katie was told never to do drugs. If I built cars and she was hit by a car crossing the street, would it be my fault? She was taught to take care of herself."

"Damn it, Damien," Vicki wailed. "She's been in a dozen rehabs! We've lost her and you know it!"

Yeah, I know it. Christ, I feel like I've been punched in the gut. He felt his eyes moisten.

"Buck is all that's left of our family. I've never asked for anything before, but I'm asking now. Save him!"

"Taggart said he'd give us two days. In the morning I'll meet with Buck, then take him to see Basil. We'll get the best defence possible."

"Defence?" Vicki exclaimed. "That isn't good enough! Taggart gave us two days. That should be enough time to put that bastard in the ground!"

"It wouldn't keep Buck out of jail," Damien retorted. "The video would still be entered as evidence. The upshot would be a bunch more club members going to jail — or killed while being arrested."

"I'd go to jail to save Buck," Vicki said.

Yeah, you would, too. Damien shook his head in awe. *I love you so much.* "Listen, I'm sorry for the way I spoke to you tonight." He wrapped an arm around her waist to pull her close, but she pushed him away. "I'd care if you went to jail," he said.

Vicki looked silently up at him. Her face was blank.

"You do know that I love you, right?" he murmured.

"Sure I do, but not as much as you love your club."

Damien made a conscious effort to control his frustration.

"What about bribing them?" Vicki suggested. "It isn't like we can't spare a couple million."

"I know Taggart. He'd seize the money and charge us with bribery."

"Then I don't see any alternative." She eyed Damien briefly. "You know what needs to be done. Kill 'em!"

"That's not happening."

"Then I'll do it myself," she threatened.

Damien could no longer control his temper. "Cool it, you dizzy bitch! The club is my family and it's about to become Buck's family, too. Keep the fuck out of it!"

Vicki's mouth fell open.

Damien regretted his words as soon as he'd said them. "I'm sorry," he added gruffly. "I shouldn't have said that, but the club is my business and you know not to stick your nose into it."

Vicki was momentarily at a loss for words. She sucked in several deep breaths as a combination of rage and grief consumed her.

"Five years is the most Buck would do," Damien assured her. "Maybe less if the right judge can get involved. Either way, Buck can take his licks like a man. He's not your little boy anymore."

"You bastard," she spat out. "That's it, I'm packing a bag."

"Where you going?" Damien demanded as she turned and stomped back to the house.

"My sister's. I can't stomach being around you."

Damien stared after her. *Maybe that's for the best. Give her a couple days to cool off.*

Chapter Twenty

Jack got home at six in the morning. He tried to be quiet as he undressed, but Natasha awoke, first glancing at him and then the clock. "You working twenty-four-hour shifts these days?" she grumbled.

"Seems like it."

"Did you eat?"

"Grabbed a burger for lunch yesterday. Never had time for supper. I'm too tired to be hungry."

"You'll sleep better if you eat," she said, getting out of bed and reaching for her robe. "I'll make some hash browns and eggs."

"You don't need to. Why don't you try to sleep a little long —"

"I'm awake. It's okay."

Jack gave her a kiss, hugged her, then kissed her again. "I love you."

"I love you, too, but you stink. Take a shower and I'll make us breakfast."

Jack nodded.

"Do we have you for the next two days? You said you'd be taking today and tomorrow off. By the time you sleep, half the day will be gone."

"I know, I'm sorry," Jack replied. "I'm expecting a phone call this morning, but it should be short. How about waking me at noon and we'll take the boys to a park for a wiener roast?"

"They'd like that."

An hour later Jack had finished breakfast and was getting up from the table when he received the call he was expecting.

"Hey, Connie, to what do I owe the honour of I-HIT's ace investigator calling me at 7:00 a.m. on a Sunday?"

"Sorry," Connie said. "VPD Homicide picked up a new one last night. I got a call from Detective Wilson around midnight wanting some info. I ended up attending and haven't been to bed since. You're lucky I let you sleep this long." A couple of seconds passed before she said,. "One guess as to who was murdered."

"If Wilson called you, I imagine it involves King and Weasel, seeing as they live in VPD's jurisdiction."

"You're right. King was beaten to death and Weasel is in the hospital with a broken leg, broken collarbone, and a couple of broken ribs. Wilson found out that I tried to interview King about Dwayne's murder and called me."

"Is he handling the case?"

"He's the lead detective, but considering that it's likely entwined with Dwayne's murder, I'll work with him."

"Did Weasel say who did it?" Jack asked.

"He said three guys wearing masks came in and attacked King. Told us he had no idea who they were or why they did it. Said he tried to help King but got attacked himself. I'm sure he's lying. VPD found a witness who said she saw a group of guys going down the alley toward King's house about twenty minutes before the ambulance showed."

"Can she identify them?"

"It was too dark and she only got glimpses of movement between the boards on her fence. She was at her kitchen sink and saw a couple of vehicles go by first, then minutes later saw a group of people heading down the alley. She thinks it was about ten people, but said it was hard to tell. At the time she thought maybe someone was throwing a surprise party."

"Sounds like it *was* a surprise party."

"You told me before that Satans Wrath only planned on roughing them up the first time, then giving them a couple of days before getting heavy. With Weasel being afraid to tell the truth, I think Satans Wrath was responsible."

"Satans Wrath was involved. Of course, that's only my opinion as someone watching from the sidelines."

"Glad you agree," Connie said. "I think King ripped off their grow-op and killed Dwayne in the process. At the time he probably didn't know Satans Wrath was connected. They then retaliated by killing him — although we'll probably never prove it."

"Guess things got out of hand with whoever was sent to rough King up."

"Roughing someone up is one thing. Killing them is another. I feel guilty as hell about it. If I hadn't shown those pictures to Larry, it wouldn't have happened. Wilson and I are going to interview him on Monday — not that I expect him to admit that he told the bikers."

"Don't feel guilty. You were doing your job."

"You were concerned about Larry when we told him his brother was murdered. I remember you pointing your finger in his face and telling him to leave things to us. At the time I thought you were being a little too hard on him. Boy, was I ever wrong."

"It's not like King was an upstanding citizen," Jack said.

"Yeah, I know. At least I tried to warn him. After you gave me the info about Satans Wrath threatening his guys in the bar, I called him."

"Hope you didn't burn my source." Jack's tone was grave.

"Give me some credit, will you? I told him we got a call from someone who works in the bar."

"Good."

"Although I did pass on your info to Wilson," Connie added.

"I trust him. I've no problem with that."

"Didn't think you'd mind."

"What did King have to say about it when you warned him?"

"He laughed it off. Denied doing the rip and said he wasn't worried. He told me the bikers didn't know where any of them lived and said they'd lay low for a while."

"Sounds like you did everything you could."

"I don't know. Maybe I should've talked to him in person."

"I've heard of the horse whisperer," Jack said. "Who do you think you are? The moron whisperer?"

"This isn't funny. I feel horrible about it."

You gotta be kidding. "Sorry, Connie, but it's tough to deal with idiots. If you'd gone over to talk to him, he'd think you were trying to con him into admitting something about Dwayne's murder. King was the leader of a gang of thugs who deal dope. I'm surprised he lived this long."

"Guess that's one way of looking at it."

"You know we're running wire on some of the bikers," Jack said. "Did you call the monitors to see if they heard anything?"

"I did, but they haven't heard a peep."

"No surprise. Not the sort of thing they'd talk about over a phone."

"So you really think they didn't mean to kill King?"

"If they intended to kill him, they wouldn't have sent so many guys. That number is more for intimidation. If they wanted him killed, it would've been done by their three-three team."

"What the hell is a three-three team?"

"It's what Satans Wrath call their professional hit team. All club members belong to chapters in various cities, as do members of their hit team, but they're on call to operate Canada-wide. Unofficially they're thought of as the Canada Chapter because they take instruction from various chapter presidents."

"You mean orders for hits?"

"Yes."

"Why do they call themselves the three-three?"

"The letter *C* is the third letter of the alphabet, hence number three. So together, the two *C*s stand for Canada Chapter — or the reverse for the French."

"Nice that they're so politically correct."

"In the old days various club members used to get individual tattoos for doing a club-sanctioned hit called the Dirty Dog."

"Yeah … I remember."

"Since then they've become more professional. They have a full-time hit squad made up of guys who know their stuff. Club members sometimes refer to someone as belonging to the double three — or in the case of a victim, being double-three'd."

"How many guys belong to it?"

"I think there are four in British Columbia. Three in the lower mainland and one in Kelowna, a fellow by the name of Pasquale Bazzoli. There are about eight or nine others scattered across the country with half of those living in Quebec. For individual hits, the three-three might only use one or two guys."

Connie sighed. "When it comes to King, I'm not optimistic that I'd get anything on them, anyway. All I'd end up doing is wasting a lot of manpower that could be better tasked working on cases involving innocent victims. If you're right that it was accidental, then that makes it even less of a priority."

"And Dwayne?"

"King is dead. Maybe in a couple of weeks if we get confirmation from the lab matching the rock to his boat, I'll officially close the file then."

"It would be nice to nail the bikers. All this stuff with Dwayne and King — bikers are my priority. Mind if I stick my nose into it a little?"

"I don't see any harm in you doing that now. Especially considering it probably involves Satans Wrath.

Maybe your informant can help us out — if he wasn't one of the ones involved."

"He wasn't involved," Jack assured her, "but give me a couple of days to work on it. Who knows, maybe I'll come up with something." *Like handing you a video of the murder.*

"How do you know your informant wasn't involved?" Connie asked.

"He'd call me if he did something like that. I also believe King was killed accidentally, so there'd have been no reason for him not to have told me in advance that they were going over to do it."

"Yeah, well … if you do hear something, let me know."

"You might want to pass on to Weasel that he should disappear. Satans Wrath might be looking at him as a loose end."

"Good point. I'll tell Wilson to warn him. If it was accidental, Satans Wrath might not even know King is dead."

"I'm sure they already know," Jack said, then hung up.

Natasha looked across the kitchen table at Jack. "You told me you were expecting one short call. From the surprise in your voice when you answered the call from Connie, I take it that wasn't it."

"No, that was the call I was expecting," Jack said.

"So you're playing her."

"More a matter of not letting her see the big picture yet. I gave someone a deadline of two days. If he doesn't come through by then, which I don't think he will, I'll give Connie the full scoop."

"You mean let her in on the big picture."

Jack grinned. "The big picture in this case is more like a video." He glanced at the clock. "At the moment the only things I want to see are the insides of my eyelids."

Natasha rose from the table and gave him an affection-
ate kiss on his cheek, along with a promise to wake him
up at noon.

Jack was pulling the covers back to get into bed when
his phone rang again. Unlike Connie's call, this one was
totally unexpected. After a short conversation he hung up
and called Laura.

"What time is it?" Laura asked. "Did I sleep in? I
thought we were off —"

"No, you didn't sleep in," Jack said.

"What the heck! I've only been in bed thirty minutes!
You better be phoning to say good night."

"Get dressed and wear your Kevlar vest," he said tersely.

"What's up?"

"Vicki wants to meet."

"Vicki! At her house? Is Damien —"

"No. She wants to meet us alone. I'll give you the
details when I pick you up. Be out front of your house in
thirty minutes."

"Oh, man …"

When Jack hung up, he saw that Natasha had been
watching him from the doorway. "Sorry," he said. "Gotta
go back to work."

"Dangerous," Natasha said.

"No, don't worry about the vest thing. We're meeting
someone who says she has some information for us."

"Right. Don't worry. You haven't slept in twenty-six
hours and are heading out to a situation where you feel
the need to wear a bulletproof vest. There's nothing for
me to worry about."

"The Kevlar is simply a precaution. It's like looking

both ways before you cross the street."

Natasha didn't look convinced.

"It shouldn't take long," Jack proffered. "I doubt she'll have anything of value. More likely wants to beg me not to charge someone, or if I do, to reduce the charge. I should be home in time for lunch."

"Where have I heard that one before," Natasha muttered.

Chapter Twenty-One

The sun had been up for an hour when Laura opened the door to climb into the SUV. She wore a long-sleeved white blouse that hung over her jeans to hide her pistol and saw Jack checking her out. "Yes, I know. I shouldn't wear white after Labour Day."

"Yes, now I'll be embarrassed to be seen with you." His eyes drifted down to her chest.

"I'm wearing it," she said. "Can't you tell? Makes me look flat and fat."

"Good." Jack pulled away from the curb.

"So what's the deal?"

"Vicki phoned and said she wanted to meet right away. She also told me she was calling from her sister's place and that Damien doesn't know about it."

"Her emotions were all over the map earlier. How was she when she called?"

"Still upset, which is why I didn't want to delay meeting

her until we got some sleep. She could change her mind after she cools off."

"At one point I had the distinct feeling she wanted to put us in the ground — especially you."

"She still might want to."

"You think Damien could be setting us up for a hit?"

"No. He's upset, but I didn't leave his house with the feeling he'd murder us over it. Even if he was planning to, he wouldn't use Vicki. He loves her too much. He wouldn't risk her going to jail or getting hurt."

"So Damien really might not know about this," Laura said.

"Maybe not. She told me that she had something to give us in exchange for Buck going free, but wouldn't tell me on the phone. The thing is, I really doubt that she'd know anything about club business. Anything she could tell us would likely be general in nature and not enough to put anyone in jail."

"Are you thinking she's going to try to take us out on her own?"

"I wondered. I told her to dress in something to show she wasn't packing any weapons — but we'll search her regardless."

"So where do we meet her?"

"I'll rent a hotel room. I told her I'd call her back and direct her to a specific location on a street. I told her at that point we'd be able to see her, but she wouldn't see us. Then I'd call her again and give her instructions to walk to our location. Once that happens, she's not to use her phone again unless it's to answer a call from me. I also warned her that she'd still be searched."

"Did she seem okay with that?"

"No hesitation at all, but what was interesting is she asked if all these security precautions were because I'd been talking to Damien after we left their house. I told her we hadn't."

"How is that interesting?"

"I think she brought up the subject of killing us with Damien — which is another reason I don't think he's involved. If he was, she wouldn't have asked me that."

"If it isn't a trap, then what the heck does she have for us?"

Jack shrugged. "I doubt she knows any details about club business that'd allow us to arrest anyone."

"So we're wasting our time? All we'll hear is some mom begging for us to let her son off the hook?" Laura shook her head. "I could be home in bed right now."

"There's another possibility. What if Damien did send her to meet with us?"

"A moment ago you said you didn't think he did."

"I'm not talking about her or Damien wanting to kill us. Maybe, on a psychological level, his loyalty for the club is stopping him from talking to us direct. Maybe he gave her something to pass on."

"Like their new European connection?"

"Possibly. Damien could get her to say she overheard something. He knows I wouldn't jeopardize her safety, which would protect her from the club knowing." He stopped at a traffic light and glanced at Laura. "What're your thoughts?"

Laura yawned. "I'm too tired to know what to think right now."

That's the problem. So am I.

Chapter Twenty-Two

Vicki got off the elevator and walked to the end of the sixth-floor hallway in the hotel while talking to Jack on her phone. "I'm here," she said. "What room number?"

"Hang up," Jack said. He opened a door to reveal that he and Laura were inside the stairwell.

Seconds later Laura searched Vicki in the stairwell. She then brought Vicki to a room on the seventh floor and directed her to sit at a small table, which held a carafe and three coffee mugs. Jack took the only other chair available and sat facing her, while Laura sat on the corner of the bed.

Jack poured a mug of coffee and pushed it across the table.

"Not for me," Vicki demurred. "I've already had six cups with my sister. My nerves are rattled enough."

Jack slid the mug to Laura and poured one for himself. He glanced at Vicki and saw she was anxious to get started. "Talk," he said before taking a sip.

"If, uh, I give you something but … well, if you don't think it's enough to keep Buck from being charged, would you at least see to it that he gets off with probation?"

"Probation!" Jack put the mug down. "No way. We're talking murder with the commission of an offence involving a criminal organization laid on top of it. That penalty allows for a life sentence. Simple probation would never be allowed because it'd set a bad precedent."

"He could get off," Vicki argued.

"You and I both know that isn't going to happen," Jack said. "Otherwise you wouldn't be here."

"Maybe … but Damien said he'd only get five years." Vicki looked intently at Jack. All she saw was a grim smile. She turned to Laura, who rolled her eyes and exchanged a knowing look with Jack.

Jack cleared his throat. "I understand why Damien doesn't want you to worry, but Buck is your son. Your husband should be telling you the truth." He reached for the mug again and glanced at Laura. "Maybe he hasn't even told *himself* the truth yet."

Vicki looked glumly from Jack to Laura and back again.

"The reality is," Jack continued, "if Buck is sentenced to less than ten or twelve years, we'll put pressure on to have his sentence appealed." He paused to sip more coffee. "Once charges are laid in regard to a criminal organization, I couldn't arrange leniency or probation even if I wanted to."

"But the charges haven't been laid yet," Vicki said, her eyes pleading. "You said we had two days. Maybe you could charge him with something less serious."

"I could do something if you had something to offer," Jack replied, "but there —"

"Buck didn't mean to do what he did," Vicki cried. "You must see that!" She looked anxiously between them for a reaction. Nothing. "He's young and has been influenced by Damien, but he's a good boy at heart. I know he didn't mean to do what he did. He got caught up in the moment."

Jack's face was hard. "You said you had something to tell us. There's one thing you need to know. If you lie to us about anything, anything at all, then all deals are off." He paused for effect. "That's provided we do make a deal with you."

"Of course. I understand that. I won't —"

"Does Damien know you're talking with us?" Jack asked.

Vicki's face darkened. "No, of course not. Otherwise he'd be here … like he should be."

"Then that poses a problem," Jack said. "If you do have something to tell us, it has to be good enough that we could put someone in jail for it for a long time. Also, we'd have to be able to do that without anybody suspecting it was you who informed. If charges against Buck didn't proceed and Damien knew you were privy to whatever information you're thinking of passing on, he'd immediately point a finger at you."

"I don't care what he thinks if it keeps my son out of jail," Vicki replied haughtily.

"You may not, but we do," Jack said. "We have a reputation for protecting our sources."

Vicki shrugged. "I'm not sure how upset Damien would be with me. For a moment when you were talking to us in our kitchen, I thought he was going to tell you about that European connection. I could see in his eyes that he was considering it. I tried to convince him after you left … but that didn't go well."

"This is different. You're going behind his back. If he found out, I think he'd kill you. If not personally, then someone from the three-three would."

Vicki shuddered. "Maybe."

"That being said, depending on what you tell us, there are often ways we can do things to deflect the heat — but your husband is no fool. The element of danger would still be present."

"So you've heard about the three-three," Vicki said thoughtfully.

"I know about them. I wasn't sure if you did," Jack replied.

"Some of the wives and girlfriends talked about it when we were at a party. Maybe I could find out their names. One of them is from Kelowna."

"Pasquale Bazzoli," Jack said.

Vicki's face revealed her disappointment. "You already know," she said.

"That … and a lot more." Jack's tone was firm. He looked hard at her. *She's holding something back … something she's afraid to tell me.* "We don't have all day. Do you have something for us or not?"

Vicki met Jack's gaze. "Okay, I've got something else."

She's testing the water … like tossing out a low-valued poker chip. Whatever she's about to say isn't much.

"But what you wanted, that European thing, I can't help you with that. I hadn't even heard about it until you mentioned it to Damien."

"Okay, so what can you tell us?"

"When I spoke with Damien after you left, he told me that Buck might even get less than five years — if the right judge takes the case."

"We've been over that," Jack said.

"When he said 'the right judge,' he wasn't talking about getting a judge who's soft on crime. The judge he referred to is with the B.C. Supreme Court and has been in Damien's pocket for years." She smiled smugly. "I know who it is. I could give you his name."

"Don't bother."

Vicki looked crestfallen. "You know?"

"All you've got to do is read the newspapers," Jack replied. "Everybody knows who he is. He's tossed out so many cases or given such lenient sentences that it's obvious." He glanced at Laura and joked, "I wouldn't be surprised if he had a club tat on his ass to show his support for Satans Wrath."

Vicki bit her lower lip. *She's holding something back ... but what?*

"Listen," Jack said, sounding sympathetic. "I know a good mom would do whatever was necessary to protect her children. Considering that Buck will be a prime target by rival gangs in prison, I understand your concern."

Vicki looked sharply at Jack, then her eyes brimmed with tears.

Jack drank from his mug. "I can't guarantee anything, but I'll ask that he serve his time in isolation. I can't make any promises as to his safety, but I'll ask."

"What do you mean you'll *ask?*" Vicki said abruptly. "Isn't that a given? You simply explain the situation to the warden?"

Jack looked incredulous. "You must know that Satans Wrath has bought off jail guards?" Vicki's puzzled look said she didn't understand. Jack took another sip of coffee. "The same thing goes for some of the rival gangs. Ten or twelve years is a long time. Things happen … but as one parent to another, I'll do my best. Isolation would be the safest."

Vicki's jaw quivered and a tear ran down her cheek.

Jack continued to build pressure. "If he's put in isolation for that long, it's obvious he'd require years of psychotherapy when he was released, but at least — physically — he'd still be alive."

"Oh, my God," Vicki sobbed.

"I'm sorry," Jack said softly. He leaned forward and gave her a consoling pat on the arm. "I can only imagine the grief you feel now … and how that'll manifest itself with the day-by-day worry and anxiety you'll feel once he's imprisoned."

Vicki sat back in the chair, placing her hand over her mouth. Jack didn't know if it was because she felt sick or if it was an unconscious motion to stop herself from saying something. When her brow furrowed in thought he knew it was the latter.

Time to prod her again. Jack made a pretence of looking at his watch. "I feel bad rushing you, but it appears you're unable to provide us with anything of value. I'm sorry. I tried to reason with your husband and make a deal … But you were there. You saw how that went."

Vicki lowered her hand from her face. "What if I gave you him?" she said icily.

"Him?"

"Damien," she replied.

Jack's mind went numb. For a moment he was afraid. Afraid to dream. Afraid to feel any exhilaration. He tried to downplay what he might be told so as to avoid bitter disappointment later.

What does she actually know? Things she's heard from the past? Things that are too late for us to act on, once more allowing Damien to slip away?

Chapter Twenty-Three

Jack realized Vicki was studying him closely. Like a poker player not wanting to disclose his hand before taking all his opponent's money, he did his best not to show any emotion. He glanced at Laura. "More coffee?"

"Uh, no thanks. I'm afraid it'll keep me awake, uh, later."

Jack nodded, then poured himself another cup and took a sip. His mind raced. *It's not possible. Even if she does know something to put him away, he'd be bound to know she was responsible.*

"Well?" Vicki prodded.

"Perhaps I'd be interested," Jack allowed.

"Perhaps?" Vicki chortled. "Don't give me that shit."

"Make no mistake, I want him — but not if it puts you in too much jeopardy."

"Put me in jeopardy?" Vicki seemed speechless. Then she looked at Jack with disdain. "You're a fool." She threw a glance at Laura. "A couple of hours ago I begged Damien to kill the both of you." She paused to see a reaction, but didn't get one. "When he refused, I threatened to get my gun and do it myself. Now you're worrying about protecting me? That's a laugh."

Yeah, that's a real laugh. Dwayne was my informant, too, except he wasn't laughing when he called. He wasn't laughing when a bullet ripped through his guts.

Laura saw the injured look on Jack's face and rushed to his defence. "You may think it's a laugh," she snapped, "but protecting our sources is something we take seriously."

"Really?" Vicki questioned. "Are you going to protect me like you're protecting whoever it is in the Gypsy Devils who ratted?"

"What do you mean?" Jack asked.

"Damien knows that someone in that club gave you the info to set up Buck. He's giving them two weeks to find out who it was and deal with the problem. If they don't, Satans Wrath will do it for them and take out a few others while they're at it."

Hope it's the latter — except with a bunch of losers like the GDs, some innocent bystander could get hurt. He eyed Vicki. "Believe what you want, but as Laura said, if you talk to us your protection automatically becomes a priority."

Vicki looked sullen now. "Yeah, whatever. I'm a big girl. I can look after myself. If Buck stays out of jail I'll be happy no matter what."

"You need to understand that, depending on what you tell us, we may or may not act on it. Usually I come up with a creative idea to help protect someone, but again it depends on what you tell us."

"Jack's very creative," Laura added dryly.

Jack saw Laura frown and knew what she was thinking. *Creative — like pinning the blame on someone else and having that person killed. What's wrong with that?* He turned his attention back to Vicki. "You mentioned you don't know anything about the European drug connection, but do you know of some other deal we could link Damien to?"

"I don't know anything about drug shipments," Vicki replied.

Not drugs? Then what the hell do you have? "Before you tell us, there's something else I need to warn you about. The murder your son committed took place in the jurisdiction of the Vancouver Police Department. I may not have any influence on their decision if they gather evidence to have him charged."

Concern spread across Vicki's face. "Meaning you might not be able to stop Buck from being charged?"

"What I'm saying is that if you give us something worthwhile, we won't disclose the evidence we have to them, but it still leaves the possibility that they could solve it on their own."

Vicki appeared to give it some thought. "I'm willing to live with that. I bet that other guy on the sofa keeps his mouth shut. Without your evidence I can't imagine my son ever being convicted even if one of the others talked — which I doubt would happen."

I doubt it, too. "Okay, as long as we're clear on that. Tell me what you have on Damien."

"What I have is how his money is being laundered and where it's stashed."

Jack felt as if his heart had stopped. Then his brain told him it would never happen. *No way — this has to be a set-up.*

"You can get him for tax evasion, money laundering, whatever those charges are," Vicki continued.

Maybe allow us to seize a hundred thousand without getting quite enough evidence to put anyone in jail. Then if we charged Buck, Defence would claim we weren't acting in good faith and the charges would be tossed. Damn you, Damien. You did put her up to this.

"Well, what do you have to say about that?" Vicki asked.

"You say it's Damien's money," Jack replied, "but in reality, isn't it your money, as well? The two of you've been building a nest egg together for years. Are you telling me you're willing to turn it all over to us?"

"I'm not worried about money. My father's in the hospice and could die any time. I usually have lunch with him. He's a wealthy man. There'll be more than enough for my sister and me. As far as Damien goes, he could die for all I care."

Okay, I'll play along. "Until we know the details, we can't promise you anything. You're going to have to trust us."

"You wanting to protect me even after knowing I wanted to kill you — that tells me I can trust you," Vicki said.

"Then let's hear it. We need details." He gave Laura a nod and she took her notebook out of her purse.

Vicki took a deep breath and slowly exhaled. "Damien has a bank account in Vancouver. Between his safety deposit box and his actual account he's got one point two million."

Oh, yeah. I'd like to take that away, but one point two? He must have more than that. Jack knew that Vicki was trying to read his face, but he remained stoic. *She said a bank account in Vancouver. Why mention the city — unless the bastard has an account somewhere else, as well.*

"So, what do you think about that?" Vicki smiled. "Are we square? I bet your Integrated Proceeds of Crime unit would sit up and pay attention to that."

"That amount isn't bad, but it wouldn't cause anyone in I-POC to sit up and pay attention." Jack waited a beat. "At least, not the same way a jury would pay attention if they watched the video of your son beating a man to death."

Vicki's face paled.

"Furthermore, is there any possibility that Damien could explain the money?"

"Explain? In what way?"

"Don't bullshit us," Jack said. "If you know about I-POC, then you obviously have discussed ways to launder or explain your income, particularly if it's sitting in a bank account in Vancouver where it might be discovered."

"Well … of course we've talked about it," Vicki admitted. "Most of the money was laundered through a legitimate business, but out of that money, a quarter mil is in a safety deposit box. It would be difficult to explain."

Difficult — which means not impossible. Just as I thought — she's trying to scam us. "What's his so-called legitimate business?"

"He owns a string of ATMs across the country. Nobody keeps track of how much cash is being loaded or made in those machines."

"That'd be tough to do," Jack agreed. "Too many of them. Strip bars, taverns, hotel lobbies." He thought for a moment, then shook his head. "The quarter mil is chump change. What I'm really interested in is where the rest of his money is."

Vicki's body twitched like she'd been tasered. "The rest of his money?"

"You and I both know that Damien has made more money than that from all the dope the club has moved."

"I don't have anything to do with that stuff," Vicki replied defensively.

So, you're not denying the existence of more money. Jack glanced at Laura. "Wilfully blind."

"Wilfully blind?" Vicki echoed.

"You've been his wife and partner for years. You've had three children together. Don't say that your hands aren't dirty."

"They're not," Vicki protested.

"Aren't they?" Jack replied contemptuously. "You've supported him all these years and have lived a life of luxury, knowing full well where the money came from."

Vicki glared. "Okay! So what if I have? Big deal! I'm small potatoes in the scheme of things. Are you going to take my deal or not?"

"You might be small potatoes, but think of the anguish felt by parents whose children have died from drugs. Your daughter is in rehab." Jack took a sip of coffee to give her a moment to let that sink in. "Do you ever feel like an invisible hand is clawing at your heart? Katie's hand … begging for help."

Vicki swallowed.

"Then there's Buck. Don't you worry about him being involved in the drug trade? A trade where people are killing each other on a daily basis?"

"Yes, I worry about it," Vicki said quietly.

"So, the worry you have for your children, is that what you describe as small potatoes?"

"You've made your point," Vicki said. "Can we move on now?"

Okay, let's see if I can get her to crack. "They say you reap what you sow. But tell me, as a mother, are you proud of how Katie and Buck turned out? Katie is still alive, but you must wonder for how long."

Vicki's mouth opened and closed like a gasping fish, but she couldn't seem to articulate anything.

"Then there was the daughter you lost to meningitis. What was her name?"

"S-Sarah," Vicki stuttered, clearly emotional.

"I can only imagine how horrible it must feel to lose a child," Jack said. He paused to let the grief build. "So think about it. Are you really going to act out this charade, hoping to trick us — and gamble with Buck's life?"

"What charade? What're you talking about?"

"You know what I'm talking about," Jack said harshly. "The rest of the money! Is that worth more to you than Buck? Or don't you give a rat's ass about your children."

A look of rage crossed Vicki's face.

Crap. Not the response I wanted.

"So you think I'm a terrible mother," Vicki fumed. "What the hell do you know? I love my children. Fuck you! Do you think my coming here is easy for me? It goes against every fibre in my body."

Okay, time for a new approach. "The thing is, I know you're not a terrible mother." Jack spoke softly now. "I saw the fear you felt for your children when we went to your house. You love them. Really, aren't you here because you want to do the right thing by them? You're not the kind of mom to take chances with her children. I just needed you to realize that."

Vicki looked down and her body trembled. "I love them so much," she sobbed. "I keep Sarah's picture on our fireplace mantel and talk to her every day, wanting to believe she's still alive, that she still lives here." She raised her head and met Jack's gaze. "As far as Katie and Buck go, I'd do anything to save them."

"Then start by being completely truthful," he said. "Tell us what we need to know."

Vicki nodded, then wiped tears off her cheeks with her fingers. "Okay. The account I told you about — Damien used to think it was safe because he could explain it legally if you guys got into it. Eventually he ended up making so much money he knew it couldn't be explained. About ten years ago we met with a lawyer and came up with a new plan to funnel our money offshore through a phony company."

Jack believed at that moment that he could really hurt Damien. He felt his stomach knot with excitement and glanced at Laura. She stared wide-eyed back at him. He turned back to face Vicki. *It all seems surreal. A moment in time that will stay locked inside me forever.*

Chapter Twenty-Four

Laura glanced at her notebook, then cleared her throat. "We?"

"Pardon?" Vicki asked.

"You said 'we met with a lawyer.'"

Vicki shifted her gaze back to Jack and grimaced. "Yes, *we*. You were right. I knew the money was dirty but chose not to think about it. I told myself that I was still a good mother. I think it was when Katie became an addict that the blinders came off. I knew I was part of it." She paused, obviously thinking back. "Mind you, I'd wanted out before that. Meeting with a lawyer to launder money was an easy step to what I thought would be escape."

"Escape?" Jack asked.

"Retirement," Vicki clarified. "A worry-free life. Getting Damien away from the club." She paused. "They say that hindsight is twenty-twenty. Maybe it is, because I can see clearly now. Believe me."

"I believe you," Jack said.

"You mentioned an account offshore," Laura noted. "Where?"

"The British Virgin Islands. A lawyer here deals through a lawyer in Mexico, as well as one in the BVI."

"Basil Westmount?" Laura asked, not bothering to look up as she wrote.

"No. Basil says he's too well-known to you guys because he's on retainer for the club. He recommended a guy who doesn't defend criminals and so wouldn't be connected. A corporate lawyer by the name of Irving Cummings. Francesco Lopez is the name of the one in Mexico, and Charles Bentley is the one in the BVI."

"Do these lawyers launder for the whole club?" Jack asked.

"You mean across Canada?"

Jack nodded.

"Not as far as I know."

Jack felt a pang of disappointment. *Don't get greedy. Damien is the biggest fish out there.*

"I know for sure that Cummings only launders for Damien," continued Vicki. "When we first met him, Damien asked him how many other clients he laundered for. Cummings said only one. Damien didn't want to chance someone else attracting any heat. He told Cummings that if he wanted our business, he wasn't to launder for anyone else. Cummings said his other client was much smaller and dropping him wouldn't be a problem."

"And the other two lawyers ... Lopez and Bentley?" Jack asked. "Do they only launder for Damien?"

"Yes. I believe Lopez met with the east- and west-side club presidents, but that was only to introduce them to some other lawyer."

"The east and west side — Whiskey Jake and Lance Morgan respectively," Jack stated.

"Yes, but I've no idea where their money ends up or who they were introduced to. I only know they were going to meet Lopez a month or two after we did because of a comment Lopez made. When we were in his office, Damien made Lopez swear not to let anyone else in on the scam or mention Cummings's name, either, to any other investors. He didn't even tell Lance or Whiskey Jake about Cummings, which is surprising, because he's pretty tight with them."

Figures. Damien isn't stupid. "Does Basil get a share of the action?" Jack asked.

"I don't know. If he does, there wouldn't be anything on paper because they don't want to show any link between them. When he referred us to Cummings, all he said was that he heard Cummings had a way of moving money offshore. I don't think he knows any more details than that. I'm guessing that the other client Cummings used to launder for was Basil's client at one time."

"So Cummings has the records when it comes to moving Damien's money out of Canada," Jack concluded.

"Yes. The company is registered in my maiden name and I signed the documents, so I guess I'll have to be charged, too. But I don't give a damn as long as you let Buck go."

"Considering who Damien is, it's unlikely you'd end up with anything more than probation," Jack said. "Your lawyer would have you say you were forced to use your name and were afraid for your life. Not to mention, it'd be apparent that the money came from Damien's activities and not yours."

"Sort of what I figured," Vicki admitted.

"The club must have some way," Jack went on, "of sending the money back to Canada to pay off the locals, such as the Gypsy Devils."

"I suppose so, but not through Lopez or Cummings," Vicki said.

"I take it that Cummings introduced you to Lopez and Bentley?"

Vicki nodded. "When it was being set up Cummings sent us down to meet Lopez on our own. He specializes in real estate and has an office in Chihuahua. After setting things up with him, we went to the BVI the next day, where Cummings joined us and introduced us to Charles Bentley. He has an office in Road Town."

"Explain how it works."

"Well, to start with, we took two-and-a-half mil that we supposedly made in the ATM business and bought some development properties in Mexico through Lopez. In actuality, the land is worthless chunks of desert, but the pretext is that they'll be developed into large condo complexes with golf courses. Lopez has several real estate people from different firms who are in on it. Supposedly investors buy small lots back from us and we make an enormous profit. On paper it looks like we've been reinvesting and buying more development properties for condos, resorts, or whatever."

"And do these investors actually exist?" Laura inserted.

"I don't know if they all do. I think most are major dope dealers — kingpins, so to speak. They pay Satans Wrath for the weed by handing the money over to various real estate firms who deal with different Mexican lawyers. Lopez is the guy who looks after Damien's end."

"Can you remember the names of the real estate firms?" Jack asked.

"No, but there are several. Pretty easy to buy off a real estate agent down there. I don't know if the companies themselves are dirty, or just certain people in the companies."

Jack mulled the information over. "So nobody from the club has to handle the money personally during the actual drug transactions." *No wonder why we haven't been able to trace it.*

"No, I guess they don't." Vicki paused. "I suspect that some of the weed is exchanged for coke, but Damien told me that mainly they just deal in weed."

He lied to make you feel better. They're into every type of drug there is, not to mention prostitution and any other crime that preys on the vulnerable or the weak.

"At least with weed, it's not like it's really hurting anyone," Vicki said.

Weed isn't hurting anyone? Wish you could've heard Dwayne's last phone call ... although considering your total lack of remorse for what happened to King, would you even give a damn?

"Why are you looking at me like that?" Vicki asked. "Don't you believe what I'm telling you? It's all true."

Jack pushed Dwayne from his thoughts. "What you're saying makes sense. It'd also be easy to smuggle drug money from the States into Mexico. That way there wouldn't be any currency-transaction reports, which are required for amounts over ten grand."

"I guess. That part of the business isn't something I know much about. On this end we receive and send money through Cummings. It's either disguised as profits from land sales in Mexico or sent on the pretext of buying more land. Either that or to pay for construction materials, but so far, all that's ever amounted to were a couple of foundations being laid."

"How does Charles Bentley fit in?" Jack asked.

"He simply looks after the money that we send to him, either through Cummings or Lopez."

"He must know it's dirty," Laura said.

"Yeah, well, I guess he's what you'd call wilfully blind," Vicki replied, giving Jack a perky smile.

Jack didn't return the smile. "To confirm that I'm clear on things, neither Lance nor Whiskey Jake knows about Bentley or Cummings?"

"Definitely not. Damien didn't want to take any chances of anyone knowing where his money ended up."

Jack caught the concern on Laura's face and knew what she was thinking. *If nobody else knows about Cummings and Bentley, how do we bust Damien without him knowing it was Vicki who tipped us off?*

"I know you'll want proof," Vicki continued. "Damien doesn't keep any records of it in our house. He had me store some files, including a backup computer flash stick, in a safe we keep at my sister's. The flash stick has all the info, including telephone numbers for the lawyers and account details."

"You should've brought it with you," Jack said.

"I made a copy. It's in my car."

"In your car?"

Vicki bit her lip. "I didn't bring it because I was afraid you'd find it when you searched me. I was hoping you would've been satisfied with taking the one point two mil I told you about."

"We'll get the flash stick later," Jack replied. "We're not done yet."

Vicki nodded. "Damien won't be happy with you taking the one point two, but the BVI is where you'll really hurt him."

"That was going to be my next question," Jack said. "How bad can we hurt him?"

"I'd say you could hurt him to the tune of eighteen point four million."

Holy shit!

Laura gawked at Vicki for a moment, then looked at Jack. "That sounds like a lot of hurting."

Jack's mind reeled with what he'd been told. *How do I seize all that money, not charge Buck, and make Damien think Vicki wasn't involved?* He saw Laura glance at Vicki, then turn toward him and shake her head. He knew what she was thinking. *If we seize the money, Damien will kill her.* He ignored her and faced Vicki.

"So what do you say now?" the woman asked. "Is Buck in the clear?"

Jack heard Laura clear her throat to catch his attention. He continued to ignore her. *There's no way I'm allowing Damien to slip away.*

Laura cleared her throat again. Louder.

Jack smiled grimly as a plan formed in his mind.

Chapter Twenty-Five

It was noon when Jack and Laura retrieved the computer flash stick from Vicki and returned to their SUV. Once in the passenger seat, Laura swivelled to look at Jack. *He knows how I feel. He's been avoiding eye contact with me ever since he told Vicki that ridiculous plan to protect her from Damien finding out she talked.*

Jack turned to face her. He smiled and raised his hand to give her a high-five.

"Are you totally nuts?" she said angrily.

He lowered his hand. "What're you talking about? We've got him! After all these years, we've —"

"We don't have him!" she cried. "You're so bloody blinded by the notion of taking him down that you're not thinking straight! I'm sure as hell not taking part in that ludicrous plan you ran past her!"

"Oh, we've got him," he said determinedly. "Make no mistake about that. As far as my plan with Vicki goes, I know you're not happy about it, so let's talk. What don't you like?"

"Don't like?" *You jerk!* "The woman's a loose cannon! Her emotions are all over the place. You could end up dead."

"I'm not letting Damien get away," he replied vehemently. "My plan will protect her and us."

"*Us?*"

"It'll give Damien something more to think about than coming after us. Buck was one thing. This is far more serious."

"How is getting yourself killed protecting anyone?"

Jack dismissed her comment with a wave of his hand. "I won't get killed. If it works, Damien will thank us."

"What you should've said is you won't get killed if it works."

He gazed at her coldly. "If you have a better idea for how to seize Damien's money, his home, all his belongings, and avoid the charges on Buck without him thinking Vicki was involved, I'm all ears."

"Their home? Jack! What are you …? God, you never mentioned that to her! That makes it far worse. She's only thinking about the bank accounts and has her father's money as backup. You don't know how she'll respond to losing her home."

"If she's genuinely angry it'll be all the better. Damien won't think she had anything to do with it — which is another reason not to let her know until we do it."

"She'll flip out!"

"Good. It's not like she could say or do anything about it. Besides, she should pay for living like a princess all these years off blood money."

Take a deep breath. Try to reason with him.

Jack started the engine but didn't put the SUV in gear, opting instead to take out his phone. "I know you're perturbed," he said calmly.

Perturbed? Is that what you're calling it? Perturbed that I might have to drop by your house and tell Natasha and your kids that you were killed? You've no idea how —

"I admit I've got reservations about it, too," Jack said, "but like I said before, do you have a better idea?"

Laura felt her frustration grow. "No, but what you told her might not work, either."

"I only told her part of the plan. Damien's no fool. With him we'll really have to muddy the water."

"What's the rest of the plan?" she asked in a tone meant to show her displeasure.

"When we raid his home and lawyer's offices, he's going to suspect Vicki immediately. We're going to have to deflect the heat instantly. We need extra insurance to protect Vicki down the road."

Extra insurance? More like life insurance for Natasha to collect!

"Trust me, it'll all turn out," Jack said calmly, "but we need to mess with Damien's head."

"His head isn't the only one you're messing with. I'm not prone to headaches but I've got a doozy of one now."

"You're tired. Once you get some rest you'll see that I'm right."

"But the risk you'll be putting yourself in is too —"

Jack's voice was harsh. "Doing a number on Damien is worth the risk."

Laura saw the look in his eyes, defying her to say otherwise. She knew she couldn't change his mind unless she had a better idea. *Better idea? Man, I don't have any ideas.* She sighed. "You told me there was more to your plan. What's the rest?"

"I'll tell you in a minute, but first I need to call Sammy." He stabbed at the numbers with his finger. "I want to see if Bob and Roxie have delivered the weed yet."

Laura listened as Jack spoke with Sammy. It seemed the semi was still in Dallas, Bob and Roxie had not unloaded yet, and they were currently parked in an industrial area.

"Good," Jack said to Sammy. "Sounds like someone from the West 12th Street gang should be there soon. There's a change of plans. Tell the DEA to seize all the dope as soon as the semi is clear." Jack listened, then smiled. "No, the money trail is no longer a problem. Tell them to seize the dope … I'm sure, yes. It has to do with an informant. They can apply to have Bob and Roxie extradited back to the States later, but let the semi go. We can seize it later, as well." He paused to listen. "Yes, I know it'll make the case stronger if they can seize all the dope. I'll outline everything in a report. Let me know how it goes." With that he hung up.

"You're seizing the dope and letting the semi go?" Laura said. "In other words, setting Bob and Roxie up to look like informants?"

"Not them," Jack replied. "Let me take you through it step by step." He pulled away from the curb. "Vicki said Damien is blaming the Gypsy Devils for our being there and making a video of Buck. Having the DEA bust the West 12th Street gang in Dallas will add credence to his belief and help protect Weenie Wagger."

"It's not him I'm worried about. It's Vicki — and you for your cockamamie plan."

"Step by step," Jack said, gesturing with his hand for her to be patient. "Think about Weenie Wagger. We don't know what the future will bring. He's a full-patch member. I've checked his history. He ran away from home when he was sixteen. The only family he knows now are Satans Wrath. Turning on the club will eat away at him — but with luck and proper coaching, we may be able to swing him our way. Maybe someday he'll be willing to wear a wire and testify. If Damien, or I should say his replacement, clues in that the leak is in their club, our guy could be in jeopardy."

"The replacement — Purvis Evans," Laura said. "Alias Pure E, alias Pure Evil."

"They're all evil as far as I'm concerned. But back to Weenie Wagger — only two guys from Satans Wrath knew where Larry and Dwayne's grow-op was."

"Weenie Wagger and Buck," Laura supplied. "But if Buck isn't charged with murdering King, wouldn't they suspect him, instead of our parkade rat?"

"If Buck was our informant they'd know we wouldn't have shown the video to Damien. Not to mention, they'll realize we received information from someone prior to witnessing Buck."

I should've thought of that. I am so tired.

"Once we take down Damien and the lawyers, it'll end up in a conspiracy trial. We won't have to name Vicki, Weenie Wagger, and Larry, but it'll come out that we had three informants. I'm going to deflect heat onto one of the Gypsy Devils now. When it comes to court, Satans Wrath will think they've already dealt with the problem."

"Dealt with the problem? You mean killed the problem."

Jack grinned. "Glad your sense of humour has come back."

I wasn't trying to be funny.

Jack read her expression. "Okay, it hasn't come back." He ignored her glare and continued, "By having the dope seized in Dallas, I'll be putting the heat on the Gypsy Devils, and Neal in particular."

"But by letting Bob and Roxie go, wouldn't it be obvious that they were to blame?"

"Obvious is right. Too obvious. Damien knows I protect my sources. If they were really my informants I'd never let it happen like that, let alone allow them to drive back to Vancouver where they'd be killed. To add to that, Bob and Roxie were on the road to Dallas when King was killed. The break-in at the marina to get King's address happened later. It couldn't have been them who squealed."

Laura nodded. "So with the ultimatum that Damien gave, the Gypsy Devils will really be giving each other the hairy eyeball."

"Yes — and a likely suspect would be Neal. He lost a shipment of weed prior to us videoing Buck. His buddies will think we busted him with the seventy-five keys and that he rolled over — perhaps to protect his brother. By not arresting Bob and Roxie in Dallas, the bikers might think that we let them go as part of the deal."

"Meaning Neal will probably be killed soon."

"Thinking optimistically perhaps — but yes."

Yes, it's always nice to be optimistic about having people murdered. The worst part is I'm inclined to like the idea. God, what's happened to me?

"There's another reason to set up Neal," Jack said. "If the GDs don't believe that it was one of them who squealed, they could end up in a war with Satans Wrath.

Some innocent person — or kid — could be killed in the crossfire. It's not something I want to risk."

"It'd be a short war if the GDs took on Satans Wrath."

"Short, but the GDs are amateurs. I doubt they'd care about the loss of innocent life. I think seizing the weed and letting Bob and Roxie go is the right thing to do." He looked at her. "Don't you?"

I suppose it is.

"Glad you agree," Jack said, again reading her expression. "You just needed to see the big picture. When you think about it, having the GDs kill one of their own is great," he added enthusiastically.

"Damien is giving them two weeks to do it themselves."

"Yes, and from a psychological aspect, having to murder one of their own will hurt morale."

"Perhaps making some of them question the whole idea of belonging to the club," Laura reasoned.

Jack gave a satisfied smile. "They're not all that big of a club. It could be a catalyst for them to implode."

"Goodbye Gypsy Devils," she said sardonically.

"Now ... back to my plan with Damien. There's more to it than I told Vicki."

Great. Let's hear it.

"I'm going to throw a little heat on one of the lawyers."

"A little heat on a lawyer?" Laura gasped. "If Damien loses every dollar he made, do you really think that any heat will be little?"

"Probably not," Jack admitted.

Probably dead, thought Laura. *Oh, man.*

"What's wrong?"

"Having Neal killed is one thing — but a lawyer?"

Jack gave a lopsided smile. "Sounds to me like you're disparaging Neal." His tone became serious. "These lawyers are worse than Neal. At least they have the brains to make an honest living. Neal, I'm not so sure."

Laura exhaled. "Which lawyer? Lopez, Bentley, or Cummings?"

"With the corruption in Mexico, I doubt Lopez would ever go to jail. That'd make him a good suspect, except Damien will know we're behind it all. It'd be better to pick someone we could've conceivably dealt with. Shop local as they say."

"Meaning Cummings."

Jack nodded. "That's my thought. Besides, I'd prefer we get rid of the scum here. Let Mexico and BVI deal with their own scum."

"How? He'll have to be charged with money laundering. We won't have any say in that. How could you make him look like an informant once that happens?"

"I'll think of something," Jack replied.

That's what I'm afraid of.

"I know the brass will be taking a keen interest," Jack continued. "Informant safety will be an issue. I'll have to word things carefully when it comes to the, uh, finer details of how to protect them."

Yes … the finer details. That ought to go over well with the brass if they hear about those.

Jack stifled a yawn. "I'll go in and talk to Rose tomorrow. I won't need you for that, so stay home and take the day off. I think you need it."

You think I'll say something to Rose, or that she'll see I'm hiding something.

"I'm not afraid you'll screw this up with Rose," Jack said.

Laura frowned. *Can't I have a personal thought without him knowing what it is?*

"Sorry," Jack said. "I'm tired and am trying to be expedient."

Damn you. She looked out the window so that he couldn't guess what she was thinking.

"I'm only saying you don't need to be there when I tell her. You should grab a day off when you can get it. We're going to be busy."

"You're the one who needs a day off," Laura said, realizing she sounded sulky.

"I agree. Hopefully after I debrief her, I'll be back home by lunch."

"Are you going to tell Rose what's going on?" Laura asked.

"Obviously not about my plan with Vicki."

Laura spun around to look at Jack. "Gee, really?" Her voice dripped with sarcasm. "I meant about how we turned her. Will you show Rose the video we took?"

"From the sidelines as ordered — that ought to be interesting."

"So you *are* going to show the video?"

"I'll have to. Once I-POC puts in the requests for foreign assistance to search lawyer's offices, Rose will demand to know who and how we got the information. Isaac, too, for that matter. It'll be better to tell them sooner. I wouldn't want them to think we're trying to hide something."

"Heaven forbid they'd think that," Laura replied facetiously.

"We have to be careful," Jack stressed. "If they don't think we can protect our informants, they're liable to shut down the investigation. We've got Weenie Wagger, Larry, and Vicki involved. If I don't convince Rose that they'll be safe she'll pass on the concern to Isaac. They'd let Damien walk away scot-free and rich."

"How will you handle that with Rose?"

"I'll tell her about setting Neal up. When she's distracted with that I'll gloss over Vicki's safety by saying lots of people know about Damien's bank accounts. Lawyers in Canada, Mexico, the BVI — as well as real estate firms. Isaac will rely on Rose. If I convince her the informants will be safe, it shouldn't be an issue."

"If Bob and Roxie were grabbed by the DEA before returning to Canada," Laura noted, "it wouldn't really matter when it comes to seizing Damien's assets."

Jack looked annoyed. "If it did matter, I wouldn't tell them."

"Don't look at me in such disgust! I was simply thinking out loud."

"Okay, thanks, I appreciate that," Jack replied. "It saves me from having to look at you and read your mind while I'm driving."

Laura folded her arms across her chest in frustration. "You can be a real jerk sometimes."

"I know ... sorry."

Laura didn't speak for several minutes as she mulled things over, but the closer they got to her house, the more stressed she became. *This is like riding a runaway roller coaster with Jack at the helm. It's veering off the tracks — I either have to jump or stay for the ride.*

"You okay?" Jack asked gently. "I know we're both tired. Feeling edgy."

"Besides your plan with Vicki, you plan to toss Neal and Cummings to the bad guys like a couple of sacrificial lambs," Laura murmured.

"Poker chips in the game of life," Jack replied dispassionately. "Besides, neither of them are lambs. As far as I'm concerned, their choice to work for the drug trade contributed to Dwayne being murdered. They didn't pull the trigger, maybe, but they're full participants in the industry that got him killed."

"Dwayne was in the drug business, too."

"I'm not sure Dwayne really knew what he was doing," Jack replied. "You talked to the poor guy. You know how mentally challenged he was."

I know — and I feel horrible about his death, too. And responsible.

"And he was trying to help us when he got killed," Jack stated. "In a way he died a hero. I'll never forget him."

"We were really using Larry," Laura said. *At least, that's what I try to tell myself.*

"Dwayne felt like he was part of it — and I allowed him to think he was. He even called himself a deputy." Jack swallowed. "I feel sick about it. Sometimes I wish to hell I hadn't taken the shotgun away from him. Maybe he'd still be alive."

"And if you hadn't, he might have shot some innocent person who was out digging for clams or having a picnic," Laura said. "I've been over it a thousand times."

"Me, too. One thing is for sure — Neal and Cummings are not innocent. I've no qualms about putting them on the chopping block."

Laura glanced at a church they were passing and saw the Sunday-morning worshippers coming down the steps. *They were probably in there praying and singing hymns of forgiveness while we're out here deciding who should be murdered.*

"If you fly with the crows, you get shot with the crows," Jack said bluntly.

Laura glanced at Jack and felt a feeling of sadness. She thought about how she'd changed since working with him. *Perhaps how we've both changed ... protecting informants ... preventing a gang war ... setting people up to be murdered. What's the right thing to do?* She became aware that he was watching her.

"You disagree?" he asked.

"Sometimes it's hard to figure out who the good guys are," she said.

"Good guys don't murder some poor schmuck like Dwayne."

Laura sighed.

"You with me on this?" Jack prodded.

Oh, man. She turned away and took a deep breath. *Jump or stay for the ride?* She slowly exhaled and turned back to face him. "Aren't I always?"

Chapter Twenty-Six

Jack pulled into his garage and glanced at his watch. *Lunchtime. Good, made it home when I said I would.* When he switched the ignition off, Sammy called.

"Good news," Sammy said. "The DEA busted two outstanding citizens belonging to the West 12th Street gang who happened to have 250 kilos of weed with them. They arrived in a van and were arrested about two blocks away from where they loaded up. Bob and Roxie didn't see the bust take place, but I'm sure the shit will hit the fan soon."

"Perfect," Jack said.

"And somehow you know about the money trail?" Sammy asked.

"Yes, it's being laundered through a phony real estate scheme in Mexico. I'll send you a full report, but I haven't been to bed since Friday night. I need to get some sleep before I figure out how to word it. Informants are involved."

"I presume your real informant isn't in that semi," said Sammy.

"You presume right."

"Hopefully we'll hear a call between Neal and Bob once they find out," added Sammy.

"That'd be nice."

"Mind you, Benny and I already ripped Neal for the seventy-five and saw him deliver more to Bob. I'd say that's pretty good evidence for the conspiracy as it is."

"I agree, but out of curiosity, should something … say, untoward, happen to Neal, do you still think your conspiracy would be good?"

"Untoward?" Sammy questioned.

"You know what I mean."

"Yeah, I know what you mean." Sammy was quiet for a moment. "No, it wouldn't weaken the case. With the DEA seizing the two-fifty, I suspect the charges will proceed down there. With the number of years they'll get in the States, slapping their wrists up here would seem silly."

"Good. I'm going in to work tomorrow morning, but hope to take most of the day off. Regardless, call me if anything happens."

"Something is always happening when you're involved," Sammy replied wryly.

Jack yawned audibly.

"I'll let the monitors know to keep their ears open," Sammy continued. "Could be some interesting calls. You go ahead and get some sleep — but I'll be anxious to get your report," he added before hanging up.

Jack entered his house and kissed Natasha on the cheek before plunking himself down at the kitchen table. He gazed silently at his two sons as they polished off their lunch. Ten-year-old Mike was eating his favourite toasted sandwich: dill pickle, mustard, and cheese. His brother, Steve, at a year younger, had finished whatever sandwich he had and was slurping down a glass of milk.

I love you, guys. I'd do anything to protect you. Damien must love his family, too.

"Are you done work for the day?" Natasha asked.

"Yes, but I have to go in tomorrow morning to talk with Rose and do a report. It shouldn't take long. I hope to be home by noon."

Natasha's face darkened. "That's what you call a day off? Like your short call this morning that wouldn't take long?"

Jack didn't reply.

"When will you get time to be a father and a husband?"

"Yes, I know and I'm sorry," Jack answered in a groggy monotone. He continued to look at his sons. *With Vicki ... did I miss anything?*

"Want me to make you a sandwich?" Natasha asked in a tone that revealed her exasperation.

"No thanks. I'm too tired. I need to crash for a few hours."

Natasha eyed him a moment longer. "You look like you're in a trance."

"I'm tired."

"Over thirty hours without sleep — I understand why, but I've seen you work that long before. This time you seem different. Something wrong?"

Jack stayed silent.

"The way you're looking at the boys. Is everything okay?"

Jack was too tired to show any enthusiasm. "I think I'm about to get *him*."

"Who?" Natasha asked.

"The one I've been after since before you and I even met." *What, am I afraid to say his name? Would it be like the nightmare I have four or five times a week that we're being murdered in our bed and the sound of the gunshot jerks me awake? Would saying his name cause me to wake up and realize it was all a dream?*

"Not … You mean *him*?" Natasha sounded as if she was afraid to say his name, as well.

Jack saw the anxiety on her face. *All these years of wondering if I'd come home alive. Dealing with informants when I wasn't available. Doing her own heat checks when she was out shopping to ensure she wasn't being followed home — and having our two little guys with her when she did. Christ, she's probably been through more hell than I have. Damien was behind much of all that — and she knows it.*

"You're talking about —"

"Yes, Damien," Jack replied sombrely.

"The man who blew up that young prostitute when you and I first met because she was trying to get out of the sex trade," Natasha said bitterly.

"Yes. It was other guys in the club who did it, but he ordered the hit. Her name was Crystal. She was a good person."

"After all this time, you think you can nail him?"

"The next week should tell, but it's looking good."

Natasha's eyes fell on the boys. "How many middle-of-the-night phone calls have you had since Crystal was murdered? Informants or people whose lives he's destroyed?"

Jack shrugged. "You know the answer to that as well as I do. I figure he's responsible for dozens of murders over the years. Including trying to have me murdered by the drug cartel when I was in Mexico."

"So finally you think you've got him for murder?"

"No, I've got a lead on his money. It might be better than murder. Judges tend to pay attention when someone doesn't pay their taxes. They take it personal. Taxes pay their salaries."

Natasha nodded. "Follow the money."

"You've often said that," Jack noted.

"It shows people's real colours — and not only the guys who wear their colours on their backs."

Jack smirked.

"What's so funny?"

"You sound like a cop's wife," Jack replied.

"I am."

Jack felt a lump in his throat. "You're more than that. You've been my wingman all these years."

"Mom, are you talking about following the money because of the politicians?" Mike asked.

"Some of them," Natasha said.

Jack raised a brow. "You're only ten — how'd you come up with that?"

"I heard it on the radio," Mike replied. "It said some politicians have been taking money for things they're not supposed to. Personal stuff."

"Good, then you know to stay out of politics when you get older," Jack said. "Some are really good people, but others become affected by greed. It can be a dirty business."

"Like being a policeman or a defence lawyer," Steve piped up.

"Yes, don't go into those professions either," Jack replied.

"I'm going to make computer games when I get older," Mike declared.

"Me, too," Steve said.

Jack smiled. "I love you guys. Always remember that — but now I need to get some shut-eye."

"Do you want me to wake you in time for work tomorrow morning," Natasha asked, her tone rather dry.

I'm too tired to take the bait for that conversation. "Wake me before supper — otherwise I'll never get back on track." He yawned again. "Sorry about tomorrow, but Rose will need to know what happened. Searches have to be arranged here, in Mexico, and the BVI. It's not something I can tell her over the phone. She'll need to see a video I took. Still, I should be home in time for lunch."

Natasha looked worried, so he raised an eyebrow in question.

"You're not going back to Mexico, are you?" she asked nervously.

"Definitely not. The investigation is basically out of my hands now. Tomorrow I'll be turning it over to other sections."

Natasha breathed a sigh of relief — then looked concerned again. "Even if you do turn it over, Damien will find out you were behind it. Will he come after you … or us?"

"Damien's a businessman. I think his intellect precludes revenge on a police officer or his family."

"You think?"

"When I said that the investigation was basically out of my hands, I was referring to all his assets being seized," Jack replied. "There's another aspect to my plan that has yet to be played out. When it is, Damien will have bigger problems on his mind than coming after me."

"Your plan … is it something I should worry about?"

Jack understood her concern. "I won't be working in any grey areas, if that's what you mean."

"Ah … good. I won't need to worry about Internal Affairs bugging our phones or our house."

Jack chuckled. *No grey areas. Mind you, the brass would never allow it.* "Let me say that Damien is very much a family man. His loyalty to the club is beyond reproach, but in his heart, I think that his love for his family is stronger. My plan will make him realize that his own family's survival will be dependent upon my survival."

Natasha studied Jack's face. "Damien is an extremely dangerous man. I don't know what your plan is, but if it involves a threat against his family … well, how would you respond if it was you?"

Jack lowered his voice. "You know how I'd respond." *Can't you talk about something else? This isn't the kind of stuff you say out loud.*

"You'd respond the same way as Damien would," Natasha said.

"This is different — and I don't appreciate you comparing me to Damien. You've no idea of the scope of what he's capable of or what he's done."

"It's what he's capable of that scares me," she replied.

Jack met her gaze. *Yeah, he scares me too.*

"I know you're good at what you do. I have to believe that because I couldn't live with the worry to think otherwise. You've survived years of rubbing shoulders with some really bad people."

"Then don't worry now," Jack said.

"Damien's also a survivor," said Natasha. "Be careful."

"I always am."

Minutes later Jack climbed into bed and closed his eyes. He expected that exhaustion would take over. It didn't. Natasha's mention of the young prostitute tugged at his memory.

Damn it, Crystal. You really cared about other people. You shouldn't have had to die like that. He tossed off the sheets and retrieved an old notebook from his dresser, then sat with it on the edge of the bed. He didn't know why he did. The memory was all too vivid. He and his partner at the time — Danny O'Reilly — had come upon Crystal seconds after a car bomb had turned her into a human torch.

It was the look in her eyes before she died that he remembered. Danny had remarked that her eyes were questioning him — as if he was responsible for her death. Jack didn't see it that way. He thought her eyes were asking for justice. He hoped his own eyes had conveyed an unspoken promise that justice would be served.

And in part, justice had been served. The bikers who planted the bomb were killed later, but it was Damien who had given them the order and was still a loose end who'd never been brought to justice.

He found Crystal's name in his notebook, along with an account of what happened. It was like looking into her eyes again.

I've never forgotten you, Crystal, and I sure as hell haven't forgotten Damien.

Chapter Twenty-Seven

Jack arrived at his office Monday morning an hour and a half early. He prepared a brief report outlining what Vicki had told him — and his decision to have the DEA seize all the marijuana in Dallas. At 8:30 a.m. he heard Rose arrive, so he went to her office, set his laptop and the report on her desk, and took a seat.

"I thought you were taking today off," she said, glancing at a note he'd left her Saturday morning. "You said you were working Saturday and taking Monday off." She eyed the laptop and the report. "What's going on?"

"Turned out there's lots going on," Jack replied. "Laura and I ended up working a thirty-hour shift — Saturday morning through to Sunday noon. I came in to debrief you and get you to sign off on the report so it could be forwarded ASAP. I still hope to be home by noon."

Rose leaned back, folding her arms across her chest. "Who was murdered and how?" she asked sternly.

"Why would you ask that?" Jack was defensive.

"After working thirty hours, if it had been anything less you would've called to debrief me. Answering my question with another question tells me I'm right."

"Well, you're partially right, but —"

"You're telling me that someone has been partially murdered?" Rose said coldly.

Jack closed his eyes and sighed. "No, someone *was* murdered."

"Who, how, and what part did you play in it?"

"I had nothing to do with it." He raised his hands in protest.

"Really? Then I won't be hearing any coincidence bullshit about where you happened to be when it happened. Preferably you weren't even in the same city."

"Uh, let me explain. Jamie King was beaten to death Saturday night. It's in the news as a home invasion, but his name hasn't been released pending notification of next of kin."

"And you worked thirty hours on that? Damn it, Jack, you were specifically told by Isaac to remain on the sidelines. Does I-HIT know you stuck your nose into their case?"

"To start with," Jack said, gesturing to his laptop, "I've got proof that I did remain on the sidelines."

Rose glanced at the laptop and gave Jack a quizzical look.

"Furthermore, Connie called and asked for my help. It's Vancouver's case, but Wilson from VPD Homicide called her because King was her main suspect in the murder of Dwayne Begg. She's assisting him."

Rose exhaled audibly. "Sorry I sounded so cynical. You did tell Connie last Thursday that Satans Wrath had given the Cobras an ultimatum to pay up. Isaac will find it reasonable that you became involved, given the circumstances and that I-HIT called you."

Jack nodded. "Connie blames herself for King's murder because after she showed Larry Begg his picture, he told the Gypsy Devils, who then told Satans Wrath. The reason Connie called was that she knows I have an informant in Satans Wrath. She asked me to let her know if I heard anything and also gave me permission to stick my nose into the matter."

"And I presume you did," Rose said, gesturing to the report.

"I better start at the beginning," Jack replied. "That'd be Friday night. Laura and I checked out the bar where the Cobras hang out."

"That was a day before the murder. You were told to stay —"

"I know, on the sidelines. We did. I simply wanted to see if any of the Cobras were around after being threatened by Satans Wrath."

"Why? What does that have to do with anything?"

"The Cobras weren't around, which to me indicates they were unable to return the weed or pay the money. I think they would've done one or the other if they'd been the ones who killed Dwayne and ripped off the stash."

Rose appeared to mull this over.

"It's only a theory," Jack went on. "I also came up with another theory Friday night. I wondered if there was another grow-op in the area where Dwayne was murdered. If there was, then perhaps whoever had that grow-op did the murder."

"And?"

"It didn't check out. Laura and I went out Saturday morning and searched the area far beyond where Larry and Dwayne had their grow-op. There was nothing."

"Too bad," Rose said.

"The good news is that we think we found the rock that Dwayne used to pound on the boat motor right before he was shot."

"Forensics missed that?" Rose exclaimed.

"It wasn't easy to find," Jack replied, before explaining how it was found and Connie's subsequent delight.

"I don't think Isaac will criticize you for that, considering that the crime scene had been vacated," Rose noted.

"Hope not," Jack said. "We did our best to remain on the sidelines, "including what happened later." He turned on his laptop and stood beside her to watch.

Rose's eyebrows shot up. "What're you showing me?"

"You'll see, but let me explain what led into it."

"Led into what?"

"Another theory." As the laptop powered up, Jack told her about the break-in at the marina on Friday night and his suspicion that Satans Wrath did it to obtain King's address.

"So with King's murder the following night … that theory may be right," Rose said musingly.

"May be right?" Jack smiled. "Laura and I decided to video the event."

"No! Don't tell me —"

"The video is self-explanatory," Jack said.

Rose focused on the screen, with occasional quick glances at Jack as the video progressed. When it ended with King's murder and Weasel's 911 call, she turned and gaped at Jack, speechless.

"As you can see," he said, "we remained on the sidelines as ordered."

"What … what did I-HIT say about this?" Rose demanded. "The evidence — Christ, the courts will slam you for not stepping in to save him."

"I didn't expect someone to be murdered," Jack replied. "We just got lucky."

"Lucky? Don't say that in court!"

Jack struggled to hide his grin when he imagined how that'd go over.

"So what did Connie say?"

"She doesn't know. I didn't inform anyone in I-HIT."

"You didn't tell them? Why the hell not?"

"No need to raise your voice. I had a reason."

"What reason?"

"I'll tell you," he said, "but let me sit down." He closed the laptop and returned to his seat. "It was after the murder when things got really interesting."

"*Then* things got interesting?" Rose looked ready to burst. "I'd say the murder is plenty interesting enough. What happened next?"

He gestured to the report on her desk. "It's all there, but let me debrief you first."

Rose listened as Jack told of his unsuccessful attempt to get Damien to cooperate and the subsequent meeting with Vicki. When he finished she said, "I don't believe it."

"What don't you believe?" Jack asked, irritated.

"I — I'm flabbergasted," Rose replied. "I don't know what to say."

"As far as I'm concerned it went well." Jack's tone was terse. "Today is Monday. Damien retires this Saturday. That's when Purvis Evans — alias Pure E — takes over. It's also when Buck receives his full patch. I intend to nail Damien before then."

"All … all right, you have my support," Rose said finally. "I feel shell-shocked." Suddenly she groaned.

"What's wrong?"

"There's no way we can seize the money and drop the murder charge against Buck without Damien knowing Vicki turned him in."

Jack stared silently at Rose. *We can get him — but how much can I tell you without you freaking out and nixing the idea? Then there's Isaac….*

"This sucks," Rose said glumly. "Knowing what we know and not being able to do anything about it is worse than not knowing."

"What you're worried about isn't a problem," Jack said, with a brush of his hand to indicate her concern was trivial.

"Really?" Rose couldn't hide her skepticism.

"I questioned Vicki to ensure her safety. Lots of people know about the laundering. Three or four lawyers and people in several real estate firms. As far as Buck goes, I'll make it look like I didn't have the legal grounds to go on King's property. Therefore, the prosecutor would refuse to lay the charge."

"It's unlikely the lawyers would ever inform on Damien because they could go to jail, too," Rose said. "As far as the real estate agents go, they wouldn't know the details of the accounts in Vancouver and the BVI, so I don't see how that really helps."

"It's doubtful the lawyer in Mexico would go to jail," Jack replied, "because somebody there'd be bought off. I don't want the guy's office searched. It could be done right afterwards, but either way, I'm sure he'd be tipped off. If they try to search it at the same time as the others, he could be alerted as soon as someone applied for a warrant. Then he'd warn everyone."

"You're thinking that if the lawyer in Mexico is left alone, Damien might think he's the informant," Rose said.

"It's something he'd have to consider. And there's another thing in Vicki's favour. Her maiden name is on all the documents."

"So she'd have to be charged, too."

"She knows that, but it'd be obvious in court that Damien coerced her into doing it. If she was convicted, she'd only end up with probation."

Rose hesitated. "I still don't think the lawyer in Mexico would be enough to guarantee her safety."

Me, neither.

"As far as her name being on the documents goes," Rose went on, "Damien would know that she'd likely get probation, as she would. As far as the rest goes, sure, there are lots of people in on the money-laundering scheme, but very few know about the account in BVI." She frowned. "Arresting Damien so soon after King's murder, then letting Buck off the hook? Uh-uh."

"I don't like the timing, either, but this can't wait. Vicki is emotionally unstable. At one point, she wanted Damien to kill Laura and me. It's hard to know what she'll do next. If she says something to Damien, the money would disappear — and maybe her along with it."

"I don't know." Rose shook her head. "Her safety is a concern to me."

"I do know," Jack said firmly. "Trust me."

Rose stared at him. "Dwayne was your informant. Now you want to take a chance on having another one murdered?"

"You know how I feel about Dwayne," Jack said heatedly. "Do you really think I'd risk another informant's life if I wasn't confident?"

"Even for Damien?" Rose challenged. When Jack didn't respond, she added, "Your desire to nail him, especially before Saturday … well, it could be blinding your judgment."

"I'm far from blind." Jack struggled to control his emotions. "I'm not saying there aren't problems. What I *am* telling you is that Vicki will be okay — although I'd still like to muddy the water so that the wrong people won't be murdered in retaliation."

"The wrong people murdered?"

"There's a problem," Jack stated, "but it isn't with Vicki. Forget about her. She'll be okay."

"Who do you think is the problem?" Rose asked.

"Let me explain the situation," Jack said. "Once Damien is busted, I have to look down the road and think how much information will be divulged in court. If the DEA in Dallas get a whiff of the money trail, it could all end up in a conspiracy charge."

"If the DEA connects the West 12th Street gang in Dallas to any financial transactions with the lawyers or the real estate agents," Rose said, "I can guarantee there'd be conspiracy charges. Likely here and in the States."

"Exactly. It might come out that I had three informants. To follow the sequence of events, first I may have to disclose who I'd refer to as 'Informant A.' He's a full-patch member of Satans Wrath and tipped us off to the grow-op. He also told us about Satans Wrath giving the Cobras two days to pay up."

"That's the Weenie Wagger you told me about. He wouldn't have to be identified as being a member of Satans Wrath in court."

"No, but the witch hunt would be on. As it stands, he thinks he's safe, but I hope to use him down the road. If Satans Wrath later become suspicious and look at their own people, only two of them knew where Larry's grow-op was. One was Buck Zabat and the other is Informant A."

"They might think Buck's charge was dropped because he co-operated," Rose suggested.

"Buck is Damien's son. He's been brainwashed all his life that the club is his family. They know he wouldn't turn, which is why I took the video to Damien instead of trying to turn Buck. Something I wouldn't have done if Buck was my informant."

"So with that in mind, using Informant A in the future could place him in some serious trouble," Rose said.

"More like a bullet to the back of the head."

"Ouch."

"Then it might come out that I had Informant B, but as far as Larry goes, he's too low end and I'm not worried about anyone pointing a finger at him. The bikers have several grow-ops. I wouldn't supply enough information for them to figure out his identity or which grow-op Informant B may have been connected with."

"Which leads to Informant C," Rose said.

"Yes … Vicki. At first I worried that dropping Buck's charge could have the potential to make the bad guys suspect her, but —"

"The potential to suspect her? I think it'd be crystal clear."

"Crystal clear?" *It's clear to me what Damien did to Crystal. I can still see her eyes as she burned to death....*

"Are you with me?" Rose asked.

"Yes. Sorry. My mind was wandering."

"Damn it, this is serious. Pay attention. I don't see how Vicki could not be in jeopardy — or are you thinking witness protection?"

"That's not an option," Jack said. "Too many relatives in the area who'd be targeted in her place. Besides, it's not necessary. All the informants will be safe."

"I feel like we're dancing in circles here. I believe that Larry isn't an issue, but explain how you intend to protect Weenie Wagger and Vicki."

"Damien is giving the Gypsy Devils two weeks to come up with whoever was responsible for tipping me off, resulting in my videoing King. To add further credence to his belief that the Gypsy Devils are to blame, I deflected some heat onto one of them. In time, when things come out in court, the bikers will think they've already cleaned up that problem and Informant A should be safe. If I don't keep him safe I won't be able to use him in the future. Obviously."

"Exactly how did you deflect heat onto this Gypsy Devil?"

Jack told Rose that he'd had the DEA seize the drugs in Dallas and explained how that'd cast suspicion on Neal. He capped his explanation by saying, "If you disagree with the idea, it's not too late to bust Bob and Roxie in the States. They won't have made it back yet. Also, if the bikers don't suspect Neal and he lives, then farther down the road he'll likely be deported to face charges."

Rose twirled a pen between her fingers before she spoke. "I realize that Neal's a bad guy, but Isaac won't be impressed by another murder. Especially if we were the ones who pointed the finger at the victim."

"If we don't point the finger and Satans Wrath select a few of their own targets, it could result in a gang war. Some innocent person could be killed."

Rose just stared at Jack.

"You disagree?" he asked.

"No, but I feel like you've stuck me between a rock and a hard place."

"Maybe I shouldn't have told you about letting the semi return from the U.S.," Jack replied.

"Quit trying to protect me," Rose said in annoyance. "I'm your boss. I need to know what's happening under my command." She eyed him suspiciously. "What other tricks do you have up your sleeve?"

Like setting up Cummings and my plan with Vicki? Jack twirled the tip of his beard with his fingers as if he was in deep thought. "It's possible I might come up with something else to deflect heat from the informants, but that'd be fluid, depending on the circumstances as they unfold."

"What about Vicki? Seizing the dope and letting the semi go has nothing to do with protecting her."

"I told you, she'll be safe."

"Why, then, do I feel like there's something you're not telling me?"

Probably because you're right — there is. You know me too well. He gave Rose his best look of wide-eyed innocence. "I don't know what more I can say. Basically we're on the verge of taking Damien down. We should be rejoicing."

"Yes, and when I bring up the issue of Vicki's safety, you purposely try to distract me."

That obvious, was I?

She scrutinized Jack's face. "The thing is, I know how protective you are of your sources. When you first sat down to talk I was concerned that you hadn't looked at the situation closely enough. I thought perhaps you were blinded by your understandable desire to catch Damien. Now that I've spoken with you I know that you're confident she'll be okay."

"I *am* confident."

"I know — too confident. So what aren't you telling me?"

Jack leaned forward, his eyes riveted on hers. "I won't take any action against Damien unless I'm convinced it can be done without bringing harm to Vicki." His words were firm and expressed his determination.

Rose grimaced.

"Don't you believe me?" Jack asked, his anger rising.

"I believe you," Rose said evenly. "But I'm asking you *how* you protect her."

"And I'm asking you to trust my judgment. Look, I admit that Vicki's unstable. Things could change in an instant — but be assured, I've lost one informant and I don't intend to lose another."

Rose sighed. "I better schedule a meeting with Isaac."

"Do I have your support?" Jack asked.

"Reluctantly … yes."

Jack closed his eyes, raised both fists, and shouted, "Yes!"

"Don't celebrate yet. Wait until we talk with Isaac."

"Are you going to tell him that I-HIT should expect another body, one by the name of Neal Barlow, to roll their way?"

"I'll play that by ear," Rose replied.

"Yeah, he's a pretty busy guy," Jack said. "No use bothering him with trivial details. It'd be reasonable to expect he'd trust your judgment regarding what's right."

Rose exhaled noisily. "You just talked me into it. When I meet with Isaac I'll tell him how you set Neal up."

I should've kept my yap closed. Before he could respond, he felt his phone vibrate and he checked the call display. *Yes, my weenie-wagging friend, I wondered if you'd call.* He glanced at Rose. "Speaking of informants, Informant A is calling me."

"Go ahead and take it," Rose said. "When you're done with him call I-POC to get things started. While you're doing that, I'll review your report and then try to get us an audience."

Yes, an audience with Isaac. That ought to be interesting.

Chapter Twenty-Eight

"Holy fuck!" Mack Cockerill shouted into the phone. "You got a movie of Buck and the guys killin' King! Then tried to use it to get Damien to rat?"

"That's yesterday's news," Jack replied, walking down the hall toward his office. "How come you waited until now to tell me King was being paid a visit?"

"Yeah, that. I was sort of out of it. I got to partying a little heavy on Saturday and passed out."

"I warned you before about —"

"Yeah, yeah. The guys are already pissed off at me. I don't need to hear it from you, too. I've quit drinkin.'"

Jack's silence revealed his skepticism.

"Anyway, I didn't find out about everything until last night when I got word to go meet Lance."

"Lance Morgan — your chapter president," Jack said.

"Yeah. At first I was worried that maybe I was gettin' the boot from the club or somethin' because of my drinkin'. Wasn't that at all. He told me about the video you took. He said that

Damien is fuckin' wild about it and took Buck to meet the lawyer yesterday afternoon, even though it was Sunday."

"Basil Westmount?" Jack asked.

"Who else would it be?" Cockerill muttered as if that was a given.

"Any idea what Basil had to say?"

"Yeah, said it'd be best to sit tight for two days in case, uh, somethin' should happen."

"Something?"

"Well … I might as well tell ya', but don't get excited until you hear me out."

"Okay — keep talking."

"Lance didn't say word for word what Damien told him, but from the gist of the conversation, you must have told Damien that it was you, your partner, and some other cop who took the video."

"Yes, I let him know that," Jack said.

"Damien thinks it was only you and your partner … but he ain't positive."

"Why should it matter?"

"Because Basil was wonderin' if Damien was thinkin' about poppin' you both."

"And?"

"Damien told Basil that wasn't an option and said it wasn't on the table for discussion."

"Nice to hear."

"'Cause of what Lance said, I know Damien means it, but Basil ain't so sure."

"What do you mean? You said Damien told him."

"Basil figures because you gave Damien two days to think about it, that things might still happen."

"Things?"

"Damien doesn't tell Basil anything he doesn't absolutely need to know. Basil knows that. He thinks Damien could be holding back for somethin."

"Something?" Jack repeated dryly.

"If you and your partner gets, uh —"

"Three-three'd," Jack supplied.

"Shit, you know about that, too," Cockerill complained.

"I told you before that you weren't the only guy in the club talking to us. "Still, I'd like to hear your version of events. Go on."

Jack heard Cockerill swallow. "Someone is gonna get three-three'd all right — but it ain't you. It'll be someone in the Gypsy Devils."

"Why do you say that?"

"Lance had me meet Neal and arrange for his prez — Carl Shepherd — to have a face-to-face with Lance last night."

"Only Shepherd and Lance?"

"A couple guys from both clubs were there, too, but it was Lance who did most of the talkin'. He told Shepherd that —"

"They had a rat in their club and were being given two weeks to take care of it," Jack said.

"You really do got someone in the club besides me," Cockerill said.

"I told you I did — I wasn't lying to you," Jack lied, "and I'll sure as hell know if you lie to me or hold something back."

"Yeah … no shit," Cockerill replied, sounding depressed.

"Tell me how the GDs responded," Jack said.

"They were too blown away to know *how* to respond. Their sergeant-at-arms, Thor, mouthed off a little. He said if that were true, then why didn't the cops bust the semi in Vancouver? He said everyone in their club knew about it before it left. Told us there's no way the cops would let that much dope slide past, because they'd want the glory. He thinks that if there was a rat, it had to be someone who found out about the raid on King after the semi left. Meanin', it wasn't one of them."

"How'd that go over?" Jack asked.

"Lance really got in Shepherd's face over that one. Said everyone knowin' is the problem, and if everyone is the problem, then we — meanin' Satans Wrath — would see that the entire problem was looked after."

"Did Shepherd get the message?"

"Loud and clear. All of 'em did. Shepherd looked like he was about to piss himself. Then Lance told 'em they had two weeks to take care of it and we left."

Time to fish and see if he can remember anything else. "Something you forgot to tell me?" Jack used a menacing tone.

"N-no," Cockerill replied nervously. "Oh, maybe you mean after, when me and some of the guys were wondering what the GDs would do."

"Yes."

"Not much to tell you. I said the GDs would probably pick one of their prospects, but as Lance said, if they don't pick the right guy, then we'll find out and take out a couple extra as punishment." Cockerill paused, then said, "With all this shit about Buck being videoed I never asked. How'd it go in Dallas yesterday? Bet the DEA were glad to seize a semi."

"The DEA seized the weed and busted two guys from the West 12th Street gang, but let Bob and Roxie continue on without interference."

"Why the hell didn't they bust them, too?"

"I told them not to. It'll provide more protection for you by pointing the finger at the GDs."

Cockerill was silent for a few moments. *Probably mulling it over.* "They'll blame Neal," Cockerill finally said, "what with him getting ripped for those seventy-five keys."

"That's my guess. I told you I'd look after you."

"Fuckin' Jesus — if I didn't believe you before, I do now. Too bad we didn't know that last night. It would've shut Thor the fuck up."

"Which club will find out first?" Jack asked. "Your guys or the Gypsy Devils?"

"Us. I'm surprised we don't know already. Bet it's 'cause today will be their first court appearance. The West 12th might be waitin' to see if Bob and Roxie were busted before bitchin' to us."

"But they'll be contacting your club and not the GDs?"

"For sure. Except for dropping off the dope, the GDs don't have any dealings with the West 12th. It all goes through us — but I don't know who in our club handles that end. Like I told ya before, things are kept separate in case someone like me is blabbin'."

"You do what you gotta do," Jack said. "Keep in touch — and stay sober." He hung up and leaned back in his chair, then took a deep breath and called the Integrated Proceeds of Crime unit and asked to speak to one of the bosses. He was put through to an Inspector Pollock.

Pollock listened to what Jack told him about Damien's money-laundering system, then exclaimed, "You're talking close to twenty million!"

"More than that, once you seize all his property and vehicles. He lives in a mansion in the British Properties. I've been in it. Lots of expensive antique furniture."

"Your source is close enough to know for sure, or did he or she hear this second-hand?" Pollock asked.

"Close enough that I have the actual account numbers."

"Can't get closer than that."

"Yes, but time is of the essence. A deal has been struck and I don't have much time to fulfill my end of the agreement."

"I see. I presume you're talking about having a charge withdrawn for an upcoming court case?"

"Something like that," Jack said. "Any chance we could do it before the week is over? Damien retires Saturday. I'd like to do him before then."

"If it was only Vancouver we could be ready by tomorrow morning — but bringing in Mexico and BVI ... I don't know. It needs to be done simultaneously."

"I strongly suggest you leave Mexico off the list until you're already doing the searches in Vancouver and the BVI," Jack said. "Too much corruption there."

"From what I've heard about Mexico, I bet you're right. We'll prepare the paperwork for Mexico, but won't contact any of the authorities until the other searches are underway. If we do the Vancouver and BVI searches early in the morning, there's still a chance we could do Mexico later in the day."

"Sounds good," Jack said. "Guess the big question is when?"

"We could try for Friday, but that's really pushing it. I'll know more after the respective liaison officers are contacted."

"Then I'd suggest you push it," Jack replied. "There's a real concern that Damien could be tipped off if we don't move quickly."

"Tipped off?"

"I can't discuss that with you. Informant issues — and I'll ask you to keep it to yourself."

"Understood. We'll do our best to make it Friday. I'll also bring in an investigator from the Canada Revenue Agency."

"Fine with me," Jack replied. "It'll be your show, but I'd like to be part of the search team when you raid Damien's house, along with my partner, Constable Laura Secord. Damien's response may help me decide how to protect my informant down the road."

"Of course. I should let you know, however, that in a situation like this where searches and criminal charges could be laid against lawyers, we likely won't arrest anyone until a few days after the search. Everything will have to be reviewed by a prosecutor."

"As long as charges are eventually laid and the assets are forfeited, I'll be happy," Jack said.

"Also, once we do make arrests," Pollack went on, "I doubt we'll be able to hold anyone for longer than a day or two before they're released. A trial date could easily be two years away. The best we might get when they're released pending court proceedings is permission to hang on to their passports."

"That's about what I expected. For now I'll be content to see the look on Damien's face during the search when his lawyers call him to tell him he's broke. That, and later when the moving truck rolls up his driveway to seize everything he owns."

"It does tend to take the wind out of people's sails," Pollock replied.

"Shipwrecked is what I want," Jack said coldly. "There's something else. Damien has a fortified panic room inside his home, along with electronic detection and camera surveillance on his property. He knows about I-POC and if he sees officers in suits or looking like businessmen raiding his property, he could lock himself inside his panic room and destroy evidence long before we could bust inside."

"Should we set up surveillance and grab him when he's away from his house?"

"A family member could still be in his house and we'd face the same problem."

"You want my people to wear jeans that day?"

"They'd still look like businessmen. Damien is professional. I wouldn't put it past him to have had surveillance done on our members. With facial-recognition cameras … well, who knows? But we don't have to take that chance."

"What do you suggest?"

"There's something in our favour," Jack replied. "Damien thinks I might be arresting his son this week. It's over an unrelated matter involving a drug dealer who was beaten to death."

"Beaten to death? Holy smokes."

"Like I said, he was a drug dealer. Nothing to lose sleep over — but it helps us. If Secord and I were to show up at his place with a couple of narcs, he'd think we came with a warrant to look for his son. If he doesn't see any of your people, I know he'd let us in. Once we're inside and have secured the premises, then we could call your team in."

"You sure that'd work?"

"Positive. I know two Drug Section investigators who'd assist. Corporal Sammy Crofton and Constable Benny Saunders. I've worked with them before. They're both knowledgeable about bikers and meticulous when it comes to doing searches." *They'll also keep their mouths shut and go along with my plan to destroy Damien before I ever call your team in.*

"Sounds good. I'll have one of our investigators contact you as a liaison."

"Thank you." Jack hung up and gazed at his phone. *The wheels of justice, please, this once — run over Damien like a snake on the road.*

"Isaac wants to see us immediately," Rose stated, "but quickly fill me in about your calls first."

Jack hadn't realized she was listening from the doorway. "Immediately? That was quick."

Rose gave Jack a hard look, then placed the report he'd made earlier on his desk. "I told him that you and Laura witnessed and videoed a murder."

"Bet that caught his attention," Jack said as he flipped open the last page of his report.

"Yes, I signed it," Rose said, "but don't send copies out until after we see what Isaac has to say."

"Gotcha."

"So, you finished?" She nodded at his phone.

"Is that a question or a statement?"

Rose frowned. "I meant with I-POC — but your question does contain a certain verisimilitude."

"I was trying to be funny," Jack said.

"I don't think Isaac will find the situation funny. Did your informant have anything to tell us?"

"Nothing we don't already know. He confirmed that the GDs have been given two weeks to kill one of their own. I told him we let the semi go. He agrees that Neal will be picked as being the informant."

"And your call to I-POC?"

"I spoke with Inspector Pollock. Seems like an all right guy. He's excited and on board. Trying to gear it up for Friday morning."

Rose nodded. "Don't forget your laptop," she said brusquely before spinning sharply on her heel and heading down the hall.

Chapter Twenty-Nine

Isaac rose from behind his desk and pointed to a grouping of upholstered chairs clustered around a coffee table. Jack placed his laptop on the table and took a seat on one side of Isaac while Rose sat on the other side so that they could view the video together.

"I suggest you start by telling Assistant Commissioner Isaac the action you and Laura took Saturday morning that led to finding a key piece of evidence at the crime scene," Rose said.

"Which crime scene?" Isaac asked.

"Where Dwayne Beggs was murdered, sir," Jack replied.

"That was the case I told you not to become involved with," Isaac said, peering at Jack over the top of his reading glasses.

"Forensics was finished with the scene," Rose stated. "Corporal Taggart went to the area to check out a theory he had in regards to another grow-op."

"I'm listening," Isaac said, "but it better be good."

Jack told Isaac everything that happened, leading up to where he was outside Jamie King's window when the bikers arrived. "Here's what happened next," Jack said as he started the video.

Isaac watched the clip silently. When it was finished, Jack shut the computer off and glanced at his face. *Totally without expression. What the hell is he thinking? Bet he'd be good at poker.*

"To paraphrase Corporal Taggart," Rose said, "after the murder, things got really interesting. Please continue, Jack."

"One question first." Isaac focused his complete attention on Jack. "I ordered you to remain on the sidelines. If I hadn't done so, would you have taken steps to prevent this crime from happening?"

"No, sir," Jack replied. "Your order had no bearing on the outcome of what happened. I was not expecting anyone to be killed — and neither were the bikers, for that matter."

Isaac nodded. "If you'd known in advance that the victim was to be murdered, would you have prevented it then?"

"Uh —"

"Never mind," Isaac interrupted. "I should have put more thought into that question. Dealing in the hypothetical could take all day. Please continue. I'm curious to discover what you feel is really interesting — if videoing a murder isn't."

Jack then told of their attempt to turn Damien and their subsequent success in turning Vicki into an informant. When he was finished, Isaac looked at Rose to see if she had any further comment.

"King's murder took place in the jurisdiction of VPD," Rose noted. "Detective Wilson from Homicide asked Corporal Connie Crane for assistance, but as of yet, we've not disclosed what we know to either one of them."

"I left it with the informant that I wouldn't disclose any information concerning Jamie King's murder to the investigators," Jack said. "At the same time, I told her I might not be able to prevent charges from being laid if they solved it on their own."

"She was okay with that?" Isaac asked.

"Yes, sir. She doesn't think I-HIT or VPD would come up with any witnesses or evidence to convict her son without my help."

Isaac's face darkened. Jack knew he'd read enough reports over the years to conclude that Vicki was probably right.

"I did give Connie my opinion that the death was unintentional," Jack said. "I suspect the case will not be a priority."

Isaac's voice became grave. "Do you believe Vicki Zabat is telling you the truth about the money laundering? Damien has held the reins of power for a long time. He's cunning. Could this be some scheme where they'll transfer or disperse the money before we make our move?"

"Making it look like we haven't fulfilled our end of the bargain if we charge Buck," Jack replied. "Yes, sir, I've considered that possibility — but her natural instinct as a mother to protect her son came through loud and clear. I believe the emotions she displayed were genuine. At the moment, she's angry with Damien and is completely focused on doing what she can to keep her son out of jail."

"Then I'll trust your judgment on that issue," Isaac replied.

"My only concern is if she regrets her action once she's cooled down," Jack added.

"Meaning that time is of the essence."

"Yes, sir."

"I'll do what I can — but I also have concerns. The first being Corporal Crane's involvement in the investigation surrounding King's death. Despite being unlikely, there's still a chance that charges could conceivably be laid. Should your involvement be brought to the courts' attention, they may suspect the police didn't abide by the agreement."

"That's a possibility," Jack admitted.

"Corporal Crane and you have worked together in the past, which would cast further suspicion on their evidence, as it would be implied that there was a bond between you. I think it best to sever her from the investigation immediately. For that matter, it'd be best for VPD to continue without any RCMP assistance."

"That would certainly alleviate the problem."

"I fully appreciate the need for secrecy when it comes to your informant. Obviously the fewer who know about it the better. With that in mind, I don't want to instigate any undue chatter or rumour as to why Corporal Crane is being taken off the case. For that reason, would you object to showing her the video without disclosing who became an informant as a result of it? She'd see for herself that King's death was unintended. You could then explain to her that the decision to remove her from the case was a pragmatic one based on new evidence obtained to lay more serious charges."

"I've no problem with that," Jack replied. "I trust her completely. For that matter, I wouldn't object to her subsequently informing Detective Wilson at VPD about why she's being taken off the investigation. I trust him, too. If I never talk to Wilson myself about the case, it would be more difficult for Defence to taint his evidence."

"Then I'd ask you to enlighten Corporal Crane as soon as possible. Once you've shown her the video, tell her that it involves an informant who's an integral part of a much bigger picture. Inform her that she's to cease all investigation in to King immediately."

Oh, yeah. Connie's going to love this.

"Notify me once you've done so," Isaac continued. "I'll also call I-HIT and speak to Inspector Dyck. If Corporal Crane has any doubt about the situation, she can check with him."

"I'll notify her as soon as we're finished here, sir."

"Good." Isaac nodded. "Following that, tell her to notify Detective Wilson as to why she's off the case and wish him good luck in his own investigation."

"Understood, sir."

"My next concern: Vicki Zabat. Her safety is a serious issue. How comfortable are you with that?"

Here it comes.

"I've spoken with Corporal Taggart in regard to informant safety, sir," Rose said. "There are actually three informants involved. He's confident that his informants will face minimal risk."

"Really?" Isaac asked in surprise. "Including Vicki Zabat?"

"I'm confident she'll be safe, sir," Jack replied.

Isaac stared at Jack long enough to make him feel uncomfortable.

"No cash rewards are being demanded by the informants," Rose said, "and none will be entering witness protection."

"I see," Isaac said, still looking at Jack.

I bet he does see, thought Jack. *Perceptive old fart.* He cleared his throat. "I might make one or two modest payments to the informants."

"Why would you dip into our budget if it's not necessary?" Isaac asked.

"Defence often questions whether informants are paid, with a view of trying to identify who they could be. The bad guys would never believe that Vicki Zabat would be a paid informant as they would think her motive would be to keep Buck out of jail and that cash would not come into play if it were her."

"A strategy I could live with," Isaac remarked. "Okay, then. Is there anything else?"

"There's another, uh, delicate matter we need to discuss," Rose said.

Isaac raised an eyebrow.

"It involves a plan that Corporal Taggart put into action concerning the shipment of marijuana delivered to Dallas yesterday. There's something I feel you need to know."

"You're talking about the shipment to the West 12th Street gang on behalf of Satans Wrath," Isaac said. "I've read your reports."

"Yes, sir," Rose acknowledged. "As a result of what Corporal Taggart learned about how Satans Wrath launders their money, yesterday he had the DEA seize all the marijuana minutes after the transaction took place."

"I don't see a problem with that. The original plan of letting the delivery go uninterrupted so we could identify the money trail is no longer necessary."

"Yes, but Corporal Taggart allowed for the semi to continue without being stopped or its occupants arrested. His reason was —"

"You did that to make Bob and Roxie Barlow look like informants in order to protect the real informant, didn't you, Corporal?" Isaac accused.

"Uh, well, that's —"

"It's not too late to have them arrested," Rose inserted. "They could even be deported later, but —"

"They wouldn't be alive to be deported!" Isaac shouted.

Jack swallowed. "I don't expect they'll be harmed, sir. Damien knows me well enough to know that if they were really my informants, that I wouldn't let the arrests in Dallas take place immediately after the delivery — let alone have them return here afterwards."

The anger disappeared from Isaac's face. "You're saying that Damien will believe it to be so blatant that it couldn't be them."

"Yes, sir."

"Who do you think *will* be blamed?"

"I think the blame will be laid on Neal Barlow — a full-patch member of the Gypsy Devils."

"That's the person Drug Section took seventy-five kilos of marijuana from shortly before the semi left," Isaac noted. "He's Bob Barlow's brother."

"Yes, sir."

Isaac's face again registered his displeasure. "So the bikers might think Neal Barlow was arrested and cut a deal with us that allowed his brother and sister-in-law to go free."

"Yes, sir. The semi hasn't made it back to Canada. It's not too late for the DEA to seize it and make arrests, but first I think you need to —"

"So if you're correct, you propose to set up one, or possibly two or three people, who could all be murdered for the express purposes of protecting your informant?"

Sure, I do it all the time. Jack cleared his throat. "There's more to this than informant protection. What you don't know yet is that Damien is blaming the Gypsy Devils for leaking the information that allowed me to video the attack on King. Two informants say he's given the Gypsy Devils two weeks to find and eliminate the problem. If they don't, Satans Wrath will eliminate some of them. At this time the Gypsy Devils do not believe there is an informant amongst their ranks. The two clubs could conceivably go to war."

"We don't need a gang war taking place on our streets, Corporal," Isaac said icily. "Innocent lives would be put at risk."

"My thoughts exactly, sir. The Gypsy Devils would readily kill one of their own if they thought he was an informant. As of a few minutes ago, the bikers are not yet aware of the seizure in Dallas — but my plan, if allowed to proceed, would direct them toward one of their own."

"They don't know about the seizure yet?" Isaac asked. "Wouldn't the West 12th Street gang have alerted them immediately?"

"I suspect the bad guys in Dallas are still trying to figure out what went wrong before making any accusations. Today they'll be appearing in court. Once they confirm that Bob and Roxie were not arrested, the finger-pointing will begin. If Damien —and therefore the Gypsy Devils — suspect that Neal Barlow is the informant, it'll be an easy decision."

Isaac leaned back in his chair and stroked his chin thoughtfully. A moment later he spoke. "With what you've said, if we have Bob and Roxie arrested in the States, it would ensure their safety — but would mean that someone else would be murdered, with the good possibility of a gang war erupting here, which could result in numerous murders. If I allow your plan to continue, then Neal Barlow will most likely be murdered, and he could be murdered regardless if a gang war breaks out."

"Yes, sir. That's it exactly."

"We're damned if we do and damned if we don't," Isaac said gruffly.

"The deadline Damien gave is two weeks away," Jack noted, "but the semi could be crossing the border back into Canada within the next twenty-four hours. I'm not trying to rush your decision, but we have little time to decide."

"What if we warned Neal Barlow that his life could be in danger?" Isaac suggested. "Do you think he'd cooperate? Either flee or perhaps wear a wire if he's going into a situation where he thinks his life might be in danger?"

"Neal's a hard-core biker. I'm certain he wouldn't cooperate."

"He's the subject of a wiretap order now," Rose put in. "It's possible that if someone is luring him into a trap that we might hear about it."

"His brother and sister-in-law are also named," Jack noted, "but with what has happened, the bikers will be on heightened alert. I'm dubious that we'll hear anything over their phones. We do have a car bug in a limo owned by one of them, but to overhear someone in the limo planning to murder Neal would be a real fluke. Also, if we try to do any physical surveillance to protect him, I'm sure it'd be spotted. That would add further credence to their belief that he's an informant and likely serve to hasten his demise."

Isaac took off his glasses and massaged his temples. When he spoke, he stared straight ahead. "A gang war puts innocent people at risk. Second-guessing the actions that criminals may take with one another does not supersede what must be the primary safety of the public." He looked at Jack. "In other words, I concur with the current status of the investigation, including the wheels you've put in motion — which in this case, are the wheels of a semi." His tone was dry.

"Thank you, sir," Jack said.

Isaac looked grim, then gave the pair a dismissive nod.

Jack and Rose got to their feet, but before they left, Jack turned to Isaac. "Sir, I'm sorry to have placed you in such an awkward position."

"You haven't placed me in this position, Corporal," Isaac said sharply. "*Damien* has. Make damned certain you're successful in toppling him from his throne — preferably before he retires, which I might add, is about two weeks before I do."

Chapter Thirty

Rose glanced at Jack as the two of them exited into the hall. "That was a tough call for him to make. Considering the circumstances, he stuck his neck way out."

Jack nodded. "Isaac has always stood up for what he thinks is right. He isn't persuaded by politics. I hate to see him go."

"Likewise," Rose admitted.

"Any idea what the new assistant commissioner is like? I haven't talked to anyone who's even heard of Ralph Mortimer, let alone worked with him. I don't think he's been out West before."

Rose looked around to ensure they had privacy. "I called a friend in Staffing, who pulled his file. When he left the academy he was sent to red-serge duty in Ottawa for two years. After that it was five years on VIP Security, five on Customs and Excise, and then seven years in Montreal on Commercial Crime. That's where he received his commission and was transferred to headquarters where he was assigned to Procurement and Contracting for eight years before being transferred here."

"From guarding the tulips to opening doors for politicians, then Customs, Commercial Crime, and an admin job?" Jack shook his head in disbelief. "Who the hell decided he was experienced enough to handle the job of Operations Officer in Charge? Bet he's never encountered the kind of criminals we deal with. At best he may have had someone throw a fake Rolex at him in Customs or threaten him with a calculator when he was on Commercial Crime."

"Don't slam-dunk the guy before you've even met him," Rose said.

"I don't think I *want* to meet him."

Rose decided to change the subject. "Back to the matters at hand. You'll call Connie pronto, show her the video, then take the rest of the day off?"

"That's the plan. Why do you ask?"

"Because I'd like to think the rest of the day could pass without you doing something to worsen my headache."

"Maybe there's a bug going around," Jack said. "Laura mentioned she had a headache yesterday."

"Yeah, a bug named Jack."

He smiled, then returned to his office. He was about to call Connie, but an incoming call stopped him. *Second informant to call me within the hour. What is this? The year of the rat?*

"Hey! So I hear King got beat to death Saturday night," said Larry gleefully. "Guess he won't be rippin' off any more stashes and killin' people.

"How'd you know King was killed?" Jack asked.

"'Cause that lady cop you came to the hospital with …

her and some cop from Vancouver PD came by to talk to me about it."

"She told me she'd be meeting with you."

"Nice of her to keep me informed all the time," said Larry facetiously.

"What do you want?" Jack asked. "Why are you calling?"

"Well, with what happened, my brother being killed, I figure you and I should be even. Now with the guy who did it dead, I'm thinking of goin' back to the rock."

"You can go back to Newfoundland as far as I'm concerned," Jack said, "but as far as Corporal Crane and Detective Wilson go, it might be another matter."

"They got nothin' on me," Larry told him. "Ain't no way they can say I had anything to do with what happened to King."

"When do you plan to leave?"

"As soon as I can. I want to sell my boat first. It and all my hydro shit. I've put it all on eBay. The boat runs good if you're interested. I'll even throw in my crab traps and fishin' gear. Real cheap."

"I'm not interested."

"Yeah, well, if you hear of someone, lemme know. Hopefully I'll sell it all soon."

"Where'd you get your hydro equipment from?" Jack asked.

"A place called Aaron and Chuck's Hydroponics. I already called 'em. They won't take it back."

"Listen, Larry ..." Jack paused. *Should I tell him I don't think King murdered Dwayne? For what purpose?*

"Yeah?"

"I'm sorry about Dwayne. I mean it."

"Yeah, well …" Larry's voice cracked and he coughed. "Was me who got 'im into it," he blurted, then hung up.

You'll live with that for the rest of your life, Jack thought as he made another call.

"That didn't take long for the lying little bastard to call you," Connie said upon answering.

"I just hung up from him," Jack replied. "I take it he didn't tell you anything?"

"No. Denied that he told the Gypsy Devils anything about King."

"The bikers wouldn't have told him details about their visit to King, regardless," Jack said. "Even if he wanted, he wouldn't be able to tell you who did it."

"If it was the bikers," Connie replied. "The Cobras have a lot of other enemies vying for their turf."

"Are you with Wilson at the moment?" Jack asked.

"No, I'm on my way back to my office."

"I'm going home, but there's something I need to show you," Jack said. "How about we meet halfway? It won't take long."

"What is it? I'm busy as hell."

"Isaac ordered me to show you something. You need to see it in person."

"Isaac? What the hell? You're kidding, right? Can't you just read it to me over the phone or tell me?"

"No — and the sooner we meet the better."

It was 11:30 a.m. when Jack drove into the strip-mall parking lot. He placed a quick call to Natasha, promising he'd be home in an hour, then hung up when Connie arrived. He smiled to himself as Connie got in. *All work and no play makes Jack a dull boy. Time to have some fun.*

"You better not be bullshitting me," she said grumpily. "I don't have time for jokes these days. Did Isaac really tell you to show me something?"

"Yes, it's a video I took." Jack flipped open his laptop and readied it to start the video before passing it to Connie.

"What of?" she asked, placing the computer on her lap.

"An integral part of the big picture. Push start."

Seconds later Connie looked sharply at Jack. "It's King and Weasel!"

"Yes, I thought it was them," he replied.

"Where'd you get this?" Connie demanded.

"I took it myself from outside their window," he replied nonchalantly.

"You were outside their window? No! Were you there when —"

"Yes, but I was careful to stay on the sidelines." He pointed to the laptop, "Look, here comes that surprise party your witness spoke about."

Connie watched slack-jawed as the bikers rushed into King's living room and beat him and Weasel with baseball bats. "Son of a bitch." She turned to Jack. "You got this on film? Why didn't —"

"Shh, keep watching and listening."

When the video was over, Connie turned to Jack, her face furious. "Why the hell didn't you tell me?" Wilson and I were up all night investigating. I even waited until morning to call you because I thought you were sleeping. How did you even know?"

"Well —"

"You should've told me! We would've scooped these guys up immediately. There'd have been blood on their clothes. Maybe we would've even got the weapons. Who are they? At least two were Satans Wrath. You must know them."

"The rest are Gypsy Devils," Jack said. "I can identify all of them, but the video and what you've seen and heard here can't be used."

"Bullshit it can't be —"

"Furthermore you're not to tell anyone about it. You're now officially off the investigation."

"What the hell? You can't order me off a case!"

"Orders from Isaac. By the time you get to your office, he'll have informed Inspector Dyck. Isaac wanted me to explain it to you first so you'd understand. Pretty decent of him, really."

"Understand? Understand what?"

"To use Isaac's words, the situation involves an informant who's an integral part of a bigger picture. In a nutshell, this informant is supplying information to pursue more serious charges on another matter."

"More serious than murder?"

"What you saw on the video clearly exposes that it wasn't a premeditated murder," Jack said.

"Why'd you wait until now to tell me?" she demanded. "If I'm being jerked off this case, I could've saved a lot of time if I'd known."

"I'm sorry I couldn't bring it to your attention earlier, but it was after this incident that the informant supplied me with information. Information that's more worthy of what the people in this video would receive if convicted."

"So you turned one of these sons of bitches into an informant in exchange for immunity," Connie said, gesturing to the laptop.

Jack nodded, more out of a natural instinct to protect his informant than anything else.

"Well, if that don't beat all," Connie muttered.

"If you're upset that a murder case has been taken away from you, I suspect that one of the bikers in the video will be murdered soon — and that action will be premeditated." Jack gave a friendly smile. "If you like, I can give you his name."

"What?" Connie almost yelled. "Are you serious?"

Jack nodded.

"Damn you, Jack! What is it with you? Why do you keep doing this to me?"

"Because you work Homicide and because I trust you enough to tell you."

"And now you're sayin' that someone else might get whacked?"

"Probably."

"Who?"

"Neal Barlow." Jack gestured to the laptop. "He was the big fat greasy-looking guy with the braided goatee. He's a full-patch member of the Gypsy Devils."

"Him? Why?"

"They might soon think he's an informant," Jack replied.

"You're setting him up?" Connie accused.

"I'm just letting the chips fall where they may, so to speak."

"Damn you," Connie said again.

"Mind you, I'm not sure what jurisdiction they'll be in when it happens. Perhaps it won't be your case."

"They? I thought you said one guy?"

"Sorry — Freudian slip. I spoke with Isaac this morning and discussed the possibility of two others being murdered. Bob and Roxie Barlow. Bob is Neal's brother, but in my opinion the heat will fall on Neal."

"So Isaac knows and approves this?" Connie sounded astonished.

"It's a delicate matter — but yes."

"I don't believe this," Connie said. "Does Neal know he's being targeted?"

"Not yet. Bob and Roxie dropped off two-hundred-and-fifty keys of weed yesterday in Dallas, Texas. I had the DEA seize the weed but let the semi go."

"And you think they'll blame Neal and not his brother and sister-in-law?"

"I'm confident that the blame will go to Neal due to other things that have taken place. If it was Bob and Roxie, they wouldn't be coming back here. Once Neal hears the details about the bust, he might clue in, but it's hard to say. He's not known as cerebral."

"And of course you wouldn't even think of warning him."

"Actually I discussed that with Isaac," Jack said.

"Really?"

"Of course." Jack shook his head. "Sometimes it's hard to figure out how you think, Connie. Sure, the Gypsy Devils dress a little different, but really, when you see them as I have, sitting in a pub with their girlfriends, they're actually just a fun-loving bunch of guys who enjoy a beer and a good laugh once in a while. Really nice people if you get to know them."

"Up yours." Connie became sullen. She looked out the window, then turned back to Jack. "So Isaac told you to warn him?"

"No. We discussed it, but there's more involved, including public safety." Jack then explained how the murder of Neal might prevent other deaths.

"Jesus," she said under her breath, then, "Maybe I should set up surveillance on him myself. If —"

"As much fun as I know it is to video a murder, I don't —"

"Fun?" Connie interrupted him.

"Come on, where's your sense of humour?"

"Fun?" Connie repeated. Her tone expressed exasperation.

"Okay, let me say that the idea of protective surveillance was also discussed with Isaac. I'm sure you'd be spotted — which would confirm the bikers' belief that he's the informant. We do have a wiretap order on him and others in the club. The situation could change, depending on what we hear — although I'm not optimistic that we'll hear anything."

"So you're telling me to sit back and watch some guy get murdered — without lifting a finger," Connie said.

"Believe me, his death won't be any loss to society."

"Yeah … well, it's not like I need the extra workload."

"Considering that you now have a glimpse of the big picture, it'd be better if you were left out of that investigation, as well," Jack said. "There'd be too much tippytoeing you'd have to do in court. That's if he *is* murdered, of course."

"If?" Connie opened the door and got out, then turned to look at Jack. "Don't give me that crap. With you involved, there'll be no *if* about it."

"It's not guaran —"

Connie slammed the door shut.

Chapter Thirty-One

Forty minutes later Jack was having lunch at home when his phone rang. He mumbled an apology to Natasha and answered.

"Corporal Taggart, this is Mr. Basil Westmount. I'm representing —"

"Yeah, I know. Whaddaya want?" Jack intentionally slurred his voice as if he was inebriated. "I'm off today."

"I'm calling to advise you that I'm representing Mr. Buck Zabat," the lawyer replied.

"Yeah? What're you representing him for? Has he been charged with something?" Jack asked facetiously.

"I don't have time to play games, Corporal. I met with his father, who you rousted out of bed in the middle of the night."

"Yeah, I was nice enough to let 'em know."

"Nice enough? You intentionally got this poor couple out of bed in the dead of night and maliciously led them to believe that one of their children had been killed. I can hardly think of a more despicable thing to do. Then you accuse Mr. Zabat of being involved in illegal activity — a man who doesn't even have a criminal record. You slander him in front of his wife and try to coerce him into providing you with information. All because you are under the impression that you have evidence against my client. Evidence that, I suspect, will not stand up to the test of admissibility in court once —"

"Under the impression that I have evidence?" Jack snorted. "That's a good one. What I have will take more than having one of Buck's sluts sitting in the front row with a pillow under her blouse to fake a pregnancy in order to con a jury into letting him off."

"I've no idea what you're talking about," Basil said crisply.

"Guess your memory isn't as good as mine."

"I'm calling to inform you that I will personally bring my client in to face any charges," Basil sneered, clearly irritated. "You said you would wait two days before arresting him. Tomorrow will be that deadline. I would like to arrange a time to bring him in. Here I am doing you a favour, yet by your tone you —"

"A favour? You really are a funny guy. What you want is to impress a judge that your client isn't a flight risk and to ensure that he says nothing to the police."

The tone of Basil's voice went beyond irritation to anger. "As his lawyer, I'm instructing you not to talk to him without my presence! Have you got that?"

"Yeah, well, I haven't had time to show the prosecution what I have," Jack replied. "Did I tell ya I'm off today?"

"Yes, you told me."

"I'm so hungover from celebrating that I feel like pukin'. Anyway, tomorrow's too soon. By the time I do go into work, tear my bosses away from their coffees and newspapers, and show 'em the video, then run it over to the prosecutors … well, you know what lawyers are like. They'll wanna know every blinkin' detail about everything. If it all goes well … I dunno. Christ, what day is it now? Monday? It'll probably be next week."

"Then I wish to make it clear to you that when you do obtain a warrant, you're to call me and I'll arrange a time and place for Mr. Zabat to come in."

"How, when, or where I arrest little Bucky Zabat will be my decision," Jack said with mock indignation.

Natasha eyed him curiously as he hung up. "What was all that about? Or can you say? I'm beginning to wonder if I married an idiot."

Jack gave her a lopsided grin. "No. I was simply prepping him to protect an informant. I want him to hate and disrespect me. Later, when a charge doesn't proceed, he'll be inclined to believe the evidence was tainted due to my incompetence."

"Think your charade worked?"

"It might."

Natasha nodded.

Unfortunately Damien is a lot smarter. Tricking him won't be so easy.

Chapter Thirty-Two

Damien opened a sliding glass door that allowed access to his swimming pool and the yard beyond. He gestured for Purvis Evans to go ahead of him. Technically Pure E wouldn't officially become the national president of Satans Wrath until next weekend, but unofficially, he was already at the helm.

Damien eyed him after they passed the pool and entered a stone pathway. *For a man considered pure evil, he's not physically large — except for his ego.*

Pure E was half-a-head shorter than Damien and at forty-two, seventeen years younger. At first glance one might guess he was a businessman who worked a Monday-to-Friday job. His curly black hair was relatively short and he was clean-shaven. Women found him handsome and if they stirred his desire, he could be charming, but generally he preferred the company of women who were paid with either cash or drugs.

Purvis Evans was a sociopath in the true sense of the word. He was convicted of his first violent sexual assault when he was just fourteen. His subsequent stay in a juvenile detention facility helped to educate him in the ways to meet his criminal aspirations.

Pure E cast a sideways glance at Damien. "Well, Gramps, I gotta say, things are really falling apart with the club."

Damien thrust out the heel of his hand, hitting Pure E's shoulder, sending him stumbling backward. When Pure E regained his balance he locked eyes with Damien, who looked at him with disdain and growled, "You ever call me 'Gramps' again I'll put my fist down your throat and next time you see your teeth they'll be in the toilet."

Pure E's rage was briefly reflected on his face. Then he gave a smile that didn't reach his eyes. "Don't be so touchy. I was only teasing."

"No, you weren't," Damien replied evenly. "You were being cocky and disrespectful."

Another flash of anger on Pure E's face. "If that's how it's to be between us, fine by me."

"Your position demands respect. Start thinking and acting like you're worthy of it."

Pure E's lips curled and he opened his mouth to speak.

"Don't say something you'll regret," Damien warned.

Pure E stopped. He took a breath and slowly exhaled. "You never backed me for taking over. Ever wonder why the majority voted for me?"

"Like me, they figured it was time to put a Frenchie in the position — but Quebec is in turmoil over what'll happen with the corruption inquiry. Your mother, however, was French — you're bilingual and spent a lot of time liaising with our boys in Quebec. Can't say as I was surprised you won."

"Maybe that's part of it, but too many outside players are moving in on our turf. Especially here on the West Coast. I've made it clear I'll change that."

"The only ones infringing are bit players," Damien said. "If any of them start making real money, they'll be told to work for us. In the meantime, chasing around wannabe gangsters isn't worth our while. It attracts heat and has the potential to put our members at risk. Right now the cops have reassigned most of their people in the Anti-Gang Unit to combat terrorism. It's wise not to alert the politicians that they need more manpower."

"You have the gall to talk to me about risk?" Pure E looked at Damien with contempt. "Under your watch, your own son is about to go down. This morning we find out we lost two-hundred-and-fifty keys in Dallas yesterday."

"As far as Buck goes, I took immediate action," Damien replied. "Yesterday the Gypsy Devils were given two weeks to clean up the problem. The incident in Dallas highlights that need."

"Two weeks makes it a week after you retire," Pure E noted. "Talk about passing the buck."

"Ferreting out the rat could easily take that long. As far as passing the buck goes, I view the Gypsy Devils as a small problem — one I thought you'd be capable of dealing with."

"Oh, I'm more than capable," Pure E said.

"It'd also be nice to prevent negative feedback."

"Negative feedback?"

"At the moment the Gypsy Devils don't believe that one of their guys ratted. They're not aware of the bust in Dallas yet. They need to be told about it immediately. It'll be a little added incentive for them to take a hard look at themselves and prevent some idiot in their club from doing something stupid toward us."

"You're calling a loss of two-hundred-and-fifty keys 'a little added incentive'? I'd call it a lot more than that."

"Come on," Damien said in annoyance. "That amount of weed is nothing. The cost of doing business. It happens and should be expected to happen once in a while. Our club will move on and find another means of moving it."

"It isn't nothing!" Pure E declared adamantly. "Someone talked … about your son and the weed."

"Yes, which is why I gave the GDs the order to deal with the matter."

"Yeah, and you talk to me about a lack of respect? Open your eyes. We've got a major problem with our image when a couple of truck drivers aren't afraid to rat us out."

"It wasn't the couple in the truck who talked," Damien said. "They were on the road when Buck was filmed and wouldn't have known about it. I also know the cop who took the video. His name's Jack Taggart. Believe me, he's not stupid enough to burn someone like that. I'm positive those two aren't his informants."

"Then who ratted? Someone inside the Gypsy Devils? The same club you gave the go-ahead to sponsor?"

"The Gypsy Devils have their use like any other group who works for us. It's not like we'd ever allow more than one or two of them to prospect for us. As far as who talked … well, the truck driver's brother is a Gypsy Devil. His name's Neal Barlow and he lost seventy-five keys of weed last week. He said he was robbed."

"So you already know who the rat is. The cops used his brother as leverage to get him to rat."

"Maybe, maybe not," Damien replied.

"What do you mean, maybe not? Neal Barlow is the rat. Why dick around?"

"As I said, Taggart is smart. Maybe he set this up to make us think that. My advice to you is that if he's involved, never be too sure about anything. As a result of what happened in Dallas, I'd recommend we plant a few bugs and do our own surveillance. Let's make sure the Gypsy Devils get the right person."

"You told me that only the GDs and a couple of our guys knew about the visit the cops videoed. Same for the weed in Dallas, I presume. How much more obvious could it get?" Pure E shook his head. "The time for pussyfooting around is over."

"I'm only suggesting you make sure first."

"I *am* sure. Hell, even if I wasn't, I'd still send a special message to shut up anyone else who might be inclined to rat."

"Special message?"

"I don't want it to be a simple hit. It has to be done right. I want one or two of our guys involved to make sure it goes down the way I want."

"Why put our guys at risk?"

"To show that we still have balls," Pure E replied. "Don't take this the wrong way, but the club is under new management. Things are going to be different."

"That's your prerogative as the new boss," Damien said.

"Do we have any business with the Gypsy Devils in the next two weeks?"

"No. Normally in a week or so they'd expect to be paid, but if we're blaming the bust in Dallas on them, then I'd demand they pay *us* for the loss."

"For sure, but I want to make an example out of the rat," Pure E said emphatically. "I'm going to contact Lance and talk to him about it."

Damien sighed, then nodded.

"Now for more important matters," Pure E said. "How are things going with Europe?"

"First delivery should arrive in about ten days, but there's always a possibility the boat could be delayed due to bad weather."

Pure E smiled. "When it does dock, that'll be a day worth celebrating." He paused a moment. "Too bad it didn't work out to coincide with your send-off party on Saturday."

"It is what it is," Damien replied. "For me, the big moment will be seeing Buck get his full patch. That means more to me than the boat."

"Still, I think our new venture in Europe is worthy of a party. The guys will be wondering."

"Not too many in the club know the exact details," Damien said, "At least as far as the delivery date or what country the shipment's arriving at."

"I know, but I think I'll call a meeting to coincide with the day it arrives. It'll be safe enough at that point to let 'em know we're officially doing business. Ten days from now will work. I'll tell everyone the meeting is for me to introduce myself to the troops. Then when the boat is being unloaded, I'll let them know Europe is in our pocket and crack open the champagne. They still don't need to know the exact details."

Damien nodded.

"That'd also be a good day to educate the Gypsy Devils on how to take care of rats." Pure E smiled. "My new management style is going to hit everyone like a nuke. Talk about shock and awe."

Damien eyed him briefly. "About Europe, bear in mind that Taggart asked about it when he came to my house with the video."

"Yeah, I wonder how the fuck he got wind of it."

"Probably rumours," Damien said. "Considering that we've got a chapter in Colombia and several chapters in Europe, it wouldn't take much to make that presumption. Once the product hits the streets over there, they'll know soon enough. The important thing is he doesn't know anything now."

"How do you know he doesn't?"

"He wouldn't have mentioned it otherwise. Not with us being so close to delivery. If the cops were really on to it, he wouldn't chance ruining their investigation."

"Makes sense." Pure E stopped to grind his heel on an ant. "So ... you think Taggart is smart. Think he's smart enough to stay out of my way?"

Damien looked at Pure E in frustration. "If you plan on killing a cop, it'll bring heat down on the whole club. Not to mention the fact that Taggart doesn't play by the law. Play dirty with him and he'll play dirty back. I'm sure he has friends who do, too."

Pure E scowled. "I appreciate your concern for the club. I'm not saying I'm going to have him killed immediately. Perhaps he could be dissuaded from pestering us if he received the right message. One that's personal. Is he married?"

"Yes, with two kids, but he isn't the type to respond to a message the way you'd want," Damien replied. "Particularly if you make it personal."

"Guess we'll soon find out — because in about ten days I'm going to give him one."

Damien kept his thoughts to himself. *Either you, Taggart, or the both of you will end up dead — and quite frankly, I couldn't care less.*

Chapter Thirty-Three

Jack was preparing a Caesar salad for dinner when he received a call. *Weenie Wagger, don't you ruin my day.*

"Thought I better let you know I went with Lance this afternoon for another chat with Carl Shepherd," Cockerill said as soon as Jack answered.

"That doesn't surprise me," Jack replied. "I imagine your club is a little upset about what happened in Dallas yesterday. Who's being blamed? How'd it go with Shepherd and his boys?"

"His boys weren't there. We did a surprise visit to his house. Shepherd is a mechanic and works out of his garage. It was only the three of us. Lance told him about the weed being taken down in Dallas as soon as Bob and Roxie pulled away."

"How'd that go over?"

Cockerill gave a snort. "Shepherd damn near shit himself. Both him and Lance figured it had to be Neal."

"Which is what I expected," Jack replied.

"Yeah, well, it sort of made me feel like shit."

"Why you?"

"Makes me feel guilty. Standin' there and listenin' to them talk about Neal when it was me who blabbed."

"Better than you standing in Neal's shoes," Jack said. "Is Neal still above ground?"

"Yeah. Lance told Shepherd to stay mum and not tell any of his guys about the bust in Dallas. He's to tell his guys that we no longer think they had anything to do with you getting that video."

"Why?"

"Dunno. He's to tell 'em the cops were already watching because King was suspected of killin' Larry's brother. Lance also told him to say that the West 12th Street boys have a leak and that business with them will be on hold until it's straightened out."

"Stay mum about Dallas for how long?" Jack asked.

"About ten days."

"Ten days?" Jack echoed in surprise.

"Lance said Pure E is waitin' till Damien officially steps down on Saturday. Then he's gonna call a general meeting about a week later to talk to us about his leadership style. Lance thinks Pure E is going to make an example out of Neal at the same time."

"Wanting to show what a tough guy he is and start his new leadership role with a bang — literally, as far as Neal is concerned."

"Sorta what Lance thinks." Cockerill cleared his throat. When he continued, his voice was nervous. "When Neal gets whacked, they want someone from our club to oversee it."

"Someone?" Jack asked.

"It could be me."

"You? Why not the three-three?"

"A couple reasons. One is 'cause I'm the liaison guy. Neal wouldn't suspect nothin' if he was told to meet me. The other is 'cause they're still pissed at me for drinkin' too much. I think this is where I'm supposed to redeem myself. Someone from the three-three might be there too, but I dunno for sure."

"Why risk you or one of the three-three on something like that? If the GDs are convinced Neal sold them out, they won't have any problem putting a bullet in his head."

"Lance says Pure E wants us to be more hands on in the future. Show we ain't afraid of nothin' or nobody."

Good. Sounds like Pure E isn't as smart as Damien. "When you find out, let me know."

"Will do." Cockerill paused. "I know you probably don't want me involved in that, but I don't know how to get out of it."

"I don't care if you're involved. I won't direct any heat toward you — but if you screw up and get caught, don't plan on having me save you, either."

"Okay … as long as you're not pissed at me."

"Not as long as you're straight with me."

"That eases my mind." Cockerill paused again. "Then we got Damien's party on Saturday. Are you gonna be collecting plate numbers or are ya leavin' that to the gang unit?"

"The Anti-Gang Unit will cover that," Jack replied, "although their priorities are more with the street gangs these days."

"Yeah, it's nice to have 'em shootin' each other up. Takes the heat off us. That and the terrorists. Lance said we should send them all thank-you cards."

"Will the GDs be working security for you at the party?" Jack asked.

"Yup. They can babysit our hogs. That and being errand boys." After a moment he added, "Hopefully the weather'll be good for ridin.'"

The weather will be good? What the hell? "What are you holding back? There's something on your mind."

"Damn it, I'll tell you what's on my mind," Cockerill blurted. "I've given you a lot of shit. How much longer am I gonna have to talk to you?"

"There are some things happening with your club in the next couple of weeks that I'll want to know about. Keep me up-to-date on everything, and I mean everything, and then I'll cut you loose."

"Oh, you mean like the meeting about Pure E's new management style," Cockerill replied. "That I can handle."

"And details about Neal," Jack said.

"Yeah, I know that."

"Along with any other things that might crop up." *Like Damien being squashed like a bug on a train track.*

"I'll be kept in the loop about Neal 'cause I'm the liaison. Even if the three-three do it, they'll want me to contact him to set 'im up." Neal sighed. "Yeah, another coupla weeks. I'm okay with that."

Jack was putting his phone back in his pocket when he received a call from Inspector Pollock of the Integrated Proceeds of Crime unit.

"I have some news that should make you happy," Pollock said. "We're set to go Friday morning."

"Make me happy?" Jack replied. "I'm elated!"

"Good. Our Liaison Officer handling the British Virgin

Islands is in Miami, but an investigator from here will go to the BVI on Wednesday. They'll be in position to go Friday morning at the same time we search Damien's house."

"Fantastic," Jack said. *Damien, I can't wait to see the look on your face.*

"I also spoke with our L.O. in Mexico. Like you, he suggested we don't get a warrant signed for the lawyer's office in Chihuahua until after the other searches are underway. If the paperwork's done in advance, he's still optimistic that the search warrant could be executed there late Friday afternoon."

"By then Lopez might already have been tipped off," Jack said.

"I know, but there isn't much we can do about it."

"No worries. I'm sure what we'll get here and in the BVI will be plenty to hang Damien. I'll drop by your office tomorrow to go over the finer details."

"Sounds good," Pollock replied. "I expect Friday will turn out to be a bad day for Mr. Damien Zabat."

After hanging up, Jack thought about Lopez's office in Mexico. Then his thoughts turned to El Paso, Texas. Specifically to a U.S. Customs special agent he'd worked with before. John Adams was a man he trusted. *In fact, we're considered birds of a feather.*

Chapter Thirty-Four

The next few days ticked past slowly for Jack. Thursday night he went to bed early, but the closer the clock moved to Friday morning, the more his adrenalin pumped — and the more he thought about how Damien would respond. He had set his alarm for 6:00 a.m., but was up and dressed long before then.

At 8:00 a.m. Jack and Laura arrived at the entrance to Damien's estate with Sammy Crofton and Benny Saunders parking behind them.

Jack switched off the ignition and glanced at Laura. "This is it."

"I know, I've been counting down the minutes all week," she replied.

"You and me both. I've been waiting for this moment since before we were partners." Jack took a deep breath, then slowly exhaled. "It's showtime. Let's do it."

Sammy and Benny climbed out of their car. "All set with I-POC?" Sammy asked as Jack approached the intercom mounted on a stone pillar beside the gate to Damien's estate.

"They've got a team of four guys," Jack replied. "I had them park four blocks away. They'll expect a call when we go in, so in about twenty minutes I'll tell them you finally arrived and that we're entering — then again about fifteen minutes after that to say the house is secure so they can come in."

"Sure, put the heat on us," Benny joked. "Everyone will say we're tardy."

"You ugly mutt," Sammy said. "Calling you tardy would be the nicest thing anyone could call you."

"Hey, I resent that remark." Benny pretended indignation.

Sammy gave Jack a nod. "So we should have about thirty minutes inside before I-POC arrives. Ought to be enough time."

"If it all goes according to plan," Jack said.

"No worries about Damien seeing Sammy and me?" Benny asked.

"No. Your long hair and Sammy's goatee — he'll know you're Drug Section and presume you're helping us locate Buck. You don't look like the type of guys who'd be dealing with financial institutions. No insult intended."

"None taken," replied Sammy. "I hate wearing suits. Speaking of which, didn't I-POC wonder why you wanted them to park so far away?"

"I actually told them the truth about that. Damien has security cameras all over his estate, some of which I'm sure monitor the street. He also has a panic room in his house. I doubt that we'll find much of value, but if there is something and Damien sees the suits, he could destroy it long before we got inside. His place is like a fortress."

"Something to bear in mind if things don't go as planned," Laura said. Her distaste for Jack's plan was evident in her tone.

Jack gave Laura a solemn look, then pushed the button on the intercom.

A moment later Damien's gruff voice was heard. "What do you want, Taggart?"

"Good morning, Damien," Jack replied. "This time we're back with a warrant. I suggest you let us in — or do you want us to drive through your gate?"

"Goddamn it. Buck moved out of our house when he turned eighteen."

"Yeah, sure he did," Jack said sarcastically. "Open up."

A second later the front gates swung open and the team got back in their vehicles and drove through.

Damien, wearing his housecoat, stood at the front door as they approached. He stepped aside to allow them entrance to the foyer, where Vicki stood dressed in her housecoat.

"Here's the warrant," Sammy said, holding the document toward Damien.

Damien slapped it away and pointed his finger at Jack. "Basil called you. He told you he'd bring Buck in."

"Anyone else in the house?" Sammy interrupted.

Damien glared at Jack, then turned to Sammy. "Only the two of us," he answered, with a nod toward Vicki. "Buck hasn't lived here for years."

"Then the two of you take a seat in the living room," Sammy ordered, gesturing to a leather sofa that faced a floor-to-ceiling stone fireplace. "Keep your hands where they can be seen."

Damien and Vicki both sat on the sofa.

While Jack stood guard, Sammy, Benny, and Laura disappeared to make a quick search of the house to ensure nobody else was present.

Damien glowered up at Jack. "You know he isn't here. This is straight harassment."

Jack just smiled.

"You think this is funny?" Vicki fumed. "Thinking you can just bust in on us any time you want."

"Take it easy," Damien said, placing a hand on her knee. "The more Corporal Taggart acts like an ass, the more he'll pay for it when Basil Westmount tears him apart in court."

Vicki sighed hugely, then sat back with her arms folded across her chest.

Minutes later Laura, Sammy, and Benny returned to advise that there was no one else in the house.

"Told you," Damien said. He glanced at a clock on the fireplace mantel. "Basil will be in his office in twenty minutes. Call him then and he'll bring Buck to your office. Or if you want I can call him now. I've got my cellphone on me." He patted the pocket of his housecoat.

"Actually I think I'll arrest Buck tomorrow," Jack said.

"You dirty son of a bitch," Damien seethed. "You know tomorrow is when he'll be receiving his patch."

"What a shame. Not to mention missing your retirement party. However, that's not the reason we're here."

"What do you mean?" Before Jack could reply Damien said, "Let me see that warrant."

Sammy showed Damien the warrant. After scanning the document, he looked at Jack and gave a bemused smile. "You're searching for documents related to money laundering ... tax evasion? What is this? One desperate last-ditch attempt to hang something on me before I step down?" He shook his head. "Didn't realize you were that pathetic. Go ahead and search. Be my guests." He raised his hands, palms up.

"I don't think you'll be smiling in a moment," Jack said. "This isn't the only search that's taking place. We're also — Hang on, my phone." He took his phone from his pocket. "Team two," he said to Laura before answering.

Damien listened intently to what Jack said as he spoke on his phone, unaware that no call to Jack had actually been made.

"Yes, we're inside now, but haven't started to search yet," Jack said. "How are things on your end?" With appropriate pauses, he continued, "Great. Any news from down south? ... No? ... Well, let me know. ... He does? Sure, I want him to call Damien. Besides, he's their lawyer. He probably has a right to." Jack smiled in Damien's direction. "I want to see the look on his face. Make sure that's the only call he makes, though, until we get confirmation from team three. I'll get his number and confirm it, then you can dial it for him." He lowered his phone and looked at Damien. "What's your cell number?"

Damien gave Jack his phone number, which Laura copied into her notebook.

Jack spoke into his phone again. "I'll call you right back." He hung up and dialled the number Damien had given him.

Seconds later Damien said, "It's vibrating."

"Answer it," Jack ordered.

Damien took his phone from his pocket and answered.

"Good, number confirmed." Jack smiled as Damien hung up. "Don't bother putting it away. You're going to find your next call really interesting. It'll be from your lawyer."

"Basil is going to have a field day with you," Damien said, placing his phone on the coffee table.

"Basil?" Jack asked. "Hang on, another call." He looked at his call display, glanced at Laura, and said, "From team three. I have to take it. Call team two and give them Damien's number."

Laura dutifully took her phone from her purse and pretended to make a call as she walked to the far side of the room.

Jack, pretending to have received another call, allowed Damien to hear bits of his conversation. "Yes ... that's great. I spoke with team two a minute ago. They're viewing the files as we speak. How about you, are the files there? ... Perfect. Thank you. If you're sitting on the beach later, have a margarita on me. I'll pay for it when you return."

Damien's face revealed concern and he glanced suspiciously at Vicki, then back at Jack.

Jack beamed with delight. He dropped his phone into his inside jacket pocket and sang out, "'Oh, what a beautiful morning, oh, what a beautiful day.'"

"Jack," Laura said urgently from across the room, still gripping her own phone to her ear.

Jack appeared not to hear as he smiled at Damien and Vicki.

"Jack!" Laura repeated, then spoke into her phone. "Give us a minute. I'll have him call you back." She put the phone back in her purse.

"What is it?" Jack asked joyfully.

"I need to see you alone," Laura replied.

Jack crossed the distance between them and playfully placed one hand on her shoulder. "Laura! I'm a married man!"

Laura's expression said she wasn't amused. She slammed the palm of her hand on his chest, shoving him backward. "There's a problem at team two," she said tersely.

Jack tensed, then gestured for her to follow him to the foyer where they could talk in private. As they did so, Damien's phone vibrated on the coffee table. Upon hearing the phone, Jack looked back and said, "Go ahead, answer it."

Damien picked up his phone. "Hello?" He saw Jack watching him from the foyer while talking quietly with Laura. "Hello?" he repeated.

It was Jack's voice that Damien heard on his phone. He heard Jack whisper to Laura, "So what's up? Team two told me the files were there exactly as we'd told them."

Damien had seen Jack put his phone in his inside jacket pocket before Laura shoved him. Now he believed that Laura had accidentally hit the redial button on Jack's phone.

"It's not that. It's Cummings," he heard Laura say.

"Look, Cummings is talking to Damien now." Jack and Laura looked over at Damien. "He looks white as a ghost," Jack noted.

"So would I if I were about to lose every dollar I ever made," Laura said.

"So what's the problem?" Jack asked, turning to face Laura.

"Cummings wants to be charged," Laura said.

"What do you mean, he wants to be charged? I told him we'd make it look like there wasn't enough evidence to prove he knew he was laundering money."

"He got cold feet," Laura replied. "He thinks if he isn't charged, Damien will clue in that he ratted. He wants us to charge him."

"What about the other guy he was laundering money for? The deal was we wouldn't charge him or Cummings."

"No change there," Damien heard Laura reply. "If we charge him, Damien might clue in as to how we found out about Cummings."

"The plan was that we'd make Damien think it was the Mexican lawyer who ratted him out," Jack said.

"Cummings is afraid that isn't enough."

"Charging him would certainly tie in with the conspiracy charges," Jack said, turning to stare across the room at Damien, who had his phone glued to his ear. The combination of angst and anger upon Damien's face was clearly evident.

"It's hard to believe that Cummings would risk going to jail and losing his licence. He must be really scared," Laura said.

"My guess is he's gambling that he'll beat us in court," Jack replied.

"Perhaps from his point of view, it's a small price to wager if he thinks it'll save his life. What do you want to do?"

"Do? This is great. I never liked the idea of letting Cummings off in the first place. Call team two back while he's still on the phone with Damien and tell them to slip him a note to say he's being charged, too."

Laura pretended to make another call while Jack walked back into the living room. As he did Damien hung up. "Hanging up so soon?" Jack asked.

"I heard what I needed to hear," Damien replied gruffly. He then sat back on the sofa and folded his arms across his chest in an apparent attempt to control his emotions.

"Somebody want to tell me what the hell is going on?" Vicki demanded. "What's this bullshit about money laundering and tax evasion? What's that got to do with Buck?"

"This isn't about Buck," Jack said. "It's about Damien — and you, considering your name's on the business documents we found."

"What're you talking about?" Vicki demanded, casting an anxious glance at her husband.

"Right now we're conducting searches here, Irving Cummings's office, and at the office of Charles Bentley in Road Town, BVI."

Vicki gasped, then looked at Damien.

"Keep quiet," Damien cautioned. "Not a word until we speak to our lawyer."

"Which one?" Jack asked facetiously. "Basil Westmount, Irving Cummings, Charles Bentley … or Francisco Lopez in Chihuahua, Mexico?"

Damien's nostrils flared like an angry bull and the muscles on his jaw rippled as he clenched his teeth.

"Oh, by the way," Jack said, "we're not searching Lopez's office immediately, because of all the corruption down there." He glanced at Laura and added, "As much as I really hate to see some guy like that get away with what he's been doing."

Laura exchanged a knowing look with Jack, then gave an almost imperceptible nod, as if that comment was something to be ticked off a list.

Damien's eyebrows knitted together, heavy creases forming above them. One lip curled above an eye tooth like a dog about to attack ... but he said nothing.

Jack hid his smile. His comment was intended to make it appear that he was trying to make Lopez look like the one who talked in order to protect Cummings. By the expression on Damien's face, Jack knew he'd succeeded. *Cummings, I'd suggest you get your affairs in order.*

Chapter Thirty-Five

"So we're being arrested?" Vicki asked.

"Not at the moment," Jack said, "but I expect you will be within the next week once formal charges are laid." He smiled. "Perhaps that'll give you time to find a good legal-aid lawyer, seeing as we'll be seizing everything you own, including your money, passports, vehicles, all your possessions … and your house."

"What do you mean, our house?" Vicki screamed.

"Proceeds of crime," Jack replied bluntly. "You'll be allowed to live here for a short time while the paperwork makes its way through court. We'll kindly leave you your bed, kitchen table, and two chairs in the meantime."

"You can't do that!" She leaped to her feet and turned to Damien, who sat in stunned silence. "Do something! I'm not going to stand here and watch this happen! This is our house!" She gestured to the family photos on the fireplace mantel. "We raised our children here, for God's sake!"

"You don't have to watch us," Jack said. "You're not under arrest and as the search teams are already doing what needs to be done, you're free to leave. Considering how upset you are, I think it'd be a good idea."

Vicki ignored Jack and continued to stare at Damien. "*Do* something!" she cried again. "He can't get away with this!" When Damien didn't respond immediately, she asked, "Can he?"

Damien took a deep breath and slowly exhaled. "They've got a warrant to do what they're doing now, but I'll be talking to a lawyer. In the meantime why don't you go to your sister's and I'll call you later."

Vicki swung to face Jack again. "You bastard!" she shouted. "You're not going to get away with this!"

"I'd suggest you heed your husband's advice and leave," Jack said. He glanced at Laura. "Go with her and watch her get dressed. Don't let her near any computers."

Laura nodded, then escorted Vicki up a large staircase to the second floor, where they walked down a hallway open to the living room below. A moment later they disappeared behind a set of French doors.

"Okay, so where do we start?" Sammy asked as he glanced around the living room.

"I'll call I-POC and tell them to come in," Jack told him. "The ball will be in their court as to how they want to proceed. I suspect they'll be videoing and documenting everything, as well."

"I'm used to looking for dope," Benny said. "This is something new for me."

"I doubt you'll find any dope here." Jack glanced at Damien for confirmation, but the man was staring off into space, apparently lost in thought. His face was dark with rage and a vein on his temple pulsed visibly. *Good, you bastard. Hope you have a heart attack.*

Jack went to the foyer, where he would not be overheard, and called Corporal David Cash, the guy in charge of the I-POC team awaiting access to the house. To cover standard procedure he told Cash that Sammy and Benny had arrived and that they were currently being let into Damien's estate. He said that he'd call again once the house was secure.

Jack returned to the living room at the same time Laura brought Vicki back down the stairs. He ignored the look of hatred on Vicki's face and glanced at Sammy and Benny. "I-POC will arrive in a couple of minutes. I told them we were letting Vicki leave and they could enter at the same time she heads out the gate." He swung his gaze to Vicki, who was retrieving her coat and purse from a hall closet, then turned back to Sammy. "We may as well hang tight until they get in, then decide how to break up the search team."

"So what exactly will I be looking for?" Benny asked.

"Any financial documents," Jack replied. "And any computer flash sticks that might be hidden."

"Computer flash sticks," Sammy murmured as he gazed around. "Talk about a needle in a haystack."

"You're right about that," Jack agreed. He walked over to the fireplace mantel and looked at the family pictures. Amongst the grouping, he saw a framed picture of their daughter Sarah, who had died a few years earlier from meningitis. He remembered what Vicki had told him. *I keep Sarah's picture on our fireplace mantel and talk to her every day, wanting to believe she's still alive, that she still lives here.* He picked up the picture and glanced at Benny as he turned it over. "A flash stick could be hidden in something as innocuous as the back of this." As he spoke he carefully slid the black cardboard backing from the frame to take a look.

"You don't touch that!" Vicki screamed from across the room. "Damien! He's not getting that!"

"Calm down," Jack ordered. "We can take or search anything — Oh, crap." The picture fell from his hands, landing face down on the tiled apron in front of the fireplace. There was the sound of breaking glass. "I'm sorry," he said, squatting and carefully picking up the frame with both hands in an attempt to keep the broken glass from falling out.

"You did that on purpose!" Vicki bolted across the living room toward Jack.

Jack concentrated on the picture as he rose. "No, I really didn't. I'm sorry if —"

Damien jumped to his feet with an outstretched arm. "Vicki! No!" he roared.

Jack glanced up. Vicki was nearly upon him and Laura was in close pursuit. He was too late to defend himself. Vicki had flung her purse to the floor and he felt the muzzle of a pistol being rammed into his chest over his heart — then heard the blast when she pulled the trigger.

The blast was only one of a cacophony of sounds in the room. The air burst from Jack's lungs, making a horrible wheezing sound as his lungs fought to regain oxygen. The picture smashed to the floor again while he gasped and clutched his chest with one hand.

At the same time Laura screamed and grabbed Vicki's wrist while tackling her to the floor. The thud of them landing was echoed by another thud of Jack's body collapsing face down beside them.

Sammy and Benny drew their pistols and aimed them at Vicki, only to hesitate when they saw she was sprawled on her back with Laura sitting on top of her.

Damien, mouth agape, took a step forward. He stopped when Sammy pointed his pistol at him and yelled, "Hands on your head and don't move!"

Vicki still held the gun, but Laura had her wrist pinned to the floor and Benny took a step in their direction to help. It wasn't necessary. Laura glanced at Jack's prone body, then emitted a scream of retribution and drove her fist hard into Vicki's sternum. The pistol fell from her hand.

Chapter Thirty-Six

Corporal David Cash, sitting behind the wheel of his car parked four blocks away, glanced at his watch. Three other I-POC team investigators sat in the car with him. "What the hell is taking them so long?" he grumbled.

"Jack and Laura have a long history with this guy," said the investigator beside him. "How much do you want to bet that they're sitting around the kitchen table with him having a coffee while trying to gain some so-called intelligence?"

"Yeah, things like, gee, when does the next annual Labor Day ride take place?" chimed in a third voice from the back seat.

A few chuckles broke out.

Benny scooped up Vicki's pistol from where it had fallen as Laura pulled back her fist to strike again. She then caught sight of Benny. "Don't just stand there!" she screamed. "Call an ambulance! Start CPR!" She looked at Vicki. "I'll deal with this bitch."

Vicki coughed and gasped for air while squirming and twisting her body in an attempt to protect herself.

Laura hesitated, then lowered her fist and pinned Vicki's other wrist to the floor as her own body convulsed with sobs.

Benny fumbled to take his phone out of his pocket.

"Sit back down and keep your hands on your head!" Sammy yelled, gesturing with the muzzle of his pistol for Damien to return to the sofa.

Damien sat down as Benny punched in the first number on his phone.

"Wait," Jack gasped. "I … I think I'm okay."

Laura gave an unintelligible cry.

"Oh, God, thank you," Damien uttered.

Jack groaned and slowly rose to his hands and knees on the floor.

"You're not hurt?" Benny questioned, dropping to one knee beside Jack.

"Looks like I picked a good day to wear my vest," Jack replied. He then sat back on his haunches and pulled up his sweater. A bullet hole was visible on the Kevlar vest over his heart. He shoved his hand inside, then slowly removed it and looked at his fingers. "No blood," he announced, getting to his feet.

"Oh, Jack … Jack, I'm sorry," Laura said.

Jack looked at Laura and his face darkened with anger. "What the hell were you doing allowing her to grab her purse without searching it? You knew she was pissed at me!"

"I — I'm sorry. It was my mistake. It happened so fast I —"

"You're damn right it was your mistake! The kind of mistake that gets people killed!" He rose to his feet. "Get off her and cuff her," he ordered. "It could be the last arrest you ever make. Once my report goes in, you'll be spending the rest of your career pushing a pencil. That's if you still have a job."

Laura opened her mouth to speak, but no words came out. The hurt in her eyes and the tears on her cheeks spoke for her. She closed her mouth, nodded, then stood up while emitting a sob.

"Come to think of it," Jack said, "Benny, you arrest Vicki and bring her in. Laura doesn't deserve the honour." Laura emitted another sob and he jabbed her in the chest with his finger. "Go wait in the kitchen! I don't want to even look at you."

Silence descended on the room as Laura hurried to the kitchen. Benny then grabbed Vicki by the arm and pulled her to her feet.

Damien stared up at Vicki as she was being handcuffed. "Why?" he asked. "Why'd you do it?"

"Because ... because ..." Vicki started to tremble. "He smashed Sarah's picture," she cried. "He's taking all our money ... our house ... okay. Maybe I could deal with that. But smashing Sarah's picture ..."

"We've scanned copies of it on the computer," Damien said.

"I know but ... it's like she died all over again and he killed her!" she blubbered. She shook her head in self-recrimination. "Oh, Papa Bear, what've I done?"

The pain on Damien's face was obvious. He squeezed his eyes shut, but when he opened them, it was as if his emotions had been flushed away. "She has the right to a lawyer," he stated firmly. "I demand to call a lawyer immediately and have him there when she's brought in."

"Maybe makes you think you should've accepted my offer with Buck the other night," Jack commented. "You've destroyed your whole family. Vicki, if she's lucky, will spend the next ten or fifteen years in jail. Buck will be going to jail. That leaves your daughter, Katie, who's in rehab. Considering that you're about to become penniless … well, who knows what'll happen to her."

"Quit trying to screw with my head," Damien snarled. "I'm demanding a lawyer. Or haven't you heard of the Charter of Rights?"

"I'm familiar with it," Jack replied. "I was simply wondering why the big rush. She tried to shoot me in front of three police witnesses. Do you really think a lawyer will be able to help her? Why not wait until we're done our search? You're not being arrested — at least, not today. Come visit her in jail later and bring a lawyer then."

"I'm not leaving her to you hyenas," Damien said angrily. "She needs one now and I'm demanding that she be allowed to exercise her rights and obtain a lawyer immediately." He looked at Sammy and Benny. "You two are witnesses to what I just said. Write that down in your notebooks."

"You should let us put her in touch with a legal-aid lawyer," Jack said callously. "We're seizing everything you own. You won't have money to pay a lawyer."

"I'll borrow the money if I have to," Damien snarled.

"Fine — have it your way. Do you have Basil on speed dial?"

"He'll have his hands full handling Buck's case," Damien replied. "I'll get someone different for Vicki. I'd like to call Edward Gosling."

Wise choice, Jack thought. Gosling was a top-notch lawyer who was respected by police, prosecutors, and judges alike. Unlike Buck's case, where the admissibility of the evidence could be argued, with Vicki there'd be little doubt of a conviction. Gosling had a reputation for being reasonable and his recommendations for sentencing carried considerable weight. *Particularly with a mother who overreacted upon seeing a photo of her deceased daughter smashed. If anyone could gain some measure of sympathy from a judge, he could.*

"Well?" Damien asked. "Can I look up his number on my phone?"

"No, because our searches are still underway and I don't trust that you won't text someone. We'll look up his number and dial it for you."

Jack glanced toward the kitchen and then looked at Sammy and Benny. "You think I was too hard on her?" he asked them.

Benny shrugged. "Maybe, but then again, it wasn't me who was shot."

"The brass will find out when this goes to trial," Jack said. "It's not like I plan on running in and tattling on her."

"We're not saying you are," Sammy said. "I know the two of you've been through a hell of a lot together. She made a mistake. Shit happens. We're not blaming you … or her."

Jack sighed. "I was pretty upset," he admitted. "Maybe I did overreact a little. I'll talk to her." He gave a nod toward Damien. "Look up Gosling's number and dial it yourself.

Keep an eye on him, but at the same time give him space to talk in private."

"Will do," Sammy replied as Jack went to the kitchen.

Laura remained seated at the kitchen table while Jack slid out a chair to sit beside her.

"Things aren't going as I planned," he whispered.

"No kidding," Laura said in a hushed voice. "She was told to shoot you in the stomach, so that if there'd been a flaw in your vest you'd at least still be alive. That bitch put it right over your heart!"

"Maybe she got so caught up that she overacted," Jack suggested. "Speaking of which, you gave an academy-award performance out there. I really thought you'd lost it when you punched her in the gut."

"That wasn't acting. I thought you were dead," Laura said, making no effort to hide her anger. "The plan was for both of us to grab her and wrestle the gun away!"

"Shh, keep your voice down," Jack cautioned. "When I was hit, it completely knocked the wind out of me and spun me half-around. You had her instantly, so I thought it'd look more realistic if I did what I did."

"Too realistic!" Laura hissed. "I figured the bullet either stopped your heart or pierced the vest."

"Ah, come on. Have a little faith" Jack lifted his sweater to look at the vest again. "I've heard these things are guaranteed. If the front panel doesn't stop the slug, the back panel will."

"That's not funny. You really scared me."

"Damien's response wasn't funny, either," Jack said, tugging his sweater down.

"He didn't take the bait?"

"He's demanding a lawyer immediately. I threw out a reminder of the offer we made the other night to let Buck off, but there was no sign he wanted to make a deal now, either. He's determined to get Vicki a lawyer."

"Guess the pretend butt call worked," Laura noted. "Maybe it wasn't necessary to have her shoot you."

"Damien will be going over everything that happened bit by bit. If he starts to question the butt call, I think her shooting me will alleviate any suspicion."

"Sure hope Basil and Damien will believe we're not charging Vicki to protect me from getting in trouble."

"The good news about that is Damien didn't call Basil. He wants to hire Ed Gosling. He's probably on the phone to him now."

"Why is that good?"

"Basil's loyalty lies with Satans Wrath. If he knew that Vicki turned informant, he'd burn her to the club. Gosling wouldn't do that. "

"And Damien? What if he gets suspicious?"

"He's so worried about her — plus he knows you and I are close — that at the end of the day he'll want to believe we didn't charge her in order to protect you."

"But even with him thinking that both Vicki and Buck are going to jail, he still won't deal," Laura said.

"Maybe that was too much to hope for."

"So what now?"

"I haven't totally given up hope. Let's play it out a little longer."

"We won't have much time," Laura said. "One … maybe two hours by the time she's taken back to the office and talks to Gosling."

"I know, but despite his outward appearance, Damien has to be pretty shook up. Let's see if we can turn up the heat."

"How? We're already seizing everything he owns. He thinks his wife and son are going to jail. What more can —"

"Hang on … my phone," Jack said. "It's I-POC." He answered it. "I was about to call you. We're in. The house is secure and only Damien and Vicki are home, so come on in."

"You took longer than I expected," Dave said. "Any problems?"

"Not really. Vicki tried to assault me and has been arrested. Benny is taking her back to the office."

"She tried to assault you?" Dave said.

"It's no big deal. I accidentally broke a picture of their deceased daughter and she became upset. We're arresting her more to get her out of our hair than anything. Benny will be at the gate in a moment and you can drive through at the same time."

"Shooting you is no big deal?" Laura questioned when he hung up.

"I'll cover that off by telling Sammy and Benny in front of Damien that I don't want to embarrass you in front of I-POC with what really happened. I'll add that I'll need time to figure out how to word things. Stay here, then I'll call you in."

"Then what?" Laura asked. "How can we turn up the heat more than we have?"

"I don't know," Jack admitted. "We'll watch him while the search takes place. Maybe if I chat him up, he'll come around, but you pretend you're upset—that'll lay the groundwork for me to change my mind about charging Vicki."

"That'll be easy," Laura replied. "After what happened in there, I won't need to pretend."

Chapter Thirty-Seven

Benny left with Vicki in his custody and minutes later, the I-POC team entered. Jack and Laura stayed in the living room ostensibly to keep an eye on Damien while the other investigators began their search. Jack's attempts to engage Damien in conversation were met with silence.

Thirty minutes later Jack received a call from Benny. When he hung up, he looked at Damien. "Gosling is talking to Vicki. I'll let him call you when he's finished."

"Thanks." Damien appeared to brood for a moment. "Would it be okay if I get dressed? Or are you seizing my clothes, too?"

Jack ignored the sarcasm, but called out to Sammy to come with him as Damien got dressed. The three of them went upstairs to the bedroom, where a female officer was searching. "Find anything?" Jack asked.

"He buys his wife expensive jewellery," she replied. "Diamond bracelets, pendants, earrings. Definitely worth seizing."

"It's all just stuff," Damien said, then defiantly, "I couldn't care less if you take it."

Jack asked the policewoman for a few minutes of privacy while Damien dressed. She obliged and closed the door behind her.

"My pants and shirt are in the closet and socks are in the dresser," Damien said.

"Any weapons in the room?" Jack asked.

Damien let out a snort. "Yeah, I've got a jackknife in my top dresser drawer, but despite its name, it isn't meant for you. Other than that, I've got a gun locker in the panic room — but everything there's legally stored."

"Too bad Vicki didn't do the same with her gun," Jack commented.

A flash of pain crossed Damien's face. "Ever since the Colombians grabbed her that time, well … Enough of that. Can I get my clothes?"

"Go ahead."

"Fantastic bedroom," Sammy said as Damien gathered his clothes. "Great view of the mountains and the ocean. You won't be seeing that from your cell."

Damien was not about to give in to his emotions. "Like I said before, it's all just stuff." He took off his housecoat and sat on the edge of the bed in his underwear to put on his socks.

Jack saw five teddy bears lined up on the dresser. Two larger ones on each end and three smaller ones in the middle. Two of the smaller ones wore skirts and a blouse, while the third was dressed in pants and a T-shirt. Of the larger teddy bears on each end, one was dressed to represent the mother and the other the father. He remembered what Vicki said to Damien in the living room. *Oh, Papa Bear, what've I done?*

Jack gestured to the teddy bears. "Your family, Damien?"

"I gave one to Vicki each time one of our kids was born," Damien explained.

"Which one is this?" Jack asked, pointing to one in the centre.

"That represents Katie."

"Your youngest, who's in rehab. May as well put her face down," Jack said, toppling it over.

Damien winced.

Jack's finger lingered over the head of the next teddy bear. "Which would make this one Sarah … but she's dead." He toppled it over. "Besides you, I guess that leaves Mama Bear and Buck." Jack picked them both up and tossed them onto the bed. "You believe in omens, Damien?"

"What're you talking about?"

Jack took the jackknife out of the dresser and opened the blade, then tossed it onto the bed between the two teddy bears. "Pick up the knife, Damien."

"I'm not touching it," he said, standing up to distance himself from the knife. "You'll shoot me."

"No, that's not why I told you to pick it up." Jack gestured to the dresser. "The ones on the dresser are done for, but think of all the people with mental health problems who're in jail. Some will be seeking attention and I'm sure Vicki and Buck, because of who they are, will stand out as celebrities. I want you to stab one of the ones on the bed. Just for fun, see if it turns out to be an uncanny prediction for which one might get shanked in jail. Then again, maybe you'll want to do a clean sweep of your whole family and stab them both."

Damien looked at the two teddy bears lying face down on the dresser, then at the two on the bed with the knife between them.

"You're in charge of their fate," Jack said. "Figuratively speaking, the knife is still in your hands. This is your last chance. Once they're incarcerated, who knows who'll be holding it? Go ahead." He paused, then, "Are you going to stab them?"

Damien sucked in a lungful of air — then a pitiful moan erupted from the big man's throat. His legs wobbled and he sat down hard on the bed. Tears seeped from the corners of his eyes.

Sammy gave Jack a surprised look.

"Step out in the hall for a minute, will you, Sammy?" Jack asked.

Sammy nodded, then left the room and quietly closed the door behind him.

Damien looked at Jack. "I'm such a rotten fuck. My family … Vicki … she's never deserved what I've done to her." He shook his head in remorse. "I don't understand."

"Understand what?"

Damien made no effort to wipe the tears from his face. "Why I'm the way I am." He breathed heavily. "What's wrong with me that I'd allow this to happen to my family?"

"The thing is, you don't have to let it happen to your family," Jack replied. "It's not too late to save Vicki and Buck. You, yes — them no. I could still put a stop to it." He waited a beat. "Providing I had something to show for it, of course."

Damien's eyes searched Jack's face. He appeared to be trying to gain control of his emotions. "You couldn't stop it now. It's too late."

"Like I told you before, with Buck I can make it look like I didn't have the grounds to go on King's property and take the video. Without that, there'd be no evidence."

"Buck yes. But Vicki? She tried to kill you — in front of witnesses."

"Yeah, in front of witnesses. I would've thought you'd have taught her better than that," Jack said facetiously.

"Her name's on corporate documents in Cummings's office, too," Damien admitted.

"I'm sure you could take the heat for that," Jack replied. "Maybe make a deal with the prosecution. Regardless, that's nothing in comparison to the trouble she's in now. The important thing is that formal charges haven't been laid yet. The only witnesses to her trying to kill me are people I trust."

"You really think they'd keep their yaps shut?"

"If I told them to, yes."

"Oh, God." Damien wiped his eyes with the back of his hand, then mumbled, "I don't know what she was thinking."

"The point is moot unless you can give me something," Jack said coldly.

Damien looked at him. "She's the mother of my kids," he said earnestly. "She's not a killer."

Jack tapped his sweater over his heart. "You might have a tough time convincing a jury of that. If we're going to play Let's Make a Deal, you'll need to bring something better to the table than someone shooting a cop."

Damien stared briefly at Jack, then his face hardened. "Something better — like severing a coke connection to Europe. That's what you're after, isn't it?"

"Yes, but not without the bodies behind it — and I'm not talking about the idiots at the bottom end."

Damien stared at Jack for a few seconds. "Yeah, all right. I'll give you what you want — our European connection."

"And the bodies to go along with it?"

"Four full-patch from our club and several high-level Europeans to boot. That, along with a metric ton of coke should be enough to satisfy you."

"Possibly," Jack said.

"Possibly?" Damien sounded contemptuous.

"My bosses would have to know," Jack replied. "If it were simply in exchange for letting Buck go, I know they'd go for it. But Vicki's matter will be viewed as more serious. What she did wasn't accidental. You might want to consider sweetening the pot as much as you can before I speak to them."

Damien shook his head. "If I give you more, then the club would figure it out. I'd rather risk they go to jail than what might happen to them if the finger got pointed in my direction."

"To them? You mean you," Jack stated.

"I don't care about myself," Damien replied. "We're under new management. I've a feeling that the new guy is … well, more vindictive than I'd be."

"You're talking about Pure E."

Damien nodded. "So what I'm offering is what you get."

"Hopefully the brass will go for it."

"Go for it? You're full of crap," Damien growled.

"What do you mean?"

"You won't even tell them about Vicki. You'll lay it all on Buck. Now that you've cooled off, you're hoping to save Secord her job."

"Maybe."

"So don't give me any bullshit about having to check with your bosses about Vicki. Do we have a deal or not?"

"Will I have the bodies in jail and dope in the locker before the weekend's over?"

Damien grimaced. "It'll be another five or six days before the players are in position for you to do that."

"I can hold off that long." Jack nodded. "There's one other thing I want to find out about."

"I told you, I'm not giving anything else up," Damien said firmly.

"This isn't about your club. At least, not directly. I'd like to know the details about any grow-ops that were ripped off within the last year or two."

"You interested in that homicide that took place on Bowen Island?" Damien asked. "Considering the bust in Dallas, you obviously know we had investment interests in it."

"I-HIT asked for my help," Jack said.

"We've been interested in finding out, too." Damien reached for his pants and began to pull them on. "I'd be willing to help you, but I don't know much about it. Besides the one on Bowen, last year we had two others ripped off."

"I'd like to know the details of who was running those so I can try to cross-match any names or phone numbers with the operation on Bowen Island."

"I don't know details like that," Damien replied. "If I were to ask, especially now that I'm retiring, it'd definitely arouse suspicion."

"I understand," Jack replied.

"I can tell you that one of the grow-ops ripped last year relocated to Aldergove. It was being run by a Vietnamese couple and was busted three months ago by your uniform people. As far as the other grow-op goes, it was relocated to Kelowna."

"Vietnamese tending the crop in Kelowna, as well?"

"No … and we looked for a connection there already. I was told that the guy running the Kelowna operation is white and had no connections whatsoever with any Vietnamese." Damien reached for a shirt and pulled it on. "Guess it's possible that more than one set of guys ripped us."

Jack nodded.

"So do you want to hear the details of our European investment or not?"

"Yes — we've got a deal," Jack said.

"Figured so." Damien began buttoning his shirt. He didn't speak.

"I'm ready to listen. Talk."

"I will, but …"

"But what?"

Damien sighed, his hands falling to his sides. "You've destroyed everything I've ever stood for. Don't get me wrong. I don't hate you. I know you're just doing your job, but turning on my own brothers, losing every dollar I've ever made after years of fighting to stay on top … well, I never thought it would end like this."

"At least you'll still have Vicki and Buck," Jack said.

Damien nodded. "Guess I should be thankful for that."

Chapter Thirty-Eight

It was noon and Jack and Laura were pulling into their office parking space when Jack received a phone call from U.S. Customs Special Agent John Adams.

"Well, you all were right about Lopez," Adams said as soon as Jack answered.

"John, sorry, I should've called you this morning," Jack replied. "Things got a little busy here. I sort of forgot about you."

"Forgot about me?" Adams asked. "I get up at four o' fucking clock in the morning and drive down to Chihuahua to park my ass outside Lopez's office and you forget about me? What were you doing? Sitting around drinking that olive soup of yours or out feeding your horse?"

Jack chuckled.

"You might be interested to know that at eleven this morning, Lopez hustled out of his office with two file boxes and stashed them in his trunk. Then he drove over to some little hole-in-the wall real estate office called Realty Rápido.

He came out with a guy and put the boxes in his trunk."

"Were you able to stay with the boxes?"

"Yup. Lopez took off and the other guy drove in the opposite direction. I followed him to a vacant house that's for sale. He carried the boxes inside, then left."

"Good going," Jack said.

"So right now I'm northbound and should be back in El Paso in about two hours. What do you want me to do with 'em when I get there?"

"You've got them?" Jack asked excitedly.

"Yeah, well, I'm not as smooth as you at opening doors. You never did teach me how to pick locks, but the sole of my shoe seemed to work okay. The place didn't have a stick of furniture in it, so it didn't take me long. Found 'em stashed in a cupboard."

"Did you get a chance to look at them?"

"No, I popped the lids when I found them, but kind of thought I shouldn't hang around. Besides, they're in Spanish. I speak a little but don't read it that well. When I get back, I'll have my wife go through them."

"How is Yolanda?"

"Doin' good. There's a lot of paper so it might take her a week or two."

"I'd be interested to find out the details. Considering how you got them, I couldn't use them in court, but I'd still like to know the details."

"You couldn't use 'em even if they were sent to your office anonymously?"

"I doubt it. Defence would start calling everyone to ask them about it. Wouldn't take long for them to get around to calling me."

"Might work down here. What with them dealin' with the West 12th Street gang, I could send them anonymously to our office in Dallas."

"If the evidence supports conspiracy charges down there, that'd be fantastic. Damien might get some real jail time compared to what he'd get here."

"I'll let you know once Yolanda reads them."

Jack passed on the information he'd received to Laura as they walked to their office. They hadn't arrived yet when Jack received another call. This time from Ed Gosling. After a quick introduction Gosling said, "I'm representing Mrs. Vicki Zabat and have just spoken to her husband. He didn't say much, but told me to call you."

"What can I do for you?"

"I've been told that serious charges against Mrs. Zabat are being held in abeyance pending the veracity of new information you've been provided?"

"That's correct. Do I need to emphasize the need for secrecy?" Jack asked.

"I'm fully cognizant of Mr. Zabat's reputation and realize the need to keep this between us. You may rest assured that I'll be keeping the file in my personal safe."

"Glad to hear that."

"I understand that the situation may be resolved next week. At that time I'd like to receive confirmation. If it turns out that charges are to proceed, I'd ask you to provide me with fair warning so that I may properly address the matter with my client."

"I promise I'll let you know," Jack said, before hanging up.

Jack and Laura then went directly to Rose's office. They found her tucking her glasses into her purse. "Back so soon?" she asked. "I was about to go for lunch. How are the searches going?"

"Great," Jack replied as he and Laura sat down. "We've heard from the BVI and they've seized all sorts of financial records and have put a freeze on the bank account. Turns out Vicki underestimated what was in there. The figure is closer to eighteen point seven million, not eighteen point four."

"Super!" Rose replied. "And here?"

"Cummings had all the records exactly like we were told," Jack replied. "There's little doubt that he'll be charged once everything is reviewed by the prosecutors." *If he lives that long.*

"That's great. What about the house?"

"Nothing ... with the exception of a crack pipe found inside a brass bedpost of what had been their daughter's room. She's apparently in rehab in Italy. The pipe has probably been there for years."

Rose looked quizzically at Jack. "Okay ... so out with it."

"Out with what?"

"You know what. How'd Damien handle it? Was he giving Vicki any hard looks?"

"Not at all," Jack replied. "If anything, he was protective of her. We did mention that we weren't in any hurry to search the lawyer's office in Mexico due to corruption."

"You think he bought that?" Rose said. "I would've thought he'd have been smart enough to realize you were trying to pin the blame on Lopez."

"I told you I wouldn't chance busting Damien if it put Vicki at undue risk," Jack said.

"Yes, I remember quite distinctly. You said that I needed to trust you."

"There's more." Jack was starting to feel uncomfortable with Rose's tone. "To save his son from going to jail, Damien finally decided to co-operate. He gave up their new connection in Europe."

"Are you serious?" asked Rose in amazement.

"Yes. Very."

"That's fantastic!"

"They've spent over a year setting it up and making inquiries with different European connections," Jack said, while taking out his notebook to look at what Damien had told him. "Their first shipment, which is a metric tonne of cocaine, is —"

"A metric tonne? Wow!"

"Yes, it's due to arrive on a sailboat next Wednesday or Thursday at a marina on the French island of Saint-Martin-de-Ré. It's a small island joined to the mainland of France by a bridge."

"Next Wednesday or Thursday ... I better jot this down." Rose removed her glasses from her purse and scribbled notes on a pad.

"Want the spelling?" Jack asked.

"No, phonetics is good enough for now. I'll get your report later, but I want to call Isaac and let him know. Continue."

"One full-patch Satans Wrath member from the Eastside chapter in Vancouver and one from their chapter in Bogotá will be on board. Meeting them when they arrive will be another Eastside Vancouver member, along with a member from the chapter in Holland. I've got all their names ... but it probably doesn't mean anything to you."

"Not really. Knowing they're full-patch is enough," Rose replied, not bothering to look up.

"Having four full-patch Satans Wrath there is a one-time thing to celebrate the inaugural voyage. After that, the plan is to turn over future shipments to prospects and other criminals."

"There must be more Europeans involved than the one biker from Holland," Rose said.

"There is," Jack replied. "I've got eight other names in my notebook. Representatives from Germany, France, Spain, Great Britain, and the Netherlands. Damien wasn't sure how many of them will actually be there when the boat arrives, but expects at least half of them will show up. As far as Satans Wrath goes, only the ones directly involved know the exact details."

"So he really put himself at risk by telling you."

"Enough Europeans know that we can deflect the heat there," Jack said. "Damien knows that and is okay with it."

"Good. Go on."

"He said that a few days before the boat arrives, everyone will be booking into the Hôtel de Toiras, which overlooks the marina."

Jack put his notebook back in his pocket, but waited until Rose finished writing. "That's about it," he said when she glanced up.

Rose put her pen down. "This is totally unexpected," she said. "I'm absolutely astounded that Damien rolled over — even if it was to save his son from jail." When neither Jack nor Laura replied, she leaned forward, clasping her hands on the desk. "Is there anything else that influenced his decision to talk?"

It's that tone again. She knows something. "Like what?"

Laura jumped in. "He knows he can't do anything with the charges that'll be brought against him from today. All his money, assets, home ... everything will be seized. None of that was part of the deal."

"Yes, the deal," Rose said. "Odd that you offered him that deal last weekend and he refused."

"Maybe he needed time to think it over," Laura suggested.

"Or today, was it including Vicki as part of that deal that convinced him?" Rose asked.

Jack was taken aback. *Crap. How'd she find out?* He and Laura exchanged glances.

"Cut the theatrics," Rose said. "The two of you've done terrific work. Don't spoil it now. Inspector Pollock called me earlier to give me an update." She focused on Jack. "He told me that Vicki had been arrested for assaulting you. I was told you weren't injured but that she'd been brought in and was meeting her lawyer."

"Oh, that." Jack brushed it off with a wave of his hand. "It was nothing. I had her arrested to shake Damien up."

"Nothing?" Rose raised an eyebrow. "I was told the lawyer was Edward Gosling. High-priced help — for nothing."

"I was checking a picture frame as a possible hiding spot for a computer flash stick. Turns out the picture was of considerable emotional value to Vicki. It was a photo of the daughter who'd died. She yelled at me and I dropped the picture and the glass broke. She reacted by giving me a pretty good shot in the chest."

"I see," Rose said.

"Laura grabbed her and calmed her down," Jack added.

"Is that how you saw it too, Laura?" Rose questioned. "Exactly as Jack said?"

"Absolutely," Laura replied, locking eyes with Rose in response to her intense scrutiny.

"So, yes, I guess you could say that Vicki was part of the deal," Jack said. "I told Damien that neither Vicki nor Buck would be charged. Provided, of course, that arrests and seizures are made in Europe as promised."

"If that happens, I'd say we got the best end of the deal." Rose looked satisfied.

"He also gave me some info on a couple of grow-ops that were ripped last year. He doesn't know much in the way of details, but said one the grow-ops relocated to Aldergrove and was busted by uniform three months ago. I'm going to get Laura to see if she can cross-match any names or numbers with I-HIT's investigation into Dwayne's murder. Maybe find a common link. While she's doing that, I'll get the ball rolling with Interpol to deal with the investigation in France and give them the names of the players involved."

"With the boat arriving in five or six days, it doesn't give us a lot of time," Rose noted. "I'll let Isaac know, but I'd like a full report on my desk by the end of the day."

"You'll have it," Jack promised.

"It's also Friday," Rose said, "which means by normal standards Ottawa won't even see your report before Monday. I'll ask Isaac to pull some strings."

"Good point. I'll get started on the report." Jack stood up to follow Laura out the door.

"Oh, Jack, there's one more thing," Rose said.

Jack paused in the doorway. "Yes?"

"About the bullet hole in your sweater ... directly over your heart. I'd agree with you when you said it was a pretty good shot — and obviously planned for."

Jack peered closely at his sweater. "Funny, it does look like a bullet hole. Come to think of it, I did see a moth fly out of my closet."

"Moths don't leave powder burns. I'd suggest that you don't try to get the force to pay for the damage. It might not bode well for your career."

"I, uh, don't know what to say." Jack felt like an idiot.

"I do," Rose said harshly. "If you pull a stunt like that again, I'll kick you in the nuts so hard you'll need a surgeon to retrieve them."

Chapter Thirty-Nine

"I agree with Rose on that," Laura said, as they walked down the hall. "Except I thought nuts swelled up if they were kicked. I was thinking you'd need a wheelbarrow to walk around with."

"Forget the wheelbarrow. I'm not going through that experience again." When they entered their own office he put his hand on Laura's shoulder, causing her to face him. "We've finally caught Damien!"

"I know." She smiled and squeezed his hand. "To heck with this, I feel like a hug. Maybe even dance a jig."

"The hug I'll do."

"After all these years, the loose ends are tied up," Jack murmured as they hugged. He then stepped back and spoke solemnly. "If I never catch another criminal, I'll still be content knowing we brought that monster to his knees."

"That's how I feel, too," Laura said. "Ever wonder how many murders he's been responsible for?"

"We'll never know. Sometimes I wish I wasn't an atheist."

"Why?"

"So I could fantasize that when he dies, he'll burn in hell."

"Speaking of murder, what about Cummings? Are we going to leave him hung out to dry?"

Jack frowned. "Tomorrow's the big day for Damien to step down and Buck to get his patch. Maybe the club will kill Cummings as a retirement gift for Damien."

"Should we warn him?"

"If we warn him and he tells Damien we did, wouldn't Damien clue in that the butt call was a set-up?"

"I don't think he would," Laura replied. "In Damien's mind Cummings is panicking. Damien might think it's a desperate attempt by Cummings to feel him out to try and get assurance that he doesn't suspect him. It could make Cummings look even guiltier."

"I think you're right. It will also make him look guilty if he flees."

"More added protection for Vicki," Laura noted.

Jack sat at his desk and called Cummings's office. I-POC were still there, but an investigator put Cummings on the phone and Jack identified himself.

"I'm not talking to anyone without the presence of my lawyer," Cummings said abruptly. "If you've something to say, I suggest —"

"I suggest you shut up and listen," Jack said. "I heard from a reliable source in Satans Wrath that you're being blamed for Damien's money being seized."

"Me? That's preposterous!"

"If you don't believe me give Damien a call and feel him out. You're a lawyer. You should be smart enough to sense what he thinks of you. I wouldn't recommend meeting him in person, though. They're calling in their hit team to take you out — and I'm not talking for dinner."

"I know I'll … I'll be charged, as well," Cummings stammered. "Why would they think that?"

"Possibly something either Lopez or Bentley said. As far as you being charged, the bikers think that's a ruse. They think your charges will either be withdrawn or that a deal will be struck where you don't go to jail. The thing is, it doesn't matter. You wouldn't be alive long enough for it to go to trial. Are you married and do you have children?"

"Married but no children."

"You could be murdered as soon as tonight or tomorrow."

"Tonight! Jesus. Then I … I need protection!"

"But not your wife? I suppose you have her insured for a bundle," Jack said.

"I meant her, too, of course."

"Let me think about this," Jack said sarcastically. "You want us to use up our budget to protect you, a criminal, from the ramifications of your own criminal activity. Yeah, right."

"You can't tell me this and not do something!" Cummings cried.

"If we did protect you it'd really look like you're working with the police. Not to mention these guys have long memories. If you did manage to stay alive until you were incarcerated they'd think you received a reduced sentence in exchange for your co-operation — and reduce your life accordingly."

"Then … then what should I do? I —"

"If it were me, I'd disappear immediately. Considering what you've stashed away for Damien all these years, I'm guessing you have a similar offshore account for yourself. This might be a good time to cash it in. I heard that property on Baffin Island is really cheap."

"Is this a ruse to find out if I have such an investment?" Cummings asked suspiciously.

"That's a really good question," Jack replied. "Maybe you should wait around for a few days to find out. Goodbye."

Laura's desk faced Jack's and she'd heard Jack's side of the conversation. When he hung up she asked, "So? Is he heading for Baffin Island?"

"I don't know. Remind me to read the obits next week to find out."

"I think you'd hear before that," Laura replied. "Most likely in an obscene phone call from Connie."

"Connie ... yes, that reminds me. Call Aldergove and find out what grow-op they busted. Then have them send a copy of every name and phone number they may have seized. After that, have I-HIT do the same with the file on Dwayne. See if there's a match. While you're doing that I'll prepare a report for Ottawa. I also need to do an informant-debriefing report. Isaac will want to know the details."

"Bet you never thought you'd be saying that," Laura said.

"Saying what?"

"Referring to Damien as your informant."

Jack felt taken back. "That asshole isn't ... well, I guess technically he is." He smiled grimly. "That, however, will be short-lived. If the boat is on time, by the end of next week he'll be finished."

"He's still an informant, though," Laura persisted. "Kind of like Dwayne technically was."

"Dwayne died being a hero. There's no similarity."

"Damien is risking his life to save Vicki, which isn't all that bad, either. He isn't doing it to save his own skin."

"Yes, he did it to save Vicki." Jack's smile widened. "That's what I think is hilarious. If only he knew."

Late that afternoon Jack had his report approved by the brass and forwarded to headquarters. Within minutes he received a call from the Interpol office in Ottawa. When it was finished he gave Laura a thumbs-up. "It pays to have Isaac involved. That was Ottawa. They've contacted Interpol in France and promised to contact me immediately with any updates."

"Wish we could be there for the takedown," Laura said. "It's going to be a long week sitting around here waiting for it to happen."

"I know how you feel, but I'm sure the police in Europe will be tripping over each other as it is. I also told Damien to contact me day or night with any updates. I want to be able to meet him face to face if need be."

"I understand that — but it'd be fun," Laura replied.

"It would be more fun to see the look on Pure E's face," Jack said. "This bust will be taking place within a week of when he takes over."

"He's going to be one unhappy camper."

Jack nodded. "How'd you make out with the grow-ops?"

"A member in Aldergrove scanned and sent me everything they had. The grow-op was in an apartment building and uniform busted it after the manager went in when water broke through the ceiling into the apartment below. All the names they sent me were Vietnamese. Lots of cell-phone numbers as well, but the majority weren't registered and are no longer in service. The few numbers that I could track down are also Vietnamese."

"No matches from Connie's file?"

"Nope. There weren't any Vietnamese names in her file."

"And no English names in the Aldergrove file," Jack said.

"No … well, there were a couple of names on a slip of paper, but it was the receipt from the store where they bought their hydroponics."

"What was the name of the store?"

"I've got it here," Laura said, scrolling down on her laptop. "Here it is … Aaron and Chuck's Hydroponics. Looks like it was rubber-stamped on the receipt. The payment was done in cash."

"Aaron and Chuck's Hydroponics," Jack repeated slowly. He took out his notebook and flipped back through the pages.

"Does that mean something to you?"

"When Larry called me a couple of days ago, he told me he was selling his boat and hydro equipment. I asked him where he bought the equipment — bingo!" Jack tapped his notebook and looked up. "Same place. Aaron and Chuck's Hydroponics."

Laura's face showed her excitement. "We've got the connection!"

"There are only a couple of hydroponic stores around, so it could be coincidental — but I was never one to believe in coincidences."

"Coming from you, that's funny."

"Aaron and Chuck's could be selling them the equipment, then somebody could be following them when they leave," Jack said.

"Or perhaps providing hands-on, expert advice," Laura suggested.

"Not with the bikers. Satans Wrath would've clued in to that one. My guess is the customers were followed — but in Larry's case that person or persons needed a boat."

"Larry probably made several trips to the store. Maybe they arranged to get one or simply rented it at the marina like we did."

"We'll find out," Jack said.

"Should we tell Connie?"

"Not yet."

Laura made a face.

"What's wrong? Connie gave us permission to stick our noses into this after King was killed."

"Only because she thinks King was responsible. Plus she knows the grow-ops are biker-controlled."

"I promised to sit back and let Connie solve it," Jack said. "I don't think she has. If Dwayne's killer is still out there I want him found. We'll talk to Rose, but I don't want to tell Connie about it until we get something to show we're on the right track."

"What do you have in mind?"

"One thing for certain. We won't be sitting on our asses waiting for a boat to arrive in France."

Chapter Forty

Rose agreed to Jack and Laura making an initial probe into Aaron and Chuck's Hydroponics provided that any positive results were immediately passed on to I-HIT.

Aaron and Chuck's Hydroponics was located in a small strip mall in North Vancouver and their website said it closed at 6:00 p.m., which was what time Jack and Laura were watching from the parking lot. Two men exited the store and one locked the door. He was tall and thin with a pockmarked face and short blond hair. His companion was stocky and ruddy-faced with a shaved head and a pot belly.

Moments later the taller man unlocked the door on a bright yellow Corvette Stingray and they both got in.

"Have my doubts they'd be following anyone in a car like that without being noticed," Jack remarked, pulling out to follow as the Corvette drove out of the lot.

"Maybe they have friends," Laura suggested. "Could delay the customer in the store and give whoever it is time to get here."

"Maybe. Run the plate and check for CR and warrants."

After deciding that there was too much static on the police radio, Laura phoned in the licence plate and asked for a criminal-record check and any outstanding warrants while Jack drove. Minutes later she wrote the details into her notebook, then hung up. "The registered owner is an Aaron Goldsmith. Thirty-six years old with four convictions for drug trafficking. His address is on Marine Drive."

"We're on Marine now," Jack said. "What's the number?"

"Suite one oh nine at —"

"Right here," Jack said, as the Corvette pulled into a driveway leading to the rear of the apartment building.

Jack parked out front and they watched to see if any lights came on in the suites. When none did, they drove behind the building and saw where the Corvette was parked. "Take a look," Jack said, indicating a red Corvette parked beside the yellow one. "Doesn't look like it's been driven for a while."

Laura wrote down the licence plate as Jack found an empty stall and parked. In moments she had the details. "Registered to Charles Atwood of the same address. He's thirty-seven years old and has one conviction for drug trafficking and three for driving under the influence. His licence is currently under suspension — but get this," she added, shaking her head.

"What?" Jack asked.

"He has one conviction for causing a disturbance and three for assault. Going by that fat little tummy and how short he is, the guy must be a masochist."

"Probably a classic case of small-man syndrome," Jack replied. "Likely manifested with his drinking. They figure they've nothing to lose by taking a swing at a bigger guy. If they get smacked back, they look like victims. If they get in a lucky hit and win, they think they're heroes."

"Wow ... how pathetic can you get," Laura said.

Jack gestured to the rear of the apartment complex. "There are a few lights on in the ground-floor units. I'm going for a walk. If the owner of this parking spot shows up, drive around and pick me up out front." He then got out, pulling his jacket collar up to his ears and keeping his head down, as he walked.

A moment later he returned to the car. "They're in the unit down at the end," he said. "I caught a glimpse of them through the living-room window. There are empty beer bottles and glasses all over the coffee table and a couple of cheap girly posters on the walls."

"Aren't all girly posters cheap?" Laura chided.

"By the looks of these guys, it's probably the best they can get." Jack took out his phone and punched in a number.

"Who you calling?" Laura asked.

"Tina Chan in Drug Section. According to the store's website, its open tomorrow, then closed Sunday and Monday. I'm going to see if she's available — add a little Asian heat to spice things up."

"Spice things up?" Laura repeated, sounding far from enthusiastic. She'd doubtless guessed what was coming next.

"I want her to act as a date for one of these guys," Jack said as he held his phone up to his ear.

"Right — for one of these guys."

Jack stared at her.

"Oh, man," Laura muttered.

"No answer," Jack said. He left a message, then looked at Laura. "I know how you must feel, but these guys may be the ones who murdered Dwayne."

"I know. Don't get me wrong. I'm not complaining. It's sort of like having a root canal. I may not like it, but I know it's necessary."

Jack smiled. "Will it make you feel better if you get first choice?"

"What? At shooting them?" Laura joked.

Jack's smile disappeared. "Let's find out if they're guilty first."

Chapter Forty-One

Jack and Laura worked Saturday in an attempt to link either Aaron or Chuck with renting or owning a boat. Their effort was futile. Tina Chan did return Jack's call. She was available to work undercover on Tuesday when the store reopened. In light of that Jack decided that they'd take Sunday off.

Jack was playing his usual weekly game of chess with his ten-year-old son on Sunday afternoon when he felt his phone vibrate. He glanced at the call display and saw that it was Cockerill. "Have to take this," he apologized. "It's an informant."

"That's okay, Dad," Mike shrugged. "I think you've only got four moves left, anyway."

Jack ignored his son's prediction and answered the phone.

"So, you're officially the party-pooper," were the first words out of Cockerill's mouth.

"Damien wasn't smiling at his retirement party last night?"

"Fuck, you really did a number on him. The only time he smiled was when Buck received his full patch."

"Did you get drunk?"

"Nah, I told ya' I quit drinking."

"Good. Anything else I should know?"

"There's some talk going around that you didn't have grounds to go on the property and take that video of Buck."

Perfect. Damien has already planted the seed.

"Any truth to that?" asked Cockerill.

"Hope not," Jack replied. "I'm still waiting to hear from the prosecutor. Guess someone being killed accidentally isn't high up on their priority list. Anything else going on?"

"Not really. Pure E said he wants to have all the B.C. chapters get together next Wednesday or Thursday for a talk, but that's about it. Rumour is that some of the guys from Alberta might show up, too."

To celebrate when the boat arrives in France, which Cockerill doesn't know about yet. "He could have done that last night," Jack said, not wanting Cockerill to ever know he already knew the real reason.

"Guess he didn't want to steal the show away from Damien. Mind you, you already did that."

Pure E steal the show? More likely he plans to announce that their ship has come in — literally — and grandstand for the credit.

"I expect things are going to be different," Cockerill added.

"Oh, yeah?"

"Pure E is concerned about our image. He feels we've been too laid back and that we don't have the respect we once had. Says that's why punks are moving into our space an' why some people are no longer afraid to rat us out."

"Speaking of that, is there anything new on Neal?"

"Haven't heard anything. As far as I know, he's still being taken out the day Pure E meets with us. If I hear somethin' different, I'll call ya."

"You do that."

Jack hung up and turned his attention back to the chessboard. He made four more moves and was checkmated.

"Another game, Dad?" Mike asked.

"No, losing three in a row is enough. Time to restore my shattered ego on the pool table with your brother."

"Everything okay at work?" Mike asked, looking concerned.

Jack smiled to himself. He was so evenly paired with his sons at chess and pool that it was rare that any of them lost three in a row. When his sons did, he knew something else was on their minds and they'd talk about it. Now the shoe was on the other foot. "Sorry if my mind wasn't on the game. I've been thinking about a couple of bad guys I want to catch." He winked. "At least, that's my excuse."

"That's okay. Maybe next Sunday."

Sunday night after the boys had gone to bed, Natasha snuggled up with Jack on the sofa, then made eye contact. "The boys are worried about you."

"About me? Why?"

"They came to me after they got ready for bed. It was kind of cute. They both had such serious looks on their faces. Steve said he beat you three out of three in pool and Mike said he did the same in chess. They're worried that you're doing something dangerous."

"They're great kids. Pretty perceptive."

"*Are* you doing something dangerous? You told me you nailed Damien hard. Are you worried that he might —"

"No. Not at all. Damien has other things on his mind besides me. I'm distracted because I may have a possible lead on who killed Dwayne."

"The mentally challenged man who —"

"Yes, him. I've got a couple of suspects and will be doing a UC — but it's nothing dangerous."

"Right, undercover's not dangerous," Natasha said skeptically. "You're saying that even though they may have murdered a man less than two weeks ago."

"They'll find dealing with me a little different." Jack looked at her. "I'm not like Dwayne. That poor guy couldn't even tie his own shoelaces."

"You do realize, don't you, that you wear slip-on shoes yourself?"

Jack was about to protest, but Natasha kissed him, muffling his response.

Jack and Laura spent Monday morning in the office. At noon Jack received a call from Ottawa confirming that European investigators had converged on the Hôtel de Toiras in Saint-Martin-de-Ré, France. It was confirmed that a Satans Wrath member from Vancouver and one from Holland had each reserved a room. Electronic listening devices were planted in both rooms shortly before the bikers checked in.

Jack felt triumphant as he relayed the news to Laura and Rose. "Right now the two of them are drinking in a nearby bar. France is nine hours ahead of us, so it's evening there."

"It confirms what you were told," Rose said. "What now?"

"Nothing for us to do but wait," Jack replied. "While we're doing that, Laura and I are going to see what Aaron and Chuck are up to."

"If there's any indication they're involved in Dwayne's murder, I want I-HIT informed immediately," Rose insisted.

"Of course." Jack's phone vibrated and he glanced at the call display. "Dave Cash from I-POC. I better take it. He was in charge of the search at Damien's on Friday."

"Or thought he was in charge," Rose said dryly. "I heard that he and his team were waiting outside the house when you were allegedly attacked by Vicki."

Jack ignored her. "What's up, Dave?"

"I heard you called Cummings on Friday to warn him that the bikers might blame him for what happened."

"Yes, I had the impression that Damien was suspicious about Cummings. For me it's good news because the real informant is safe, but I still thought I should warn him."

"What did Damien say that made you think he was blaming him?"

"Damien isn't the type to advertise what he's thinking, but the look on his face when Cummings's name was mentioned said it all. Very few people knew about his hidden bank accounts. When it comes to blaming someone, I think Damien put Cummings at the top of the list. Even if Cummings is charged, the bikers might think a deal was struck. I felt it morally right that I should warn him."

"Morally right?" Rose mouthed.

"Both he and his wife have disappeared," Dave said.

"Are you thinking that he and his wife have both been murdered?" Jack saw Rose glare at him. *Shouldn't have worded it that way.*

"No, whatever you said must have scared the hell out of him," Dave replied. "We pulled his credit-card receipts. They checked into a hotel Friday night and bought tickets to fly to Indonesia on Saturday. I'm waiting to hear back from Airport Special Squad to confirm, but I feel confident that they're gone."

"So he's alive but on the run," Jack said, more for Rose's benefit.

"Yes."

"I thought you guys would've seized his passport."

"We never found it. This morning we discovered he had a safety deposit box that we didn't know about. He was into it Saturday before they left."

"There's no extradition in Indonesia," Jack noted.

"His house, their cars … all left behind," Dave said.

"Guess he figured his life was worth more. Perhaps my hunch that Damien suspected him was right. Cummings must have thought the same thing."

"Well, if you hear anything from your sources about him, please let us know."

"Will do," Jack replied.

"Your hunch that Damien suspected him?" Rose asked the second he disconnected. "What did you say to him?"

"Who?"

"Cummings!"

"I called him on Friday to warn him that Damien suspected him of being the informant. I guess he listened to me, because credit-card receipts indicate that he and his wife fled to Indonesia on Saturday."

"You said or did something to make Damien suspect him, didn't you?"

Jack nodded. "I thought it better for Damien to suspect him, rather than Vicki."

"Which is why you were certain Vicki would be safe when you first told me about the bank accounts. You knew then what were you going to do?"

"It's basic psychology," Jack replied. "If a tragedy befell you like it did Damien, who'd you rather suspect was responsible? Your spouse or some lawyer? I simply thought it prudent to warn Cummings that he might be under a certain degree of suspicion for —"

"And you felt it morally right to warn him!" Rose said.

"I'm sorry," Jack said. "You're right. Cummings is a degenerate — even by defence lawyer standards. I was probably wrong to warn him. You're right to be angry with me."

Rose looked dumbfounded. "I'm not angry about your warning him!"

Jack glanced a Laura and winked.

Rose spotted it. "You might find this funny, but I don't! How funny do you think you'll find it when you're kicking your Stetson up the Trans-Canada to Chilliwack Freeway Patrol?"

Jack sighed. "Okay … you're upset because you think I didn't trust you."

"I'm *very* upset."

"It's not that I don't trust you," Jack said.

"Then you were protecting me from knowing — which means that whatever you did was wrong. Same as your bullshit attempt to tell me a moth was eating your sweater."

"That was different. At worst I could be judged as having taken a foolish risk. Cummings is more what I'd call a grey area."

"How grey?"

"Damien overheard what he thought was a butt call."

"A butt call condemning Cummings," Rose said flatly.

Jack nodded.

Rose briefly closed her eyes while she pinched the bridge of her nose. "I would've gone along with it," she said quietly. "You should've told me."

"I'm sorry," Jack said. "I felt like my very existence — my sole purpose as a police officer — was to catch Damien. I didn't want to chance anything going wrong. If I never make another arrest, I'll be content with the knowledge that he's truly finished."

Rose gazed silently at Jack, then gripped his shoulder to emphasize what she was about to say. "Promise me you'll never hold out on me regarding stuff like that again."

Jack met her gaze solemnly. "I promise," he said, honestly believing he was telling the truth.

Chapter Forty-Two

It was early afternoon on Tuesday when Jack, driving a Mercedes with a rental sticker on the bumper, parked in front of Aaron and Chuck's Hydroponics and went inside. Laura and Tina remained in the car, but could see him through the store's large glass windows.

A small bell over the door announced his entrance and Chuck appeared from down an aisle. "May I help you?"

"How you all doin'?" Jack replied, glancing around the store. There were no other customers. He saw Aaron at the end of another aisle holding a clipboard and checking inventory.

"Doing fine, thanks," Chuck replied. "And you?"

Jack paused to turn and give a friendly wave to Laura and Tina. "We're doing great! Love it up here. More beautiful than California. A little cooler, but man, those mountains are fantastic."

"What can I do for you?"

Jack made a point of looking around the store as if to

ensure they were alone, then lowered his voice. "I know you sell hydroponics."

"Yes," Chuck replied, gesturing at the aisles. "Nothing wrong or secret about that."

"Well, the thing is, B.C. has a reputation for growing the best, uh —" Jack raised his hand to his lips, the thumb and forefinger pinched together to simulate smoking marijuana "— you know, tomatoes. I'm hoping you could put me in touch with someone who, uh, grows tomatoes. My brother lives in Alaska and I'd like to bring him two hundred pounds. Or I guess you call it metric up here. Whatever two hundred pounds is in metric."

"I'm sorry," Chuck replied. "I don't understand why you came here. Maybe try a grocery store. We only sell the equipment for growing plants. What people grow is none of our business."

Jack scratched his head, pretending to ponder the situation as he gawked at the items on the shelves. Then he gestured toward Aaron. "What about him? Think maybe he could help me?"

"No, I really doubt that —"

"Yo, big brother!" Laura called as she and Tina entered the store. Both wore skin-tight jeans, high heels, and open windbreakers that revealed low-cut blouses stretched tightly across ample cleavage.

Jack saw Chuck glance at the women. *Perfect. You suddenly became a mouth breather.*

Laura approached Jack. "We didn't come all the way to Canada to spend the day sitting in a car. You promised you'd take us someplace where we could meet some guys and party."

"There's lots of time," Jack replied. "It's still early."

"Yeah, but we want to shop for some clothes first. Can't this business stuff wait until tomorrow?"

Tina didn't appear interested in the conversation and she smiled at Chuck. He was quick to smile back.

"Yeah … okay," said Jack. "I'll take you shopping in a minute. Wait here a moment." He looked at Chuck. "Can I speak to you in private, maybe in back?" He set off in that direction.

Chuck followed Jack halfway down an aisle, where Jack stopped, before giving a nod toward Aaron at the end of the aisle. "I'll talk to him in a moment and see if he can send me someplace other than a grocery store, but first I want to ask you something."

"What?"

"I don't know Vancouver too well. Is there any place you can recommend where I can take my sister and her friend out tonight? Tina is celebrating her divorce and my sister broke up with her boyfriend last week. Both of 'em want to cut loose and go someplace where they can meet a couple of guys."

Chuck glanced toward the front of the store and Tina gave him another smile. He turned to Jack. "Actually my friend and I are single."

"You are?" Jack replied, sounding surprised. "I don't suppose … I know it's a lot to ask … especially at last moment like this, but would you mind being dates for the girls tonight? I'd pay the shot … dinner and all."

Chuck looked like he'd won a lottery. "Give me a minute to talk to my buddy."

"If you're too busy —"

"No. Maybe ... maybe we could help you out on that other thing, too," Chuck said anxiously. "Wait here a sec."

Jack watched as Chuck went and whispered to Aaron. As they talked Aaron made several furtive glances in Laura's and Tina's direction. Chuck then took out his phone and placed a call while Aaron approached Jack.

"My name's Aaron," he said, sticking out his hand.

Jack shook it. "My friends call me JB."

"Where you from?"

"California," Jack replied.

"Don't they grow tomatoes down there?"

"Not as good as B.C.," Jack said. "Plus bringing them across the border into Canada and then back into the States is a risk. Besides, I used to deal with a guy up here before and I'm already set up when it comes to paying."

"Set up?"

"My sister already has a bank account and safety deposit box in Vancouver. I prefer to pay by having her hand the money over in the bank at the same time I receive the goods elsewhere. Once I'm clear, then whoever Laura is meeting leaves the bank."

"To prevent rips."

"You got it. In the end I trusted my other source enough that we didn't bother with the bank. The problem is he got married and his wife made him quit. He did give me the name of a guy who lives in another city, but it'd be a nuisance to go there. I'd rather do business in Vancouver if I could."

Aaron nodded. The sound of Laura and Tina giggling distracted him and he saw Laura adjusting Tina's long black hair. "Wait a minute, I gotta get something from the till."

Aaron ambled to the front of the store and opened the cash register. While he rummaged around he glanced at Laura and Tina, who smiled at him. He then returned to where Jack stood.

"Do you think you'll be able to help me out?" Jack asked. He glanced at Laura and Tina. "With the tomatoes, I mean, not my sister and her friend."

Aaron grinned. "There's a guy we know who, uh, might be able to help you out. Chuck is trying to reach him." He gestured as Chuck approached.

"How did you make out?" asked Jack.

Chuck shook his head. "I phoned around but couldn't reach the guy, so I ended up leaving him a message on his voice mail."

"I really appreciate the effort," Jack said. He then introduced himself to Chuck as JB before adding, "If it works out, tell him I'd like to do a similar run every couple of months."

"I'll let 'im know," Chuck replied. "We've got coffee on in the back. Do you want a cup and see if he calls back in the next half-hour?"

Jack smiled. "That'd be great."

"You mentioned your sister and her friend are looking to party," Chuck said.

"Yes." Jack glanced toward the front of the store.

"Aaron and I know this city like the back of our hands. We'd be glad to show them around." He looked at Aaron. "Wouldn't we?"

"Sure, I happen to be free tonight," Aaron said nonchalantly.

Asshole. I'm sure you're free every night. "Give me a moment to check with the girls and make sure they, uh, haven't changed their minds. Like I said, if they're up for it, dinner's on me tonight."

Aaron's and Chuck's faces were each the picture of hope as Jack went to the front of the store. He whispered to Laura and Tina, who gave an enthusiastic response. Jack gave Aaron and Chuck a thumbs-up and they beamed.

Introductions were made and moments later, everyone settled around a plastic patio table in the back room while Chuck busied himself making a fresh pot of coffee.

"Where are you staying?" Aaron asked Jack.

"At the Pan Pacific. Room five oh six. Laura and Tina have their own room down the hall from me."

"Posh hotel," Chuck said, glancing at Aaron.

"The hotel recommended a Italian restaurant on Robson Street called CinCin," Jack told him. "How about we meet for dinner at eight o'clock, then go from there?"

"Sounds great!" Chuck replied enthusiastically.

"I've also picked up a cellphone," Jack said. "I'll give you the number in case something comes up and you can't make it. If you don't reach me on the cell, phone my room. You can also pass it on to whoever you called."

Aaron retrieved a pen and piece of paper.

"We can't make you any promises," Chuck said as Aaron wrote the number down.

"I understand. I appreciate you trying."

"So where in California are you guys from?" asked Aaron.

"Santa Rosa," Jack replied. "It's about an hour north of Frisco."

"I've been to San Francisco several times," Aaron said. "My sister lives there and is married to one of your countrymen."

"Great place to visit," Jack said, secretly glad that he'd done his homework. "Easy drive to the Napa Valley if you like wine."

Over the next hour the conversation centred on climate and sightseeing in northern California. Jack felt he was able to handle the conversation without arousing any suspicion from Aaron.

During that time, Jack noted that Aaron and Chuck took turns going to the front of the store. *Business is slow — but not so slow that they can't each drive a Corvette Stingray.* Eventually Jack made a pretence of looking at his watch, then raised an eyebrow in Chuck's direction.

"This guy is sometimes hard to get hold of," Chuck said. "Bad cell connections where he hangs out. Hopefully I'll know by eight tonight."

"We wanna go shopping," Laura pouted.

Aaron and Chuck walked outside the store with them and as they climbed back into the Mercedes, they called out, "See you at eight!"

"That went as well as could be expected," Jack said as he backed out of the slot.

"Don't even think about inviting them back to the hotel tonight," Tina warned.

"Ditto on that," Laura added, giving a friendly wave to Chuck and Aaron as they drove away.

Aaron and Chuck went back into the store and Aaron opened a laptop computer. They both stared at the screen.

"The tracker's working well," Chuck noted.

Chapter Forty-Three

Aaron and Chuck entered CinCin on time and joined Jack, Laura, and Tina, who were seated on an patio overlooking the street one storey below. It was a romantic setting and outdoor heaters took away the coolness of the late-September air.

After greeting everyone and sitting down, Chuck looked at Jack. "I still haven't heard back from that guy. Maybe later tonight I will."

"No problem," Jack said. "Would you guys like a drink?"

"You bet I would," Chuck said, his ruddy face eager. He scanned the table to see what Jack, Laura, and Tina were drinking.

"I'm having olive soup," Jack told him.

"Olive soup?"

"A martini," Aaron explained, giving Chuck an annoyed glance.

"Oh, yeah. Olive soup. That's a good one. What's in a martini?"

"Gin and vermouth," Jack replied. "These days people make them all sorts of ways, but I like mine with gin, vermouth, and three olives."

"I'm having something they call an Autumn's Kiss," Laura said. She smiled at Aaron. "It's really good. Not sure what's in it. I think they said pear and ginger vodka, along with cinnamon syrup and lemon." She glanced at Tina beside her. "You really should try one. Maybe it'd make you feel better."

"I better stick to the soda," Tina replied.

"Something wrong?" Chuck asked. He gawked at her and breathed through his mouth, which was open wide enough to hold a baseball.

Tina grimaced and moved slightly in her seat as if in pain. "I started getting cramps and feeling feverish late this afternoon when we were shopping. I had a glass of water about an hour ago and thought I was going to lose it. Maybe the nausea'll go away in a while."

"Airports and airplanes," Laura said. "Packed with all those people from everywhere on the planet. Who knows what bug you might have caught."

"I'll be okay," Tine replied. "I'm counting on having fun tonight. I'm sure if I take it easy for a bit I'll be okay."

"Hope so," Chuck said.

"I'm ordering a bottle of wine," Jack said. "As much as I love my olive soup, they're kind of strong."

"Yeah — wine, that's what I'll have," Chuck said.

Aaron nodded in agreement and Jack ordered a bottle of Pinot Noir, Kettle Valley Reserve from the Okanagan Valley. Everyone then ordered an appetizer of wild-mushroom-and-chestnut soup with mushroom crostini, to be followed by the main course.

It was the most delicious soup Jack had ever tasted and it paired well with the wine. He gazed across the table at Tina. She'd lost the coin-flip to Laura and was toying with her soup. *Too bad you have to pretend to be sick. The food is fantastic. Note to self — bring Natasha here someday.*

While waiting for their entrees, Aaron smiled at Laura. "So you're heading up to see your brother in Alaska?"

"Actually he flies a seaplane, so — Ouch!" Noise under the table indicated that she'd been kicked. She made a face at Jack.

"They call it family business because it's supposed to stay in the family," Jack warned.

Aaron and Chuck gave each other a knowing look.

"I guess I'm not supposed to talk about my other brother," Laura said. "Too bad, 'cause he's the nice one."

After an uncomfortable silence Jack said, "How about I order another bottle of wine?"

"I'm all for that," Chuck said.

When the entrees arrived, Jack was pleased with his choice. Like Aaron and Chuck, he'd ordered steak and it was perfectly done. Tina waited until Laura had finished her halibut before excusing herself to go to the washroom, leaving her own plate of roast chicken only half eaten.

Ten minutes later Laura expressed her concern and went to check on her. When she returned she said, "She's in there being sick. I'm going to take her back to the hotel."

Disappointment was evident on Chuck's face.

"Are you coming back after?" Aaron asked hopefully.

Laura shook her head. "Sorry, no, I think I should stay with her." With a nod toward Jack she added, "If things work out, we'll be coming up here every couple of months."

"We don't know yet, Laura," Jack said. "They're still waiting to hear back from someone."

Laura gave Aaron and Chuck an apologetic smile. "I sure hope it works out and that you give us another chance. I know Tina feels really bad, too."

"How long do you plan on staying in Vancouver?" Aaron asked.

"Let's see what tomorrow brings," Jack replied. "I was given the name of someone else that I can talk to — but he lives in Penticton. Vancouver would be more convenient, but I guess that's life. If I have to go elsewhere, I will."

After Laura and Tina left, Jack enjoyed a milk-chocolate mousse with chocolate-almond crunch, roasted almond, and dark chocolate. *Yes, I'll definitely be bringing Natasha here.* He glanced across the table at Aaron and Chuck. *Am I wasting my time with these goofs? Even if they do connect me to someone, who's to say any of them had anything to do with Dwayne's murder?*

Chuck drained the heel of another bottle of Pinot Noir into his glass, then looked at Jack questioningly.

"Sure, why not?" Jack said and gestured to the waiter. *Laura and Tina had the easy job. I'm stuck with these two.*

It was 11:00 p.m. when Jack said that he was calling it a night. He paid the tab and they descended the stairs to the street.

Chuck's voice was slurred and he swayed on his feet as they stood on the sidewalk to say goodbye. "I'll call ya tomorrow. Don't know why that guy hasn't called back yet. Betcha he does in the morning."

"Whatever. You've got my number," Jack said.

Aaron had stayed relatively sober during the evening. "Thanks for a great meal. Hopefully we can do it again. Next time we'll pay."

"Yeah, the food was great," Chuck said. "Too bad Trina and Laurie missed out."

"It's Tina and Laura," Aaron corrected him.

"Really?" Chuck looked surprised. "Anyway, JB, call ya tomorrow."

"Either that or I'll drop by the store," Jack suggested. "Speaking of which, hope you guys don't have headaches when you open in the morning."

"I'll be okay," Aaron said.

"Me, too," Chuck said. He giggled, gesturing with his hands apart like he was telling a fishing story. "I only drank this much!" He staggered backward.

One of four men passing by behind was bumped and Chuck flailed his arms to maintain his balance. By the looks of the men, they could easily pass for professional football players, Jack thought.

"Hey, careful there, little buddy," the man said.

"Who ya calling little?" Chuck shouted. "Ya big dumb ape!"

Jack grabbed Chuck by the upper arm. "My apologies, gentlemen. His girl left him tonight and now he's had too much to drink. I'll deal with him."

"No worries," the man replied and continued on his way.

"Those guys were huge," Jack said as he let go of Chuck's arm. "They could have turned us all inside out if they wanted."

"Fuck, I don't care!" Chuck looked at Aaron. "Ya hear that guy diss me?"

"I heard everything," Aaron stated. "You're drunk. Let it go." He looked at Jack. "Good night, JB, and thanks again."

"Good night, guys," Jack replied.

Aaron gestured for Chuck to follow him and headed down the sidewalk.

Chuck paused, scowling in the direction of the man he'd bumped. "That's one fucker I'd enjoy seeing gut-shot and capped in the skull," he muttered.

Chapter Forty-Four

Jack knocked on Laura's and Tina's hotel-room door. As he waited Dwayne's last sobbing words replayed in his mind. *He shot me, Officer Taggart … in my tummy. I'm going to die, aren't I?* The sound of the second gunshot echoed in his mind. His body jerked when Laura opened the door at the same time.

He saw Laura glance down the hall. "No, I didn't invite them back. I need to make some notes and write down something Chuck said. When I'm done I'll be back and making us all a martini."

"Celebratory?" asked Laura.

"Chuck was there when Dwayne was murdered."

Laura looked at Jack in surprise.

"I'll explain when I come back. Give me twenty minutes."

Laura understood the need for Jack to write down as much conversation as he could recall as soon as possible. Every minute of delay was ammunition for a defence lawyer to say the notes weren't accurate. She glanced over her shoulder. "I'll get Tina out of her sickbed and explain the olive-soup tradition. Hurry, I can't wait to hear."

Laura and Tina listened raptly as he, busy preparing the martinis, described how the evening had gone. When he reached the part where Chuck staggered into a man on the sidewalk, he paused and handed them their glasses.

"What do you think?" he asked Tina with a nod at her drink.

Tina took a sip. "Not as bad as I expected."

"That's what I thought the first time," Laura said. "Jack told me they were an acquired taste. Work with him and they tend to grow on you — perhaps out of need, I'm not sure."

Tina smiled, then looked at Jack. "So? Come on! Don't keep us hanging here. What happened? Did the little fart get his ass kicked? What makes you think he was there when the murder happened?"

"Unfortunately he didn't get his ass kicked," Jack replied, reaching for his notebook. "But when the guy walked away, Chuck said, and I quote, 'That's one fucker I'd enjoy seeing gut-shot and capped in the skull.'"

Laura and Tina looked at each other in shock.

"He said he'd like to see the guy gut-shot, which Dwayne was, before he was likely 'capped in the skull,'" Jack said. "To me that indicates Chuck was there but didn't do it himself. Otherwise he'd have said, 'I'd like to gut-shoot him.'"

"You think maybe Aaron did it?" Tina asked.

"Whoever did it had a boat," Jack said. "It's possible it was Aaron, but so far we haven't connected either one to a boat. "Dwayne told me there were three guys. I'm thinking whoever pulled the trigger was someone else. But I bet Chuck and Aaron were both there."

"How'd Aaron respond to Chuck saying that?" Laura asked.

"He was walking away at the time. Chuck muttered the words, so I don't think Aaron heard him."

"Muttered, eh?" Tina said. "Meaning, Defence will say you didn't really hear what he said, either."

"Exactly," Laura agreed. "A defence lawyer could convince a jury that Chuck said something along the lines of 'The guy with the big gut who shot his yap off is someone I'd like to slap on the skull.' Then it would be intimated that you either lied or just hadn't heard properly."

"Only takes one in the jury to believe the Defence version," Tina noted.

"It doesn't matter," Jack replied. "We'll continue the UC until we get all the details."

"Hopefully we'll find out who the third man is soon." Tina glanced at Laura. "What a fun job. I get to date a drunken little bald guy who likes to pick fights — although your sweetie isn't any better."

"Yes, who knew that working UC could be so glamorous," Laura said. She looked at Jack. "So what's next?"

"We'll stay here tonight. If I don't hear back from them in the morning, I'll drop by their store around noon and put a little pressure on them. I'll say you both feel bad for bailing on them. Then I'll talk business and threaten to go elsewhere if they don't get their act together soon. I think they'll do their best to accommodate me."

"Hope they do it fast," Tina said. "If I have to see them again, I won't be pretending to be sick."

It was 2:00 a.m. when the three of them decided to call it a night. Jack was heading for the door when he received a call from the Interpol office in Ottawa.

After hanging up, he smiled at Laura and Tina. "Six major European players arrived at the Hôtel de Toiras in Saint-Martin-de-Ré. Investigators managed to pick up conversation between three of them, along with both Satans Wrath members. The boat is expected to arrive at about ten o'clock tonight their time, which will be one o'clock this afternoon for us."

"Eleven hours from now," Laura noted. "Any mention of the cocaine?"

"Not specifically, but plans were discussed to unload the boat at six the following morning — which would be nine tonight here."

Laura looked reflective. "Even if we're stuck dating Goofus One and Two at that time, I'll still be smiling."

"Likewise," Tina said. "A metric ton ... what do you think it's worth?"

"Once it's seized, I'd say it's worth about four martinis each," Jack replied.

The bed was one of the most comfortable Jack had slept on, but the first half-hour passed with him fretting about the investigation in France. When he finally put that to rest, the events of the evening, along with Dwayne's cries for help, replayed in his mind.

It was 3:30 a.m. when his thoughts returned to having coffee with Aaron and Chuck in the backroom of their store.

He recalled Chuck going to the front, ostensibly to look after a customer. *Funny. I remember thinking I never heard the bell over the door — but heard it twice before he returned.*

"Son of a bitch, I'm stupid!" He sat bolt upright in bed.

Ten minutes later he crawled under his rented Mercedes and spotted the tracker. He cursed himself for not thinking to look earlier. He'd thought because Chuck had been unable to contact whoever he was trying to reach, taking that precaution wouldn't be necessary.

He gave a grim smile as he stared at the tracker. *Thanks for the confirmation, assholes. You think you're tracking me? Better look behind you. I'm on your trail — and the end is near.*

Chapter Forty-Five

Jack left the tracker where it was and returned to bed, but sleep eluded him for the better part of two hours. It was 5:30 a.m. when he finally drifted off to sleep.

Two hours later, he was awakened by an incoming call on his regular phone, which he had left on the bedside dresser beside the cellphone he had purchased for the UC.

"I've got an update," a man said, not bothering to say hello.

Jack recognized Damien's voice. "I'm listening."

"The boat is due to arrive before midnight Wednesday their time. Unloading is to take place at six the next morning."

"You sure?" Jack asked, not wanting to disclose that he already knew.

"I'm sure. Pure E is calling a meeting with everyone for tonight, including some from Alberta. He's gathering the executive members at nine o'clock to tell them. With the time difference, that'll be when the first shipment hits the docks. He wanted to know if I was coming."

"Are you?"

"My presence would put a damper on the party." With that, Damien hung up.

Jack managed to go back to sleep, but at ten past nine his regular phone vibrated again. The call display blocked the details of the caller, but he answered with a sleepy hello.

"Jack, are *you* still in bed?" His caller was a woman.

"As a matter of fact I am," he replied, trying to put a name to the voice.

"At the Pan Pacific Hotel?" she asked.

"Uh … yes."

Jack heard her speak to someone in the background and say, "Yup, it was Jack." She turned back to the phone. "Still in bed … tsk, tsk. Too many olive soups, I bet."

"Who is this?" Jack asked.

"You don't even recognize my voice? Typical man," she said. "Last time I had olive soup with you was in a hotel room in Edmonton. After that you never called. You never wrote. Bet you found some other girls — like Laura and Tina — to keep you company."

"Vivian Mah!" Jack smiled. Vivian was a civilian member who worked in Victoria, where she was responsible for monitoring wiretaps. They'd worked on a joint project years earlier that had taken a group of them to Edmonton for a court case. It was there that he'd introduced several of them to his olive soup. "How've you been?" he asked.

"Good. Same old, same old. "And you? How are Natasha and the boys?"

"Good. We're all good. I presume Rose told you I was here."

"Rose?"

"My boss. Rose Wood."

"No, it wasn't her," Vivian replied. "I monitored some conversation this morning about some hotshot by the name of JB who drinks what he calls olive soup, stays at the Pan Pacific, and has a good-looking sister whose friend is Asian. I had a hunch it'd be you."

Jack immediately swung his feet over the side of the bed. "You got Chuck or Aaron on wire?" he asked.

"It was a Chuck who called initially," Vivian replied. "We don't have him identified any more than that. That call came in at one-thirty yesterday afternoon."

"His name's Charles Atwood."

"Atwood … okay. Then another call came in last night at eleven-thirty from a different guy saying they'd had a great dinner and that Chuck was drunk."

"That'd be Chuck's partner. His name's Aaron Goldsmith. I'll give you the pertinent details in a moment. Who were they calling?"

"Our primary target. A fellow by the name of Todd Doringer who a source says is running B.C. bud down to the States."

"I don't imagine you'd know if the source is in tight with him, would you?" Jack asked.

"The investigator who got the wiretap is in court at the moment, but from what I heard, the source is connected to someone Doringer sells to and not to him directly."

"Too bad."

"Do you want to hear the calls?" Vivian asked.

"Give me the gist of them now. That'll be faster. I don't know when the bad guys will be calling me and want to be prepared. I'll listen to the calls and make notes later."

"Okay. There isn't much. We only got Doringer hooked up yesterday morning." Vivian snickered. "I think it's pretty funny that the first call we get would involve you. The investigators will be happy. You've made the wire positive right off the bat."

"Peaks and valleys," Jack said. "Sounds like I hit a peak. What's interesting is yesterday afternoon I was with Chuck at one-thirty. I was trying to score and he said he'd call someone. I saw him use his phone, but he told me he couldn't reach the guy and left a message."

"He lied," Vivian said. "Chuck told Doringer that he met an American who was looking to buy two king salmon."

"Make that two hundred pounds of marijuana," Jack said brusquely.

"Sort of what we figured. He said he —"

"Vivian," Jack interrupted, "interesting he uses a code like that. Does Doringer have access to a boat?"

"More than access," Vivian replied. "He lives on a boat."

Jack found himself staring at his knuckles. They had turned white as he gripped the phone. He didn't know if he was going to let loose a tear or scream with delight.

"It's old ... about a fifty-footer with a wooden hull," Vivian continued. "He's an ex-navy guy and calls it *Awol.*" She waited for Jack to respond, then asked, "Why? Is that important?" There was still no response. "Jack? Are you there?"

Jack took a deep breath, slowly exhaled. "Yes ... yes, I'm here."

"I asked if Doringer having a boat was important?"

"Important? Viv, I could kiss you right now."

"Why? I mean, other than the fact that I'm sexy and used to men throwing themselves at me."

Normally Jack would've joked back, but an unwanted flashback to Dwayne's dying moments precluded any joviality. "I didn't approach Chuck and his partner to catch them dealing dope," he said. "They're suspects in the murder ... the murder of ..."

"Sorry, I didn't hear," Vivian said. "Who was murdered?"

Jack swallowed. "An informant of mine. He was looking after a grow-op on Bowen Island when three guys did a rip. He was on the phone to me when it was happening. I heard the shots and ... it was, uh ... he was killed before I could get much in the way of details." He paused to gain better control of his voice. "Whoever did it came and went by boat."

After a moment Vivian said, "Jack ... I'm sorry. That must have been awful."

"Where does he keep his boat?" Jack asked, intentionally shifting the subject. He didn't want his professionalism being overruled by emotion. Vivian would understand, he knew.

"At a marina in Brentwood Bay," she replied.

"Next door to the Butchart Gardens," Jack noted, more to himself than Vivian.

"Yes, the Gardens are just a short drive away."

"A fifty-footer — it must have a tender on it, then," Jack stated.

"I'm sure it would. Hang on, I'll radio one of the investigators." When she came back on the phone she said, "Yes, he has a dinghy."

"With a motor or oars?" Jack asked.

"A motor."

Jack felt like his chest was momentarily paralyzed with adrenalin. "My informant was trying to bust their boat motor with a rock before he was shot. I-HIT has the rock. Could someone walk past on the pier and see if there's damage to the motor? Perhaps scrape marks on the cowling or something?"

Vivian spoke on the police radio, then said, "Apparently the dinghy's strapped down under a tarp. Besides keeping a pit bull on board, Doringer knows a lot of people at the marina. Boaters are a pretty friendly bunch. They tend to watch out for each other when it comes to strangers nosing around. This time of year there are people at the marina during the day. At night the place is basically deserted, but that's when Doringer's on his boat."

"Damn."

"We haven't even had the opportunity to put a bug on the boat, but we did manage to get a boat to use as an OP."

"How close is this operation post?"

"Directly across the wharf from him. Maybe the opportunity will arise to get a peek at the motor later. Doringer normally keeps the dog inside, and the tender is laid over the engine compartment on an open deck at the stern."

"Taking the tarp off would require a warrant," Jack said. "Then, even if we got it, it could be later quashed in court on some technicality and out would go the evidence."

"Yup, there's always a chance of that," Vivian said dispassionately.

"I want this guy bad. I'm going to try to hedge the bet."

"Hedge the bet?"

"Have him invite me onto the boat and allow me to see it."

Vivian hesitated, then she spoke, her voice grim. "Jack, there's something you need to know. Doringer's a real nutcase with a long record of violence."

"If he's the one who murdered my informant — that goes without saying."

"I know, but from what I've heard from the investigators, he's more dangerous and unstable than your average murderer. When he was in the navy he spent most of his time in the stockade before being dishonourably discharged. He was diagnosed with some kind of mental disorder. A thing called ODD."

"Oppositional defiance disorder," Jack said.

"Yeah, that's it. He has a hair-trigger temper. Apparently a lot of his type don't fit into society too well and tend to do the opposite of what they're told."

"Then maybe it's time to remove him from society," Jack said coldly.

Chapter Forty-Six

Tina's sleepy voice told Jack that she'd been sleeping when he called. He didn't bother to apologize. "Tina — you, Laura, get over to my room now and bring your phones and notebooks," he said tersely. "We're getting a conference call in fifteen minutes. I'll need to debrief the both of you first."

"A conference call? From who?"

"One of the monitors in Victoria." Then he ordered, "Hustle."

Four minutes later Laura and Tina arrived in Jack's room. They hadn't even taken seats before Jack started, "After you two went back to your room last night, I went down to the parkade and checked the Mercedes. I found a tracker that Chuck slapped on it yesterday afternoon when we were having coffee in the store."

"No!" Laura said, her face mirroring the shock on Tina's face. They slowly sat down. "What made you think to look?"

"Couldn't sleep and mulled things over," Jack replied, sitting down on the bed. "It's my fault. I remembered thinking I hadn't heard the bell above the door ring when Chuck left — but heard it twice before he returned. I was so intent on maintaining our cover story with Aaron and chatting about life in California that I didn't listen to my subconscious trying to warn me."

"All three of us are operators," Tina said. "We all missed it."

Laura nodded. "In a way, its good news. Helps confirm we're onto the right guys."

"Yes, and it gets better. Chuck did connect to the guy he called yesterday while we were in the store. The call was monitored on the other end. Victoria had the guy's phone tapped. A fellow by the name of Todd Doringer — who lives on a boat."

"Oh, man ... Eureka!" Laura yelled, raising her hand.

High-fives were exchanged, then Jack continued, "Vivian Mah called me this morning and —"

"Wait a sec," Tina said. "How'd Vivian know to connect it to you?"

"Aaron mentioned my olive soup."

Tina looked at Laura for an explanation.

Laura shrugged. "It's world-famous. Everyone who has worked with Jack knows he's the master martini maker."

"Listen, you two, I've only got a few minutes before Vivian calls back," Jack said. "She's going to play the calls for us. So far there've been two. One when Chuck called him while we were at the store, and a second when Aaron called him after dinner. Let me explain what I've been told so far and what my plan is."

Minutes later they were apprised of the situation, but before Jack could discuss what he wanted to do next, they received their conference call.

After a few quick hellos Jack said, "I've updated Laura and Tina as to what you've told me. Before we listen to the calls, though, I'd like to talk to you about a few things in case Chuck or Aaron call me. Also, I'd like to get a sense of what you think of their conversations."

"What I think?" Vivian asked.

"Not so much as what's said, but what the person is thinking," Jack replied. "Subtleties in the tone of voice. Nuances that might not be heard by us when you relay the call over our phones."

"Maybe you'll want to be talking to one of the investigators," Vivian suggested.

"Viv, you've listened to more psychopaths, assorted nutcases, and run-of-the-mill bad guys than twenty seasoned cops put together. I'd prefer your opinion over anyone else's."

"Wow … thanks, Jack. It's good to be appreciated. So far, though, the calls are fairly straightforward."

"When Chuck told Doringer that he met an American wanting two king salmon, what did Doringer say?" Jack asked.

"Doringer said he only had a couple of sockeye on hand."

"Likely ten- or fifty-pound lots," Jack said. "Sounds like I asked for too much."

"Our info says that Doringer deals up to a couple hundred kilos at a time. I think you simply caught him shorthanded. By the way, how'd you meet Chuck and Aaron?"

"They own a hydroponics store in Vancouver," Jack said. "It was a cold approach. We walked in and I hit them up trying to score." He glanced at Laura and Tina. "Well, maybe not exactly a cold approach. There were a couple of hot women involved."

Vivian tittered. "Yes, I'm familiar with the scenario. Okay. To start at the beginning, in the call that Doringer got from Chuck at one-thirty, Doringer was wary and told him to check you out good."

"He tried, too," Jack said. "While we were at the store, Chuck slipped out and slapped a tracker on our car."

"No kidding?"

"Like a fool, I didn't clue in to it until the middle of the night when everything was going through my mind. Fortunately we didn't drive anywhere that'd have blown our cover story."

"Phew, that's good." Vivian paused. "A grow-op store … That's interesting because up until now, we've had no idea where Doringer was getting his weed."

"I think Chuck and Aaron identify the grow-ops for him, then do rips to get the dope," Jack said.

"By using a tracker to follow the customers," Vivian concluded.

"You got it. So besides being wary, how receptive was Doringer when Chuck called?"

"Not overly. He grilled Chuck on whether or not you could be a cop. He mentioned something about your timing."

"My timing?"

"Hang on, I've got the log in front of me. Doringer said: 'The timing on this stinks. This guy shows up right after we did what we did?'" Vivian swallowed. "Your informant?"

"Murdered two weeks ago yesterday," Jack said.

Vivian sighed. "It fits. That could be what they were talking about."

No doubt in my mind, Jack thought bitterly.

"That was basically it for that call," Vivian said. "The next one to Doringer was at eleven-thirty last night from the guy you identified as Aaron. He went into detail about what a great dinner you bought them. That's when he mentioned that you drink what you call olive soup and said that Chuck was really drunk." Vivian paused. "You'll be relieved to hear that Aaron also said how gorgeous his date was and, uh, he made some mention of what he'd like to do to you, Laura, sexually … from behind."

"Gee, that's nice to know," Laura said. "I was wondering how I was going to make up for ditching him last night."

"It's a visual I'd rather not think of," Vivian responded. "After that he went on to describe how Laura slipped up and said her brother flew a seaplane in Alaska. That really peaked Doringer's interest. It also caused him to question again whether or not you could be a cop."

"Thought it would peak his interest," Jack said.

"Aaron went out of his way to assure him you weren't a cop."

"Guys will say anything if they think it'll help them get laid," Tina commented.

"Is Doringer going to meet me?" Jack asked, adrenalin fuelling his optimism.

"I don't think so. At least not yet."

Peaks and valleys … back to the valley.

"Aaron tried to convince him that perhaps you'd settle for the sockeye, but he said he didn't feel like making the trip over for that. Overall I'd say he was really curious about you, but in the end I couldn't tell if it was in a good way or if he was simply suspicious."

"How was it left? Are Aaron and Chuck going to turn me down?"

"Aaron doesn't want to do that. He's hoping to stall you and come up with some more fish, as he put it."

"Sounds like it would be through someone else," Jack said. "Do you know how Doringer is running the weed down to the States? Is he using his boat?"

"Yes, we think he gets close to the border, then anchors and scoots over to the San Juan Islands on his tender."

"With heighted border security these days, he's taking a risk."

"Yeah, well, I told you what a nutcase he is," Vivian said. "I don't think looking at the consequences of his actions has ever been his strong point."

"Maybe I could use our seaplane conversation to entice him."

"Maybe," Vivian allowed. "So what are you going to do?"

"I've got an idea to meet Doringer," Jack said determinedly. "Viv, Laura, Tina — hang up. I'm going to try something. Viv, you'll probably know what's happening before I do, so stay tuned. I'm calling the bad guys."

Chapter Forty-Seven

Jack called the store and Chuck answered.

"Hey, Chuck, how's the head today?" Jack asked.

Chuck groaned. "Bloody awful. I feel sicker than a dog. When Aaron and I got home last night, we stayed up for another two hours. Bad idea."

Jack snorted a laugh.

"It was good of you to spring for the restaurant," Chuck said. "How's Trina?"

"That's Tina, you moron!" Aaron yelled in the background.

"She's okay now," Jack replied.

"You gonna swing by the store?" Chuck asked, sounding hopeful.

"Well, uh, I know you're trying to introduce me to someone, but the thing is, the girls want me to take them to Vancouver Island today."

"They're going over to the Island," Chuck called to Aaron.

"We're going to try to catch a ferry that leaves at one," Jack continued, "stay overnight, and come back tomorrow.

There's some sort of big flower garden they want to see."

"The Butchart Gardens," Chuck said, enunciating the words slowly as if his brain was connecting them with an idea.

"Yeah, that's the name," Jack replied.

"It's huge. People from all over the world go to see it."

"Yeah, well, I'm not really into wasting my afternoon walking around and looking at flowers. My allergies would drive me crazy. I'm going to drop Laura and Tina off, find a bar to sit in, then pick them up again at five. We've booked rooms at the Empress Hotel in Victoria. We'll see what that city has to offer, then come back tomorrow."

"Listen, JB, can I call you back in a couple of minutes? I need to, uh, deal with a customer."

"I'm about to have a shower. Guess I could call *you* back in twenty minutes."

"That'd be great. Don't go without calling me."

"Yeah ... okay," Jack replied, sounding less than enthusiastic.

Vivian phoned Jack less than five minutes later. "Well, you've caught Doringer's attention."

"In a good way or a bad way?"

"You'd probably think it was a good way," Vivian said. "I wouldn't if it was me. He told Chuck to give him your number and said he'd call you."

"Perfect," Jack said, giving Laura and Tina a thumbs-up.

"Chuck asked if he was going to call you right away. Doringer said no, that it'd be better to see where you go first. I presume they're talking about the tracker."

"I'm sure you presume right," Jack said happily. "I love it when a plan comes together."

"Jack." Vivian sounded grave. "The call was really short and I'll let you listen to it, but you said you respected my opinion when it came to subtleties in the tone of voice."

"I do," Jack replied.

"Then listen to me when I tell you that Doringer is really suspicious."

"I expected he would be," Jack said, "but even if he doesn't trust me enough to sell me any dope, all I want is to get on his boat and have a look at his tender. I should be able to do that without him freaking out."

"Yes, but … being suspicious is only part of it. I get the feeling he's vengeful."

"Vengeful? I haven't done anything to him — yet."

"It's more of an attitude. Like a mindset that says nobody is going to put anything over on me — or if they do, they won't live to talk about it." She paused but Jack didn't respond. "Maybe that's me acting like a mother hen. From what was actually said, there's nothing to justify how I feel."

"I trust your senses, Viv," Jack said solemnly, "and will heed your advice. You said you had a boat to use as an OP right across from his?"

"Yes. You could go from one boat to the other in about two leaps."

"Then don't worry, I'll make sure there's a cover team hidden in the OP."

"Good. Tell them to stay awake."

Jack chuckled. "I'll pass on your thoughts about Doringer, not to mention his history with the navy and having ODD. I'll be okay. Besides, I've got you on my side if he makes any calls concerning my credibility — or is someone else handling the lines tonight?"

"There is, but I'll stay, too. Wouldn't want to miss out on any olive soup after."

Moments later Jack called Chuck again.

"Good news," Chuck said. "Since we spoke, I was finally able to reach that guy."

"And?"

"Turns out he's going to be on Vancouver Island today, too. I gave him your number and he said he'd call you at about three this afternoon. Maybe you'll be able to get together."

"Hey, that's great," Jack said. "What's his name?"

"Uh, I just call him Bud."

"As in Buddy?"

"Yeah. So you and Tina and Laura will be back tomorrow?"

"That's the plan."

"Maybe we could all get together again?"

Jack winked at Laura and Tina. "Yes, the girls mentioned they're looking forward to seeing you again." *In handcuffs — and no, you won't like it.* He grinned when Laura shook her head and Tina pretended to choke herself to death.

Rose took a call from Jack and listened as he updated her on the Doringer investigation, including what Damien had told him about the cocaine arriving in France. When they hung up she called I-HIT and told Inspector Dyck about Aaron, Chuck, and Doringer.

Inspector Dyck was pleased to hear what had been discovered and said he'd immediately relay the information to Connie.

Rose's next call was to Isaac. His tone was brisk and strictly business. As soon as she told him Taggart was involved in an undercover role with someone who may have murdered Dwayne Beggs, he ordered a meeting in his office to take place as soon as I-HIT could make the drive over.

One hour later Rose was walking down the hall to attend the meeting when Jack called again. "What now?" she asked. "I'm about to enter Isaac's office."

"I just received a call from my weenie-wagging friend telling me that Pure E scheduled a meeting and party for this evening."

"It's good he's keeping you up-to-date, but we already knew that," Rose said.

"There's more. The Gypsy Devils are supplying the usual security and acting as gofers at the hall Satans Wrath rented for the meeting. Weenie is to meet the GDs first at the Barlow farm and go over their duties. After they all go to the hall Weenie is to meet someone from the three-three and then take part in disposing of Neal after the party."

"What time and where do you think the hit will happen?" Rose asked.

"Considering how late the party will go, I don't expect it'll happen much before two or three in the morning. Weenie doesn't know where yet. I told him that I wouldn't interfere or do or say anything that might jeopardize him, either with Satans Wrath or from possible prosecution. He thinks the GDs will be forced to do the actual hit, but it'll be under the supervision of the three-three. Hopefully Weenie will be able to limit his role to that of spectator, but it's not guaranteed."

"I appreciate you telling me," Rose replied. "I realize that disclosing this makes you uncomfortable."

"Yes, it makes me nervous," Jack admitted, "but I made you a promise to be straight with you and I'm keeping it. That being said, I don't believe there's anything we can do about it without jeopardizing Weenie. I hope you trust my opinion on that."

"I do and am content to let the chips fall where they may, so to speak. I'll mention it to Isaac — but trust my judgment on that. He's already concurred and I'm confident that the protection of your informant will supersede any interference on our part."

"Thank you."

"I know your brain will be spinning today, Jack, what with the imminent seizure in France, your undercover role with Todd Doringer, and now worrying about your informant being involved in a hit."

"It's called multi-tasking — I don't need reminding. But you're right, my head is spinning. I feel like I need to be cloned so I can be everywhere at once."

"No matter what happens, stay focused on Doringer. The other two matters are out of your control. Try not to think about them. Doringer is a dangerous man. I want you to be at the top of your game."

"Thanks, I appreciate what you're saying," Jack replied.

"And by the top of your game, I don't mean by having the coroner pick up his body when you're finished," Rose added dryly.

"Gotcha. You'd prefer his body never be found."

"Don't even joke about —" Rose quit talking when she heard the dial tone. A moment later she was ushered into Isaac's office and she nodded cordially to him.

Her thoughts were still on Neal Barlow as she took a seat beside Connie and Inspector Dyck. When she looked at Isaac, behind his desk, his steel-grey eyes were on her. *Bet he senses something is up.*

"Something else happen?" Isaac asked abruptly.

Yup, he knows. Rose cleared her throat. "I just received an update from Corporal Taggart on an unrelated matter."

"An unrelated matter?" the assistant commissioner asked. "I would've thought he had a full plate today as it is. Is it in regard to the cocaine shipment being intercepted in France later?"

"No, sir. It involves the, uh, delicate matter we discussed last week," Rose replied. She caught movement in her peripheral vision. It was Connie, tensing. *How did she clue in?*

Isaac became more sombre. "I see. Has the anticipated action taken place?"

"Corporal Taggart received word from his informant that the matter will be dealt with late tonight. There'll be some involvement required on the part of the informant. As such, Corporal Taggart feels there's nothing we can do without endangering his life."

Isaac grimaced. "Please keep me informed on the matter."

"Yes, sir." *Good. He won't interfere. Jack, your trust in me is deserved.*

"On to the matter at hand." Isaac looked at Inspector Dyck. "I gave instruction for Corporal Taggart not to become involved in the homicide investigation of Dwayne Beggs unless requested by your unit. Was such a request made?"

Inspector Dyck glanced sideways at Connie. "After the beating death of Jamie King, Corporal Crane spoke with Corporal Taggart. At that time she told him she was going to deprioritize her investigation into the Beggs homicide. She then gave him permission to look into the matter himself."

Isaac addressed Connie. "Was this because you thought Jamie King was responsible for the murder of Dwayne Beggs?"

"Yes, sir," she admitted. "That and knowing bikers were involved, which is Jack's, uh, Corporal Taggart's specialty."

"And in light of this new information we received this morning, do you still believe King was responsible?" Isaac asked.

"Sir, Corporal Crane had not closed her investigation on Beggs," Inspector Dyck said. "She simply deprioritized it. Her decision to have Corporal Taggart involved, due to his sources of information in the biker community, was prudent, given the information we had at that time."

Isaac turned to Connie again. "Corporal Crane, I suggest you always protect this man." He nodded his head in the direction of Inspector Dyck.

"Sir?" Connie said in obvious confusion.

"Because Inspector Dyck protects you," Isaac said flatly. He glanced at Inspector Dyck. "Yes, I understand that cases evolve — but I have not availed myself of all the notes, details, or wiretap logs concerning this matter, let alone become aware of the gut instincts of the investigators involved." He focused on Connie again. "So Corporal

Crane, do you feel that Corporal Taggart may well have the person responsible for the murder of his informant within his sights?"

Within his sights? Rose tried not to cringe.

"Yes, sir," Connie replied. "The evidence is circumstantial, but two of Doringer's associates own a hydroponics store and planted a tracker on Corporal Taggart's car when he met with them. Doringer lives on a boat, and coupled with his background of violent behaviour, I'd say there's a strong likelihood that he is, in fact, the murderer."

Isaac swung his gaze to Rose. "So Corporal Taggart's stated objective is to work in an undercover capacity and receive permission from Todd Doringer to board his boat, where he then hopes to see the motor on the tender."

Stated objective? Sir, are you implying — Rose's thoughts were put on hold when Isaac continued with a comment directed at Inspector Dyck.

"The tender, I am told, is covered with a tarp. Even if Corporal Taggart receives permission to board the boat, it does not give him carte blanche to view objects not in sight."

"Sir," Inspector Dyck replied, "Corporal Taggart is a seasoned undercover operative. I'm sure he's most familiar with what the legal requirements would be."

"Yes, I'm sure he is, too," Isaac said, returning his attention back to Rose. "Nevertheless I'd like to ensure — for court purposes of course — that all his actions are corroborated." Isaac paused, but continued to stare at Rose. "As the investigation into Doringer has now become a murder investigation, I want Corporal Crane to take charge and be part of Corporal Taggart's cover team to witness or respond to any, shall we say, unforeseen events."

Rose returned Isaac's stare without blinking. She was well aware that his eyes were remaining purposely fixed on hers, not Connie's. *Yes, I understand completely. You won't go along with Jack saying that Doringer fell on a fish gaff and died from having it rammed up his ass.*

Chapter Forty-Eight

Jack, with Laura and Tina, drove onto the one-o'clock ferry as planned. Awaiting their arrival on Vancouver Island would be a surveillance team comprising members of the Victoria RCMP Drug Section, who'd be responsible for their protection. The team was under the leadership of Corporal Willy Mineault, a trained undercover operative and a good friend of Jack's, but his command would be relinquished to Connie if any operational decisions were to be made. Connie had boarded the same ferry as a foot passenger and would join Willy in his vehicle.

As Jack got out of the car on the ferry, he received a call on his regular phone from Vivian Mah.

"Contact made?" he asked.

"Yes, Aaron just hung up. He told Doringer that you boarded the ferry."

"Looks like their tracker is working well," Jack said. "Is Doringer on his boat?"

"Yes, there are three members in the OP monitoring him and they'll provide you cover or surveillance if need be."

"Good. Make sure you tell Connie, as well. She'll be riding shotgun with Willy so you can relay through him on the radio. Technically she's in charge."

A moment of silence, then Vivian said, "Technically ... right, I understand, but seeing as it's your ass on the line, technically I'll be phoning you first."

Jack grinned. "You'll do or say anything for an olive soup. Talk to you later."

At two-forty Jack, Laura, and Tina drove off the ferry at the Swartz Bay terminal on Vancouver Island while Connie hustled out to the area for foot-passenger arrivals and met up with Willy.

Fifteen minutes later Jack turned off the Patricia Bay Highway and was heading west on Mt. Newton Cross Road toward the Butchart Gardens when he received his next call.

"Still live monitoring," Vivian said. "This time Chuck called Doringer. Told him that you turned off the Pat Bay on the Newton Cross Road toward the Butchart Gardens."

"Doringer's response?"

"He said it sounds like you're who you say you are."

"Any mention when he might call me?"

"He didn't say, but I presume he will shortly. At the moment he's out of his boat and heading down the pier."

"I'm going to drop Laura and Tina off at the Butchart Gardens. They'll have their phones and will be in contact with the cover team. At that time I'll stash this phone in the trunk and switch over to the other phone."

"I've got the number. Chuck gave it to him."

"If Doringer hasn't called me by then," Jack said, "I'll drive to the Quality Inn at the intersection of Pat Bay and Newton Cross and wait in the pub."

"Gotcha."

"Once I meet him, if there's a real emergency call me direct."

"Real emergency?"

"Like if he calls Chuck or Aaron and tells them he thinks I'm a cop. Bear in mind that if I'm with him, we may have to code the call."

"Code the call?" Vivian questioned again. "I'm a monitor, not a UC operator."

"You've spent years listening to bad guys code their calls," Jack told her. "You'll figure something out if you have to."

"Tell you what. I'll keep it simple. I'll yell, 'Run, you stupid bastard! Run!'"

Jack laughed. Minutes later he dropped Laura and Tina off at the Gardens and then drove to the Quality Inn. As he pulled into the lot, his phone rang.

"JB?" It was Doringer.

"Yes."

"I'm a friend of Aaron and Chuck. They suggested I give you a call."

"Oh, that's right. Chuck said you were going to be on the Island today, too."

"Where are you now?" Doringer asked.

Like you don't already know. "I dropped my sister and her friend off at the Butchart Gardens and was about to go for a drink. I just pulled up to someplace called the Waddling Dog."

"Yeah, I know the place. It's at the Quality Inn. Listen, I'm at a restaurant in Brentwood Bay. It's about a ten-minute drive from the Gardens. I've already ordered a drink. How about coming here and joining me?"

"Sounds good," Jack replied.

"I'm at the Blue's Bayou Café."

"Hang on while I punch it into the car's GPS," Jack said.

"It's right on the water. I'm outside on the patio."

Seconds later Jack said, "Got it. Looks close — see you shortly."

Moments later Vivian relayed Jack and Doringer's conversation to Willy and Connie.

"It'd be a good move to have Laura and Tina hop in the surveillance van," Willy suggested.

"Why?" Connie asked. "You seem to have lots of manpower already."

"They're both trained operators and Laura has worked with Jack for a lot of years. She knows his facial expressions, gestures, hidden hand signals. She'd be able to read his situation better than anyone."

"But we can't risk her being seen," Connie said. "She's pretending to be his sister."

"They won't be seen in the van. Who knows, we might even be able to sneak her into the OP if it looks like Doringer is taking Jack to his boat later on. Laura would be of a lot more value there than waiting at the Gardens. If I'm wrong and he goes with Jack back to the Gardens we can take Laura and Tina back and easily drop them off without being seen."

Connie mulled it over. "UC isn't my bag, so I'll rely on your judgment. Go ahead." She watched Willy dial

Laura and as the phone rang, she asked, "Do you know Jack fairly well?"

Willy grinned. "Oh, yeah. He introduced me to his olive soup years ago. We go way back."

Connie nodded. *Why do I get the feeling I'm outgunned over here? Damn you, Taggart.*

It was 4:00 p.m. when Jack stepped onto the café's outdoor patio. The view overlooked a marina and he saw Doringer sitting by himself. They made eye contact and Jack approached and held out his hand. "Hi, I'm JB."

"Yeah, I'm Todd," he replied, not moving from where he sat slouched back in his chair. He eyed Jack's extended hand briefly before leaning forward to shake it.

Good. At least he trusts me enough to give me his real name. Jack slid out a chair opposite him and sat.

Despite the crisp autumn air, Doringer had his jacket slung over the back of the chair and was wearing sandals, a dark green T-shirt, and shorts in a multi-green camouflage design.

Jack unzipped his windbreaker but raised the collar to protect himself from the breeze. He saw Doringer staring at him. "Cooler up here than in California," Jack said. "Looks like it doesn't bother you."

"Been on the sea most of my life. You get used to it."

Jack nodded and took in Doringer's physical features. He knew he was thirty-seven and had a long record of violence, but now Jack could size him up one on one. Even though the man was sitting, Jack could see he had a stocky muscular build, powerful-looking arms, and a bit of a beer gut. He had a thick short neck and his black hair was cropped close enough to reveal most of his scalp. It was evident he hadn't shaved for about a week and his skin was weather-beaten. His nose looked like a sausage that had been chewed on by a dog. *This guy has been in a few brawls over the years.*

Doringer was silent as a waiter brought Jack a menu. When the waiter left he said, "I understand you're in the tomato business."

"Straight to the point. I like that." Jack smiled. "I'm in the green business. Green, as in money."

Doringer nodded. "You'll appreciate that I don't know you, and what you're requesting isn't exactly chicken feed."

"Trust goes both ways," Jack replied. "I didn't just fall off the banana truck from Mexico. I was ripped off once and don't ever plan to let that happen again."

"Nobody wants that," Doringer said, his expression not giving as much as a flicker.

You lying scum. "And of course, there's always that other thing," Jack said.

"What?"

"It's not just rips — and I don't want you all to take this personal, but a few years ago a good buddy of mine got set up by the DEA. It's made me paranoid as hell." He paused, eyeing Doringer suspiciously. "Like you said, we don't know each other and that's a two-way street."

Doringer took a slurp of his drink and studied Jack over the top of his glass before putting it down. "So where do you propose we go from here?"

"To start with, let's get to know each other." Jack gestured to the glass. "What're you drinking?"

"Lamb's Navy and Coke."

"Sounds good. I'm going to order some food, as well. We can get to know each other a little better before discussing business. You ready for another?"

Doringer gulped down the last of his drink. "I am now."

At 4:30 p.m. Willy tapped on the rear door of the surveillance van parked in a nearby lot. Laura opened the door a crack and peered out.

"You'll both have to sit tight for the moment," said Willy. "Doringer can see the marina from where he's sitting. At the moment he's the only one who stays on his boat overnight, so anyone going onto the pier this late in the day would attract his attention. Especially as the OP is so close to his boat. It gets dark about seven-thirty. Maybe you can sneak out to it then."

"Seven-thirty? Do you think they'll be there that long?" Tina asked.

"I've got someone on foot who has the eye," Willy replied. "Jack's been with Doringer for thirty minutes and they're on their second round of drinks. I don't know, what do you think?"

"Martinis, beer, wine, or cocktails?" Laura asked.

Willy clicked his transmitter and relayed the question. "Cocktails."

"If it was olive soup, they'd be staying until closing time," Laura said.

"Yup, been there," Willy replied, shaking his head as if recalling something from the past.

Laura felt her phone vibrate and looked at the display. "Speak of the devil. Everyone be quiet." She answered. "Hey, big bro, what's up?"

"I'm with that guy Chuck and Aaron know. I'm going to be a while. You and Tina grab a cab to the hotel when you're done sniffing flowers. I'll catch up to you later."

"How much later?"

"I don't know. Shouldn't be too long," Jack replied, then disconnected.

Laura looked at Willy and Tina. "Got a feeling it's going to be a long night."

The next few hours slid past with Doringer and Jack sharing idle conversation, mostly Doringer talking about his time in the navy and Jack telling jokes and making up stories about life in California.

At 7:30 p.m. Jack looked at his watch. "Man, look at the time. Too many jokes and too many drinks. The girls are going to be pissed off. I should go, but I'm going to need a cab." He glanced around. "We're also the only customers. Bet the restaurant wants to close up."

"We haven't talked any business yet," Doringer said. "We've got time. The restaurant doesn't close for another thirty minutes."

"Yeah, okay, let's talk. For starters, are you able to handle the amount I want?"

"Maybe. How soon did you want it?"

"I'm meeting my brother in two days. I was hoping to know by then so I could talk to 'im about it."

"You're heading up to Alaska this soon?"

"No." Jack eyed Doringer. "I reckon Chuck or Aaron already blabbed to you that my brother flies a seaplane."

"They mentioned it."

Jack frowned. "My sister shouldn't have said that. But yes, Jim-Bo flies tourists on sightseeing trips and sometimes takes 'em to remote fishing lodges. He also makes regular runs down to Seattle, so I —"

"He flies by here?" Doringer exclaimed.

"He has to on his way to Seattle," Jack replied. "He's got a trip coming up in the next couple of days and will land in Vancouver for a visit. I'm hoping to be able to have something to tell 'im by then."

"Christ, I'd really like to meet 'im," Doringer said. "The three of us should talk."

Jack studied Doringer's face closely.

"What's wrong?"

"I find this suspicious," Jack stated.

"Suspicious?" Doringer furrowed his eyebrows. "What're you talking about?"

"That you happen to be here on the same day as me. I'm not a guy who generally believes in coincidences. Now you wanting to meet Jim-Bo ... well, makes me wonder."

"Oh, Chuck and Aaron." Doringer shook his head. "I'd forgotten what they were to tell you."

"Forgotten what?"

"I live here," Doringer said, gesturing outward with both hands.

"Oh. They made it sound like you being here today was a coincidence."

"I told 'em to say that because I wanted to meet you before deciding whether to do business with you."

Jack nodded. "Okay, but there's no reason for you to meet my brother."

Doringer grinned. "That's 'cause there's somethin' else you don't know."

"Which is?"

"I live on a boat."

"You do?" Jack feigned surprise.

"Yup." Doringer leaned back and stuck his thumbs in his waistband, looking smug.

"Are you serious?"

"Yup." He smiled. "Wouldn't you say that a guy with a boat and a guy with a seaplane — who are both in the green business — should get to know each other?"

"Is your boat near here?" Jack asked. "Can I see it?"

"Sure. It's straight down the pier." Doringer waved a hand at the marina. "Join me on board. I got a bottle of Lamb's. I'll pour us a drink and we can talk about it."

"Let me phone my sister and tell her I'll be late," Jack said.

"No problem. I gotta go to the head." Doringer stood and grabbed his jacket. "Don't worry about the tab. I'll get it."

"Let me split it with you," Jack offered.

"Don't worry about it." Doringer grinned. "I'll add it to the cost of the first shipment." He then disappeared inside the café.

Jack phoned Laura. "Thangs are going well here, lil' sister."

"Your voice sounds a little slurred," Laura noted. "You drunk?"

"I've been trying to sound American, but you're right. I won't be driving, that's for sure. The asshole can really hold his booze — keepin' up wasn't easy. The good news is he just invited me onto his boat."

"Where is he?"

"He went to the washroom and after we clear the tab, we're going to his boat."

"Hang on," Laura said. "Willy and Connie have been waiting to sneak out to the OP. I'll tell them that —"

"They know and are mobile," Jack said, on seeing Willy and Connie hustle down the pier. "How about you? Are you nearby?"

"Tina and I are in a surveillance van, but not close enough that I'd risk making a run for the OP at this point," Laura replied. "Not only that, the marina is fenced off and I'm told Willy has the only other key."

"Too bad."

"I'll grab some binocs and we'll go out on foot. There's a place that overlooks the marina, so we'll be able to watch from there."

"Sounds good."

"Any signal in mind if you need help?" Laura asked.

"Yeah, if you see me ram Doringer's head through a porthole and slice his throat open, send for help — but make sure you put enough postage on the envelope."

Chapter Forty-Nine

Jack followed Doringer down the pier. When they reached the end, Doringer gestured to his boat. "So whaddaya think of 'er?"

"She's beautiful," Jack replied. He did his best to pretend he was admiring the boat, rather than studying the tender. The dinghy was strapped down under a tarp over a knee-high wooden structure that covered the engine compartment near the stern. The front of the dinghy was about three paces away from the entry to the boat's cabin. The propeller on the dinghy's motor protruded outside the tarp close to stern, beckoning to him like a shiny lure to a hungry fish.

"She's old, but seaworthy," Doringer commented. He unlatched a waist-high door in the gunwale, then motioned for Jack to follow him on board.

Jack stumbled a little when he stepped off the dock. *Laura was right. I'm pretty drunk*. He glanced at the boat moored opposite them. It was in darkness, but an opening in the curtains over a small sliding window in the cabin told him where the cover team was watching from. He then bent down to take his shoes off.

"Don't worry about your shoes," Doringer said as he fumbled with his key trying to unlock the cabin door. There's somebody I need you to meet." He tried to jam the key in the lock, then pulled it out, turned it over, and tried again.

Good. I'm not the only one feeling the drinks. "You got a lady?" Jack asked.

Doringer chortled.

"What's so funny?" Jack asked.

Doringer unlocked the door. "Matey ain't no lady, so it's best not to let 'im hear you call 'im that. It's also healthy to stay on his good side. Ain't that right, b'y?" He was holding the pit bull by the collar and petting it.

Jack cautiously held out his hand for the dog to smell. A moment later Matey licked his fingers.

"Looks like you two are going to be friends," Doringer said. "Come on in and make yourself comfortable."

Jack followed Doringer inside and shut the door behind him.

Doringer flung his jacket on a chair, then opened a cupboard and took out a bottle of Lamb's Navy Rum. "Go ahead, grab a seat," he said, indicating a horseshoe-shaped bench that ringed a wooden table.

Jack took a seat and beckoned Matey, who seemed to enjoy it when Jack scratched him behind the ears. *Good boy. Get to know me in case I need to return later.*

"Damn it, I'm out of ice," Doringer said, peering into a small bar fridge. "Make yourself comfortable. I'll be back in ten minutes. Matey probably needs a piss, too, so I'll take him with me."

"Not a problem. I'll wait where it's warm." Jack glanced around. "Man, I'd love to own something like this. Do you mind if I take a look around while I'm waiting?"

"Go ahead."

Jack watched Doringer through the window. When he disappeared down the pier, Jack stepped out onto the rear deck and gestured to his mouth as he faced the OP.

"What's he doing? Telling us Doringer went for food?" Connie asked from where she hid in the darkened cabin of the boat.

"He wants to talk," Willy said, sliding the window open.

Jack's hushed voice came across the pier. "He's gone for ice. I figure I've got about ten minutes. I told him I'd like to own a boat like this and asked for permission to look around while I was waiting. He told me to go ahead. Connie, it's your call. Does that cover me legally to take a look at the tender?"

"In my mind it does," Connie replied. "Hurry!"

"Cover me." He quickly examined how the tarp was tied down. One rope encircled the bottom of the tarp, weaving its way in and out of the eyelets. The ends of the rope were knotted under the leg of the propeller.

Jack undid the knot, then lifted the tarp and bent over the motor to look. The motor was tipped in the "up" position for being removed from the water. In the darkness he was unable to see if the front of it had any damage. His hands fumbled for the lever to lower the motor so he could have a better look.

Connie's panicked voice roused his attention. "He's coming back! He's coming back!"

Jack peered over the gunwale and saw that Doringer was seconds away. *Son of a bitch. I know time seems to go fast when I'm drinking, but that couldn't have been ten minutes.*

He pulled the tarp back over the motor, but didn't have time to tie it down. He stayed bent over as he crept to the front of the dinghy with the idea of distracting Doringer's attention.

As Doringer was looking down to unlatch the door in the gunwale, Jack slowly stood up on the opposite side of the boat. He tried to look nonchalant, as if he'd been standing there the whole time.

"What're you doin' out here?" Doringer asked, startled by his presence as he stepped on board. "I thought you were cold."

Jack pulled the collar of his jacket tight to his neck. "I am, but I feel a little queasy, so came out for some air. Do you have the ice already?"

"Nah, I remembered I left my wallet in my jacket. You too sick to drink now?"

"Hell, no. I get this all the time. I've got a peptic ulcer, but I'll be fine by the time you're back with the ice." He smiled reassuringly at Doringer and felt a light breeze sweep across the boat. *Hope the damn tarp stays in place.*

Doringer nodded, then ducked into the cabin.

Jack glanced at the dinghy. The rope running through the eyelets on the tarp had slackened and drooped from eyelet to eyelet. *Oh, crap.* He'd little time to think about it as Doringer stepped back out onto the deck. *Okay, yawn and stretch my arms high over my head to divert his attention. Keep him talking so he's looking at me.*

Doringer's focus did remain on Jack, but he had neither his jacket nor his wallet in his hand. What he had was a .45-calibre Glock pistol that he pointed straight at Jack's face. "You're either a cop or a rat and I don't give a fuck which, because you're dead!"

Chapter Fifty

Over her earpiece Connie heard Laura's panicked alert. "Gun! Gun!"

She was too busy to reply. Although Doringer had his back to her and the gunwale prevented her from seeing all but the top half of his body, everyone in the OP had heard his harsh declaration to kill Jack. She'd already stuck the barrel of her Smith & Wesson 9mm semi-automatic pistol out the window and was aiming down the sights — dead centre between Doringer's shoulder blades.

"Police! Drop it!" she yelled. "Drop it!"

A simultaneous barrage of yelling and noise erupted from the other four officers in the OP as they scrambled out the rear cabin door while drawing their weapons.

Doringer glanced in Connie's direction. It was something she'd relive in her nightmares forever. His glance was only a second, but even in the shadows cast across his face, she saw the look of rage. She knew in her heart that he wasn't going to comply with her command. As he turned to face Jack again, his right shoulder lifted slightly as his elbow straightened to shoot.

Connie knew what she had to do. Her brain automatically shut off all the noise and commotion as her vision zeroed in on Doringer's back. Time and motion seemed to slow … and she squeezed the trigger. She was aware that her aim had been diverted slightly higher due to the movement caused when the cover team leaped off the OP onto the pier. *A head shot is okay. Maybe even better.*

Her finger was still wrapped around the trigger as she stared down the barrel, the sound of the shot echoing in her ears. Her training commanded she fire a second shot and her finger twitched as her brain told her not to. "Oh, God! No!" she screamed. It wasn't Doringer she saw in that brief instant when her gun first discharged. It was Jack's face as he tackled Doringer.

Connie stood, gaping in horror as both figures fell from view.

Chapter Fifty-One

Laura was still yelling a warning into her portable radio when she heard the gunshot. She jammed the binoculars back into her eye sockets. The gunshot had sent the dog running down the pier toward safety while four members of the cover team swarmed across the pier. Jack was no longer visible. She envisioned his body lying on the deck below the gunwale.

"What happened?" Tina demanded.

"I don't see Jack!" Laura cried. "I think Doringer shot him — the cover team are boarding."

"No, oh, no." Tina stood on her tiptoes, trying desperately to see what was happening below — but the light was too dim and the distance too great.

Laura glanced at the high fence with the locked gate blocking entrance to the marina, then raised the binoculars again. She saw Connie, with her weapon hung loosely by her side, cross over from the OP and peer over the gunwale of Doringer's boat. Whatever Connie saw caused her to put her hand over her face. Even from that distance, Laura could tell that her body was shaking.

Willy was the first of the cover team to leap over the gunwale. A wretched gurgling sound emitted from the surface of the deck. Jack was lying over Doringer, clenching his Adam's apple in a talon-like grip while pinning his head to the deck. Doringer's body convulsed in a desperate need for air. He clawed in vain with one hand trying to loosen Jack's hold. His other hand was pinned to the deck as Jack held his wrist.

Willy saw Doringer's pistol lying on the deck and quickly picked it up. "Got it, Jack. You can let him go. I've got him covered."

Jack continued to dig and twist his fingers deep into Doringer's throat as if trying to rip his Adam's apple from his neck. In response, Doringer's legs thrashed wildly and his feet pounded the deck.

"Jack, I've got his weapon, so you can let him go," Willy repeated more loudly. Jack paid no heed. Willy glanced at the other three officers watching. "Jack! You're crushing his larynx! You're going to kill him!"

Jack looked up without releasing his grip. "Hey, Willy. Nice of you guys to drop in. There's a bottle of rum inside on the counter. How about you all go in and mix some drinks? I'll be done in a minute."

"Christ, Jack, let go before you kill 'im!" Willy pleaded.

"The bastard had a gun," Jack replied. "I'm acting in self-defence."

"Wrong!" Willy said.

Jack hesitated, then let go. "Yeah, okay, I know. Sure felt good, though." He rose unsteadily to his feet as two members of the cover team bent down to handcuff Doringer.

"He's okay! He's okay!" announced Laura from her viewpoint.

"You sure?" Tina asked excitedly.

"Yes, he stood up."

"So it was Doringer who was shot," Tina said.

"Probably. No, they're standing him up. He's cuffed, bent over like he's hurt."

"Shot?"

"I can't tell. Two members are holding him up by each arm. I'll radio Connie and have her open the — Wait!"

"What's wrong?" Tina asked anxiously.

"Connie's hugging Jack. Wow. I never knew she felt that close to him." After a pause she muttered tersely, "Enough already, Connie. He's my partner, not yours."

Jack was surprised that Connie had responded so warmly to him. He patted her back as she held him, the side of her face tight to his chest. *Is she glad I'm alive — or pleased that we solved Dwayne's murder?*

Laura's voice was audible over Connie's earpiece. "Hey, Connie, did you forget about us up here? Open the gate!"

"It's Laura," Connie said, stepping back from the embrace.

"I heard," Jack replied. "I'll come with you. We should talk about what's happening."

"What's happening?" Connie repeated.

Jack gave a nod toward Doringer. "Without him listening."

Connie nodded.

"I expect you'll be busy for a while, collecting evidence and getting Forensics over," Jack said as they strolled along the pier toward the gate.

"Yes ... yes, of course," Connie replied.

"The thing is, I've got some things happening back on the mainland."

"With Chuck and Aaron?"

"Chuck and Aaron? No, it's nothing to do with them. You should scoop them up for interrogation right away and grab the computer they're using. And don't forget to grab the tracker off my car."

"I'm going to," Connie said. "I ... I'm ... sorry. My mind is still back on what just happened." She quickened her pace to keep up with Jack. "You've got something else?"

"Yes. In about an hour Interpol is going to take down some Satans Wrath members in France with a metric ton of coke. At the same time, the new national president for Canada is giving a speech in Vancouver. I expect he'll be bragging about their new European connection."

"Oh, that. I was with Rose this morning and Isaac mentioned it. Rose also talked about your informant taking part in murdering Neal Barlow tonight."

"She said that?" Jack was shocked that Rose would divulge that information.

"Not exactly. I heard her describe it to Isaac as that 'delicate matter' they'd discussed earlier — which was how you described it when you told me Isaac knew that Neal

Barlow was going to be murdered. I only presumed that was who they were talking about."

"Oh … I see." Jack glanced at her curiously. *Her voice sounds so monotone … as if she's in a trance. It's not like her to talk about someone being murdered like it's nothing.*

"It's all about the big picture, as you like to call it," Connie added flatly.

"Exactly. So with what's happening, I want to get back as soon as possible. I've got about three hours' worth of notes I need to make immediately. It's too late to catch the last ferry tonight — but I want to be on the first ferry out tomorrow morning at seven. Don't know if that's too early for you to head back?"

"No, that's fine. I'll be up."

Jack glanced at Laura and Tina standing under an overhead light, anxiously peering at him through the chain-link fence. As Connie reached to open the gate, he said, "Connie, are you okay?"

Connie glanced at him. "Yeah. I'm okay." Her voice sounded tired.

"What happened?" Laura demanded as soon as she was face to face with Jack.

"Doringer clued in that I was looking at the tender and pulled a gun," Jack replied.

"I heard a shot — I thought maybe you were dead." Laura's voice caught and she was trembling.

"Nah, still above ground," Jack replied. "Sorry to scare you."

Laura took a deep breath and exhaled slowly. "I should be getting used to feeling like this when I work with you, but I swear my hair is going white. Wonder if I can claim hair colour as a needed expense."

"So then, what happened?" Tina asked.

"Connie saved my bacon is what happened. She yelled and fired a warning shot to distract him — then I tackled him."

"A warning shot? No, that's not what I did!" Connie cried, her monotone gone.

"No? Maybe it was Willy then," Jack replied. "Somebody did."

Connie grasped Jack's arm. "It was me who shot, but I meant to kill —" She gawked at Jack's collar. "Oh, my God. Oh, my God … your collar. Oh, my God."

"My collar?"

Laura looked at the collar on Jack's windbreaker. Her face blanched. "You've got a bullet hole through your collar — about a finger's width away from your throat."

Jack took his windbreaker off and looked. *So that's why Connie is acting weird.*

"Jack, I … I …"

"You tried to kill me, Connie? Christ, I know you disagree with the way I investigate sometimes, but —"

Connie burst into tears.

"Hey, I'm sorry," he said quietly. He embraced her and rubbed her back. "I was only joking — trying to get you to lighten up. Shit happens."

"I tried to kill him," Connie sobbed, "but when I fired … your head appeared in the sights. You saved his life, but I almost killed you instead." She pushed Jack away. The windbreaker Jack held became like a magnet for her eyes.

"If you hadn't distracted him," Jack said, "I'd probably be dead. I owe you my life."

Connie's eyes remained glued to the windbreaker. "No, but —"

"No buts about it." Jack stared at Connie. "You tried to kill him?"

Connie refocused on Jack's face while using her fingertips to wipe her cheeks. "I was sure he was about to shoot you."

"Me, too, but I figured you wouldn't shoot him until after he fired, so I jumped him." He paused. "Believe me, it wasn't to save his life — it was to save mine."

"That's good to hear," Laura said wryly. "For a moment I thought you tried to save him. I was worried about what happened to the real you."

Jack ignored the comment and continued to look at Connie. "Are you okay?" he asked softly.

Connie let out a big sigh and folded her arms across her chest in an attempt to stop shaking. "I ... I just need a moment."

"Never let the guys see you cry," Tina advised. "They'll be on you like a pack of weasels going after a wounded chicken."

"Yeah, I know," Connie replied, trying to sound gruff.

Jack eyed the bullet hole in his windbreaker. "Guess I could claim this expense as friendly fire." He glanced at Connie. "Or, how about I toss it out and in the report claim you fired a warning shot to distract him, thereby saving my life."

"You don't lie in your reports," Connie admonished him.

"Ah, Connie." Jack shook his head. "I don't know whether to be proud of you for trying to kill him or frustrated that you won't fudge a report."

"I tried to kill him and almost killed you. That's what my report will say."

Jack grinned. "That ought to catch Isaac's attention. He assigns you to keep an eye on me and I save the bad guy from you killing him." He shook his head. "Yup, the word will be out. You've got homicidal tendencies. Maybe they'll team us up together."

Connie smiled. "Don't even suggest that, you son of a bitch."

Jack chuckled. "Glad you're back to being you again."

Chapter Fifty-Two

Later that night Jack was in his hotel room writing notes of what had transpired when he received a call from the Interpol office in Ottawa. The news was good. Four full-patch members of Satans Wrath had been arrested, along with three high-level European criminals. An estimated, but as yet not verified, metric ton of cocaine had been seized. The news media in France had already picked up the story. There was little doubt it would quickly go international.

Jack could barely conceal his delight. He tried to imagine how Pure E would respond. *By now you'll have tried to impress everyone with the direction the club will be going under your leadership. Crossing the threshold into Europe with promises of bigger and better things to come. Yup, open the champagne, boys. Wish I could be there to see the look on Pure E's face when he gets the news.*

Two hours later Jack was putting his notebook away when he received another call. This one gave him an inkling of how Pure E responded.

"I don't have much time, but thought I should let you know," Cockerill said. "That's if you don't know already."

"Know what?" Jack asked. "Are you still at the party?"

"Yeah, but it ain't exactly a happy time now," Cockerill said soberly.

"Oh? I thought Pure E would give a little speech and then everyone would have a good time."

"It started off that way. Pure E gave us a 'one for all and all for one' kind of talk with promises of great things to come. After that, he called all the exec members to huddle around. Then word spread that our ship had come in … literally. We were told that we were taking over a huge chunk of the European market and that somewhere in Europe a boatload of coke was being unloaded at this very moment. Everybody was lookin' at Pure E like he was a superhero."

"A boatload? Know any details about it?"

"No, but I'll get to it. After we were told about it, the party went into high gear. Guys were drinking their faces off."

"Except you?"

"Not a drop. Besides, I'm going to be working later … you know … Neal."

"Right. We'll talk about that in a minute. Continue."

"Everybody was happy and havin' a good time until a few minutes ago, then Pure E went crazy. He started swearin' and smashed his glass against a wall … kickin' fuckin' chairs an' tables over."

"I wonder what brought that on," Jack said musingly.

"Word is, our boat got taken down in France."

"You're kidding!"

"Nope."

"I'll have to check into it later. So tell me about Neal."

"I'm to pair up with someone from the three-three when things are done here and take my instructions from there. I think it'll be Pasquale Bazzoli."

"Your man from Kelowna," Jack noted. "Why do you think it'll be him?"

"'Cause he ain't drinkin', either. Listen, I better go. Someone might wonder who I'm talkin' to seein' as most everyone's here. Especially with Pure E havin' just thrown a tantrum."

"Call me as soon as you're done tonight," Jack said.

"Yeah, will do. If I'm paired up with someone, it might not be until morning before I get clear."

Twenty minutes later Jack entered Laura's and Tina's room where a party was underway. The first one to greet him was Connie.

"Chuck and Aaron have both rolled over already," Connie said, then gave a broad smile.

"That's great news, Connie."

"We sure as hell couldn't have done it without you, Laura, and Tina. I was ready to shelve the investigation until you guys did what you did."

"So Chuck and Aaron confessed," Jack stated.

"Yup. They were picked up and immediately separated. Both gave almost identical statements saying they saw Doringer shoot Dwayne. They also admitted to helping him load concrete blocks into his dinghy and tow the body out to sea where they weighed it down and let it go. We've got a really strong case."

"How much time do you think Doringer will get?" Laura asked.

Connie shrugged. "I don't know. I suspect Defence will see that a conviction is probable and negotiate for a guilty plea to get a reduced sentence — unless the bad guys go through legal aid, and then it could be drawn out for as long as possible so the lawyers can make some money." Connie paused a moment. "Which might be better because they'd likely end up serving longer sentences."

"Doringer has a boat and probably money from dope," Jack noted. "Aaron and Chuck also own a business. They'll be hiring good lawyers."

"Yeah, you're right." Connie nodded. "In that case, considering that it wasn't premeditated, I'd say Doringer's looking at serving from six to eight years of actual time."

"I'd say our success calls for a drink," Jack said, intentionally ignoring the clamor in his brain that said Doringer's likely sentence was not nearly what he deserved for killing an innocent man.

"Did I hear someone say a drink?" Vivian asked as she approached. "What about me? Everyone forgets about the poor girl stuck in the monitor room."

"Vivian, how the hell could I ever forget about you?" Jack gave her a hug. "You're the one who pieced it together."

"Yeah, I told everyone the project is now code-named 'Olive Soup.' You going to make me one?"

"Damn right." Jack poured two martinis, one for himself and one for Vivian. After taking a sip he grinned at Vivian, then took Laura aside.

"Have you heard from France?" Laura asked anxiously.

"Yes, it's a done deal." He quietly updated her on what had happened, including Cockerill's description of Pure E's response.

"Perfect," Laura said. "It's the icing on the cake. Not only did we destroy Damien, but turning on his own guys will stick in his craw for the rest of his life."

"I feel like a lifelong mission is complete," Jack replied.

Laura raised her glass. "I think we can call this a good day. A murderer behind bars, a ton of coke seized, and a bunch of bad guys in jail."

Jack smiled and they clinked glasses.

"And you still being alive," she added solemnly, before taking a sip.

Up till then, Jack had been too busy to think about how close he'd come to dying. "That too," he replied. *I almost died today … again.* He took a sip of his martini and thought about what was the most precious to him. *Natasha … Mike … Steve … I love you guys so much. How many times have I tempted fate?*

"What're you thinking?" Laura asked.

"That maybe my work in the fast lane is done," Jack replied just as solemnly.

Chapter Fifty-Three

At 8:45 a.m. Jack drove off the ferry on the Vancouver side. Laura sat beside him and Tina and Connie were in the back seat. He'd barely cleared the terminal when Connie received a phone call. Her polite hello and brief explanation to say she'd just arrived changed to anger. "Where?" she abruptly asked.

Jack made eye contact with her in the rear-view mirror. She scowled at him. *What the hell? Last night you were hugging me.*

"He's with me right now," Connie said, "and I'm positive the message is for him."

Message? Cockerill hasn't called yet. Did he get caught and is hoping I can get him off?

"Yeah, we'll be there in fifteen minutes." Connie hung up.

"We'll be where in fifteen minutes?" Jack said. "If you're talking headquarters it'll take —"

"We're going to a murder scene." Connie spoke harshly. "That was Corporal Lyle Roster on the phone. He's with I-HIT and is waiting for us."

"I've got a lot of reports to do back at the office," Jack replied. "I think I should —"

"It involves you!" Connie snapped.

So … they found Neal's body. "I explained to you before that I can't assist in, uh, certain homicides," Jack replied. "Also, if it's who I think it is, neither of us can get personally involved in the investigation."

"You'll want to see this," Connie said. "There was a personal message left for you at the scene."

Jack was momentarily too stunned to speak. "Where to?" he finally asked.

"The Barlow farmhouse."

"What happened? What's the message?"

"You need to see it for yourself," Connie replied. She folded her arms across her chest and stared silently out the passenger window.

Fifteen minutes later Jack drove along the gravel road leading to the farmhouse. Smoke billowed high in the sky. Once they arrived he saw that the barn was completely engulfed in flames and being attended to by the fire department.

"Park here," ordered Connie, gesturing to an empty spot behind a row of police vehicles.

Jack did as instructed. "I presume we need to wait until they douse the flames."

"It's not the barn you need to see. Follow me," Connie replied.

Jack followed Connie and ducked under the yellow plastic tape protecting the crime scene. Laura and Tina trailed behind. When they arrived outside the front door to the farmhouse, Connie spoke briefly to a member of the Forensic unit. Then she looked at Tina. "This doesn't involve you. Wait here."

As Tina nodded her reply, the roof on the barn collapsed and everyone turned to watch. Smoke and ash billowed into the air but nobody commented. Then they looked at one another. The tension was almost palpable.

The member from Forensics handed out shoe covers to preserve the integrity of the scene inside the farmhouse. Connie, Jack, and Laura quietly put them on. As they did, Lyle Roster appeared in the doorway. "Glad you're here, Connie. I should warn you. It's a stomach churner."

Jack and Laura exchanged a glance, then followed Connie and Roster into the living room. The stench of burned hair and flesh hung like a sticky clammy mist in the air. It clung to their clothes and skin.

It was a smell Jack recognized from years earlier when the young prostitute Crystal was murdered. He knew that his clothes and body could be washed, but it was what remained in the fibres of his brain that would last forever.

They were led through the living room to the kitchen. The first thing Jack saw were two blackened grotesque figures tied with duct tape to kitchen chairs. He realized the long charred braid on one figure belonged to Roxie. Her crotch and chest had been burned. In some places the fabric of her clothing was melted into her skin. Her throat and face were charred and black with soot. Remnants of tape were still stuck to her mouth.

He stared at the burned and twisted figure in the chair facing her. He only realized it was her husband, Bob, when he saw Neal's body trussed up on the floor. Neal had not been burned. His death had come from numerous knife wounds — accompanied by disembowelment.

"Over there," Connie pointed across the room.

Jack stared at a bloodied broom lying on the floor, then his eyes drifted up the wall. The broom had been used to paint a message in blood. It read "4 U JT."

Jack heard Laura gasp, then saw her charge back out through the living room. *Is she going to vomit, or just trying to escape from hell?* He swallowed the bile that had risen to his throat, then looked at Connie.

"Is this what you call 'a delicate matter'?" she screamed in anger.

Chapter Fifty-Four

Basil Westmount had barely arrived at work when his secretary told him she had a woman on the phone who worked at Edward Gosling's law firm and wished to speak to him about Buck Zabat. "Put her through," Basil said.

"Good morning, Mr. Westmount. My name is Veronica Daley. I understand you're representing Mr. Buck Zabat?"

"I will be if he's ever charged," Basil replied.

"The reason I'm calling is that Mr. Gosling is undergoing a tonsillectomy in the hospital today and I've received a call from a client of his who sounds somewhat distressed. She wants to know if all charges have been dropped against her and her son, Mr. Buck Zabat."

"Your client is Vicki Zabat?" Basil was astonished.

"Yes, and going by some notes on Mr. Gosling's file, it would appear that potential charges against her and her son would be dissolved once it was verified that her husband had performed his end of a deal with the police."

"A deal with the police," Basil repeated slowly.

"Yes, a Corporal Jack Taggart with the RCMP. Apparently Mr. Damien Zabat provided information in regard to a large shipment of drugs in exchange for charges not being laid against his wife and son. I'm told that the seizure took place last night — actually I think I heard about it on the news this morning. It was that thing in France where several members of Satans Wrath were arrested along with —"

Basil interrupted her. "What was Vicki being charged with?"

"It's alleged she tried to shoot Corporal Taggart during a search last week of the Zabat home."

"She tried to murder him?"

"Yes, it sounds serious."

"I'll say it is."

"So the police haven't contacted you yet to say the matter has been dropped?"

"Sometimes these things take time," Basil replied. "I spoke to Corporal Taggart recently concerning Buck. I've not heard anything new since, but will make some calls and find out. It's not even nine o'clock yet, so I'm not sure if their office is open. Regardless, I'll get hold of him as soon as possible. When I do, I'll let you know." Basil abruptly hung up, then pushed speed dial.

"Yeah?" Pure E answered.

Chapter Fifty-Five

Jack and Laura sat in the front seat of the Mercedes. Billowing smoke and ash added to the chaos of the police and fire department personnel trying to work around each other. Neither Jack nor Laura paid any of it much heed. Both were lost in their own thoughts. Even when Connie retrieved her suitcase and slammed the trunk, Jack didn't move.

"Uh, Connie has her bag," Tina said from the back seat, then added a bit impatiently, "Looks like we can go now."

Jack glanced at Corporal Lyle Roster. He looked bewildered as he stood beside their car. Connie had told him they were under orders not to assist with the investigation. Roster was a seasoned investigator, but never in his long career had he heard of such a thing.

Jack didn't blame Connie for opting to catch a ride back to her office with someone else. He shared her anger, but while she chose to direct her anger at him, his anger was directed at the man responsible. The man who gave the orders for the torture and murders. The man who made it personal by seeing that a message was left on the wall. *Yeah, I got your message. Wait 'till you get mine.*

He put the car in drive and was about to pull out when he received a call. "Weenie Wagger," he said tersely to Laura.

"I just got free," Cockerill said. "You heard yet?"

"I'm at the scene now," Jack replied. "What the hell happened?"

"Okay, to start with, when —"

"Why?" Jack yelled, unable to control his emotions any longer. "Why all three? Was it because Pure E was in a rage over the boat being seized in France?"

"Fuck, don't yell at me," Cockerill yelled back. "You think I enjoyed watchin' 'em screamin' an' chokin' while they was burnin'? I still got the stench in my mouth."

You're not the only one. Jack resisted the urge to wind down the window and spit. "Sorry," he said. "I'm not blaming you. I just want to know why."

"Yeah … okay. Pure E was real pissed off about the boat, but what happened with Neal, Bob, and Roxie had been planned before then."

"How do you know?"

"'Cause when the party was endin' last night, I went with Pasquale out to the farm. There was no way I could call you. He shut his phone off and made me shut mine off as a security precaution to prevent us from ever being tracked."

"I'm not pissed off about you not calling. Tell me how it went down."

"Well … before we left the party, Pasquale already had eight cans of lighter fluid."

"Eight cans — one for each member of the Gypsy Devils," Jack said.

"You got it. There were nine GDs, but Neal ain't with 'em now."

"No shit," Jack replied sarcastically.

"Yeah … so anyway, the GDs thought we were havin' an after-party at the barn and a quick talk about how they handled things for us. When we got to the barn Shepherd told Neal to go to a gas station back out by the highway and round up some ice. As soon as Neal left he told everyone that Neal was a rat. He said Neal was never robbed, but got busted with the weed. He then told 'em about the bust in Dallas and said Neal squealed to save Bob and Roxie from goin' to jail. He also said Neal tipped you off about King, which was why you were there and got the video."

"Then what happened?"

"Fuck, everyone went nuts. They wanted to take Neal away someplace and do him, then later tell Bob and Roxie that Neal disappeared while doing a deal."

"Which is what I expected to happen," Jack said.

"It didn't. Shepherd looked at Pasquale, who gave 'im a nod like he was urgin' him on, then Shepherd told his guys they had to send a message to stop anyone else from ever rattin.'"

"A message," Jack repeated.

"Yeah. By the time Neal got back with the ice, Bob and Roxie were tied to the kitchen chairs with their yaps taped shut. When he came in the house to see what was goin' on … well, lots of screamin' and shoutin' went on. Then his own guys kicked the shit out of him and hog-tied 'im with tape. Then they sat him on a chair facing Bob and Roxie. Then … then, uh …"

Jack was patient. He knew Cockerill was still fighting the horrible images in his memory. Eventually he suggested, "Don't hold it in. Get it out. Then what?"

"Then, uh, that's when everyone got kinda quiet. Pasquale handed a can of lighter fluid to each of the GDs. He told 'em all to take turns, startin' with Roxie. They splashed her first so Neal could watch. Then …" Cockerill's voice had become shaky and he stopped.

"Stay focused," Jack said. "Quit thinking about her eyes."

"How'd you know I was thinkin' about her eyes?" Cockerill asked sombrely.

"Years ago I watched a young woman burn to death after Damien ordered her car blown up because she wanted to quit being a prostitute. It wasn't pretty."

"Yeah … neither was this." Cockerill paused. "After she died it was Bob's turn. They did Neal last."

"Neal wasn't burned," Jack stated.

"No. Shepherd told Thor to use a blade on 'im."

"Norm Thorsen, the sergeant-at-arms for the GDs," Jack said.

"Yeah, him. It didn't take any urgin' by anyone, either. Thor went at 'im like he was enjoyin' himself. Then when he was done, Pasquale found a broom and used it to write you a message on the wall. I asked him about it later. He said that Pure E wanted you to know what would happen if you got any more rats."

"Why did you set the barn on fire?"

"Two reasons. One was to burn out the truck with the secret compartment. They knew you already knew about it, but decided it might help get rid of evidence if you wanted to use it down the road in case some bits of weed were still inside. The second reason was Pure E wanted you to see things when everything was still, uh … fresh, I think is the word Pasquale used. That was just to attract your attention."

"Well, they've got it," Jack said.

Chapter Fifty-Six

It was almost noon when Jack finished telling Rose everything that had transpired. Grim-faced, she looked at him across her desk, then asked, "The message written in blood ... do you feel it represents a danger to you personally?"

Jack glanced at Laura, then at Rose again. "Not at present. The message was written to scare me in the hope I'll back off or be transferred. If that happens Pure E will be more inclined to take extreme measures in the future with whoever replaces me. That's where the danger lies."

Rose nodded. "I agree."

"I almost lost my breakfast when I saw what they did to those people," Laura said.

"Me, too," Jack admitted, "and I can't blame the ferry food."

Laura's voice was shaky. "What was done ... I ... I feel that we're responsible."

"Neither of you are responsible," Rose said firmly. "What you're responsible for is solving a murder, causing major damage to Satans Wrath's connection to a notorious gang in Texas, and severing a major drug pipeline to Europe."

"But nobody, criminal or not, should have to die the way those three died," Laura said.

"I agree with you there," Jack said bitterly.

Rose nodded. "I appreciate you're both exhausted from what you've been through, but Isaac has already been apprised about the Barlows by I-HIT. He called me an hour ago and wants to talk to you. We're booked to see him at three this afternoon."

"Bet he's upset."

"He is, but not with you, Jack. Ultimately it was his decision. He has to live with the consequences." She eyed Jack and Laura. "I know you feel responsible, but what happened … happened. Everyone did what they thought was in the best interest of the public. Hindsight is —"

"Pure E made this personal," Jack said coldly. "The bloody message was directed specifically at me. Even Damien would have never done such a —"

"I've a message for you, too," Rose interjected. "You can't always control or predict the actions of others. Abhorrent behaviour is just that — abhorrent."

Jack stared silently at Rose. *Message received — but I'll also have a message for Pure E. One that's more personal.*

It was noon and Jack and Laura were entering their office when Jack received a call. "Basil Westmount," he said, looking at the call display.

"Bet he wants to know if you've received any messages lately," Laura said sarcastically.

"I'll find out." Jack answered. "What do you want, Basil?"

"Hello, Corporal Taggart. I thought you'd like to know that I just got off the phone with Veronica Daley."

"I don't know a Veronica Daley," Jack said.

"Then let me enlighten you. She works for Ed Gosling."

Jack felt the bile rise to his throat for the second time that morning. "Ed Gosling?" he repeated.

"She told me she was filling in for Ed because he's undergoing a tonsillectomy at the moment, but let me know that they're representing Mrs. Vicki Zabat. She asked if all potential charges against her and her son, Buck, are finished now that Damien has fulfilled his end of the bargain."

"His end of the bargain? I don't know what you're talking about." *The son of a bitch knows! Who am I fooling?*

"Let me refresh your memory. Damien provided you with information that allowed for the seizure of that boatload of cocaine in France." Basil paused, no doubt savouring the moment. "So is the matter with Vicki and Buck closed now? May I inform my client that there's no need to worry any further?"

Jack didn't bother to reply. He hung up and immediately punched Damien's number into his phone.

"What's going on?" Laura asked.

"They know!" Jack shouted. "Basil found out that Damien talked to us! I have to warn him!" He turned his attention back to the phone when his call was answered. "Damien, it's —"

"Ah ... Corporal Taggart. I thought it might be you."

"Who's this?" Jack demanded.

"Purvis Evans. I'm afraid Damien is not available — but I'll let him know you called. Goodbye."

———

Damien was seated on a log in a wooded area near Abbotsford. Six men were with him, four of whom were members of the three-three. The fifth man, Purvis Evans, sat across from him. He smiled as he hung up the phone after speaking with Jack.

Ignoring the sixth man, who was pointing a pistol at his face, Damien looked at Purvis and smiled.

"You think it's funny?" Purvis asked.

Damien's chuckle was sincere. "Yes, Purvis, I do. I'm looking forward to greeting you in hell — which will be much sooner than you think."

"Fuck you, you piece of shit." Purvis gave a nod. "Do it."

The shot was muffled by a silencer — but was no less deadly. The bullet entered Damien's forehead. He was dead before his body slumped sideways off the log.

"I fell for it!" Jack moaned. "Christ!" He began to jab Vicki's number on his phone.

"Fell for what?" Laura asked. "What's going on?"

"I've got to warn Vicki," he replied anxiously. "Damien's dead — I've got to warn her."

"Damien's dead?"

"Goddamn it! Her phone's no longer in service. I'm going to call Gosling's office. Maybe they have a new number for her."

"Damien's dead?" Laura said again.

"Yes, I already told you that!" Jack yelled.

Rose heard the commotion and hurried into their office. "What's going on?"

"I don't know," Laura whispered. She gestured to Jack, who was punching another number into his phone. "He told me that Damien's dead and he's trying to reach Vicki and warn her."

Jack listened to the voice-mail message at Gosling's office, then disconnected. "His office is closed for lunch and doesn't reopen until one," he said.

"What the hell's going on?" Rose demanded.

Jack briefly closed his eyes and clenched his fists in anguish, then looked at Rose. "Damien was accidentally burned by someone who works for Vicki's lawyer."

"How?" demanded Rose.

"Ed Gosling is getting a tonsillectomy today. A Veronica Daley from his office took it upon herself to call Basil Westmount — she wanted to confirm that the charges against Vicki and Buck had been dropped now that Damien gave us the boatload of coke in France."

"Oh, fuck!" Rose exclaimed.

"It gets worse," Jack said. "Basil called me a moment ago to say he just hung up from talking with Veronica. Like a fool I immediately called Damien to warn him."

"Were you able to warn him?" Rose asked.

"Warn him?" Jack snarled. "It was me who put the final nail in his coffin. Damien never answered. Pure E did."

"Oh, no," Laura uttered. "No."

"Pure E said he *thought* it might be me who was calling," Jack continued. "I'm sure Basil got the call from this Veronica hours ago."

"That son of a bitch," Rose swore.

"I tried to reach Vicki just now. The number I have for her is no longer in service. I tried to reach her through her lawyer's office, but it's closed for lunch." He glanced at Laura. "Sorry I yelled at you. I screwed up, not you."

"With what happened, I feel like yelling myself," Laura said.

"Grab your coat," Jack ordered. "Let's see if she's home. On the way I'll call I-HIT to explain the situation. Maybe they can trace Damien's phone."

"I'm coming with you," Rose said. "I might spend my day behind a desk, but if the shit hits the fan, I still remember how to shoot."

Chapter Fifty-Seven

At twelve-thirty that afternoon Buck entered his parents' house. He was surprised to see Vicki in the kitchen. "Hey, what are you doing home?" he asked. "When I called earlier you said you were heading out to see Grandpa. I thought you were having lunch with him."

"I decided he could have lunch on his own today. What are you doing here? Everything okay? You look tense."

"I came to gather up some of Dad's things."

"Why? Where is —"

"We need to talk," Buck interrupted her. "Let's go for a walk."

A moment later they were walking along the path at the back of the mansion. Vicki glanced sideways at her son. "So? What's up?"

"What's up is we found out you tried to shoot a cop when they raided the house," Buck said.

"What?" Vicki exclaimed. "Where'd you hear that?"

"Dad told me." He kissed her on the cheek. "In a way I'm proud of you. He also told me what he did to keep you … and me from being charged."

"Where's he now?" Vicki asked bluntly.

"That's what I was sent over to tell you. The club had an unexpected opportunity to sneak him out of the country. I came over to grab some of his stuff and pack a suitcase."

"He went without even telling me?"

"It was a last-minute thing. I'm sure he feels awful that he couldn't tell you in person. He'll be able to pass on messages to you later. The good thing is the cops never found all his money. He's got lots to live on."

"Is that what the club is being told?" Vicki asked.

"What do you mean?"

"I suppose that's a better story. It wouldn't be good for morale if they knew their top guy ratted."

"Why are you saying that?" Buck demanded.

"I was home. I heard you arrive and then argue with your dad downstairs. Then I heard the guys from the three-three come in and take him away."

Buck's face revealed his shock. "You were here? You didn't go to Grandpa's?"

"I told you that because I wanted to watch. I was upstairs looking out the window when you loaded him into the van."

Buck was aghast. "H-how'd you know about it?" he stuttered.

"Who do you think placed the call to Basil pretending to be my lawyer's secretary?"

"You! Oh, God, Mom … why?"

"Because I've had enough of the bullshit, that's why! My whole life with him has been a sham! We were never a family. The only thing I had left was you — and he was going to let them take you away. All for the sake of the fucking club."

"Mom, you set Dad up to be killed!"

"Damn right I did."

Buck clenched his fists in anger. "You could've gotten us both killed!"

"What're you talking about? It was your dad who ratted."

"Jesus! You stupid stupid bitch! You dunno nothin', do you?"

Vicki slapped him hard across the face.

His eyes blazoned with fury. "Do that again and I'll drop you like the piece of shit you are!"

"You wouldn't dare," Vicki challenged.

"Wouldn't I? Who the fuck do you think wore the wire to get Dad's confession this morning while the three-three listened outside?"

"You wore a wire?"

"Yeah, and who the fuck do you think wasted the rat bastard afterwards?"

Vicki stared open-mouthed. Her voice became a whisper. "They made you kill him."

"I had to prove who my real family was," Buck replied. "If I ever had any self-doubt, I sure as hell don't anymore, not after talking with you."

Vicki watched in silence as he walked away.

Jack, Laura, and Rose were parked down the block from Damien's estate. When they first arrived they'd seen Buck drive through the main gates and now they were waiting for him to leave.

"What if he takes Vicki with him?" Rose asked from the back seat.

Jack's fingers drummed nervously on the steering wheel. He glanced at Laura, who was watching the gates through binoculars, then made eye contact with Rose through the rear-view mirror. "If he does I'll pull them over. Make it look like an arrest scenario until we sort things out."

"If she's still alive," Rose noted. "There could be a body in there."

"If she's dead I don't think we'll find her body," Jack said. "With as brazen as Pure E was, I'm sure Damien's body is well hidden, too. They'll probably try to make it look like he fled to avoid charges. It would be too embarrassing for them if word got out that he was an informant. The Europeans wouldn't be impressed."

"And I-HIT doesn't think they can trace his phone for another hour or two?" Rose asked.

"Doesn't matter." Jack's tone showed his frustration. "I'm sure wherever it is, or was, has long since been cleaned up. Pure E and his three-three team wouldn't chance it otherwise."

"When you think that Pure E had Bob and Roxie killed for no reason, who knows what they might do to Vicki," Laura said.

Jack grimaced. "I've been thinking about it. Buck is a member of the club and that might change things. I doubt he'd stand for having his mother tortured to death simply to torment Damien. Also, as far as Buck goes, the club wouldn't want to kill one of their own when he had no idea what was going on."

"So you think Vicki will be okay?" Rose asked.

"I'll feel better about it when I talk to her." He looked at his watch. "Almost one." He redialled Ed Gosling's office. This time a female voice answered.

"Good afternoon. Law firm of —"

"I need to speak to Veronica Daley," Jack said tersely.

"I'm Veronica. What can I do for you?"

"It's Corporal Taggart from the RCMP. Your phone call to Basil Westmount this morning has put people's lives at risk — including your own client, Vicki Zabat. It's extremely urgent that I contact Mrs. Zabat, but the number I have is no longer in service."

"But I've never made any calls to Basil Westmount," Veronica protested. "Perhaps you should speak to Mr. Gosling. One sec, and I'll transfer your call."

"He's there?" Jack asked in surprise. "I was told he was having a tonsillectomy today."

"Unless that procedure is being performed in his office," Veronica said dryly, "he's been here all morning."

Jack's mouth flopped open. *Someone pretended to be from Gosling's office and knew Veronica Daley worked there. Who would do that, yet try to hide their involvement from either me or the club?* Vicki's anger at Damien the night he and Laura showed them the video came back to him, along with what she said later when they met her in the hotel room. *As far as Damien goes, he could die for all I care.* Jack felt stunned. *How could you do this? He died saving you ...* "You bitch," Jack said aloud.

"I beg your pardon?" Veronica said sharply.

Jack came back to his senses. "Sorry, not you. Don't bother transferring my call," he added before putting his phone back in his pocket.

"What happened?" Rose asked. "You look perturbed."

"Perturbed?" Jack said. "I'm not perturbed, I'm angry."

DUNDURN

VISIT US AT

Dundurn.com
@dundurnpress
Facebook.com/dundurnpress
Pinterest.com/dundurnpress